LOVER
FORBIDDEN

J.R. WARD

LOVER FORBIDDEN

• THE BLACK DAGGER •
BROTHERHOOD SERIES

GALLERY BOOKS

New York   Amsterdam/Antwerp   London   Toronto   Sydney/Melbourne   New Delhi

Gallery Books
An Imprint of Simon & Schuster, LLC
1230 Avenue of the Americas
New York, NY 10020

First Gallery Books hardcover edition September 2025

GALLERY BOOKS and colophon are registered trademarks of Simon & Schuster, LLC

Simon & Schuster strongly believes in freedom of expression and stands against censorship in all its forms. For more information, visit BooksBelong.com.

For information about special discounts for bulk purchases, please contact Simon & Schuster Special Sales at 1-866-506-1949 or business@simonandschuster.com.

The Simon & Schuster Speakers Bureau can bring authors to your live event. For more information or to book an event, contact the Simon & Schuster Speakers Bureau at 1-866-248-3049 or visit our website at www.simonspeakers.com.

Interior design by Erika R. Genova

Manufactured in China

10 9 8 7 6 5 4 3 2 1

Library of Congress Cataloging-in-Publication Data is available.

ISBN 978-1-9821-7996-0
ISBN 978-1-9821-7998-4 (ebook)

Dedicated to:
The both of you—
what a *magical* love story.

GLOSSARY OF TERMS AND PROPER NOUNS

abstrux nohtrum (n.) Private guard with license to kill who is granted his or her position by the King.

ahvenge (v.) Act of mortal retribution, carried out typically by a male loved one.

Black Dagger Brotherhood (pr. n.) Highly trained vampire warriors who protect their species against the Lessening Society. As a result of selective breeding within the race, Brothers possess immense physical and mental strength, as well as rapid healing capabilities. They are not siblings for the most part, and are inducted into the Brotherhood upon nomination by the Brothers. Aggressive, self-reliant, and secretive by nature, they are the subjects of legend and objects of reverence within the vampire world. They may be killed only by the most serious of wounds, e.g., a gunshot or stab to the heart, etc.

blood slave (n.) Male or female vampire who has been subjugated to serve the blood needs of another. The practice of keeping blood slaves has been outlawed.

the Chosen (pr. n.) Female vampires who had been bred to serve the Scribe Virgin. In the past, they were spiritually rather than temporally focused, but that changed with the ascendance of the final Primale, who freed them from the Sanctuary. With the Scribe Virgin removing herself from her role, they are completely autonomous and learning to live on earth. They do continue to meet the blood needs of unmated members of the Brotherhood, as well as Brothers who cannot feed from their *shellans* or injured fighters.

chrih (n.) Symbol of honorable death in the Old Language.

cohntehst (n.) Conflict between two males competing for the right to be a female's mate.

Dhunhd (pr. n.) Hell.

doggen (n.) Member of the servant class within the vampire world. *Doggen* have old, conservative traditions about service to their superiors, following a formal code of dress and behavior. They are able to go out during the day, but they age relatively quickly. Life expectancy is approximately five hundred years.

ehros (n.) A Chosen trained in the matter of sexual arts.

exhile dhoble (n.) The evil or cursed twin, the one born second.

the Fade (pr. n.) Non-temporal realm where the dead reunite with their loved ones and pass eternity.

First Family (pr. n.) The King and Queen of the vampires, and any children they may have.

ghardian (n.) Custodian of an individual. There are varying degrees of *ghardians*, with the most powerful being that of a *sehcluded* female.

glymera (n.) The social core of the aristocracy, roughly equivalent to Regency England's *ton*.

hellren (n.) Male vampire who has been mated to a female. Males may take more than one female as mate.

hyslop (n. or v.) Term referring to a lapse in judgment, typically resulting in the compromise of the mechanical operations of a vehicle or otherwise motorized conveyance of some kind. For example, leaving one's keys in one's car as it is parked outside the family home overnight, whereupon said vehicle is stolen.

leahdyre (n.) A person of power and influence.

leelan (adj. or n.) A term of endearment loosely translated as "dearest one."

Lessening Society (pr. n.) Order of slayers convened by the Omega for the purpose of eradicating the vampire species, and led by his son, Lash.

lesser (n.) De-souled human who targets vampires for extermination as a member of the Lessening Society. *Lessers* must be stabbed through the chest in order to be killed; otherwise they are ageless. They do not eat or drink and are impotent. Over time, their hair, skin, and irises lose pigmentation until they are blond, blushless, and pale eyed. They smell like baby powder. Now inducted into the society by the Omega's son, they no longer keep jars for their hearts, as they did in the past. Women now may be inducted.

lewlhen (n.) Gift.

lheage (n.) A term of respect used by a sexual submissive to refer to their dominant.

Lhenihan (pr. n.) A mythic beast renowned for its sexual prowess. In modern slang, refers to a male of preternatural size and sexual stamina.

lys (n.) Torture tool used to remove the eyes.

mahmen (n.) Mother. Used both as an identifier and a term of affection.

mhis (n.) The masking of a given physical environment; the creation of a field of illusion.

nalla (n., f.) or *nallum* (n., m.) Beloved.

needing period (n.) Female vampire's time of fertility, generally lasting for two days and accompanied by intense sexual cravings. Occurs approximately five years after a female's transition and then once a decade thereafter. All males respond to some degree if they are around a female in her need. It can be a dangerous time, with conflicts and fights breaking out between competing males, particularly if the female is not mated.

newling (n.) A virgin.

the Omega (pr. n.) Malevolent, mystical figure who targeted the vampires for extinction out of resentment directed toward the Scribe Virgin. Existed in a non-temporal realm and had extensive powers, though not the power of creation. Exterminated by the Brotherhood, and succeeded by his son, Lash.

phearsom (adj.) Term referring to the potency of a male's sexual organs. Literal translation something close to "worthy of entering a female."

Princeps (pr. n.) Highest level of the vampire aristocracy, second only to members of the First Family or the Scribe Virgin's Chosen. Must be born to the title; it may not be conferred.

pyrocant (n.) Refers to a critical weakness in an individual. The weakness can be internal, such as an addiction, or external, such as a lover.

rahlman (n.) Savior.

rythe (n.) Ritual manner of asserting honor granted by one who has offended another. If accepted, the offended chooses a weapon and strikes the offender, who presents him- or herself without defenses.

the Scribe Virgin (pr. n.) Mystical force who previously was counselor to the King as well as the keeper of vampire archives and the dispenser of privileges. Existed in a non-temporal realm and had extensive powers, but stepped down and gave her station to the fallen angel, Lassiter. Was capable of a single act of creation, which she expended to bring the vampires into existence.

sehclusion (n.) Status conferred by the King upon a female of the aristocracy as a result of a petition by the female's family. Places the female under the sole direction of her *ghardian*, typically the eldest male in her household. Her *ghardian* then has the legal right to determine all manner of her life, restricting at will any and all interactions she has with the world.

shellan (n.) Female vampire who has been mated to a male. Females generally do not take more than one mate due to the highly territorial nature of bonded males.

symphath (n.) Subspecies within the vampire race characterized by the ability and desire to manipulate emotions in others (for the purposes of an energy exchange), among other traits. Historically, they have been discriminated against and, during certain eras, hunted by vampires.

talhman (n.) The evil side of an individual. A dark stain on the soul that requires expression if it is not properly expunged.

the Tomb (pr. n.) Sacred vault of the Black Dagger Brotherhood. Used as a ceremonial site and, previously, the storage facility for the jars of *lessers*. Ceremonies performed there include inductions, funerals, and disciplinary actions against Brothers. No one may enter except for members of the Brotherhood, the Scribe Virgin's successor, or candidates for induction.

trahyner (n.) Word used between males of mutual respect and affection. Translated loosely as "beloved friend."

transition (n.) Critical moment in a vampire's life when he or she transforms into an adult. Thereafter, he or she must drink the blood of the opposite sex to survive and is unable to withstand sunlight. Occurs generally in the mid-twenties. Some vampires do not survive their transitions, males in particular. Prior to their transitions, vampires are physically weak, sexually unaware and unresponsive, and unable to dematerialize.

vampire (n.) Member of a species separate from that of *Homo sapiens*. Vampires must drink the blood of the opposite sex to survive. Human blood will keep them alive, though the strength does not last long. Following their transitions, which occur in their mid-twenties, they are unable to go out into sunlight and must feed from the vein regularly. Vampires cannot "convert" humans through a bite or transfer of blood, though they are in rare cases able to breed with the other species. Vampires can dematerialize at will, though they must be able to calm themselves and concentrate to do so and may not carry anything heavy with them. They are able to strip the memories of humans, provided such memories are short-term. Some vampires are able to read minds. Life expectancy is upward of a thousand years, or in some cases, even longer.

wahlker (n.) An individual who has died and returned to the living from the Fade. They are accorded great respect and are revered for their travails.

whard (n.) Equivalent of a godfather or godmother to an individual.

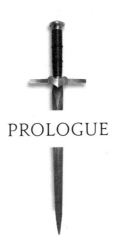

PROLOGUE

Thirty-one years, eleven months, and twenty-nine days ago . . .

Explain to me how it's your birthday and you're doing all the cooking?"

As the Black Dagger Brother Qhuinn, mated of Blaylock, son of Rocke, tossed that rhetorical across his in-laws' kitchen table, he reached to his blind side for his daughter. When a heavy, squirming bundle landed in his hands, he knew he'd gotten his mini-me, dark-haired son instead. Either was good with him, but man, you could tell the difference without looking.

Like expecting a can of soda and getting a bowling ball.

"I tried to help my *shellan*." Next to him, his father-in-law, Rocke, glanced over with his characteristic genial smile. "But she has her standards."

The older male shifted around toward the center island, his attention lingering on the female who was taking a pan of homemade lasagna out of the wall oven. Gone was the retired accountant's earnest seriousness; in its place, that even-featured face melted into something worthy of a fairy tale. Sure, Rocke, with his pocket protector, mild manner, and earnest affect, wasn't the Don Juan type—certainly not at this well-past-middle-aged era in his life, and maybe not ever—but as his mate noticed him looking, the answering blush on her cheeks said she still liked his eyes on her.

"I do have standards, it's true," the elder Lyric said as she put the pan on the counter and smoothed her apron. "That's why I mated you."

Rocke's button-down shirt stretched over his chest as he took a nice big inhale with masculine pride. "You did me such a favor when you agreed to be mine."

"Hardly." She started running a knife through the pan at right angles. "I was the lucky one."

Shaking his head, Rocke smiled again. "No, *I* was the lucky one. Still am."

The exchange was a reminder that HEA in real life didn't require a perpetual setting sun and the couple from that ancient Cialis ad holding hands in their non sequitur outdoor bathtubs. What you actually needed were two people who still gave a shit about what the other guy had to say after the passage of time—and not just days and nights. Not months. Not even years.

Decades.

Or, in the case of vampires, centuries.

Qhuinn looked in the opposite direction. At the end of the table, his Blay was flanked by two high chairs, like he was the king of babies everywhere. In the crook of his arm, the young Lyric—the one who wasn't cooking her own birthday dinner—was nestled in a pink blanket, happy as a clam after her bottle.

The male's bright blue eyes lifted sure as if his name had been whispered, and Qhuinn's body just stopped whatever it was doing—including the whole breathing thing.

At least he managed to keep hold of their son.

Even after all these years, his *hellren* had the ability to put the brakes on the world. Red-haired, broad-shouldered, and with a voice that was smooth as a good grenache, Blay was the sort of person who anchored a room. Never showy, always thoughtful, quick with a smile and a compliment, the guy was not just a male of worth, he was the sun around which all things gravitated and by which they were warmed and sustained.

At least in Qhuinn's universe. And for everybody else at this table: His parents had always adored their son, something Qhuinn hadn't gotten and was so glad his mate had.

Hell, they loved him so much that when the kid had shown up on their doorstep with a scrawny pretrans who had an impeccable pedigree, but an untenable genetic defect, they'd welcomed Qhuinn and his mismatched eyes into their home and hearts, no questions asked.

"Here we are." Lyric swooped in. "Your favorite, dear."

The feast for the senses and the belly set down in front of him was indeed a thing of beauty: five layers of lasagna noodles, tuck-pointed with meat sauce, mozzarella, and cottage cheese—the latter instead of ricotta because he couldn't handle the ricotta.

He was a tough male, a fighter for the species, a killer who never backed down. But he had the taste buds of a four-year-old.

"This is . . . amazing." Except then he frowned at all the other platters and casserole dishes on the table. "Although we already have the roast and the mashed potatoes and the—"

"I made this just for you." She put her hand on his shoulder. "You missed family dinner last weekend because you were out in the field, and I heard you were disappointed."

Qhuinn put a hand over his heart. "You know, if I weren't happily mated to your son—"

"Now, wait a minute," Rocke spoke up. "She's mine—"

"—I'd marry this lasagna."

They all laughed. For sure it was a dad joke, but then again, he was a dad. And so was Blay. And so was Rocke. Funny how things had changed.

He still had all his piercings, though.

And he hadn't traded his Hummer for a minivan—

"I think someone wants you," Blay said with a smile.

Sure enough, Lyric was reaching for him, so they traded bundled young. Good timing. She was easier to do the one-arm, eating-hold with, and Rhamp was okay getting put in his high chair and given a teething ring to gnaw on. With that settled, the adults passed serving pieces around and filled plates, and between the bites and sips that followed, the conversation was heart-wrenchingly normal: No one's tragic death was ruminated upon. No new bad, Lash-related news for the Lessening Society was reported. No seismic shifts on the Other Side were dissected.

Instead, they chatted about the human Christmas season and the recent snowstorm. The ice dam upstairs in the guest bedroom that everybody told Rocke not to even *think* about getting the ladder out for. There was also a discussion about how pretty the full moon had been the night before, and then came the most important open question following the presentation of the sainted lasagna:

"What kind of cake is for dessert?" Blay asked.

"Carrot," the elder Lyric said.

As a cheer went up, Qhuinn toasted her with his beer. "Your cream cheese icing is a food group as far as I'm concerned."

More laughter. More chatter . . .

It was all very nice. Too nice, in a way.

He paused with his fork. He'd been to this house out in the countryside around Caldwell's suburban necklace of developments countless times . . . had sat in this chair, always this chair, since the first meal he'd had right after they'd helped Blay's parents get moved in.

There was an expectation—never spoken by him or anybody else— that Family Dinner, a.k.a. Sunday's Last Meal, would continue forever.

But that wasn't the way it worked for mortals, was it.

Wrath's death two years ago had taught him that. Taught everybody that.

As he felt a familiar ache coming on, he stared down at his daughter's face. She was so like her *mahmen*, Layla, with tiny, perfect features, big pale eyes, and a dusting of blond hair. He'd heard that human children grew out of this proper baby/toddler stage after just twelve months, but he was glad vampires took much, much longer. He loved this bundle-of-joy shit, he really did, and given that it was impossible to imagine what their Lyric was going to be like when she was older, when she didn't need him or any of the other parents in her life, the fact that he could still cradle her against the bulk of his biceps like this made him feel as if time was frozen.

Sure, that was nothing but a delusion. It beat worrying that any one of them could be gone in an instant, though.

Maybe by a bomb, set by the enemy . . . at the door to a house, regularly visited.

He tried not to think about how Wrath had been murdered—

As he forced himself to focus on Lyric again, he had to tell himself to quit checking her irises. There were so many reasons not to worry about whether they were going to be mismatched like his own, but as with tracking his son's occasional dark moods, he couldn't help it. He'd had that vision, when he'd been at the door unto the Fade . . . a daughter with one blue eye and one green.

Right now, she was showing no signs of his heterochromatism, and he'd be lying if he said he didn't want it to stay that way.

But that was just his own PTSD talking, wasn't it.

"How's my girl?" he murmured.

She offered him a little stretch and a big gummy smile in return, and as that happiness wafted up at him like a warm breeze, it got hard to breathe. He couldn't imagine ever shaming her for whatever color her eyes ended up being, or hiding her from other people, or shutting her out of the family. He'd been just like her once, born into the world needing gentleness and love. And protection.

Not what he'd gotten, but that was aristocrats for you.

Fortunately, neither of his kids needed to worry about being cast out. Hell, if anybody *ever* tried to hurt either one of them, he would go bare-knuckled, bloodbath—

"You okay, son?" Rocke asked softly.

Qhuinn jerked his head up. The others had paused in various eating positions, the elder Lyric in the process of lifting her glass of water, Rocke in mid-bread-tear, Blay putting his fork into his mashed potatoes. They were staring at him with their eyebrows at full mast—

Oh. He was growling, his fangs tingling as they descended.

"Sorry," he murmured as he forced a tight smile. And then he felt like he had to tack on some kind of explanation. "Do you sometimes wonder what you would do to protect your children?"

There was a heartbeat of silence.

After which all three adults answered grimly: "No."

He glanced around at each of them, the *hellren* he'd bonded with, the father he'd never had, the *mahmen* he'd always wanted . . . and then also these kids who he now couldn't live without. He thought also about the other two parents who were part of the deal, Layla, the twins' *mahmen*, and her male, Xcor.

His life was so complete, so perfect, that it seemed as beautiful and unique as a snowflake falling from the sky.

And just as goddamned fragile.

Qhuinn looked back down at his daughter. Moving her closer to his heart, he stroked her soft cheek.

Shaking his head, he said in a low, nasty voice, "Neither do I."

CHAPTER ONE

Present Day
Bathe Nightclub
Market Street, bet. Sixteenth & Seventeenth
Caldwell, New York

The statistical probability of being killed by a falling billboard on a city street is nearly incalculable. Something south of .00000071 percent, considering that math contemplated all objects going Sputnik on you, not just billboards.

But this was something Lyric, blooded daughter of the Black Dagger Brother Qhuinn and the Chosen Layla, adopted daughter of Blaylock, son of Rocke, and Xcor, leader of the Band of Bastards, wouldn't think about until later on in the night. And even then, her one-in-a-million would just be a pebble on the shore of much, much more important things.

Fortunately, as with most stuff having to do with fate, she didn't know what was coming.

At the moment, she was standing in the grungy city snow in a pair of Louboutin stilettos—and she wasn't worried about crapping up her shoes, either. It was the shit coming through her cell phone she'd had enough of.

"Marcia." She pronounced the name "MAR-see-ah," as opposed to the Brady Bunch, normal way, under protest. "Can you just stop so I can get a word in—"

"This is a *huge* opportunity for you. She wants you to come for the *first* day of the conference, *free* of charge. There's a backstage *photo op*, and an *interview* with her—this is going to level your brand up, I'm *telling* you."

The emphasized words were like a strongman working his way through a bench press, and you had to wonder if there was a minimum set count and rep number. Like if the woman missed it, did she stand in front of her bathroom mirror and go at her grocery list just to finish the workout?

Lyric turned so her back was to the strong, shifting wind—and what do you know. Down the alley and across Market Street, there was a huge purple advertisement for the Resolve2Evolve conference.

Like Valentina Disserte was a stalker.

"*Hello?*" came through the phone.

Okay, fine, it was—*was*—a hot invite. R2E had real momentum as a self-actualization movement for women, and no one could argue that its leader wasn't making the most of her fifteen minutes of fame. If the great Valentina kept stalking those stages and proselytizing about the priority of the personhood, the woman was going to be this generation's love-yourself messiah.

The problem? It all just seemed a little too pretty-purple-bow'd to be real. Life through a filter of sound bites, rather than the real thing.

Closing her eyes, Lyric thought about what was happening in her grandparents' house. Maybe even a month ago, she might have bought into the R2E message herself. Now?

Then again, maybe she needed the distraction.

"Fine." As the wind came barreling down the alley with a big shove, she shivered and turned to the club's fire door. "But can we get through tonight first before you ask me about anything else?"

"So *where* are you?"

"Out in the alley—"

The dented metal panel swung wide, and MAR-see-ah Rotterdam, social media manager to the stars, made her appearance with a stress-flourish. Clocking in at barely over five tall and fifty pounds if she'd just had another Diet Coke, the fact that the woman had two cell phones up to her ears made her look like she was ducking an explosion.

"No, *Ron*." She motioned with the phone on the left as she hung it up. "You go to L.A. *tomorrow* for the *collab*. Look, I'm at an *exclusive* event and I have to *go*. I'll call you in the *morning*—when you better be on that *fucking* jet."

Marcia hung up phone #2. "Beautiful, but *dumb* as a box of rocks. Fortunately, he just has to *stand* there for *selfies*. Well, *look* at you."

Lyric glanced down at herself and remembered that she did like her dress. Low-cut, strapless, and black, the thing was set with four-inch strings of iridescent beads so if you swung your hips back and forth, there was a halo around your body, the show both light and dark. Plus the sound was fantastic, a hush of applause.

Of course, Rhamp called it her car-wash getup—

"You know *what*?" Marcia announced.

Oh, God, no. Not another bright idea—

"I'm calling *Vogue*. You're not *big* enough for the U.S. *channel*, but I think I can get us into one of the *European* ones. *Remember* when it was a *magazine*? Too bad we *can't* do stills to show those *eyes* of yours. Blue and green, and not contacts. With the *blond* hair, come *on*. Are you just going to *stand* there? And you've *ruined* those shoes."

As Lyric walked into the back of Bathe, she felt herself recede until she became nothing but a pinprick, only a tiny reflection of who she really was peeking through the velvety drape of what she looked like. Back in the beginning of all this influencer stuff, she had been incandescent.

Now she wasn't even a spark.

The definition of burnout was not a complicated one. The tricky part was what you did about it when all that no-shit-Sherlock, *Merriam-Webster* came and found you. Successful careers, like all bright ideas that by some miracle worked, assumed a velocity of their own, but unlike things such as cars, airplanes, or space shuttles, there was no safety equipment to buffer a sudden braking.

So here she was. Surrounded by people who thought they knew her, a paper idol who was the only one who seemed to know she wasn't actually hot as hell. She was flammable.

And there was a world of difference between the two—

Marcia stepped up, stepped in, stepped all over everything. "*You* stand over *there*, and we *bring* the line through *here*—let's get moving *now* so you know *where* you are before I bring your *people* in."

Her people? As if she'd written her name inside their clothes and was taking them to some kind of existential summer camp?

As Lyric let herself get positioned like a vase on a shelf, she glanced at the step and repeat. Set against a pink and pale green background, her Lyrically Dressed logo, with its little music bars forming a dress, alternated with the Trash Panda makeup brand's—which featured a panda and a trash bin, go figure.

Glancing out past the VIP room's archway, she measured the crowd and was shocked by how many had come. It was a surprise she'd felt before, and at least that was one part of the job that still felt fresh. First it had been ten thousand subscribers to her Zideo account, then came a hundred thousand. When she'd crossed a million, she'd thrown herself a party, and felt like she'd had a purpose.

Now she was hovering at just under five million, and she had brand deals, an appearance schedule, and a manager—

"That *light* needs to be re-angled." Marcia barked out a command and then went guided missile on some poor man in overalls. "Yes—*you.* I'm talking to *you.* That is *wrong!* She needs it *softer* on her face."

Make that, *manager.*

As Lyric was left in the dust, she looked around. The VIP part of Bathe had been reserved for the event, and a snaking series of ropes had been set up to keep the line organized. Seeing the special-access lounge empty of its usual crowd of top-shelf-drinking highfliers made the setup look like an egg carton for fancy shitfaced people: Twelve sunken seating areas were split in the middle and separated by an aisle you could strut down if you were so inclined. Lit by different shades of blue, from Tiffany's signature paler shade to sapphire to seafoam, the circular couches were comfortable, liquid-resistant, and the site of many a poor decision.

And even more empty wallets.

She knew the place well. She and her friend group were regulars, and over the last year and a half had staked a claim to the back sofa by the emergency exit. The blue-black light was great for keeping things low-key, and if you tended to dematerialize as opposed to Uber out at the end of the night, the alley access by way of that emergency fire door was convenient.

What would Marcia think if she found out she was managing a vampire—

Off to the side, the woman poked her forefinger up into the face of the overall guy like he'd insulted every mother in her bloodline.

Christ, if Marcia knew the truth, she'd probably sell the rights to a tell-all as soon as she got a podcast going.

Nosfer-chat-u.

On that note, Marcia dropped the bone of the lighting and brought over a very tall, very slender woman with very long black hair extensions. It was as if Chas Addams had tossed one of his drawings into the next century, and Lyric pinned a smile.

"Of course *you* remember *Svetlana?*" Marcia did a flourish thing. "She *is* Trash Panda. Svet, you look *amazing*—let's get the two *girls* of the *hour* together."

Marcia clapped her hands, like the world ran on her own personal lights-on-lights-off switch, and then it was cue the small talk as the photographer rushed over in a clear attempt to avoid what the lighting guy had had airmailed at him: Svet complimented Lyric's dress, and Lyric hit the blessings-ball back over the net with an honest appreciation for the other woman's shoes—because hey, even though they were the size of toasters and must have weighed ten pounds apiece, at least

they were dry. Then came the hair-compare and associated fluffing—
at least on Svet's side—followed by the obligatory what-mascara-is-
that.

"Trash Panda all the way," Lyric mumbled. Even though she was
wearing Maybelline.

"Smile!"

Lyric front-and-centered at the lens, but her eyes returned to the
VIP lounge's entrance as the flash went off. The pair of suited sentries at
the archway were looking above-it-all, and the faces on the far side were
a tide they were holding back with a satisfaction that made Lyric want
to spill wine on them.

As someone else was brought over, Lyric stared out from her private
abyss, and talked about nothing, and smiled when she was supposed to.

This time, when the flash went off, she blinked hard.

And thought about what her brother, Rhamp, was doing right now.
He and Shuli, and all the other fighters, were not standing around
posing for pictures. When a bright light went off around them, it
was because they'd stabbed one of the *lessers* who hunted and killed
vampires, and sent the fucker(s) back to their maker.

Their brilliant flashes were a sign they'd won a battle, saved a civilian, made a difference.

Done something courageous and worthwhile—

"And *here*, Lyric, before we *start* things, you have to *meet*—"

Marcia shoved another person in for advance photos, an interviewer
with some kind of podcast, who was followed by another influencer
with "an *insane* amount of followers"—

And that was when Lyric caught sight of a familiar face. Over by the
emergency exit.

A shy, reserved, familiar face attached to a lanky body garbed in just
Levi's and a t-shirt, in spite of the cold.

"Oh, Allhan!" Lyric broke out of a four-person lineup. "Hi!"

"Wait, *what?*" Marcia demanded. "*Where* are you *going*—"

"Hey!" As she rushed over to the male, her smile was an honest one.

That she hoped wasn't as desperate as she feared it might be. "What are you doing here?"

Allhan looked at the floor, and even in the dark blue light, she could see the flush race up his thin neck and bloom in his hollow face.

"I mean, I'm so glad you came." She touched his arm. "I'm just surprised, is all. This is not your usual kind of place."

As a pretrans, Allhan was about twenty-five years old according to the human calendar—no one was sure exactly when his birthday was, not even him—but he was as scrawny as a twelve-year-old human kid. And then there was the frizzy dark hair. No matter what the season, it was like he'd rubbed a balloon on the crown of his head in the middle of winter and done nothing about the static electricity.

Then again, the guy was live-wire smart. Maybe he actually had straight hair and the heat generated by all that IQ was what had permed up all his—

"*What* are you *doing?*" Marcia stepped in between them. "You *need* to be back there—"

"Oh, it's okay, I'm just saying hi. This is my friend."

Marcia's narrowed eyes did an up-and-down on the male, and somehow her wooden expression was more of an insult than if she'd said the words she was clearly thinking:

Less than. Not worth the effort.

Forgettable.

"That's just *great*." The woman linked arms with Lyric and started walking away. "That's *wonderful*. We *love* friends, just *not* right now."

As Lyric threw out her anchor, she wondered whether, if it had been her brother or, like, Shuli, for godsakes, things would be *different*. But of course they would.

"You need to give me a minute—"

"No, *now*. This is *work*."

"Let me at least say goodbye." She turned back around. "Listen, Allhan—"

He was gone, the emergency door just shutting.

Lyric put her hands to her face, and felt like screaming. "Hold on, Marcia. I have to go say—"

"You don't need to worry about the likes of *that.*"

Later, much later, Lyric would know that it all really started at that moment, with that one syllable, spoken in that tone. Something just snapped.

"All of *this* is going to wait," Lyric shot back. "While I go and make sure you didn't offend my friend."

Marcia hopped in front and put her arms wide like she was trying to stop a train. Speaking in a rushed hush, she said, "You have two hundred of your followers out there, who paid forty-nine dollars to stand next to you and get their pictures taken. The event is starting at seven. So no, you're not going—"

"There are things more important than work."

"Not tonight there aren't."

As the little woman stared up at her, that Botox-frozen face straining to reflect all kinds of inner horror, it dawned on Lyric that this thing with Lyrically Dressed, which had started with all the casualness of a sneeze two years ago, had taken on a life of its own.

And it was like feeding a monster now.

"You're *so* wrong about that," Lyric muttered as she pushed the woman out of the way. "Life doesn't last forever, you know."

She hit that fire door like it was a solid obstacle.

And as she stepped out, the cold slapped her back just as hard.

"Allhan!" she cried out. "Wait!"

CHAPTER TWO

15 Windsor Lane
Caldwell, New York

If you were going to be a traitor against Wrath, son of Wrath, sire of Wrath, two things were guaranteed to happen. One, every worldly possession you had, whether it was stocks, bonds, or cold hard cash or the house you lived in or the clothes on your fucking back, was confiscated unto the King.

And two—

Qhuinn re-formed in a snowbank and looked up at a modern version of the kind of stately mansion he grew up in.

"We're gonna hunt you until we find you," he finished.

Fucking aristocrats. Always planning shit.

Taking out a copper key, he mounted the shoveled front steps and unlocked the heavy door. As he opened things up, the alarm that had been installed a week ago started to tick down, and while he traded that slip of rosy-colored metal for a big-ass block of Beretta, things were turned off back at headquarters.

He did not shut himself in as he stepped over the threshold.

While he flipped the safety off his gun and glanced around, all he wanted to do was get his hands around Whestmorel's pencil neck and snap it off the spine at the ascot. The aristocrat had proven to be craftier than expected, however. He'd made his threat—and then done what most members of the *glymera* could not handle.

He'd gone underground and stayed there, quiet as a mouse.

Not the move of an amateur, and no doubt the snob wasn't just twiddling his thumbs.

"You'll have to come up for air sometime," Qhuinn muttered.

Sooner or later, there would be a tip-off. A financial flare sent up through the web that Vishous could trace. An associate who blabbed to somebody, a sighting at an event, a mistake that led to a crack in the conspiracy.

Or . . . an actual attempt made on the King's life.

That last one was the contingency everybody least wanted.

And the reason he felt like jumping out of his own skin.

Stalking forward into the drawing room, he looked at the vacant spot over the fireplace—and wondered what kind of oil painting had been boosted on Whestmorel's way to the exit. The guy had taken all computer components, cell phones, and security monitoring equipment with him. Safe was also empty—the Brotherhood'd figured that out when Zsadist had blown the door off. And there were all kinds of vacancies on the walls and the shelves that suggested some of the choice art had been taken on the evac, too.

What the hell were they going to do with the rest of Whestmorel's shit? The male's daughter had renounced her own bloodline—to the point that she'd even left her things behind in the house, in spite of the fact that she was totally innocent and had been offered the chance to take what she wanted.

So the rest of this was just high-class junk, really, all of which needed to be sold or donated so they could put the mansion on the open human market and cash the fuck out.

"Or we can just light this bitch on fire." He paused by a gilt-framed mirror and deliberately moved it off-kilter. "And get out the marshmallows—"

"Did someone say 'Stay Puft?'"

He swung around with his weapon pointed at chest level—but was already lowering it before Rhage shoved a grape Tootsie Pop into his mouth and put his palms up.

"You can keep your s'mores," Hollywood maintained. "Just don't shoot me before I get my licks in."

Qhuinn cursed. "You could have made a little noise—"

"I did. I asked you about the Stay and the Puft. Very important stuff."

The Brotherhood's golden boy lowered his hands and crunched down into the chocolate center. That he was eating was no surprise. And go figure, he was still resplendently handsome, big as a house, blond as a sunny day.

Then again, he'd been all that long before Qhuinn had even been on the planet.

"Entering," a deep male voice announced.

"See?" Qhuinn pointed at Zsadist as the brother came in. "*That's* how you do it."

Rhage popped the lollipop stick out of his mouth and pointed with it. "You know what I like about you, kid?"

It seemed stupid to remind the male that he was mated and had two full-grown young of his own. "Tell me."

"You always follow the rules." Rhage clapped Qhuinn on the shoulder. "Which means you're good backup."

Qhuinn blinked. He'd been called a lot of things in his life. Rule follower . . . ?

As some of the other brothers filed in, he reassured himself that his piercings were all in place.

Even—discreetly—his Prince Albert.

"I'll clear the first floor," he announced, getting his second gun out.

Walking fast, he put both weapons up as he continued through the standard category of formal rooms, all of which had their drapes drawn. Even though the whole place had been camera'd and mic'd up ever since they'd assumed ownership last week, no one could take any chances tonight.

They already knew shit was clear. But again, that didn't matter.

He wasn't about to trust a bunch of cameras with what was coming. None of them were.

Opening up his senses, he sent a healthy dose of paranoid out into the drawing room. The study. The library. The music room. As he went along, refreshing his memory of the silk-covered furniture and the museum quality antiques, the Persian rugs on the floors and the portraits on the walls, he heard the others walking around upstairs through the bedrooms, the closets, the laundry room. Another team went all the way to the attic, and a final one dove into the basement and the garage.

As he came to the kitchen, he tracked every shadow thrown by the bright ceiling lights. In contrast to the rest of the house, which was a showcase for *glymera* visitors, back here it was all business, the appliances stainless steel, the pans hanging on racks in descending size, the ladles and knives and utensils all organized and within reach of the cutting boards, the stoves and ovens, the service line.

Big-ticket setup for a house that catered to a big-ticket master.

After checking the walk-in refrigerator and then the freezer—because hey, aristocrats, like all snakes, were cold-blooded—he did a pass through the pantry, and came out into the dining room.

That was when he stopped.

The table was what pulled him up, that long, glossy run down the middle of the formal room with all those chairs tucked in tight like soldiers called for inspection: twenty-two chairs, the two at the ends sporting arms.

"Now is not the time," he said under his breath.

Nonetheless, his memory banks coughed up a hairball of the past, the room before him replaced by a what-once-was. Instead of this grand setup, he saw a downright imperial one, and instead of empty chairs, there were familiar faces in candlelight . . . the Brotherhood, their mates, and the fighters, along with the First Family. And all the young were there, too, everybody eating, drinking . . . being merry.

It was so clear, so painfully clear. Even though it had been thirty years and change since they'd gathered in that gargoyle'd royal house up on Great Bear Mountain, he could picture the amalgam of countless Last Meals vividly, like it was a dream he was in, rather than a memory that stalked him.

A lingering nostalgia registered as pain in the center of his chest. There had been problems back then for all of them, issues in life that ranged from the little annoyances to the big worries to the outright terrors. And the war, always the fucking war.

But things seemed simpler—

He went to rub his pounding head, then remembered he had a loaded gun in each hand with the safety off—and now was so not the time to shoot himself in the dome for a dumb reason.

And not just because it'd ruin all this pretentious gold-leafed wallpaper.

On that note, he thought of another table, a totally different one— and this time, it really was from memory, not some post-traumatic mental spasm that he couldn't seem to move past: A cozy family table now, in an open, casual kitchen that was ringed with windows overlooking a meadow and a pond. No butler and waitstaff. No sterling or crystal. No swooping drapes or heavy chandeliers.

No brothers, either.

Just his immediate family: Blay, and the male's parents, Lyric and Rocke, with the twins, Lyric and Rhamp, in high chairs. The Last Meal spread was served in mismatched dishes and steaming with warmth, but the plates were as yet empty because there was one more dish being brought over. Meanwhile, snow was falling outside, and the decor was red and green for Christmas, even though there were no humans in the house . . .

Rocke saying something about his *shellan* and looking her way. And Qhuinn also glanced over to the stove.

The elder Lyric was there, with her apron on and her hair pulled back sensibly. She was cutting up the lasagna she'd made just for Qhuinn, the light fixtures over the island catching the planes of her lovely face.

Healthy. Whole. With life still in front of her—

"One minute out."

Qhuinn jerked around to the archway. Rhage was standing there, filling the double doorjambs, and there were no more lollipops in sight. It was game time, so he had a gun in each hand.

Still, the guy asked, "You okay?"

No, he wasn't. But Hollywood—just like everybody else—knew that already, and knew the reason. Some things you just didn't want to say out loud, though.

My beloved mahmen-*in-law is dying* was still not a statement he was prepared to make. And the same was true about the inevitable add-on: *And it's killing everybody.*

So he pivoted on his reply. Even though now was also not the time for him to get a hair across his ass because someone who lived off Fluffernutter sandwiches, chips, and ice cream suggested that maybe he was halfway following rules.

"Just so we're clear." He touched the silver hoop in his lower lip, even though his Beretta nearly poked him in the eyeball. "I'm still who I've always been."

Rhage chuckled. "You mean a badass?"

"Yeah, exactly." He cleared his throat. "But enough about me. How is this happening?"

"It was *not* my idea," Hollywood muttered. Then he called out, "Basement and garage, clear."

Qhuinn put volume into his voice as well: "First floor, clear."

From out in the foyer, Z answered with, "Second floor, clear."

And Phury chimed in, "Attic, clear."

A vibration went off inside Qhuinn's leather jacket, and when the text was answered—the countdown started. Exactly thirty Mississippi's later, headlights washed across the front of the mansion, the hard beams penetrating a seam in the heavy, closed curtains like an adversary that'd found a weakness.

"Let's get this over with," he gritted as he headed for the foyer.

Joining the other brothers who were milling around beneath a crystal chandelier, he rolled his shoulders and then cracked his neck by cranking his head from side to side. Everybody was double-dipping into their holsters, but no daggers. Those vicious black blades had all stayed put.

A gun was better in this situation.

Two forties were even better.

Tohr was the one who opened things up, and the cold air came in before him, the dark night on the other side like a void he'd somehow managed to step out of. Vishous was next, the goateed brother looking like he was ready to fight, his hands up at chest level, the pair of Glocks in them the perfect accessory to all his black leather and fuck-off.

And behind him, the male of the hour.

Wrath, the great Blind King, was taller than everybody—or at least it felt that way. With those wraparounds hiding his eyes, his cruel, aristocratic face, and all his long black hair falling from that widow's peak, he single-handedly validated the human bullshit mythology about vampires. He was the real deal, the last purebred of the species left on the planet, a force of nature, a stone-cold killer, and a shrewd leader.

Whose side hustle was rank impatience.

The second he was past the threshold, John Matthew and Xcor entered in his wake and shut the front door with a resounding *thud*. The two of them had twin sets of guns out as well, and both put their backs to the wood. There was a brief silence, as if everybody in the foyer was taking a moment.

"Relief" was the wrong word.

No, relief wasn't going to come until they were back at the Audience House. Safely, with all of the King's fingers and toes accounted for.

Instead, this pause was what happened when a group of males were determined to keep their yaps shut—and choking on the fucking effort.

As Wrath's nostrils flared while he tested the air, Qhuinn leaned to the side and traced the blind corners in that drawing room he'd just gone through. And then he glanced back at the front entrance, even though there was no reason to worry about the exterior. The Band of Bastards was covering the property lines, and they did not need primers on how to shoot to kill.

Still, he felt like his balls had crawled up into his lower abdomen—and turned into grenades.

Then again, the last time Wrath had left the house to go anywhere except for audiences with civilians, three decades of hell had ensued. Frankly, he was surprised that Beth had gotten on board with the plan, but that was none of Qhuinn's business—although he could imagine how the conversation had gone.

Good times, good times. J/k.

When Wrath finally stepped forward and Tohr fell in beside him, the latter holstered one of his guns and put his hand behind the King's elbow to subtly guide him. The brothers then fanned out, and Qhuinn went with the flow, the lot of them like a living organism with a single mind, a single body.

No components, only the whole.

It was an ancient tradition, the Black Dagger Brotherhood not only protectors of the race, but the private guard to the King . . . prepared to lay down their lives in service to the male who mattered most.

Fucking hell, Qhuinn thought as he continued along. *Let nothing go wrong tonight.*

CHAPTER THREE

The Otto Building
Corner of Market Street and Sixteenth Avenue

The guy's down a quart. Look at him. Don't say nothin', don't talk to nobody. He's a goddamn—"

"*Stop.*" Bob Knolls, proud LiUNA member and foreman of this particular Wabash Construction Company site, shot a glare over his thermos of hot chocolate. "Just cut it with that language, okay. It's offensive."

"Oh, 'scuse me, word police." Petey McCord, resident shift-prick, bristled on the other side of the picnic table and spoke up even louder over the din of a jackhammer. "Didn't know you were so fucking sensitive—"

The winter wind barreling up from the river hung a left directly over the break area, the chain-link fence rattling, the mesh panels flapping against their ties. The only good news was that the shit cut Petey off, although one thing everybody had learned over the last month was that the asshole of this particular job wouldn't be down for long.

As the commentary started up again, Bob put his palm forward—and wondered why he couldn't be the type of foreman who ruled with an iron hammer. Fist. Whatever.

"What the *fuck* do you care so much about him, Petey? Clock your time, cash your check, live your fucking life —"

"—over there, workin' through the break and makin' us look bad—"

Bob curled up a fist and slammed it down. "Leave Big D alone."

The other guys jerked to attention, even the ones at the neighboring tables, all kinds of would-ya-look-at-that faces lifting from lunch boxes and travel mugs. Hard to know whether they were surprised by the particularly nasty edge of Petey's bitching or if it was that their go-with-the-flow foreman was actually doing something about it.

And meanwhile, that jackhammer droned on.

Bob got back to his hot chocolate because it was the only thing keeping him warm at this point. Goddamn, he hated eating out in the cold, and it was ridiculous that OSHA standards required them to be outdoors to protect their lungs. Yeah, 'cuz pneumonia was better than a little chemical exposure here and there. At least the arctic chill was an improvement over the hot months when you couldn't drink enough to keep up with the sweat—

"Big D," Petey mimicked as he tore into his sub like he was chewing off an animal leg. "Fucking Frankenstein motherfucker. Oh, *sorry*, am I allowed to use that f-word? Wouldn't want to *offend* anybody. Or Dick himself, over there."

"His name is Dev," Bob muttered.

Instead of doing something else with a fist—like coldcocking the smartass and losing his own job and benefits—Bob set into his wife's meatloaf sandwich and thought, *God bless that woman.* As he chewed, he couldn't decide if the fact that opening his lunch box was the highlight of his work night was a good or bad commentary on his life.

Better to have the home thing going right, he decided. You could always find another job.

As the tone and volume of that asphalt assault got higher and even louder, Bob shifted his eyes over the field of dumpsters, construction equipment, and debris. In the noon-bright glare of the cage lights, real-name Devlin was bearing down on the jackhammer like the piece of equipment better get him to the center of the earth or he was going to throw the hunk of crap into the Hudson. Steam rose off a set of weight-lifter-worthy bare arms, his reflective bib and t-shirt all that he was wearing—unlike the rest of them, who were so layered, they were basically human Gobstoppers.

And yeah, okay, fine. Big D's intensity was a little weird, and the never-taking-a-breather stuff on shift was pretty stupid. The collective bargaining agreement for the union guaranteed you two fifteen-minute breaks as well as a thirty-minute lunch, but if you didn't take them, it wasn't like you got overtime. Still, the guy rarely sat down, and not because he was some tweaking kind of drug user. He just seemed to want to work, and between that drive and all his strength, he could do in an hour what three regular guys took half a shift to get done.

Which was why motormouth with the slurs had a problem with him.

Not that Big D cared. He just ducked his head and—

The jackhammer's engine got cut, and Big D easily put it aside. Then he bent down and picked up a chunk of sidewalk the size of a car hood. As he walked off with the load, he might as well have been strolling through a park, and when he tossed the section over the lip of a dumpster, there was no grunting, no groaning—

"Hey, Dick! You know we got a lift for that shit!" Petey called out.

Bob went back to his sandwich with a grim fixation. The skyscraper they were renovating was a hundred years old and had last been updated about four decades ago—so they were in the total demo stage of things, ripping and tearing out every square inch of carpeting, all of the cubicle walls, and any fixture there was down to the faucets and toilets in the bathrooms and every goddamn fluorescent ceiling bar that had ever been made. Of course they were behind schedule, but he wasn't allowed to let Dev stay inside and keep cranking. The rule was, when it was break time, everyone had to vacate whatever level they were on and come out here into the open air as a group.

Big D had started working the jackhammer on the sidewalk just this week, and he'd already made it about a quarter of the way down the building's block. After he was finished? Well, he could start on the front entrance's stone stairs if he wanted to—

"Yo, Big D!" Petey shouted over again. "How 'bout you bend over some more. You look like you want a fucking date!"

As the nitpick continued, a couple of the guys grumbled and looked over pointedly. At Bob.

"Yeah, yeah," he said under his breath. "I got it."

Except before he could figure out his next move, Petey shot to his feet and marched away from the break area, a greasy string bean on a bad-idea mission.

Toward Big D.

Bob polished off the last of his sandwich and extricated himself from the bench. As he jacked up his insulated work pants, he was reminded of why he hadn't really wanted to become foreman. Too bad the pay was so much better, and it looked like tonight he was going to be forced to earn the extra ten bucks an hour.

"Can we *not* do this—"

The wind whipped around again, caught a drywall bucket, and sent the damn thing right into his shin. As he cursed and hobbled, Petey stepped in front of Big D while the other man headed back for the jackhammer.

"Say somethin'," Petey barked. "Fuck, speak wouldya!" Big D just stared down at the guy. Like all the noise at his feet was a walkie-talkie that had been dropped.

"That's it? You just gonna look at me? That's all you got, you motherfuckin'—"

As the slur was dropped for a second time, what happened next was something that Bob would replay for the rest of his life:

Big D still didn't respond, so Petey palmed up and punched the guy right on the pecs. The double strike was like a toddler tantruming a brick wall.

And that's when Big D, the strong, silent type, finally reacted.

That heavy right arm snapped out and he grabbed Petey's throat like a rope. The lift that followed wasn't exactly a surprise, but when was the last time anybody'd seen a full-ass grown man dangling from a fist grip, with his work boots clapping together as if they approved of the find-out after all the fuckin' around?

Bob hurried his own Timberlands up, but he had to dodge another tumbleweed bucket, a flag of netting that had torn off one of the pedestrian barriers, and something that could have been a panel of particle board—or might have been a fantastical flying beast, because this shit was surely some kind of screwed-up fever dream.

By the time he got to the problem, Petey was clawing desperately at the hand around his neck, his jowls all basset-hound bunched up, his already ruddy face barn red and getting worse.

Bob tried to put some authority into his voice: "Hey, Big D, how about you put him down—"

His voice dried up as the guy's head cranked toward him. Those eyes . . . so unremarkable before . . . had a soulless gleam to them that made them unforgettable: There was nothing behind the ice-cold stare. Not a scrap of humanity, and no recognition, either.

And as the other dozen or so guys on shift came over from the picnic tables, Bob stopped them with a glare. A pile-on might be a good solution in another situation. In this one? He was worried that Big D might snap Petey's fucking neck and then get to work on the rest of them.

"Hey, D," he said in what he hoped was a reasonable tone, "let's put him down, 'kay? You don't want to go to jail over him. He's not worth it. Plus he's sorry, ain't you, Petey."

Petey did what he could do to nod as tears welled and started to fall from his bulging eyes. Whether that was emotion or the precursor to him going empty-socket, it was impossible to know.

"You hear me, Big D?" Bob took out his cell phone and waved it in the guy's general direction. "If you hurt him, I'ma have to call the police. So let's not escalate this—"

Petey's eyes rolled back in his head, only the whites showing, and his boots abruptly stopped kicking.

"Devlin, you gotta let him down!" The wind was so loud, Bob had to shout over it. And then there was the alarm that had started to scream in his own head. "Come on, man! You want to go to jail for the rest of your l—"

The metal-on-metal creaking was the kind of sound that, after twenty years working construction, you instantly knew meant two things: One, it was something big. And two, gravity had a helluva hold on whatever the hell it was.

So a different kind of danger had just shown up to the chat.

And it was on such a scale that everyone, even Big D, looked to the roof of the building next door.

It was that goddamn purple billboard, the one with that brunette's face on it and some stupid logo. The vicious wind had caught the panels, turned them into a sail—and was in the process of peeling the bitch right off its support scaffolding.

Bob did a quick trajectory check. The gusts were going to take it away from the construction site and the bib'd-up, hard-hatted men who were standing around watching the show.

That was the good news. The bad news? Those people clustered around the glow of that club Bathe's entrance were fucked.

Not his problem, though.

Bob went back to what *was* his issue: "Put him down, Dev. Or I'm calling the police."

CHAPTER FOUR

Allhan, stop!"

Lyric tripped and flipped her way through the salted slush and frozen snow of the alley, knowing full well that it was going to be a miracle if she didn't break all of her ankles—because surely she had more than two if she was still upright.

"Allhan, hold up—"

With a squeak, she went full modern dance, her rhythm chiropractic, her sense of balance far outstretching her coordination. The damn Louboutins were somehow backup, though, the spiky heels like stakes on a tent, anchoring her even as she blew all around. Meanwhile, Allhan spun to a halt at the head of the lane, the crazy wind billowing his baggy shirt out from his soda-straw body, his frizzy hair remaining utterly unaffected by the maelstrom.

"Are you okay?" he shouted as he ran back for her.

As soon as he was in range, she grabbed on to his arm and yanked her heel out of its hold in the slush. "Yes, sorry—"

"Here, lean on me."

Grabbing on to his other shoulder, she went wisdom-tooth extraction on her stiletto, and then settled onto some salted pavement.

"Look, I'm sorry about my manager. She just is—"

"It's okay."

"No, it's not."

Allhan shrugged. "I'm used to people being like that with me. It really isn't a problem."

Lyric opened her mouth. Shut it. Then she cleared her throat. "Were you meeting someone here?"

His eyes drifted away. "No."

"Then why did you come?" When he didn't immediately answer . . . that was clearly the answer. Especially as his face tightened with a fragile composure. "Oh . . . it was for me?"

"I've got to go." Allhan started stepping back. "Have to be at work. Very busy."

The cold wind swirled around them, and she had a sudden thought that she had missed it. Somehow, she'd missed the crush he'd developed on her. Then again, though she'd never been cruel, she had certainly never *seen* the male properly.

And lately, she'd come to know what being invisible felt like.

Reaching out, she took his trembling, thin hand. "Allhan, thank you. For coming. I've been feeling alone."

"But you have all those people." He glanced at the tail end of the wait line in surprise. "Here to see you."

"They're not . . . real."

Neither am I anymore, she thought.

Abruptly, he tugged his hand back and turned away. "Gotta go. See you later—"

"Wait." Except what could she say? "Hold on a sec—"

"You are *embarrassing* yourself, right now. And *me*, too."

As Marcia's voice cracked like a whip, Lyric knew exactly why the male had gone into retreat mode.

Shaking her head, she didn't even bother to look at her manager. "Gimme a minute."

"No."

Lyric wheeled around and loomed over the woman. Narrowing her eyes, she gritted out, "*Yes.*"

Then she once again took off after Allhan through the snow and ice. There was no dematerializing for a pretrans, and that meant he'd either Ubered here or been dropped off by someone—and considering he didn't hang with anybody, he was clearly headed out into the wilds of Caldwell where he might or might not be able to get a car on a cold night like this.

And if anything happened to him?

"Allhan!"

"Get *back* here!" Marcia hollered.

Off in the lead, Allhan glanced over his shoulder at the woman and started flat-out running. Which meant Lyric started running. Which meant Marcia started running.

It was like something from a fucked-up rom-com, two women in high heels, one guy gunning for his life to get away, all of them slipping and sliding down the dark alley in the dirty city snow. And because the "zany hijinks"—which were feeling really desperate, actually, on all accounts—needed to be witnessed by a crowd of astonished strangers, the wait line congregating in the blue-and-green glow of Bathe's entrance checked that box as that peanut gallery pulled a collective pivot.

Instantly, the for-the-most-part-female congregation recognized Lyric—*OMG! It's HER!* —and order broke apart as they grabbed their phones and rushed forward to take pictures.

As Allhan got to the head of the alley, he skipped right through the gathering gate of people, but as Lyric closed in, she knew she wasn't going to get away with that kind of magic trick—so she started in with the sorrys way ahead.

"I'll be right back!" she told them, waving her hands. "Thankyou'scusemethankyou'scuse me—"

Give her a football and she was a Heisman candidate as she threaded through the spaces between the young human women, dropping apologies as fast as her feet were poking holes in the crusty slush with those heels. As she broke through and burst out onto Market Street, the wind lashed at her and her long blond hair tangled around her face. By the time she got the strands free from her eyelashes, three things were true: Allhan was gone. She was in the middle of the four-laner with cars honking and swerving around her.

And what the *hell* was that screeching sound?

The noise was so loud that it cut through the roar of the icy gusts and the high-pitched fuck-you of the horns.

Spinning around, she looked up.

The purple billboard was mounted on the roof of the old-fashioned building diagonally across the intersection, and even though it had been secured with metal supports, the panels had been caught by the power-ful wind and were ripping free.

Had ripped free.

It took only a split second to calculate where the impact was going to be as gravity took over what the gusts had started—and that logo and the face that went with it were the punchline to the fact that Lyric was standing at ground zero.

Or maybe they were a message from the universe that her priorities were going to kill her.

Lyric hauled ass.

Digging into the crusted hump between lanes, she rechecked the sky as she tried to avoid being crushed.

The Resolve2Evolve logo was getting bigger by the second, the face of the woman at the head of the movement on a zoom-in that was down-right deadly. Ducking the eye contact, Lyric changed directions in hopes of getting out of the line of fire, heading for a brightly lit construction site and a gaping group of men in orange vests and hard hats inside a fence.

But it was like the damn thing was coming after her.

In the mirrored windows of the building that was being renovated, she saw the billboard zeroing in on her in the wash of aqua light from Bathe's facade—and also got a good snapshot of herself running for her life in the shimmering dress she loved so much. And then there were all the people from the wait line screaming while the cars hit their brakes and careened into snowbanks, lampposts, and storefronts.

The only thing she didn't see was her savior.

Out of thin air, there was suddenly a mammoth man right on her. He grabbed her waist, spun her off her feet, and curled his massive body around her in a protective tuck—

The crash was so loud, her ears rang, and there was a *whoosh!* of cold air with all kinds of debris falling like weird snow.

After that? Just breathing.

Hers. His.

She took a deep breath—

"Are you okay?" the man asked in a low, deep voice. Which was oddly quiet.

Before she could respond, a glow surrounded them, like something in the universe had preordained both the near miss and their meeting—

Nah, it was just a delivery truck fishtailing while it tried not to run them over.

It was then that the man started to straighten. And straighten. And . . . there was also some cursing. Then again, he was holding the entire billboard over them as well as half its ugly-duckling strands of scaffolding.

With one arm.

As he released her so he could put two hands into the effort, she was transfixed. The face staring down at her from what surely was outer space was something she instantly committed to memory, from the low brows to the strong jaw to the lips that were tight with exertion. It was . . . a harsh, hard face. One that reflected age, without showing the passage of years by way of wrinkles or thinning hair.

Old eyes. Ancient . . . remote . . . eyes. In the visage of a man in his prime. And they bored into her, a different kind of headlights.

"Who are you," she whispered.

What she got in return was a grunt, as he somehow picked up the load and swung the entire billboard above his head, knocking off his hard hat.

Resolve2Evolve. With the famous brunette's face big as an SUV, her smile wide as a doorjamb.

Lyric cursed to herself. Attempted murder by the very thing she was pursuing—or being pursued by, depending on the way you looked at it.

Before she could start her thank-yous, the man walked off with the damn thing in an impossible display of strength for a human—and what do you know. The crowd that had surged forward from the wait line parted in awe for him as he headed for the side of the street. After he dumped the signage out of the way on the curb, he seemed to pause to take a look at the imagery, his head tilting to the side as if wondering, *What the hell?*

Then again, he was not Valentina's core audience, for sure. And hey, his moment of confusion turned into Lyric's advantage because she could take him in properly.

His hair was dark and fairly short, with no particular style, and his reflective bib and work boots were likewise worn from hard use, as if he pulled a lot of hours at his physical job and didn't worry about anything other than the functionality of his wardrobe. No parka, which meant his incredible arms showed like it was August, not January, the muscles wrapping thick and corded around heavy bones.

Was that *steam* rising up off his skin?

Yet he'd smelled clean, and as the wind whipped around again, the subtle spice of his scent tickled into her nose and drowned out the mix of perfumes, body sprays, and hair product wafting up from all the women with the cellphones—

Marcia jumped through the garland of gawkers. "Oh, my *God!* You're *alive!*"

For a split second, Lyric wondered who the woman was talking to. But then she was tackled in a hug, and the waterworks were ridiculous. Like they were sisters who'd been separated by a world war, and there was an Oscar nomination in play.

Then again, they did have an audience, and as the crowd let out a collective *awwwww*, those phones swung back up.

Ah, yes. Content.

"You almost *died!*" Marcia announced. "We need an *ambulance!* Someone call *nine-one-one!*"

Lyric glanced back at the man who'd saved her. He was returning to the construction site, his strides long as a mile, his bare shoulders shifting with a roll of coordinated muscle, his hands relaxed by his sides—like he hadn't just thrown all that weight around. Across the back of his bib, the words "Wabash Construction Co., Ltd." were an arch that had plenty of room given the size of him.

Look at me, she thought at him. *Stop and look at me again.*

When he did no such thing, she felt cheated. But come on, it wasn't like they knew each other—

"It's a miracle, Lyric of Lyrically Dressed," Marcia cried out, "that you're still alive—"

"Oh, shut up, Marcia," she muttered as she shucked the woman like a bad coat.

Then she took two steps over, bent down . . . and picked the man's hard hat up out of the snow.

CHAPTER FIVE

After Devlin dumped the billboard out of the way of traffic, he took a moment to look at the advertisement. Then he shook his head and started back to the construction site. There was going to be no glancing over his shoulder. No final check that the blonde was okay. Absolutely no more talking to her—

His eyes staged a mutiny and shot to her once again. Like she was the only thing in Caldwell he could focus on.

She was still standing in the middle of the street where he'd left her. In the glare of the cars and trucks that had pulled up short, those flaxen waves of hair danced on the wind currents and flashed like strands of pure gold, and likewise her iridescent dress gleamed, as moonlight on restless water. The club's wait line had closed in on her, as if she were the nucleus around which an entire atom's components spun, and a small, dark-haired woman jumped about waving her arms like she was a crossing guard who'd been ignored.

In spite of the chaos . . . the blonde was calm.

And focused on him as she held his hard hat in her hands.

Even though he should go back for his shit, he forced himself to keep on walking. He felt better when he reminded himself that it had been a long time since he'd been with anybody, felt a breast brush his chest, smelled sultry perfume. He was used to living the life of a monk, nothing but solitude, sustenance, and work.

So maybe he needed to color outside of the rigid lines he'd set over the last couple of years some night. God knew there were countless options for scratching any kind of itch in this city—

The second he stepped back through the construction site's pedestrian barrier, he stopped. Bob, the foreman, who wasn't a bad guy, was standing at the head of an isosceles triangle of inconvenience, the other workers drafting behind his middle-aged paunch.

Jesus Christ. People thought old ladies were nosy? Broads in house-dresses and Depends had nothing on a bunch of men with hammers and hard hats—and he'd really fed that gum-flapping beast tonight, hadn't he.

"How 'bout we say it all comes out even," Dev offered to the foreman.

Bob's bushy eyebrows popped. Then he took off his own hard hat. "How you figure that works, Big D?"

"I saved a woman from certain death over there."

"I don't think that matters for our purposes."

"I'll apologize to Petey then."

On that note, he glanced in the guy's direction—and Mr. Big Mouth took a couple of steps back, his hands going to his throat like he was remembering exactly how hypoxia worked.

Wonder what the half-life on that reflex was going to be, Dev thought.

"He deserved it, and he knows it."

Bob stepped between them and held his cell out like a penalty flag at a football game. "I'm sorry, D. I have to call the police. It was an assault, no matter what he said to you, and I gotta follow union and company procedure—"

"I won't do it again." He met the man's tired eyes. "How about we just get back to work—"

"This ain't personal, Dev. I like you, I really do. You're a good worker and no trouble until now, but if that billboard hadn't fallen, we'd be havin' a different conversation, wouldn't we. 'Cuz there'd be a dead body on this property."

Dev slowly shook his head. "We're already behind schedule. You think the CPD showing up is going to help that? It'll just make the delay worse, and cut into your performance bonus." As Bob put a hand to his head like something had started thumping up there, Dev tacked on, "Besides, I promise to keep my hands to myself, and I don't think Petey's saying shit to anybody anytime soon. Right?"

Petey nodded like he had a gun pointed at him.

"See? It's all done—and you won't have to fill out any paperwork."

The foreman stared down at his phone like he was expecting advice from it.

"Tell the boys to go to work now," Dev said softly. "So we can get back on schedule."

Bob cleared his throat. Then he shoved his phone back into his Carhartt jacket. "Finish your lunches, boys. Break's done."

In a lower voice, he added, "You better not make me regret this."

"No problem, boss."

As the other fellas muttered their return to the picnic table area—with Petey heading for his turkey sub like it was a Bible he really needed to be studying—Dev turned back to the jackhammer.

"Hello! Hi!"

At the sound of the female voice, Dev closed his eyes and pictured the blonde in that sparkly dress floating into the gritty construction site on a pair of shoes better suited to a ballroom's marble floors than the bald, frozen earth he was standing on.

The idea the other men were surely looking at her had him thinking fondly of strangulation again, and the surge of aggression was a surprise. For all his triggers, what was up with some woman had never been one, and not because he was into dudes. He wasn't into anybody—

Oh, God, she smelled like heaven, he thought as the wind changed directions again.

"You left this," she said from right behind him. "In the street."

Dev opened his lids, and as another gust hit his chest, he let the force of it turn him around.

She was so close. Too close—

Man, her eyes were something else, one blue, one green . . . both boring right into his soul.

"Sorry," she murmured when he kept silent. "I just thought you'd need it."

As she put out his hard hat, he stared at the thing like he'd never seen one before, tracing the scratches in the fluorescent banding, the dent in the short brim, the Wabash logo on the side.

"It's your hat. Isn't it?"

Dev looked the woman up and down, lingering on her bare arms and her long legs. "It's too cold for you out here."

Before he could stop himself, he walked over to where he'd propped the jackhammer and picked up his waterproof, weatherproof jacket from off the building's front steps. Going back to her, he swept the folds around her slender shoulders, and then took his stupid hat—after which, he promptly wondered what the hell he was thinking: He'd just wrapped a beauty queen up in some worn-out Carhartt bullcrap that was logo'd with "Wabash Construction Co." She was probably allergic to anything that didn't have a fancy label—

The woman curled her red-tipped nails around the rough canvas lapels and brought the two halves closer to her throat.

"But now you're cold," she said in a husky voice.

Yeah, the fuck he was cold when he was looking at her.

"Nah, I'm good." He nodded across the street, at that club's neon entrance. "You better get back to—"

"What did you say your name was?"

He glanced at the break area, and all the men who were NOT LOOKING, LIKE AT ALL. "I didn't."

"Oh. Well . . . I'm Lyric." A slender hand extended out of the folds of his shitty jacket. "Pleased to meet you, and thanks for saving my life."

He put his palms in the air, like it was a stickup. "I'm dirty."

"I don't care."

"Skin's rough."

"That doesn't bother me." Her half smile was like a bomb going off in his chest. "And if you tell me you've never had a manicure—"

"Dev. Short for Devlin." But he didn't dare touch her. "And I'd take my hat off, but I already did—or you wouldn't have had to bring it back to me."

"Are you always so formal?" she murmured.

"You're a lady. And my mother taught me certain manners."

That smile got a little wider. "She's certainly someone with standards and how lucky to have a son like you who—"

"She's dead, and I didn't like her."

The blonde's face froze, and, yup, he was reminded of why the monk thing for him was really the best option. For so many reasons.

"This is *fantastic*! Let me get a *picture* of you both!"

That little dark-haired woman with the bullhorn voice barreled through the pedestrian barrier like a tank, and what do you know: The crowd that had gathered out in the street followed her right in, all floodwaters after a dam burst.

He put his arms wide, knowing Bob was going to fricking love this. "You people got to get outta here—"

The brunette looked up at him like she'd never seen a stop sign, red light, or hold-your-horses hand motion in her life.

"Just a picture," she said in a suddenly level voice. "With the jacket around her standing next to you—"

"Marcia," the blonde started, "this is not the time or place—"

. As the flashes from all those phone cameras blinded him, he knew he had to bolt—hell, he shouldn't have gotten involved with this circus in the first place.

Yeah, except then she'd be dead in the street, and what a waste.

"Keep the jacket," he told her gruffly. "And go back where you came from."

"Wait, you should take it—"

"I have another," he lied as he walked away.

He didn't head over to the jackhammer because he knew she'd just give things another go with the give-back, and bring her entourage along with her. Instead, he two-stepped the stairs and went inside the old, cold building—and made sure the door couldn't be opened behind him.

"Fucking . . . hell," he muttered as the wind howled outside.

The lobby was nothing more than a ripped-clean cavern of dust and debris, the pathways through the buildup on the floor created by bins being dragged or equipment getting pulled or workers traipsing through as tributaries running off from the headwater of the entrance.

The sixth floor was waiting for him, and yet he stayed where he was, hands on his hips, head down . . .

. . . as the specter of his past stalked around him in the drafts, having no mercy while he screamed in his head.

He'd been so good at leaving himself behind and getting lost in the present.

And a chance meeting with that blonde wasn't going to change that track record. He was still a ghost for all intents and purposes, and he was going to damn well stay that way—

The main door opened behind him, and as the roar of the weather blasted into the lobby, all kinds of particles hit the air and spun up into tiny gray twisters.

Dev pivoted around grimly.

It was Bob, not the blonde. And that wasn't much better news, was it.

CHAPTER SIX

S
ome fifteen blocks due east and a little south, Shuli was deep down an abandoned avenue and having a great fucking night. The cold had eaten under his clothes, his bad hip was acting up—and he was really fucking tired of playing babysitter for a heavily armed, cranky toddler. Oh, and he also had black *lesser* blood all over his face—which meant the oily shit was in his mouth.

Nothing like a little spoiled sushi whipped up with some old school Johnson & Johnson baby powder.

He wasn't turning his head away, though, even to spit. And he certainly wasn't moving either of his hands to wipe at anything.

The slayer he had pinned against a filthy brick wall was bleeding out. The lower part of its leg looked like the thing'd been in a mangler, and of course, the fact that L.W.—a.k.a. Wrath, son of Wrath, the great Blind King—had his fingers shoved into that open wound like he was looking for his car keys was having the opposite effect of plugging the leak. But that wasn't even the worst of the undead's injuries.

Still, the *lesser* remained dangerous, its shrewd, nasty eyes alert and looking for its best chance for retaliation.

"*Where.*"

As L.W. spat out the word, he was kneeling at the feet of the enemy as if he were about to propose. The position was not the norm for the hulking male, who was no more likely to bow down than settle down, but needs must and all that jazz.

On that note, the heir to the throne leaned in closer, his bicep thickening under his leather jacket, his upper lip peeling all the way off his fangs. In response, the *lesser* moaned in pain, the dead head lolling on its shoulders, the torso jerking and not getting far.

Thanks to Shuli.

He resecured the hand he had locked on the base of the slayer's throat, but the other was doing just fine as it was: It was cranked around the hilt of the steel blade he'd impaled that abdominal cavity with—which was how he'd gotten his facial. Lot of sputtering involved when you disrupted the GI tract like that.

"*Where*, you fucker," L.W. growled as he relented a little.

And then went right back into the meat of that leg.

As the second verse of suffering bubbled out of the *lesser*'s mouth, Shuli glanced around. The alley they were in was on the fringes of downtown. With abandoned apartment buildings on both sides, no CPD civilian monitoring systems in play, and empty streets all around, this was where the war between the Lessening Society and the vampires had played out for the last century.

Privacy mattered. It was the only thing both sides agreed on.

So they were not likely to get interrupted by anything other than backup for the piece of shit—and this was what Shuli was worried about.

"Not . . . telling . . ." The *lesser* drew in a ragged breath. ". . . shit."

The former human still had the dark hair and hazel eyes he'd been born with, which meant his induction was fairly recent, i.e., within the last couple years. The longer the inductees were in the Lessening Society, the more they lost their natural pigmentation until they were pasty white and had OxiClean locks growing out of their heads. The discoloration thing was a good barometer for how advanced their training and technique was going to be, so yes, the bitch had been pretty easy to overtake. But it also meant the *lesser* wouldn't have been let out alone.

Sooner rather than later, whatever it'd been partnered with was going to show up.

"Let's move on." Shuli glanced over to the left as his instincts prickled. "This is going nowhere—"

"Where's your master." L.W. outed a steel dagger. "You're gonna fucking tell me—"

"Hold up," Shuli hissed as he narrowed his eyes on the far corner of the decayed apartment building. "We've got fucking company."

Overhead, cloud cover was choking out the moonlight, and it wasn't like there were any outside lights to go by—or inside ones, either. But at least there was enough ambient bleed from the rest of the city that he could see well enough . . . to know that there was a shadow lurking at the end of the block.

As the slayer started laughing in a series of gurgles, Shuli moved his grip up and cut off that windpipe completely.

"Stab the fucker or I will," he whispered to L.W. "We gotta get out of here."

Unlike this undead, backup for him and his boy was going to be harder to come by tonight. He wasn't about to pull a Fredo and speak candidly against the family in front of the enemy, but for some unknown reason, there was just a handful of their fighters in the field this evening, both the Brotherhood and the Band of Bastards being tied up at the same time. The reasons for whatever it was were totally above Shuli's pay grade, although he knew without asking that it had to be something to do with the King.

Except who gave a fuck about the why's, if they got ambushed by a squadron of slayers.

L.W.'s head cranked to the left as the male assessed what kind of bad news had shown up on that street corner. And then the movement was so fast, there was no tracking it. The male jerked his arm—

Pop!

The flash was bright enough to freeze-frame the scene on the backs of Shuli's eyelids—maybe fucking permanently—and the heat was like opening the top of a grill when you were flipping a dozen burgers at once. That was it for the *lesser*. Gonzo, and not in a Hunter S. Thompson kind of way.

So Shuli fell face-first into the bricks.

He managed to catch himself right before he turned into a pug, and immediately pinwheeled around. Too late. L.W. was already jogging down toward whatever was waiting for them over there.

Because of course he was. Why hang back for the guy who was not just your assigned partner in the field, but your fucking *ahstrux nohtrum*?

Shuli started hauling ass. "Like a . . . fucking two-year-old . . . gunning for a light . . . socket."

Keeping his eye on that shadow, he got out a gun for his right hand, switching the steel dagger that was dripping black blood to his left palm. He was determined to catch up, but L.W. moved like a Ferrari even though he was built like a tank. So ground was lost over a couple of yards—

Right before the king's only heir engaged with the enemy—fucking *solo*—the figure disappeared as quickly as it had arrived. One second there, the other not, and L.W. skidded to a halt in the snow as he reached the curb.

Shuli's heart stopped even though he was running like his life depended on it: Classic ambush setup. Set the bait, draw the predator, close the trap.

L.W. was about to get riddled with bullets—or at the very least brown-bagged and shoved into a murder van.

He ran even faster through the frozen ice and—

When he arrived beside the male, he had both his weapons up and his head going owl, even though his cervical vertebrae weren't meant to function on that kind of swivel.

Nothing.

Just more decaying buildings across the street. Steam rising from a manhole. A distant horn and a siren even farther off.

"What the hell was that," L.W. muttered.

"The *worst* fucking idea"—Shuli blew out his breath in a cloud—"you've had lately."

He put his weaponed hands up on his head and walked around, panting into the cold air. "Which considering you also tried to ditch me last night is really saying something, you goddamn maniac. We're supposed to stick together. I'm your *abstrux nohtrum*—"

"That was my father's idea, not mine," L.W. said as he scanned the deserted streetscape. "Keep up—or don't. Either way, it's not my problem."

With that, the male just turned away and started walking.

"Excuse me, motherfucker," Shuli called out.

When there was no response, he jumped forward and caught the male's arm. "FYI, the pink slip that comes with this job I didn't want is my own coffin. So will you work with me here?"

"No one needs to know," the heir to the throne tossed back.

For no good reason, the big dumbass came into sharp focus. L.W. was a chip off the ol' block for sure, tall, broad, and black-haired, with a center braid keeping his long-and-straight out of his harsh face, and a set of pale green eyes that gossip said were just like his sire's. He was also highly impatient, very autocratic, and about as fun to be around as a bag of Tannerite two seconds before the bullet hits.

Shuli poked the guy in the chest. "*You* need to stay with me."

"No, *you*"—L.W. returned the favor twice as hard—"need to be better at your job if you're not keeping up."

Don't do this, Shuli told himself. Not here, at least. Later, when they were home—

His body stepped forward on its own, closing the distance so they were chest to chest. Too bad he had to look up to meet that nasty stare.

"What the fuck is your problem," L.W. gritted.

"I'll spell it out. Most of the time I'd like to kill you, but if I do, I'm committing suicide. So I'm dealing with a really fucked-up conflict of interest—"

The vibration in Shuli's pocket was a welcome distraction. At least until L.W. shoved his hand into his own jacket and pulled out his phone, too.

Group texts were *never* good news—

"Holy . . . shit," Shuli breathed as he hit play on the video they'd been texted.

Out of the corner of his eye, he caught L.W. staring down at his screen with the same surprise. Which was saying something. Usually the guy didn't give two craps about anything other than hunting and killing. Then again, when was the last time either of them had seen a billboard go flying off a building and nearly crush somebody they knew?

And . . . maybe, on Shuli's side . . . loved.

A little.

"Oh, fuck, Lyric," he said. And who the hell was that Good Samaritan? "We got to get over to Bathe—"

L.W. shoved his Samsung away. "There's no 'we' in that. Go if you want, I'm staying in the field."

"You're kidding me, right?"

"She lived, didn't she."

Shuli tilted his head. "I'm sorry, *what?*"

"Go and roll bandages if you want, I'm working the rest of this shift—"

"The fuck you are. You're coming with me."

The arrogant look that was tossed back at him was bog standard, and even though it would get him murdered for so many reasons—and it was only a fantasy in his mind—Shuli imagined stabbing the asshole a couple of times in the gut just on principle: The only thing the pair of them agreed on was that this mandated arrangement sucked, and the fact that it meant they had to live together was a total kick in the nads.

Before the male could lay down another round of autonomy, Shuli cut in, "You're *not* going to make me choose between the friends who are all I have and the roommate I hate more than anything in this godforsaken city."

"You're right," L.W. said with a shrug. "You're not doing the choosing. I'm doing it for you."

With that, the heir to the throne ghosted away, dematerializing into thin air.

◆   ◆   ◆

As Lyric walked back to the club, she burrowed into the man's coat, smelling his scent, feeling the scratch of the collar under her chin, being weighted by the bulky, loose folds. Surrounded by women who were buzzing, and led by Marcia in front, she felt like she was part of a fucked-up marching band, and had to beat off a depressed letdown. But come on, she'd miraculously been saved! She could be dead, in the middle of the street, her body picked up by emergency-response humans who would find out what she actually was and create all kinds of problems for her fathers and the Brotherhood. She should be thanking her lucky Lassiter that that stranger had come out of nowhere—

What color had his eyes been? She couldn't seem to remember.

As a matter of fact, she couldn't exactly call him to mind. Then again, there had been a lot to be distracted by.

Maybe she'd gotten hit on the head after all.

When Marcia got to the start of the alley, she called over one of the security guys from the wait line, and he stopped the crowd from following any farther. The breathing room was good. Now she just needed even more space.

Halting, she turned to Marcia—

The woman put up a palm before Lyric could say anything. "You have *no* idea what this has *done* for your career. You're going to be *trending* on Zideo in a half hour with all that posting. If you aren't *already.*"

As the words registered in her ears, Lyric's chaotic brain couldn't translate them. "I'm sorry . . . what?"

"You can't *pay* for the kind of *exposure* you're going to get after tonight. The world lives for a good *romance* story and you gave 'em a helluva one in the middle of that *street* out there."

"There's no romance, no story." Lyric studiously ignored a flush of heat. "That was a complete stranger and dumb luck."

"Doesn't matter." Marcia's eyes went up and down the coat. "The currency you're trading in is *emotion,* and there are few things that *make* a better setup than a *damsel* in *distress* and a *fucking hot* construction worker—"

"I can't do this anymore." She looked to all the people with camera phones being held back by the bouncer's wide arms. "I'm going home and I'm closing my socials. I'm done."

Marcia's eyes narrowed. And then, for once, there was no hyperbole. No grand gestures.

In a low voice, the woman said, "You hired me to grow your business. You don't have to like me, or approve of the way I do my job. But you signed a contract with me, I arranged this event for you, and you are not going to leave those people high and dry after they nearly saw you killed. Don't do it for the views, fine. Fuck me off, too—you think that hasn't been done before? Just don't get all precious about how 'ugly' behind the curtain is when you're getting *exactly* what you asked for."

Lyric opened her mouth. Shut it.

Turned to the battered steel door that opened into the club.

"This is not how I thought it was all going to turn out."

"That's life," Marcia muttered. "If it goes otherwise, you're too dumb to understand what's happening."

The woman marched over and opened things up. And then she just stood there as the blue glow bled out into the alley along with some measure of the interior's heat and a thumping bass beat that went right into Lyric's skull.

"You can turn your new leaf over after you've met your obligations." Marcia swooped her hand, all lead-the-way-inside. "And yes, you can absolutely pretend that this is a dishonorable, exploitive way of making a living—but only after you do the job you sold to these people who paid good money to show up, in the cold, and wait for you to stand in a three-thousand-dollar pair of shoes that you're going to throw out as soon as you get home because you've ruined them in the fucking snow."

Lyric glanced out toward the wait line and again felt a hollow, ringing exhaustion. Especially because she didn't know what had happened to Allhan. She could only hope that he'd made it back okay.

"After this, I'm done."

"If I can get you out of R2E." That hand swooped once again toward the interior. "And yes, I already lined that up before you were nearly wiped out by Valentina's billboard."

Great, Lyric thought.

With dread, she reentered the VIP area. People had already been let in, with the line snaking through the cordoned pathway to the step and repeat. As soon as she was spotted, a cheer went up and cell phone flashes started going off.

The faces were excited and hopeful, the bodies jumping, the crowd sending nothing but warmth and support her way. And this was everything she had wanted . . . once.

Glancing down at Marcia, she said, "You're right. I can't leave now."

Marcia nodded in a bored way. "I'm always right. At least about this. And now for another truth bomb. The sooner you get started, the sooner it's over. Up to the step and repeat you go—oh, Svet, darling, right? *Can you believe* it? She was nearly *killed!*"

As the other woman came flying over, she had her cell phone out. "I *can't* believe it, *no!* Look what *happened* to you!"

The jealousy on her face was mostly hidden, and as she dipped in for a selfie, all Lyric could think was, *Jesus, you actually wanted to be the one out in that street?*

Taking a deep breath, she forced a smile for the iPhone, and then got to walking—in those expensive, ruined shoes that Marcia was, yup, right about: She was going to toss them when she got home, and she abruptly thought about the rest of her wardrobe. She had two closets full of beautiful, expensive clothing, all of which had been bought by exactly the kind of money that she'd brought in tonight.

The problem was not the crowd who'd come here. It was the content machine: the social media platforms, the managers, the influencers, who all worked together to create fantasy out of what was supposedly real, and turned people like her into false idols.

She thought about that man who had rushed out to help her, without any thought for his own safety.

Now that was *real*.

When she got beside the step and repeat, she went to take off his construction jacket.

Marcia leaned in from out of nowhere. "You should keep that on."

Of course. Better for the pictures.

"Let's bring the first person through," Lyric said grimly as she rolled up the big, loose sleeves.

CHAPTER SEVEN

The eeriest thing about Wrath was the way you'd swear the King was seeing things. As Qhuinn squeezed into a wood-paneled study along with the others, he watched the blind male sweep his head around like he was checking out the room's decor. Meanwhile, Tohr continued to stay at his elbow, guiding things when needed so that there was no risk of a trip and fall.

After thirty years of thinking Wrath had been blown to hell and gone, it was good to see the male with his second-in-command, the pair working together again.

What was not so hot was to have all the reunited-and-it-feels-so-good happen here at this traitor's house.

Whestmorel's den was set up around an ornate French desk with legs that had antique brass sculptures of women going breast-out in all directions. The walls were ringed with shelves full of show-off first editions, antique nautical crap, and Victorian-era mounted butterflies, and there were also window seats for reflection, a marble hearth for warmth, and as much personality as a hotel lobby.

The Brotherhood had already been through the drawers, the books, the nooks and the crannies. But again, like every other room in the house, it had been stripped clean of incriminating documents, computer components, cell phones, and identification. A couple of the art vacancies were in here, too: One behind the high-backed leather swivel chair. Another over the fireplace.

As the *tick-tock-tick-tock* of the grandfather clock in the corner seemed loud as a soldier's march, Qhuinn glanced around again. The other brothers were standing as still as he was, and he had a stupid thought that with all of them in here, it was like the room had been shrunk down to bread-box size.

Square footage, like time and beauty, was relative . . .

Meanwhile, Wrath just stood there, doing nothing but breathing in and out of those nostrils—

Someone coughed. Probably because they were choking on the urge to scream.

"We've been through the whole house," Tohr said. "Stem to stern."

No response from the male in charge. Just more of that *tick-tock-tick-tock* in the background . . .

Wonder how many of the others were dubbing in the *Jeopardy!* theme as the King stayed right where he was.

As Qhuinn felt a headache coming on, he did some quick game-out. They were at thirty minutes and change, and had gone through everything but the kitchen, the powder rooms, and the solarium. If Wrath insisted on a second floor walk-through, that was going to take another thirty. Attic? Please no.

And then there were the basement and the garage.

So, what, like an hour and a half more? Christ, he was going to lose his fucking—

Wrath's head cranked in the direction of the hearth. Then he turned his whole body that way, and took five full strides across a rug that no doubt had never had even one shitkicker on its pile, much less almost two dozen.

Shaking off Tohr's grip, the King dropped down to his haunches. The popping of the male's knees was a reminder that he had done hard graft for centuries in the field against the enemy, and as he leaned forward and rapped his knuckles on the fireplace's marble footer, his tremendous back muscles fanned out along his spine.

Rhage looked over with a shrug. So did Zsadist and Phury. John Matthew likewise joined in the collective WTF. Vishous just stood in the doorway, glancing back out into the hall like he expected Lash to show up at any moment.

Even Tohr joined in the eye hockey.

But he was right. The brothers *had* been through this house with a fine-tooth comb—

Down at floor level, Wrath tilted into the hearth itself and extended his heavy arm over the birch logs that had been stacked with a watchmaker's precision. The bulk of the King's shoulders blocked a view as to what he was doing, but the metallic rapping sound as he continued to knock along the hearth's back panel was enough of a descriptor.

"My Lord?" Tohr asked as Wrath sat back on his heels.

The King just shook his head sharply and got to his feet with a lithe surge. More with the knocking, this time on the panels where a painting had been centered, right under the mounting hooks.

Then he glanced to the left—and with a sweep of his arm, cleared the entire shelf at eye level with one shove, all those leather-bound volumes cast off like paperbacks.

As there was a bunch of clapping from the tomes, the King put his whole damn face into the vacancy he'd created. The long, deep inhales made Qhuinn shift his weight back and forth and tighten his hold on his guns. This was absolute madness—

Wrath went to the other side, rising up onto the steel toes of his shitkickers and slowly lowering back to the floor—

He performed another de-booking. Then started feeling around the seam where the shelf met the side of the hearth's build-out.

Shit got really quiet again—and Qhuinn felt stupid about fifteen seconds before there was a subtle *click.*

After which, the entire fireplace unit including the logs and the mantelpiece moved forward about three feet and then hinged out, revealing—

There was a collective metal chorus as everyone aimed into the darkness and Tohr all but tackled Wrath into the far wall to cover the King with his body.

As the stench of old blood and infected flesh wafted out like it was a crypt, Rhage nodded at Qhuinn and the pair of them went forward in one/two formation. With the light streaming in behind them, they entered a shallow hall that was painted all black and made a turn behind the chimney—

The body of a dark-haired male dressed in fine clothes was chained to a chair, blood, bodily fluids, and excrement pooling underneath, his chin down on his sternum and his shoulders slumped. It was like a Halloween mannequin at a haunt, except this shit was real—

A weak moan rippled up, the tips of the fingers moving ever so slightly.

"He's alive," Qhuinn barked as he shot forward while Rhage made a circle of the otherwise empty room. "We need a medic, STAT!"

"Calling Jane," V called out from the study proper.

"There's a seam over here," Rhage said. "Another entry—or exit."

Qhuinn kept his weapons up as he bent over and tried to get a look at the male's face. The skin was gray, the mouth lax, but there was a whistle of breath going in and out. With the muzzle of his left gun, he lifted the hair that had fallen forward.

The eyes were open and staring ahead. Unblinking, as if death had already claimed the spark that warmed and animated the flesh. Except that wasn't true. There was a little life . . . still in there.

For the moment.

"Make it fast with the medical help," Qhuinn said over his shoulder.

And then he mentally checked out for what was probably only a couple of seconds, but felt like he'd been gone an hour: In a hideous flashback, his mind replaced the unknown male and the chair before him with an oil drum filled with the black, oily blood of the Omega. Instantly, he could smell the sweet, cloying scent of the enemy, sense the hunting cabin around him, feel the cold air and the weird, tickling fear that something big was coming for him.

Something that would change him.

And that was when he'd seen the ever-so-subtle glow of gold in the depths. A signet ring. The one he had always hoped to receive from his own sire, the acknowledgment that a son was a valuable contribution to the bloodline, something important . . . something that was loved. But no, the badge of acceptance had been given to his brother, in a private celebration that he'd walked in on.

What the fuck was it doing in that drum?

That was what had gone through his mind first. And the question was answered fast: Luchas, his brother, had been in there, the male's body—that prized body, the one that had no defects—had been shriveled, pretzeled, and preserved in stasis.

He, too, had been barely alive after the torture—

"Qhuinn?"

He jerked to attention, pulling a pivot toward Tohr. "Yeah—sorry. What?"

The brother's face was set with the kind of mask that made your adrenal system wake up with bells on. And then he got the dreaded forefinger crook, the order to come-with-me.

Oh . . . shit, he thought. This could only mean one thing.

He was just vaguely aware of walking out of the hidden room, through the study, and into the hall.

As soon as they were alone, Qhuinn exhaled. "*Fuck, I should have been there.*"

Tohr frowned and shook his head. Because he was a male of worth who knew way too fucking much about missing last moments. "You didn't know. How could you have?"

Are you kidding me, he wanted to say. *It's been coming for months now.*

He glanced back into the study, at Wrath. Serving the King was a sacred duty, but he had to be there for his *hellren*.

"Can I go?" He met Tohr's navy blue eyes. "Even though I don't know how I can leave. It's just Blay's going to need me—"

Tohr reached out with a solid hand to the shoulder. "Your daughter's fine."

Qhuinn blinked. Blinked again. "I'm sorry . . . what?"

"Lyric." Tohr put his phone front and center. "She was saved by a miracle."

Trying to catch up to the conversation, Qhuinn bent in and focused on the video that was playing on repeat on the little screen. It took a couple of run-throughs before things sunk in—and when they did—

He was fucking horrified. His beautiful daughter standing in the middle of the street, in front of the club she and her friends always went to. She was looking up and to her right, her arms raising—

A huge shape bolted into the frame just as some kind of sheeting or part of a building—wait, was that a fucking billboard?—fell out of the sky, right on top of her.

Except somehow, whoever the hell had come out of nowhere managed to hold the thing off of her.

Holstering one of his guns, he grabbed his phone and checked on Lyric's location.

"I gotta go," he heard himself say as he started running for the front door.

CHAPTER EIGHT

I t was a total fucking blur.

Standing in front of the step and repeat, Lyric smiled on command as one of the event's assistants wielded yet another pair of cell phones like they were proper Nikon cameras. The two women who'd been brought up on the shallow stage were beautiful in their own right, their clothes off-the-rack versions of what was on the runways of Paris, their hair done up with extensions, their makeup flawless.

As soon as the pictures were taken, the conversation re-bubbled:

"—craziest thing I've ever seen! And I can't believe—"

"—and then he came out of nowhere—"

"—out of nowhere, this guy—"

"—*saves you.*"

Marcia ushered them off to the left with a firm tone and an engaging smile, and a threesome took their place. Which meant there was all kinds of *you go here, no I'll go there, I want to be here, wait, how about I kneel?* While they worked things out, Lyric let herself get positioned and repositioned like a garden gnome, her detachment so deep and complete, she felt like she was staring at herself from across the VIP area.

The good news? The conversation was always the same, so after stumbling through the first couple of interactions, she'd landed on some appropriate repeatables:

Yes, from out of nowhere—

I can't believe it, either—

I'm so lucky to be alive!

As with the smile she put on her face when it was time for the pictures, she made sure to inject the enthusiasm that was expected, and she was amazed at how good she was at faking this version of herself. The truth behind the branding, though, was that only one thing was on her mind.

What had he looked like?

How could she not picture that man's face? This monumental thing had happened to her, this shocking, near-death, close call—and if he hadn't shown up when he did, she wouldn't be—

"Smile!"

On command, Lyric focused on the iPhone and followed directions as she felt a woman lean in and fly the peace sign.

"—and then he came out of nowhere!" The brunette made twin ka-pows next to her temples. "I was there! I saw it and I posted it, too. It's the craziest thing I've ever seen!"

"I know, right?" Lyric went jazz hands. "*Amazing.*"

The young woman danced off, and Lyric went right back down below the surface, replaying the events again, a video on repeat—except it was something she'd lived through.

What color hair had he had? What about his eyes . . . ? He hadn't been wearing a coat, in spite of the cold, that much she was sure of.

"—sign this eye palette?"

Lyric came to. "Yes, of course!"

With a smile that didn't show her fangs, she turned to the waist-high table that had been brought over. As she uncapped a Sharpie and scribbled her name by the Trash Panda logo, she knew for certain the guy hadn't been wearing a coat, because she had a clear recollection of him going over and picking it up from where it'd been laid on some steps.

A t-shirt, plain, under a bib with reflective safety panels, had been the only thing he'd had on.

Well, that and a crapload of muscle.

"—I mean, can you believe it? You could have been killed!"

"I know." Lyric recapped the pen and held out the palette with more smiling. "It's one of the most miraculous things that has ever happened to me."

The redhead lingered, taking the makeup and holding it to her heart. "To anybody!"

Over at the front of the line, where the snaking ropes ended, the next set of women chimed in with agreement—

Marcia stepped up again and smiled with all her professional happy-happy. "Okay, let's keep the line moving—"

That was when Lyric saw the disruption, in the main part of the club on the far side of the VIP area's velvet rope. Bodies were agitating, getting out of the way of something that was moving fast—and then whatever it was hit the tuxedo'd gatekeepers.

And didn't give two shits about pissing them off.

She *knew* before she knew. She *felt* before she saw.

There Qhuinn was, taller than all the humans around him, but standing out for so much more than that height. Like there was anybody else in the club with spiked black hair, piercings on his face and ears, and an expression that made clear a decision to get in his path was going to be a mortal one?

Breaking out of her own lineup, Lyric rushed forward, high-stepping over the golden rope that cordoned off the riser and then jumping down. She almost lost a stiletto as she broke into all the people snaking down the aisle between the sunken seating areas, the collective gasping and flashes from camera phones disorientating her as hands with painted nails reached out for her arms, and women tried for selfies that were going to show just a blur of her.

Marcia hollered something, but that was in the background.

All Lyric cared about was getting to her—

"Father!" she whispered as suddenly Qhuinn was in front of her.

Jumping up, she hugged him hard enough to squeeze the breath out of a lesser male's chest, but it didn't matter. Her blooded sire was as he had always been, an absolute pillar, unbending, unrelenting. A superhero.

"Are you okay," he said in a low voice.

She held on even harder. "I am now."

As more pictures were taken, Lyric just lowered her face into his broad shoulder. The smell of leather, gunmetal, and the aftershave he always wore was the security blanket she needed. It was as if all the years he had ever been there for her coalesced into a tangible energy source that reinflated her with strength.

Sometimes a girl just needed her dad.

◆　◆　◆

Shuli re-formed in the alley next to Bathe at the exact time Rhampage, Lyric's fraternal twin, did the same. The other male was likewise dressed for the war, his black hair messed up out of its expensive cut, his handsome-as-a-devil face screwed down tight with stress, all kinds of black leather hiding all kinds of weapons. Given the lack of baby powder scent floating over on the cold breeze, the guy hadn't found any of the enemy in the territory he'd covered yet—

Fuck.

Shuli immediately holstered his knife and gun and started paddling his puss with his palms.

His face was covered with that slayer shit.

"Here."

He took what was offered without looking, without asking—and pulled up when the thing was damp and smelled like grandma perfume. "Baby wipe?"

"Sometimes you need a moist towelette." The male did a well-duh in Shuli's direction. "Are you here for Lyric?"

Shuli started scrubbing and spoke through the godsend. "I saw the video. Don't wait for me—"

"How is it we're in the field and she's the one who nearly gets killed tonight?"

All Shuli could do was shake his head. Then again, he felt like shitting his pants every time he thought about the near miss.

"Don't wait on me," he repeated as he started to work on his jacket.

There was the hiss of a vape and then a white cloud the size of a car came out of the guy's piehole. As Rhamp brought things up for a second inhale, his hand was visibly shaking.

"I don't want her to see me all—" He took another hit and exhaled again. "You know."

Shuli wadded up the wipe and shoved it in the ass pocket of his leathers. "I think she'd be offended if you weren't fucked in the head."

Rhamp grunted as they both went for the steel emergency door. "It's that meet and greet, remember—"

"Yeah, I know."

"Hold up." Rhamp froze. "Where's L.W.?"

As the guy looked around—because, sure, it was totally possible to miss something as big and pissed off as "Little" Wrath—Shuli rolled his eyes and yanked the exit open.

"I don't want to talk about it."

Stepping into the dark blue glow of the VIP section, his eyes went immediately to the shimmering galaxy of stars in the center of the packed space. The flashes of all kinds of cell phones were directed at the female he'd come to see, and goddamn him, she was as beautiful as always with that long blond hair and a shimmering dress he'd never seen her wear before. She was with her father, locked in a desperate embrace—

As sire and daughter eased back, she looked over to the far corner like she sensed her twin and him. Her shaken expression immediately perked up, and as she brushed tears from under her eyes, she started to come over. The crowd parted for her with expectation, like they were dying to see what the next heart-affirming-reconnection-after-tragedy was going to be, and Shuli fussed with his leather jacket, trying not to be obvious about passing both his hands through his hair—

As he caught a fresh whiff of spoiled sweet-and-sour sauce, he looked down at his palms. *Fuck*. He had *lesser* blood in his hair, too.

With a quick snatch, he snagged a drink off a passing waiter's tray and poured some of—oh, good, vodka and tonic. Perfect.

Be cool, he told himself as he swept the cold and limey into his 'do. *Just tell her that you're glad she's okay.*

God, if people only knew he was giving himself a pep talk right now. In their group, he was known as having stellar game with the ladies. Hell, especially when it came to vampire females, he didn't even need a smooth tongue and all the right words. His money and his bloodline did all the talking for him.

Lyric was different, though. And always had been—

His heart skipped a couple of beats as she arrived in front of them—and oh, fuck, she was looking right at him. In slow motion, her arms raised, and on instinct, he stepped forward as the trippy techno music dissolved, along with all of the people, most of his pride, and at least three-quarters of his brains—

Rhamp's shoulder bumped him out of the way as the guy caught his sister and held her off the ground.

"God, I really needed to see you," she said to her twin.

"Like I wouldn't come?" Rhamp's voice was rough as sandpaper. "You were almost crushed by a conference. In your car-wash dress."

Lyric glanced over her brother's shoulder. "Oh, hey, Shuli," she said with an offhand wave.

As the mob surrounded the pair, Shuli let himself get pushed back, and the next thing he knew he was all the way at the emergency exit. It was easy to hit the handle and open the thing. What was hard was the last look he took back into the VIP section.

Lyric was with her sire and her twin, and the three were a bubbly center around which an entire universe spun. Meanwhile, he was headed out into the cold—

Come on, what was he so bummed out about. After a near-death experience like that, of course she'd need to be with her immediates.

Shuli, on the other hand, was just a friend, and she had loads of those. Sure, later they'd probably have a nice big, friendly friend-friend hug-it-out—but he was never going to be on her short list like her brother and her three fathers and her *mahmen.*

Nor should he be.

He was just a playboy who was useful in the war because he happened to be a good shot with a gun—and because he had a vein of rage he could tap into when he needed to. He was not, and had never been, *hellren* material.

Never would be, either.

Too bad Lyric reminded him of that, every time he saw her—

Behind him, the emergency exit opened. The exhale of perfume-scented warmth had a chaser of blue light, and as he measured the shadow his body threw on the dirty city snow, he thought about this secret that he'd kept to himself.

Shit, if Rhamp knew? After all these years of debauchery they'd shared?

Yeah, he was pretty sure it was practically a law of physics that you never, *ever* fell in love with your wingman's goddamn sister—

"Where the *fuck* is L.W."

Shuli spun around. Okay, not Rhamp.

The Black Dagger Brother Qhuinn was filling the jambs of the exit, looking like he was prepared to throw hands.

And unlike earlier with the son, the father was not going to let the subject of the missing heir to the throne drop.

CHAPTER NINE

At the end of the night, after the meet and greet was over, and the crowd dispersed, and the Trash Panda owner and reps swept off in a limo, Lyric walked through the club, and regarded the place through fresh eyes.

Well, "fresh" was a stretch. Her peepers were way past whatever expiration date they were stamped with, each blink like she was in a sandstorm, her lids heavy as garage doors, her mascara flaking off and adding to the problem.

It was also a stretch for poor old Bathe. All the interior lights were on, the music was off, the rest of the patrons gone to wherever their last-call decisions had taken them.

When it was dimmed out and packed with people, the beat bumping and drinks flowing, there was always an electrical charge in the air, a sizzling, buzzy excitement. Like this? It was downright depressing, the scuffs on the black floor and the scrapes on the black walls, the smell of bleach as surfaces were cleaned, the worn-out staff counting bottles behind the mile-long bar, the kind of behind-the-curtain that reminded you image was not everything.

No shit, she thought with exhaustion—

"You did a good job tonight."

Lyric glanced over her shoulder. Even Marcia was subdued, but sure as the sun would set over Caldwell again in another fifteen hours, the Energizer media manager would be back on her A game soon enough.

Maybe she plugged herself in like a cell phone on her time off.

"Thanks," Lyric murmured as she refocused on the club's front exit.

"You serious about ending all this?" The woman paused as they finally got to the main door. "You're a natural, and you're just starting to get real traction."

She tried to remember any part of the event. A conversation. A person. A glance. Hell, she was even blanking on her father and brother stopping by. But they had come . . . hadn't they?

Lyric rerolled the sleeve on the construction worker's coat. "I am serious, yes. But I appreciate everything you did for me, especially tonight."

"You're welcome." Marcia shrugged as she opened things, the cold rushing in. "And I'll do what I can to get you out of the Resolve2Evolve thing. No promises."

"Something tells me you'll make it happen." Lyric offered a smile as they stepped out. "You can get things done, for sure."

"It's my only virtue—at least according to my mother, who wanted me married three years ago and working on baby number two by now." Marcia glanced around at the empty, snowy street. "Where's your car?"

"Oh, that's okay." She looked up to where the billboard had been mounted. Tendrils of the scaffolding were still in place, metal whiskers on the building's square head. "I'm taken care of."

The woman looked pointedly at the heavy coat. "Better not let your boyfriend see you in that."

Lyric's stare drifted to the construction site as she brought the rough lapels in closer to her throat. "I don't have a boyfriend."

There was a pause. And then Marcia's eyes narrowed. "You're going to take that thing back to him tonight. Aren't you."

Before Lyric could pull a response out of her butt, a forefinger was right in front of her face. "Now, listen, you have to be careful in this big city. A split-second lifesaver doesn't make him a saint. Do you have

Mace? Of course you don't." Marcia rummaged around in her purse and shoved a tube forward. "Here, you take this. Don't be afraid to use it. It's not legal, but who cares—and don't go back to that construction site."

"It's his coat."

"Put it in the back of your closet and let it be a memento of tonight. Or what your career could have been."

"I'm just going to do the right thing—"

"No, you're looking for an excuse to get killed." Marcia got her keys out and started striding away while she talked over her shoulder. "Call an Uber and go home. Woman like you, out on the street this late? Nothing good comes of it. Don't you get the news on your phone? Jesus Christ . . ."

One block down, the lights on an Audi flashed.

Lyric waited where she was in the cold wind as Marcia got into the SUV, started the car, and took off down Market, a lone set of red tail-lights disappearing around a skyscraper.

"Annnnd that's all she wrote." She looked down at the little canister. "Oh, bear repellent."

In case you didn't pick the man, evidently.

Wonder what MAR-see-ah would've thought if she knew she'd given the stuff to a vampire—

The unsettled wind whipped around her, like it was looking to have another crack at taking her out with a projectile, and she had a sudden foreboding that made her want to be home already.

Running her hands up the coarse fabric, she took a deep breath. The scent of the man was still on the material, and as it registered in her nose, she stepped off the curb like her name had been called. With choppy strides, she crossed the slushy lanes and thought of Rhamp. She could only imagine what her brother would say about her new security blanket—she'd never hear the end of it. One more reason to give the thing back to its rightful owner—

Lyric slipped and pulled some bad dance moves to keep on her feet. As she recovered her balance, she stopped, even though she wasn't any-where near the mile-high snowbank she'd been gunning for.

"Well . . . crap."

The worksite appeared to be shut down. There were still bright lights shining around the exterior, and the equipment and debris were in the same chaotic disarray. No men, though. Maybe they were inside? She doubted it. Unlike before, the interior of the building was dark and there were no sounds of work, no machines grinding on, no hammering or banging. No voices.

And her keen hearing would have picked up on all of that in spite of the wind.

Continuing onward, she arrived at the mini-mountain created by the city plows, and picked her way up and over the summit, using the predetermined footholds countless pedestrians had turned into steps.

On the other side, she stared up the flank of the building—

The sense that she was being watched leveled her head and twisted her around. Bathe's light-show entry had been turned off, and in spite of the familiar streetscape and all the lampposts, she suddenly felt like she was in the middle of nowhere.

Alone.

The reality of her isolation blew through her, an arctic gust from a different compass point, and it was as she shivered that she saw the shadow lurking in the alley by the club's emergency exit. If she'd had human eyes, she wouldn't have seen whoever it was, but her vampire retinas were especially good at night.

A big, hulking shape. A male? A man?

She was upwind, so there was no scent, and surely if it was someone she knew, they would have called out. Heart pounding, she took a step back—

Binnng . . . binnng . . . binnnng . . .

As the radar-like noise registered, she looked down. That the peculiar sound was coming from her left ovary was a shocker for so many reasons—at least until she shoved her hand into the pocket of the construction jacket and took out a cell phone.

While the binging continued, she glanced over at the alley again.

The figure was gone and she scented the air. The wind was still coming at her back, so no information there, but given the tingle of warning at her nape, she knew she had to get out of—

"So there's my phone."

Lyric jerked around. "Oh! It's you."

Her savior had come out of nowhere for a second time, and he'd had a shower and changed since she'd seen him last. Now sporting a SUNY Caldwell hoodie, a black parka, and hair that was wet, she focused on his face—and the fact that she didn't recognize it made her really worry about the way her brain worked.

"Are you okay?" he asked.

"Ah, here, sorry." She held his cell out. "And I want to give you back your jacket—"

He took the phone. "I told you to keep it. Did you come over here just to return that old thing?"

"And your phone." Even though she hadn't known it was in the pocket. "Everyone needs their phone. I was returning the phone."

Shut up, she told her mouth as she rechecked the alley.

His brows lowered and he glanced around. "And you're going home now, right."

"Yes."

"Good. This city is dangerous at night."

"For sure." Her eyes returned to the club again. "You never know what can fall on a person. Billboards. Maybe a piano or two. Cars . . ."

What the *fuck* was she saying.

He glanced toward Bathe. "What are you looking at?"

"Nothing. I . . . it doesn't matter."

She swung her eyes back to him, and as his stare met her own, there was a long, quiet moment.

"Go home," he told her. "You need to go home."

Good advice. The problem? She didn't want to leave this stranger undefended against whatever the hell had been over there.

Assuming it hadn't actually left. Just relocated to another position.

✦   ✦   ✦

Standing over the blonde, Dev had to be amazed by her. Somehow, she managed to suck him in again: What the hell business of his was it where she went. Stay here, go home . . . head to the North-fucking-Pole to join an elf colony. Who gave a shit.

Yet here he was, worried about what was going to happen to her if he took off and left her here.

"You got a car nearby?" he heard himself ask as he put his phone into his parka.

"Yes, sure. I mean, yes."

Interesting dichotomy, the beauty with this shy hesitancy thing, which did not seem like an act. Usually the two didn't go together, because blondes who wore shimmering dresses and came with cell phone entourages didn't operate in a world where insecurity was any kind of hallmark.

"Where's your ride." When she paused, he shook his head. "Why is this so hard? I'll walk you to your car."

"Oh, that's not necessary. I was going to call an Uber."

"Okay. I'll wait until it shows up." He cocked a brow. "What kind of man would I be if I left a lady out here all alone."

Her blue-and-green stare shifted back to that alley next to the club, and he copycatted her glance again, wondering what she was focused on. There was nothing that he could see.

"You must live close by," she said.

"Couple blocks over." When there was just the cold breeze between them, he found himself compelled to make small talk—which was akin to him volunteering for a manicure. "I couldn't find my phone and fired up my iPad. Find My Phone led me back . . . to you."

"Fate with a technology twist," she murmured.

"Is that what this is."

"I don't know. Is it?"

Dev took a step back. But he knew he wasn't leaving—and that was the problem. "Where did you say you were parked?"

"I'm calling an Uber, remember?"

"So where's your phone. Better get ordering."

Fuck. After so many years of living his own life, minding his own business, and staying away from drama, this blonde with her glittering dress and those mismatched eyes makes an unwilling hero out of him—and pickpockets half his brain in the process.

"You should also go home," she said softly. "It's not safe for anybody out here in the dark and the cold."

"Don't worry about me." He resisted the urge to curl up a twin set of biceps. "People tend to get out of my way instead of in it."

"I believe that."

As she looked him up and down in that charmingly diffident fashion, he felt something wake up between his legs and cursed under his breath.

Man, *none* of this was on his bingo card.

She swiped her hand across her face, clearing a drift of hair from her lips. "But you never can be too careful—"

"So how about that Uber. Is it coming?"

"Not yet."

"I'll take care of it—"

"You don't have to—"

Dev cut her off with a brisk shake of the head, and then never got into that app faster. As he entered the coordinates of where they were standing, he was very aware of how she was looking around and trying to hide it, and when he was finished, he reminded himself that she was not his responsibility—

"So how long you been stalked?" he asked as he shoved his phone away.

Her startle was the kind that couldn't be camo'd. But she gave it a shot: "Stalked—what do you mean? I'm not—"

"I'm a stranger. You can be honest with me. Ex-boyfriend? Current lover?" He frowned and thought of the women who'd clamored for pics of her earlier. "Or wait, are you famous?"

"No, I'm not—well, kind of, but not really—" She reached out and put her hand on his arm. "Listen, you really should go."

Mimicking her, he leaned down and laid his palm on her shoulder. "Listen, I'm going nowhere." When she exhaled in frustration, he shrugged. "You honestly think I'd leave a woman here alone, especially when she's looking around like she's expecting to be jumped? I wasn't raised that way."

"I don't need your protection."

"Fine." He pushed his hands into the front pockets of his blue jeans and rocked back and forth in his boots. "I'll just hang out and enjoy this bracing wind—which just so happened to cheat me out of five hours of pay. Two years in construction and this is the first night the foreman's had to call us off shift because of the weather. So, how 'bout those Mets."

The wind roared as if he'd offended the shit, and as the inside of his ears burned from the cold, he muttered, "Okay, wrong season for baseball. Who you got in the Super Bowl."

When she didn't reply, he took a moment to appreciate the sight of her in all his Carhartt. Having her in his big, shitty coat was like wrapping a beauty queen in Tyvek, but she didn't seem to mind—and the RCG virus he'd clearly come down with made him feel like that reflected well on her character.

Rose Colored Glasses, that was.

"I'm not budging until you're safely in a car." Hell, she was lucky he wasn't going to insist on riding along with her. "And talk to me about what kind of famous you are. If you want. Or we can just stand here awkwardly."

"I guess you'd call me an influencer." She glanced at the entrance to Bathe for the hundredth time. "But I'm getting out of that line of work."

"To do what."

"I don't know." She turned back to him. "Please—"

"Ask you more? Love to." He wished he'd brought his cigarettes with him. "What are you going to do if you leave the 'influencer' thing."

As he motioned to encourage her response, he felt like he was trying to start an old engine, and had to wonder if this was what people felt like when they were around him.

"Ah . . . I want to do something that matters." She huddled into his coat and stamped her high heels as if she was trying to get feeling back in her bare toes. "And I know that's the kind of thing somebody says when they're trying to look like a good person."

"Depends on whether you mean it. Do you? Mean it."

"We aren't here forever," she said hoarsely. "On my deathbed, I don't want my greatest accomplishment to be that I took a lot of pictures of myself and carpet-bombed the internet with them."

"Well, that's noble." Dev pointed at the center of his own chest. "'Course you're looking at a guy who jackhammers concrete and pulls up carpeting for a living. So I'm not exactly a Nobel Prize winner over here. Takes all kinds."

"That's honest work, though. A good, hard day's work. When you're finished, you've made a building look better, function better—why are you staring at me like that?"

"I'm not." Fuck, what was he saying . . . "Looking at you like anything."

The last thing he wanted to admit—to either of them—was that she was showing serious signs of being more than just a beauty queen. Meanwhile, the wind caught her hair again, pulling a blond wave out of his jacket collar as if to mock him.

Yeah, whatever, he already knew the shit was silky and gleamed like gold.

"Here's your car," he said gruffly.

As a Tesla auto-driver pulled up in front of them, he got his phone back out and offered her a hand over the snowbank. On the far side, he flashed the barcode that had been texted next to the door, and the passenger panel lifted.

"Your carriage awaits," he said as he went to help her in.

"You didn't need to do this." But at least she slid into the seat as she spoke.

"It'll take you anywhere you want to go."

Her eyes, those incredible, mismatched eyes, lifted to meet his—and he could have sworn they glowed with unshed tears. "What if I programmed it to go to Washington, D.C. Or Seattle?"

"You don't have that in you." *Shut up, Dev. Just stop there—* "But that's not why you wouldn't do it. You want to leave Caldwell right now, but something's keeping you here . . . something that's breaking your heart. And it's not your empty-ass job."

"How . . . can you see all that," she whispered.

"Goodbye, Lyric of Lyrically Dressed."

As he started to shut the car up, she leaned forward and stopped the door. "Wait, how did you know—"

"I looked you up." He shrugged. "Your pictures are good. You've got a knack for posing for the camera—"

"I lied to you." She glanced around. Then refocused on him. "I didn't come to give you the jacket back . . ."

"So it was the phone," he prompted.

"I couldn't remember . . ." Her eyes seemed to bore right through him. "I couldn't remember your face."

Dev had to laugh at that. "I'm forgettable. By design—"

"Tonight's event was a blur, and preceded by weeks and months of the same. And that's my normal amnesia, when I'm working. But you save my life, in the middle of the street, from a fucking billboard—and I can't remember you? That's just *wrong*."

"You were in shock."

"No, I was on autopilot because I'm not doing anything with my life, and when something worthless almost gets taken away, it's no big deal." She brushed a tear off her cheek with impatience. "I don't want to live like that. I just didn't know it until recently."

Now Dev was looking away—and not because he was worried anything or anybody was lurking in the shadows.

"Have a safe trip home," he said roughly. "Nice to meet ya."

He didn't wait for any kind of goodbye from her.

He couldn't.

The two of them really shouldn't have had anything in common.

Especially not the one thing that haunted him more than all the ghosts of his past put together.

He too was busy forgetting himself, every moment of every day.

And night.

CHAPTER TEN

The Black Dagger Brotherhood's training center was located deep underground, about an eighth of a mile behind the First Family's mansion. Though the big house had been abandoned, the training facility was very much in use, and as Qhuinn ripped open the steel door in from the parking area, he couldn't decide whether he needed the medical clinic, the weight room, or the target range.

What a fucking night.

Striding down the concrete corridor, he unzipped his leather jacket so the warm air could get at his cold body. The classrooms were all empty, and just as well. Considering who they'd brought into the clinic, it was better for the place to be NPO.

Necessary Personnel Only.

And of course, then there was his mood. He really shouldn't be around anybody who wasn't in the thick of this fucking mess.

All parts of it: The shit that had almost happened to Lyric, the shit that might have happened to L.W., and the shit that had definitely happened to that male they'd found in the hidden room at Whestmorel's.

After spending the last three hours threading the avenues of downtown, looking for the heir to the throne's body, he'd pulled off the hunt to come assess how this other unstable situation was going. When he was done? He was going to head to Blay's parents' house and check on everybody there, including his daughter.

Lyric went there at the end of every night.

At least she was physically okay.

Arriving at the clinic section of things, he could hear voices on the other side of the only closed door among all the rooms. Doc Jane and Tohr were in there, rapid-firing some kind of conversation, and as he inhaled through his nose, he could scent the dying male. Word had it, the patient was still alive, but that update had been hours ago.

As he leaned back against the concrete wall and waited for one of the pair of them to come out, he crossed his arms over his chest and stared down at the floor. His shitkickers had left a line of damp footprints that went all the way back to the parking garage's reinforced door. Thanks to the heat that was being blown in from the ceiling vents, soon enough there would be no evidence of his path.

A reminder, not that he needed it, of how the whole mortal thing worked—

God, he hated coming to this place. The fact that his brother, Luchas, had been a patient here . . . and then chose to walk out the emergency exit into a snowstorm—

The door to the patient room opened and Tohr stepped through, a coffee mug in his hand, a grim expression on his face. As the brother's navy blue eyes lifted, they registered surprise.

"Oh, hey, Q. What's doing?"

Qhuinn lifted his dagger hand in a hi-how're-ya. "Just wanted to come and see how things were going with that male."

"Not great. But Doc Jane is doing everything she can."

"Heard he coded twice in the mobile unit coming in."

"Three times, actually." Tohr ran his fingers over his high-and-tight. As the front resettled badly, the white streak formed a question mark. "Who's counting at this point."

There was a pause. "That coffee smells good."

"Dunkin'." Tohr took a sip. "You can't go wrong with the OG. Especially on a night like tonight."

"It's been a bitch. I'm assuming nobody's found L.W.?"

Stupid fucking question. There would have been immediate communication—

"Not yet." Tohr tilted his head. "Did you need something?"

"I should have stayed out there. I just . . ."

"You're dealing with enough right now. I told you two weeks ago that you shouldn't be on schedule."

To avoid the brother's frank stare, Qhuinn looked down to the glass door into the training center's office. He was staring in that direction, rather aimlessly, when a pattern of cracks on the concrete walling registered. It took a moment for the origin of them to sink in, and as he realized what they were, he cursed under his breath.

Oh, Christ. Did death *have* to stalk him like this tonight?

Just as the thought came to him, Tohr's broad shoulders passed through his visual field—and as the brother walked over to the spidery fissures, Qhuinn straightened with a jerk.

"I wasn't looking at . . ." He let the lie drift.

"How's Rocke doing," the brother said bleakly as he ran trembling fingertips along the pattern of veins.

You would know, Qhuinn thought sadly.

"He's, ah, he's focused on his *shellan*. What she needs, night by night . . . hour by hour. In a weird way, I don't think he really knows what's happening at this point. I can't decide whether that is good or cruel."

Tohr glanced back. "Is the elder Lyric comfortable?"

"Doc Jane has been great. Her pain's under control, and she's pretty lucid. For now, at least. I don't know how much more time we have."

"How's Blay?"

"Braver than anybody else in the situation." Qhuinn had to clear his throat to finish with: "Which is not a surprise."

"You need to stop trying to be in two places at once. You should be home with all of them. I know that's where your heart is."

"With the King's son gone, how could I not be downtown?"

As a tense silence bloomed between them, Tohr looked back at the corridor wall and Qhuinn studied the brother's profile. After his brother's *shellan* had been murdered by the Lessening Society, Tohr had disappeared for a time. When he'd come back, that lock of hair in the front had gone white and his dark blue eyes had been cold as graves. Word had it that if you committed suicide, you couldn't get into the Fade and be reunited with those you loved, and it'd been clear that that cautionary legend was the only reason he'd still been alive.

His pregnant mate, the love of his life, shot in the face.

It was too horrific to comprehend. Just like a brother who walked out into the cold night to die alone, like a daughter nearly crushed in the street . . . like a son gone AWOL in the field of combat.

"So you know about these, huh." As Tohr spoke abruptly, his stare shifted back over again. "The cracks in the concrete. How they were made."

"I . . ."

"It's okay." The brother reached out once more, and this time, there was no shaking to his hand. "What you've heard is true. This is where they came to find me, after my Wellsie and our young inside her were . . . killed. I knew, when I saw my brothers all at once—I *knew*."

"I can't imagine what that was like."

"Yeah, you can," Tohr countered. "You've been there—in your own way."

The ghost of Luchas seemed to drift between them, and for a second, Qhuinn could see his dead brother with painful clarity, his withered body, his butchered hands. They'd nursed him back to some level of health after they'd found him in that drum. But it hadn't been all the way, not by a long shot.

Then again, even if his body had been whole, the mind and the soul had been destroyed.

He thought about L.W. and prayed—*prayed*—the hotheaded sonofabitch was somewhere safe.

Tohr took another draw from the mug's lip. "I'm glad your Lyric was okay tonight. In the middle of that street."

"So am I." He closed his eyes. "It feels like death is everywhere right now."

When he popped his lids back open, Tohr was in front of him. "That's always the truth of things, though. We just can't think about the reality all the time or we'd be paralyzed by how thin the divide between us and tragedy truly is. In a split second, everything can change . . . and in the end, everyone dies at some point."

Qhuinn swallowed hard, knowing that his daughter had been saved by a fluke, and yet Tohr's first *shellan* had been killed by one, too: Wrong places, wrong time. Wellsie hadn't been a target; she'd just crossed paths with a *lesser* who'd had a gun. Meanwhile, Lyric had just crossed the street, at a particular moment, in a strong wind, when there had happened to be a billboard angled in just the right way.

Except tonight, his daughter had been spared by a quick-thinking stranger, while Tohr's—

"Don't do that to yourself."

Qhuinn shook back to attention. "I-I'm sorry?"

The brother put his hand on Qhuinn's shoulder. "It's a good thing your daughter was spared. You don't need to punish yourself just because luck was with your family tonight. I wouldn't have it any other way. No matter what happened in my own past—and I'm sure Wrath feels the same about the present."

Fuck, Qhuinn didn't want to even imagine L.W. being dead.

"I'm sorry," he croaked. "For the loss of your *shellan* and son, all those years ago. I don't think I've ever said that to you before."

Tohr's head turned back to the cracks in the cement. "You don't have to. We're brothers, remember. And you've had more than your own fair share of tragedy. Some things don't have to be spoken between survivors like us."

All Qhuinn could do was nod. He didn't trust his voice.

"On that note, your *hellren* needs you right now." Tohr took a deep breath. "And when you see your father-in-law, tell Rocke that I'm here for him. Now and . . . afterward—"

"You asked me if I needed something."

"Yes?"

Qhuinn rubbed his face. "I think I came here to find you and ask you for forgiveness. How fucked-up and unfair is that? I'm just grateful my daughter is okay and that feels wrong."

The brother slowly nodded his head. "Survivor's guilt is a pernicious kind of grief. I walk that path myself still. Time makes it better, but it never completely goes away."

Qhuinn thought of the footprints he'd tracked down the hall, slowly disappearing.

Tohr's voice got insistent. "It's not your fault that your daughter is alive, and my mate and my young are not. And no matter what happens with L.W., the two outcomes are not tied to each other just because they happened on the same night."

"I know that."

"But you don't believe it. It's not tit for tat, Lyric for L.W. You don't need to rack your brain over whether you should have traded her life for the heir to the throne's. Hell, we don't even know if he's dead."

Blinking to clear his vision, Qhuinn nodded again.

And then Tohr brought him in for a tight embrace. "Let this particular burden go. You carry enough, already."

The brother released his hold and stepped back with an incline of the head, as if they'd come to an agreement. "You are forgiven, Q. And I'm going to get more coffee. Now go home to your family."

At that, Tohr started heading to the break room. His strides, long and true, seemed a visceral reminder that he'd managed to keep going from his tragedy, and if anybody deserved another shot at love, it was the fighter.

His Autumn had healed him in ways all the time in the world couldn't have touched.

Qhuinn waited until the door in the distance eased shut.

Then he took a last look at those cracks.

God, he hoped they found L.W. before dawn.

CHAPTER ELEVEN

Given that L.W. had fucked off his *abstrux nohtrum*, he knew what was likely to be waiting for him when he went "home."

So at the end of the night, he didn't fucking go "home."

Side note: Working alone had all the perks as far as he was concerned. With his phone turned off, nobody dragging him down, and no reason for him to stop until the sun's imminent arrival, he got three more kills in—and would have kept going for another couple hours. Things got a little slice-and-dicey on that last skirmish, though, and he'd had to pull out of the engagement and up-up-and-awaaaaay'd while he still could.

And dipshits thought he was unreasonable? Come on, he knew how to take care of himself.

As he traveled in a scatter of molecules north from Caldwell's inner city, he metaphorically middle-fingered all the haters who said he was too reactive to be without a goddamn babysitter.

Re-forming in knee-deep snow, he confronted the mountain view ahead of him like it was something he could fight.

"Fucking idiots."

The fact that he had to studiously ignore the way blood dripped off the fingertips of his dagger hand was another thing that further backed up his solo career. Thank God and Lassiter and whatever other sky daddies were above that Shuli wasn't pointing out the obvious injury. Otherwise he would have had to smack the guy, and he wasn't sure he could lift his arm up higher than his own rib cage.

That frickin' aristocrat was the Toby Flenderson to his universe.

"And that does *not* make me Michael Scott," L.W. muttered.

The reminder that he knew all nine seasons of *The Office* by heart was a blast from the past he could have done without, because he hadn't volunteered for the binge-watching. When his *mahmen* had not been able to sleep in the bedroom next to his own, the episodes had played on her little TV like the audiovisual equivalent of mashed potatoes . . . so his youth had been background music'd by the show to the point where the references just popped into his brain, corks rising out of the murky stew of his subconscious with reflexive insistence.

Although it *was* true that every time Shuli walked into a room or opened his mouth, L.W. heard a chorus of *No God! No, God, please, no!*

Taking out a bandana, he made a fist and wrapped shit up, not because his hand was where the wound was, but to catch the blood. The pain was starting to ramp up, and not just from that bullet graze on the outside of his arm. All kinds of places were starting to talk to him, proof that swelling and bruising were joining the chat and making things all about them.

"What else is new."

As he turned away from the snowy evergreen view, the towering stone mansion before him loomed into the night sky like something out of the Marvel Universe. With gargoyles along its slate roofline, and enough windows for all the ghosts of the past to stare out at him, the sculptural entrance had always felt like an abandon-all-hope-ye-who-enter-here kind of thing.

Then again, his hope had been long lost well before the first time he'd come here as an adult, as a trespasser, to peel open its cathedral-like doors and wander its lonely rooms.

Proof that even the living could be dead.

Fighting his way forward through the snow, he looked down instead of up, searching for a set of footprints that had been left a number of nights before. The snowpack was all smoothed out, though, both from the additional inches that had fallen, and the gusting winds that had finally died down.

Come on, though, like he needed the additional verification that his sire was in fact back, had actually met him here just nights ago?

Aware his head was fucked, he rerouted around the fountain that was shut down not just for the season, but because no one lived on the property anymore. As he made the half circle, he glanced across at the carriage house's shuttered visage, the windows all battened down, its front door snow streaked and wedged with drifts.

It was as if centuries had passed since the last resident had shut things up and driven away with their shit, the whole property like the artifact of a previous civilization, its leftovers waiting for a decoding that would never be totally right.

When he got to the base of the mansion's steps, there was so much accumulation that the levels leading up to the cathedral-worthy facade were just an ascension, their contours buffed out of existence under the blanket of an infinity of flakes.

Just like the stars in the sky. Too many to count.

After a shuffle of bad footing, he approached the imperial door. The copper key he used to open the old-fashioned lock was something he'd stolen almost a decade before. He'd snuck into his *mahmen*'s room, and gone to the back of her closet. There, in a duffle bag, had been sacred things, things he knew he shouldn't have been fucking around with.

Because they were his sire's.

He'd violated the privacy and the secrets, though—and hadn't felt any guilt. He'd been about to go through his transition, and given his bloodline, there'd been a very good chance he wasn't going to live.

So yeah, he'd needed to see what his dead dad had left behind, and like the heavy key could have gone to any other door? It had taken him a couple of days to get out here, and he'd had to steal one of the *doggen*'s cars to make the trip. He'd also needed a map because he hadn't been completely sure where the mansion was.

But Great Bear Mountain? Well, that was easy to find, and he'd gone around all the rural roads at its base, trying every lane into the dense trees until he'd met with the *mhis* barrier. Getting through the wonky masking, fighting the disorientation and the nausea, persevering even as his heart had pounded with something close to fear . . . had been his first opponent in so many ways.

And he'd been in the habit of not quitting since then.

As he reached the mansion's portal—

A tremendous gust of wind punched him between the shoulder blades, his torso acting as the spinnaker for his lower body, the whole of him shoved face-first into the carved panel. He managed to catch himself before he ended up with a pair of black eyes and a nose that needed a splint, but the almost-assault didn't improve his mood.

Whatever did, though.

Well, he could think of one thing.

One . . . person.

Forcing the key into its slot, he cranked the shank and felt resistance as the cold tumblers shifted. When he went to work on the handle, there was a squeak of metal—and that got louder as he opened things up, the hinges that were big as a male's forearm protesting.

Fritz certainly came here and kept after the place. These frigid nights, though. No amount of WD-40'ing was enough to keep things smooth. For that, you needed to have people coming and going, in and out over the hours. Steady streams of males and females.

Like hinges, people were subject to rust, he reflected.

Sometimes he thought his anger was because he wasn't letting anybody in or out of his own life—

"Stop it."

Stepping inside, he closed himself in the vestibule and stamped his shitkickers on the marble floor. No mat to catch a male's heavy treads. There must have been one before, back when the Brotherhood and First Family had all lived here together with the other fighters and the staff.

He'd been a toddler then. So he didn't remember much. Hardly anything, really.

Why he continued to come back to this empty husk of a house was a pathetic reflex he kept hidden even as his visits were no doubt caught by all of the security cameras.

Although maybe the monitoring had been abandoned after all these decades.

Whatever, this was so much better than going home, especially on a night like tonight. And if someone wanted a piece of him? They could make the trip and kiss his ass.

Opening the vestibule's door, he looked across the acre-sized foyer to the staircase that poured down from the second level. The carpet was red as blood and wide as a river, like the elevator scene from *The Shining* had been relocated from a hotel to Windsor-fucking-Castle and set up on the second-floor landing. And talk about luxe. Even in the dull light, the gold balustrades glowed, and so did all the crystal hanging from the sconces and the light fixtures on the walls. And then there was the marble and malachite columns. And the yawning caverns on either side of him, homes to all kinds of hibernating furniture and antiques.

Worthy of a King. Built by a male with a vision that had outlived him.

L.W. shut everything up and crossed the mosaic depiction of an apple tree in full bloom. His head was on a swivel, and the looky-loo bullshit was not because he expected anyone else to be here. He just couldn't help dubbing in the members of the Black Dagger Brotherhood, imagining them before he was on the planet, walking around here, living as single fighters before they settled down. It was nearly impossible to imagine. Like all young, he was predisposed to thinking that his arrival on the planet had been the Big Bang, the origin of the universe. And that was before you threw in all the heir-to-the-throne shit—

The steel toe of his shitkicker hit the first of the steps and he pitched forward, like the house was disciplining him for being a little bitch. As with his whoopsie at the entrance, he caught himself with his palms, going push-up position.

Craning his neck, he looked up, up, up.

Why the *hell* did he keep coming back here.

As he got vertical again and started his climb, he walked straight up the center of the staircase—which made him feel like he owned the place. The lie fed some part of him that was ravenous and hangry, and when he got to the second story landing, he glanced around.

So many shadows, lurking. But he knew exactly what they were thrown by.

When he'd first started coming here, he'd memorized everything, his restless roaming taking him from room to room so many times, it got so he could have diagrammed everything down to the archways, closets, and back corridors. He supposed it had started out as a search for his father in all the nooks, crannies, and corners, his stupid attempt to fill out the picture of the great male he had never known in all the spaces of a house the guy had only lived in for a couple of years.

Except now his sire was back.

Too bad he'd stopped looking for the male years ago.

At the top of the steps, the study up ahead was the room he knew best, the pale blue walls and delicate French chairs and settees nothing he would have chosen for decor—and he was betting the same was true of his sire. Not that he knew that for sure. Not that he was going to bother asking.

But at least the throne and desk were on brand.

Come on, though, his pops had better things to do than try to color in the years that had been lost. He'd come back to a treasonous plot against him.

Hell of a welcome-home present, but that was Caldwell, New York, for you.

Entering the room, L.W. went over to the hearth. There was a fresh stack of logs, and he had to shake his head. Squeaky hinges to the contrary, Fritz really still looked after the place—and no doubt had never asked about who was coming in here and lighting a fire. All the *doggen* knew was that someone was visiting on the regular and that meant there were ashes to keep after and the need for new wood.

As L.W. got down on his haunches, he unwrapped the bandana from his hand and reached for the tub of long-tailed matches that had also been restocked. Taking one out of the cylinder, he streaked its red head across the gritty bottom, the little yellow flare bringing out the subtle veining in the two-hundred-year-old marble of the mantel. The newspaper at the bottom of what had been arranged on the iron basket was greedy for what would ultimately destroy it and the kindling was the same. The oak and maple logs were a little more standoffish, but they would succumb, too, after a time.

They always did.

Instead of getting back to his feet and going over to the couch where he usually sat, he let himself fall back on his ass. The scent of the fire was lovely in his nose, crispy, pretty autumn making an appearance in the dead of winter. The heat was nice, too.

Sticking his palms out, he fanned his fingers. Most of the blood had dried into a dark garnet color, but he must still be bleeding inside the sleeve of his leather jacket. Things were just too wet and warm in there.

That would solve itself, though.

His plan was to sleep here, get up at nightfall, and go out again— assuming no one disturbed him. And even then, he really wasn't interested in anybody's commentary about anything.

Rubbing his tired eyes, he refocused on the flames that licked and kicked over the logs. Everything was blurry and he did not know how he was going to force himself to fight again. But he had to, so he was going to.

For him, time was running out, and he didn't want to waste any of it.

He wanted to find Lash and kill the fucker.

He was the goddamn son of the King, and his father's death, which might as well have actually happened thirty years ago, was his to *ahvenge*, and no one else's.

Even if that act of retribution was not for the reasons everyone assumed.

Oh, and as for him fucking off his *ahstrux nohtrum*? His force-fed roommate was annoying as hell, but that silver-tongued motherfucker could talk his way out of anything. So no, there was no way Shuli's pink slip was going to include a coffin with his name on it, no matter how things had been done back in the Old Country.

That aristocrat was probably going to negotiate a raise to compensate himself for hazardous duty in the process.

With a groan, L.W. lay back. His spine and the muscles that were locked on it were so stiff, there was no easing onto the Persian rug. He was like the logs the butler had stacked, rigid, unbending, even though his physical pain had gotten worse with this horizontal shit rather than better.

Closing his eyes, he listened to the crackle of the logs, inhaled the fire's mellow fragrance, and tried to ignore all the aches.

Just as he fell asleep, his brain coughed up a correction.

It wasn't true that he didn't want to talk to anybody.

There was one person he wouldn't have minded speaking to right now. But she really should stay off-limits. If he thought his life was heading in a bad direction right now? It was nothing compared to what would happen if he kept seeing Bitty.

Rhage's daughter was irresistible to him, and he knew the feeling was at some level reciprocated.

Which meant she was in the path of disaster unless she came to her senses.

Good thing her mother was a therapist.

CHAPTER TWELVE

As Lyric re-formed on her grandparents' covered back porch, it seemed like the first time all night that she was not stepping through, standing on, or slipping over snow in her Lou-stupidns. Of course, the stillies were still ruined, her feet were solid blocks of ice, and her ankles and calves were so stiff, they could have qualified as stakes.

But who was counting at this point, especially as she had so much other stuff on her mind.

With a fit of paranoia, she tried to conjure up her human savior's face—and was relieved to a point when she remembered he had dark hair and had been in a hoodie and a parka.

"What color were his eyes?" she blurted.

He was forgettable by design? Was that what he'd said? Yeah, well, the problem was her, not him, and she needed to pull herself together.

Taking a deep breath, she exhaled and watched the cloud drift off.

This house that she had always loved coming to so much was located on some nice rural acreage, and the pond in the rear yard was one of her absolute favorite places in the world. Over the course of her life, the trees had all grown up and filled in, creating a sanctuary feel inside the fence line, and about five years ago, her grandfather had added a screened-in gazebo by the water. Eight-sided and topped with a red tin roof, the thing was a cheerful teapot without a spout—and her eyes misted with tears as she remembered him building it board by board, nail by nail.

It had been an anniversary present for the *shellan* he adored so much. And in the summertime, on Sunday nights before dawn, Lyric and her *granmahmen* had liked to go out there after the family Last Meal and have a listen to the whippoorwills and the crickets and the tree frogs.

It was also good when there was a thunderstorm and they'd been feeling adventurous.

When those moments had been happening, Lyric had certainly enjoyed them, but she'd never considered that they were something rare and precious . . . because there would come a night when she would be out there alone.

Bringing Dev's coat in closer, she stared across the snowdrifts at the gazebo, and as her eyes filled with tears, she had to look elsewhere. How beautiful the winter landscape was, so bright and gleaming, the moonlight filtering through the ribbons of clouds to drape the snowcapped pines and hemlocks in shades of blue, the frozen pond like a platinum plate.

There had been an evening back in early October, about three months ago, when the temperature had been unseasonably warm. The family had gone out there with baskets full of food and all the plates and silverware and drinks. *Granmahmen* had cooked, of course, and whatever had been served had been delicious . . .

Why couldn't she remember what they'd had?

And come to think of it, she couldn't recall what they'd talked about, either. There was also no memory of what she'd been wearing, or what anybody else had had on. No sweaters or fleeces, that was for sure, because of the eerily tender temperature.

God, yet another example of how much she didn't retain.

She was certain, though, that her *mahmen*, the Chosen Layla, had been there, and her father Xcor as well—and she was grateful now that it had been everyone.

Her *granmahmen* was never going to have dinner out there again.

They hadn't known it then. They'd just been there all together, enjoying the beautiful warm night, treasuring it as winter came rolling in. But you never knew when you were going to do something for the last time.

Turning away, she brushed at her eyes as she went over to the French door on the left. The other two opened up into the first floor primary suite that had been added the year before. Thank God her grandparents had planned ahead.

What a shame that what they'd prepared for had arrived so many decades before it should have.

There was a keypad next to the bolting mechanism, and she entered her registry number. The entire house was wired for sound, as her uncle Vishous put it, the cameras and motion detectors, the alarm system, the underground escape route, all engineered by him and monitored by his staff back at F.T. Headquarters, twenty-four hours a day.

She'd always been grateful the Black Dagger Brotherhood resources protected her grandparents as well.

As things unlocked, she waved up at the nearest camera, pushed the handle down, and entered her grandfather's office. Distantly, there was a chiming sound, and she was careful to make sure as she shut the door that the seal was tight and the mechanism could reconnect. Just like her uncle had taught her when she was very young.

Safety started with opening and closing, he'd always said—

Wincing, she lifted one foot up like a flamingo and loosened the straps on her stiletto. Slipping it off was a relief, especially in all the warmth. Except trouble came as she went to put her foot down, and while her arch protested going flat, she braced a palm on the wall for balance as she went to work on the other side.

And that was when she realized . . .

It was too quiet.

"Hello?" she said as she let the second one drop. "Anybody home?"

She bit out a curse as she rushed into the hall and skidded around the doorjamb. The way into her grandparents' bedroom was open and she didn't have time to brace herself emotionally as she usually did. She just careened right in—

The lamp beside the bed was on, the dim pool of light spilling onto the withered female who lay so still. Lyric, the elder, was positioned back against a stack of pillows, her lined face and thinning white hair still such a shock. With her closed eyes and her slightly open mouth and no movement at all, it was clear that what they had all been waiting for had—

The Kindle lying closed on that sunken chest went up . . . and down. There was a pause. Then it went up . . . and down again.

Letting out the breath she'd sucked in, Lyric sagged with relief, and then checked the two-way monitor that showed the sitting area off the kitchen. Her father Blay and her grandfather were out there on the sofas, both sound asleep sitting up—and who could blame them. This death vigil was exhausting, and yet she was not ready for the end. None of them were—even though it was all anybody had been thinking about for the last month.

Especially the last week.

With sad resignation, she leaned against the doorjamb and pushed her fingertips into her temples. Unlike humans, who aged on a gradual scale, when a vampire's end of life came, it was a fast descent into infirmity. The fact that just back in October, her *granmahmen* had been cooking and cleaning, raking leaves, and climbing up on a ladder to hang an autumnal wreath on the front door was unfathomable. And that she'd done all that while looking just like she had for the previous couple of decades? Only a little salt-and-pepper around her face, her posture still perfect, her eyes lively and her laugh quick as ever?

How were they here . . . now.

Her *granmahmen* came into sharp focus once again, and it was then she noticed that Ehlena, the nurse, had already taken care of changing the nightgown. Tonight it was a pale blue. Yesterday it had been a blush pink. Both complemented the pastel color scheme of the patchwork quilt and the room's flowered wallpaper.

Rocke had always said that he slept inside of a Victorian dresser, minus the lavender sachets and the intimate apparel. But he also knew his *shellan* liked the feminine decor, so he was more than happy to let her have what made *her* happiest to wake up to.

That little line had been repeated countless times. And the elder Lyric had always filled in at the end that Rocke was actually her first favorite thing to see when she roused, the flowers on the walls and the quilt she'd made were a distant second—

As Lyric's stomach let out a growl of hunger, she backed up . . . even though she kind of wanted to disturb all that sleep just as a double-check. Except breathing was enough for proof of life, wasn't it?

Unless the female had slipped into a coma—

"Well, there you are," came a weak voice.

Lyric jumped to attention. "*Granmahmen*, are you up?"

As she approached the bed, that old familiar smile appeared for a moment, and those eyes, those beautiful gray eyes, held an echo of the sparkle they'd always regarded the world with.

"Look at you," the elder Lyric said. "What a warm coat."

Holding the thing open, Lyric did a slow spin. "Do you think it goes with my dress?"

"Like peas and carrots. Wherever did you get it?"

Lyric leaned down and kissed her *granmahmen* on the cheek. "You wouldn't believe me if I told you."

"Well, then, you must tell me right the now."

That skeletally thin hand patted the quilt, and it was hard not to recall the week before when the elder Lyric could sit up with just a little help. Now she couldn't do that.

"And where are your shoes, dearest one?"

Settling on the edge of the mattress, she had to smile. "They're by Grandfather's desk in his study. I came in the door off the side porch and left them there because I didn't want to track salt in."

"You know—" An unproductive cough cut off the words, and there was a moment of recovery afterward. "You know . . . I must get up and run a mop over the floors. Your grandfather hates mopping."

"Oh, I'm happy to do it—"

"Not to worry." There was another pause as those tired eyes shifted to the open door. "I shall take care of it . . . perhaps after I rest a little more. Your grandfather is so tired, you know."

That hand swung toward the bedside table and reangled the monitor screen. Her *granmahmen* smiled again as she stared at the two males on opposite couches, sleeping in identical reclines, their hands linked over the centers of their chests, their chins up as they snored.

"They're both so tired," her *granmahmen* said.

And then the coughing started again.

As Lyric dove for the oxygen mask hanging from the headboard, the elder Lyric batted the hissing plastic cup away. "Enough . . . with . . . that . . ."

Given the refusal, all she could do was sit and wait until things quieted down again—while she wondered if she needed to go wake up her other father. But the male was indeed out like a light, and she hated that she'd added to his worry tonight. On her first break during the subscriber event, she'd been sure to FaceTime him, along with her *mahmen* and Xcor, from the bathroom to offer reassurance she was okay.

Talk about proof of life—

"Now, tell me about the coat," the elder Lyric said weakly.

She kept the face mask in her palm, feeling the stream of air against her wrist. "Well, I was doing an event at this club and . . ."

When Lyric got to the end of the story—and she cut things off before the part about her bringing the hard hat over to the job site—her *granmahmen* seemed to be breathing much better.

"So about this man . . ." the female whispered. "He must have been quite strong to hold up an entire billboard."

As Lyric's cheeks turned red, she cleared her throat. "Ah, yes, he was very strong. For a human."

"They're not that different from us, actually—and that blush on your cheeks tells me you noticed this, too."

"He's a total stranger."

"And yet you have his jacket."

Lyric ran her hand over the sleeve, feeling the rough weave of the outer layer. "Just a stranger."

"Everyone starts out that way."

"I'm never going to see him again."

Well, she supposed that wasn't exactly true. She'd see him from afar, maybe. When she went back to Bathe. *If* she went back there.

Partying suddenly didn't seem any more interesting than posting and promoting herself on Zideo.

"May I offer a piece of advice . . . as an old female who has seen a lot?"

Covering a yawn, she nodded. "Of course, *Granmahmen.*"

When that frail hand patted the bed on the empty side, Lyric had to smile. Getting up, she went around the footboard and stretched out on top of the quilt, curling onto her side and taking that thin palm into her own.

"Tell me," she prompted. "I feel as if my life is going nowhere, so I'm very open to any wisdom from you."

"Our time here is so very short." All the elder Lyric could do was turn her head, and she did that, their eyes meeting. "You need to find that man and follow that blush into his arms—"

"*Granmahmen!*" she exclaimed with a giggle.

"I haven't always been old, you realize." The elder Lyric smiled in a knowing way. "And your grandfather wasn't always an accountant."

"I . . . I don't know what to say to that." She smiled back. At least until she thought again of her meeting—Devlin, was it?—at the site. "And anyway, it was just a path-crossing thing."

"A man doesn't give his coat away to just anybody on a cold winter's night."

She remembered standing in front of him and was relieved to recall how tall he'd been. How broad through the chest and shoulder.

"Oh, I don't know," she mumbled. "Maybe he just happens to have good manners."

Hadn't he said something about his mother raising him right? Jesus, even their conversation was spotty in her memory.

"In January around here?" Her *granmahmen* made a dismissive sound. "Plus you are the most beautiful female he's ever seen."

"You are biased."

"I am accurate," came the retort. "Oh, Lyric, my namesake, my granddaughter, you have the world ahead of you because you have time at your disposal. Use that blessing. Find him and follow your heart. Everything will work out in the end between you two, and if it's not working out, you're just not at the end yet."

Okay, that was crazy talk.

Still, she brought her *granmahmen's* hand up and pressed a kiss to the back of it. "I didn't know you were such a romantic. And I hate to bring this up again, but he's a human, so there's no—I mean, there's no-where we can go with . . . anything."

"Then let it end as it does, on its own terms. Surely that is better than nothing at all? And when it's over, you can be glad you knew him, and you can keep him in your heart for when you're an old female like me and on your deathbed. You'll be so glad for that reflected warmth. It's the only hearth for old bones, those memories of when we were young."

Lyric opened her mouth to refute her *granmahmen's* pronouncement as to her condition. Except they both would know who had uttered the lie and who had had the courage to speak the truth.

As her tears started to come, she couldn't stop them. The collision of the near death she'd been spared with the certainty of what was com-ing so soon was just too much to hold in.

Her *granmahmen* reached out and brushed her cheeks with a gentle, wavering touch.

"I don't want you to go," Lyric said hoarsely.

"I don't want to go, either, but it is not my choice." That smile re-turned. "Have I ever told you how proud of you I am?"

Lyric had to laugh in a messy burst. "All the time."

"Good, I want you to remember that when I'm not here anymore."

Those beautiful, sunken eyes grew grave. "I cannot think of anybody better to carry my name on than you."

As her throat constricted, Lyric shook her head. "How can you say that? I'm not doing anything with my life . . . I'm going nowhere."

"That's just this particular stage." Suddenly, her *granmahmen's* voice grew stronger, steadier, the force of her resurging. "You'll find your stride and your path, and someday you'll think back to this moment, and you'll remember what I'm telling you. Lyric, blooded daughter of Qhuinn, heart daughter of mine own Blaylock, the future you want is waiting for you. Go out and grab it. We must live while we can so that when we go from this earth, the only thing we regret is the people we are leaving behind. Not all the things we didn't do because we didn't have the courage."

Lyric closed her eyes. "I love you so much, *Granmahmen.*"

"And I you, dearest one. Always." The deflation came on as fast as the momentary surge of strength had so unexpectedly arrived. "I'll be waiting for you in the Fade, granddaughter mine—but take your time down here. Life is . . . wonderful, even when you're confused. Promise me . . . that you'll go find the man who gave you this coat."

"I don't know. We'll see."

"Love is magic. And everybody needs magic in their heart . . ."

With that, her *granmahmen* drifted off, those eyes closing, her lips going lax. But there was breathing, slow, yet steady, and the hand remained warmed.

Taking a deep breath, Lyric followed her elder's example and gave in to her own exhaustion, drifting away until all she knew was whose palm she held on to, the tie that was soon to be broken . . .

So deep was her slumber that she missed the redheaded male who came to stand in the doorway, staring at the *mahmen* who'd brought him into the world, and the daughter he and his *hellren* lived for.

Blay had to wonder how your heart could be so full.

While at the same time shattered with sadness.

CHAPTER THIRTEEN

Déjà vu.

That's what Wrath, son of Wrath, sire of Wrath, was thinking as he materialized in the snow. With his blindness, he shouldn't have been able to see anything, and technically, he didn't. But from memory, he placed the Pit to his left, and the mansion up ahead of him, the latter being on the far side of the winterized fountain directly in front of him.

When he started forward, with his shitkickers punching through the snow, the wind's whistles orientated him, the subtle shifts in cadence and tone confirming everything he already knew to be true about the property's layout. So complete was the composite created from what his brain recalled and what his senses provided, that he was able to accurately anticipate the first step of the grand entrance's unshoveled stone stairs.

And what do you know.

Someone with big feet had already paved the way through the new drifts.

When he got to the entry, he thought of when he'd been here just the week or so before, returned from where Rahvyn had stashed him in time . . . with an old friend ready to meet him and let him in.

This time, he had the copper key, thanks to Fritz.

Letting himself in, Wrath stepped through into the frosty vestibule, and then did the same duty with the heavy weight of the inner door.

The foyer was not much warmer than the cold night.

His boots carried him across the mosaic design on the floor, and his brain supplied the delicate details of the apple tree in full bloom. Thanks to the echo of his treads, he once again knew where the first step was. Up, up, up . . . he went, and with each footfall, relief flooded through his veins.

He could smell the crackling fire. And the fresh blood of his only son. Again.

At the top, he stopped and flared his nostrils. Given the warmth that spilled out to him, he knew the double doors were open, and when there was no greeting, not even a gruff one, he satisfied himself that at least there was the soft, rhythmic snoring of someone in a deep, healing sleep.

Wrath took out his phone, and spoke at it quietly: "Text, red alert group. Start. L.W. is found. Repeat, I have found him and he is safe at the mansion. Minor injuries only. End."

He didn't call his *shellan* yet. She'd get the message, but would want so much more information.

Which he wasn't sure he'd be able to give her.

Walking forward in a straight line, he entered the study, and just as he had with the exterior approach, he pulled from his memory the contours of the pale blue room with its absurdly delicate French furniture and the antique rug and the glow from the fireplace . . . and there was something else he could visualize.

The fighter sprawled on the floor, his son.

Back when Wrath had been restocked onto the proverbial shelf of life and shown up here, the Scribe Virgin had granted him a brief return of sight so he could see L.W. The gift had been a surprise because the *mahmen* of the race was not known for her warm-and-fuzzies. But maybe as a parent herself, she'd been aware of how much it would mean for him to see in maturity that which he had known only as an infant young.

Not great news, as it turned out—and not because his offspring was weak or shifty.

Wrath didn't know what he'd expected, but the harsh, tortured reality of the male had saddened him—and he wasn't feeling any better about where things were after how many nights now? He was also no closer to figuring out how to reach his son.

At least he knew where he was, though.

Even if it was just physically.

Wake him up, he told himself. *Talk to him.*

Yeah, and say what? L.W. had proven too apt at the whole apple-falling-from-the-tree bullshit. Hell, the kid had landed right at the foot of Wrath's goddamn trunk, a brooding, aggressive fighter who stalked through spaces, rarely talked, and had moved out to Shuli's like a storm heading for new landscapes to ransack—

A creak down below had Wrath wheeling around and getting a gun out at the same time. The *mhis* still surrounded the mountaintop, the buffering making it virtually impossible for anyone to get here if they didn't know where the mansion was, but fate was a fucker, and he didn't need to learn that lesson a second time.

Except then . . . he caught the scent.

As he lowered his weapon, he released his breath. "*Leelan.*"

In the resonant quiet, he heard subdued movement in the foyer, his Queen coming across the hard stone floor and then ascending the plush carpeting.

"He's here?" she whispered as she closed in on him.

"Yeah." He held his hand out for her. "Sound asleep."

"I figured this was where you both were."

Beth halted beside him and left his palm dangling in the breeze, no doubt because she was rightfully focused on their son, and reassuring herself he was still in one piece. It was impossible not to rage at the many nights she must have had to do this alone, worrying over the kid with no *hellren* by her side. Maybe she was thinking of that, too, the scent of her sadness an acrid sting in the nose.

Cursing everything they had lost, he went to put his arm around her—

She stepped out of range. "I really want to call Doc Jane or Manny, but it only makes him mad when I do that."

Frowning, Wrath turned toward her tense voice. "Are you okay?"

"I guess we have to leave him here?" He had the sense she was looking around, and then came the pacing. "I mean, I know Vishous is monitoring the property and the *mhis* is still up, but—"

Wrath reached out into thin air, intent on finding her shoulder—but he got the position wrong, his hand bumping into her biceps. "What's going on."

When she didn't answer, he got his phone front and center. "We can call Jane and Manny right now, if it'll make you feel better? I don't care if it pisses him off." Still silence. "Fine, I'll call, right now—"

"You want to know what would make me feel better? You *really* want to know?"

"Fuck, yeah. Anything, what do you need me to do?"

"Don't lie to me," she said in a low, utterly clear voice. "That would be great."

Grinding his molars, Wrath went over to the study's double doors and silently closed them. "Listen, *leelan*—"

"Don't leave our home, and tell me you're going to the Audience House, like it's business as usual. Don't feed me a line of bullshit like that, when you're really going out into the field."

Behind his wraparounds, Wrath closed his eyes. "Let's go downstairs."

"Why? So our son doesn't hear? He's passed out on the floor in front of the fire because exhaustion and injury have done what nothing else can. I've seen this before. Nothing short of a bomb going off will wake him."

"Nice choice of words," he shot back. "And I did *not* go out to fight—"

"Yes, you did."

"I went to a private home—"

"Oh, you mean like the one that exploded when you opened a door thirty years ago? Like that? By *all* means, talk to me some more about where you went tonight, it's totally not digging you into an even deeper hole."

As his temper curled in his gut, he told himself to calm the fuck down. "It's not what you think, not at all—"

"Well, I guess the details are a need-to-know kind of thing, so yes, please, keep them to yourself. And no, none of your boys told me—they didn't have to. I went to the Audience House to bring you something, and none of you were there. Not home, not there—so I checked in at the training center. Not there, either, and I couldn't find Tohr, who never leaves your side. Where were you all?"

Wrath dragged a hand through his hair and felt like ripping the shit off his goddamn head. "I had to go to—"

"I don't care. But I will tell you that you should do yourself a favor—don't pull that again with me." She muttered a couple of choice words under her breath. "I'm going home now, and you can do whatever you want. God knows, that's the way you operate—"

He caught her arm. "I did *not* go out to fight. That was our agreement."

"You think you're going to skate on a technicality? Really? The field is *everywhere* in Caldwell."

"I was protected—"

"You still lied to me. You *promised* me you were not going to endanger your—"

"There's a plot *against* my life, Beth." He jacked over his hips. "I had to go to the asshole's house because we can't find him, and my guard was with me. You remember them, the ones with the fucking black daggers?"

"You think it's going to help me that you went to a traitor's own *home*?" Beth took her arm away and laughed harshly. "Is that supposed to make me feel better? And um, *no*, you don't get to throw this back on me. You made the choice when you left our home tonight, and I'm allowed to feel angry."

Tamping down on his volume, he gritted out, "Because I went, because of me, we now have a lead on what was a very cold trail."

"Hope it was worth it."

Goddamn it, he could practically see her taking one last, lingering look at the study doors . . . before she started back down the stairs at a fast clip, her arms wrapped around her torso, her dark hair streaming behind her.

"*Fuck.*"

His feet started moving before he gave them the command, and he grabbed on to the balustrade so he could go quicker. At the bottom, he tripped as the marble floor arrived sooner than he'd anticipated— then again, his concentration was on his *shellan*, not the information his remaining senses were feeding him. Rushing forward, he got to the vestibule just as the door was closing behind her.

As Wrath broke out into the night, the wind caught his waist-length hair and yanked his head to the side. "Beth!"

But she'd already dematerialized away from him.

"*Fuck,*" he shouted into the wind.

Lowering his head, he felt his rage swell. But it wasn't at his mate. It was at the fucking war, and the fucking *glymera*, and the fucking throne.

He'd come back after thirty fucking years to exactly the kind of mess he'd left.

The only difference being that everyone he'd loved had suffered for three decades—and his son had grown up to be as disaffected and angry as he himself had been at his worst.

Same shit, new night.

Fuck.

CHAPTER FOURTEEN

There were a lot of reasons to work the night shift—better pay, less conversation, lower profile—but if you sucked at sleeping like Dev did? Well, then it was a win-win. If he wasn't getting shut-eye, he might as well be earning money, right?

And bonus, his physical job made him so tired that his body had at least a chance of unplugging from his mind.

Not today, motherfucker. Not today.

A ghost was walking around his studio, and as much as he tried to ignore her, she was the only thing he could see.

Then again, he took minimalistic decor to a frat boy level, so there wasn't much distraction.

Thanks to his blackout drapes, he was able to get the shoebox nice and midnight no matter the hour, and that was usually the last brick in his REM wall. The others were following his sleep hygiene ritual, and damn it, he'd done everything right after work had been called for those high winds: He'd taken his shower, thrown a frozen pizza in the oven, and avoided caffeine in all its forms—Cokes in the fridge, coffee ice cream in the freezer, Green Mountain pods by the Keurig.

Seven a.m. he'd been tucked in like a good little boy, and after that, he'd given the eyes-closed thing a shot.

And gotten fucking nowhere.

Maybe the problem was the early send-home that had cheated him out of another three to four hours of working out—

"Bullshit."

That blonde was the problem. She'd danced around at the foot of his bed in that shimmering dress all fucking day long. And because she somehow had his remote control in her goddamn little hand, he'd just laid there against his two pathetically flat pillows, with his arms crossed over his bare chest and the rest of his naked body under the mismatched covers, watching the hallucination like it was his favorite frickin' TV show.

Tell me your mental health had punched out for the day without . . .

With a groan, he sat up and rubbed his hair. His eyes were sandy and his jaw cracked as he yawned on purpose, not because he had to. He also had a monster hard-on.

Quick glance at his phone: "Thank fuck."

Five p.m. Finally. Some people waited for that hour to have a drink. Him? It meant he could get out of bed and move about the proverbial cabin.

Getting up, he went into the bathroom and tried to take care of business for the benefit of his bladder. As he was sporting a two-by-four for a dumb handle, he had to brush his teeth and walk around, thinking of baseball—still not the season, but it did the trick—until things deflated enough to function. Back out in the open, he went to his dresser and grabbed his insulated running tights and his nylon socks. He didn't bother with a shirt, just pulled on his windbreaker and a hat. Brooks Glycerin 55s went on like gloves—and then he put his actual gloves on.

The last thing he did was grab his phone and his earbuds.

The text telling him there was no work again was front and center where he'd left it when it'd come in at three in the afternoon. Day shift foreman still couldn't get all the interior electric to come on after that crane at the receiving deck had wiped out the transformer as well as the generator.

Fine, he'd just try and outrun that blonde on the icy pavement. Best-case scenario his route took him to Vermont and back. Worst case? He slipped, fell, and gave himself a concussion that put him in a coma.

At least he'd get some sleep that way.

As Dev stepped out into the hall and locked his door, a voice said, "I made you the dinner then."

Closing his eyes, he flattened his lips. Then he forced a level tone. "Mrs. Aoun, I told you, I don't need—"

He shut his mouth as he turned around to find his five-foot-tall, white-haired, aproned neighbor planted directly in his path with a tray full of food. No doubt her door had been propped open—because of course it had—and he was willing to bet she'd been lying in wait for him to come out.

A kindly spider who was determined to put weight on him.

"I have the shawarma, kibbeh, rice, and fattoush. You will eat. You are too thin."

Bingo.

As she shoved forward that load of bowls that clearly had more than one serving in them, he put his palms up like there was a gun pointed at his chest. "Mrs. Aoun, you've got to stop this. You don't need to worry about me—"

"I told you. My sons are dead and I have no grandchildren. God put me here so that I could feed you and He put you there so I would have someone to cook for. That is the way of it—now take."

He accepted the calorie transfer because it was either that or he was very certain he would go to Hell as something worse than a murderous sociopath.

Oh, and there was another reason. The stuff smelled amazing.

"You bring the dishes back when they are empty. I will prepare you more."

Mrs. Aoun nodded her head once, as if they had concluded a negotiation, and then she waddled like a penguin back to her own studio and slammed the door shut.

Dev looked down at the food, and as his stomach let out a roar, he retraced his steps, and wondered exactly when he'd turned into such a pussy. Balancing everything as he put his thumbprint on the lock reader, he hipped things open and short-tripped over to his little counter. His fridge was empty except for his Coke stash, some sauce packets, and the three beers he'd intended on polishing off after his run in lieu of breakfast, lunch, and dinner.

Oh, and there was a jar of cherries he still didn't know why he'd bought a month ago.

And the coffee ice cream.

Round two with the exiting brought him immediately to the open stairwell and he jogged downward. The smells of all kinds of different cooking collected in the too-warm air, his nose failing to distinguish any of the food groups. On the first floor, he pushed through the glass door and passed by the wall of mailboxes, taking a deep breath of the cold preamble to the frigid outside.

Fine, Vermont was too far. His plan was to run across the nearest bridge and back.

Twice.

Putting his shoulder into the final door, he thought maybe he could do three times, given how much food he now had—

As things started to open, he knew before he even caught sight of what was waiting for him on the stoop . . . he just *knew*.

Dev stopped in the doorway and refused to acknowledge the flare that came alive in the center of his chest.

His blond ghost had become corporeal and was standing in the lee of the building entrance, just out of the wind. No glimmering dress tonight. She was wearing blue jeans and sensible trail boots, and had a red woolen scarf linked around her neck. Absently, he noted that her parka was a proper puffy one, its navy blue and gray contours dwarfing her body.

Good, he thought. She was warm.

"I'm not a stalker, I swear." She put a hand out like she was a cross-walk guard trying to stop a truck. "Your address was entered into the panel on the robo-cab? And I really wanted to give this back."

As she held out his construction jacket, her eyebrows were way high, as if she was the one surprised they were face to face even though, given her red cheeks and nose, she'd been waiting for him in the cold for a while.

Just take the coat, he told himself. *Take the fucking coat, and tell her to fuck off and never bother you again.*

"So here," she said hoarsely, her eyes slanting away. "As you can see, I have one of my own."

Dev watched her throat undulate as she clearly forced herself to swallow.

Meanwhile, the wind wafted around them, like a pair of arms urging them close. And even though she tucked her hair behind her ear, strands pulled free to create an aura of gold around her head.

What do you know. She might have found him forgettable the night before, but his memory was razor-sharp and had gotten it all right, the details of her lovely face and her mismatched eyes, her ripe lips and her tall body, spot fucking on.

"Is that why you came?" he heard himself say. "The coat."

She didn't meet his eyes. "Yes."

"Really."

When she just nodded, Dev took what she was offering him. Then he tossed it somewhere, anywhere.

Stepping into her, he put an arm around her waist and jerked her against him. As she gasped, he focused on her mouth.

"Bullshit," he growled.

Reaching up with his free hand, he fanned his fingers through her hair and the wind sent it on a wild, swirling ride. Then he snaked a hold up on to her nape and tilted her off-balance.

As she gripped his windbreaker, she still wasn't meeting his eyes.

But now it was because she was too busy looking at his lips like she was hungry.

Dev dropped his head, hovering his mouth right above her own. "Tell me something," he ordered her.

"Yes," she breathed. "Anything."

The pause was live-wire electric, and damn it, he knew he was being stupid with this shit. He had to live a life without complications, and he didn't need to fuck this blond to know that she was next-level complicated.

And yet he had to ask, just like he'd had to touch her . . . just like he had to kiss her:

"Do you like Lebanese food?"

CHAPTER FIFTEEN

Out in the wealthy suburbs, where the houses were monolithic and the properties were so picked and pruned their gardens had hairstyles even in winter, the daytime shutters started to rise from the windows all around Shuli's bedroom. The subtle whirring was not loud enough to wake him up. His phone going apeshit with a call coming through did the fucking job just fine.

Jacking upright in his satin sheets, he slapped his hand to his bed-side table and snapped the goddamn cell up to his ear.

"Did you find him? Tell me you found—"

The Brother Vishous's voice was deep as the low note on a Steinway and dry as a desert. "Yeah, L.W.'s been located."

"And he's alive." He kept that a statement, as if any hint of inquiry on his part would make the answer more likely to be in the negative. "He *is* alive—"

"Yeah, he is."

Shuli took a deep breath. "Thank Lassiter."

"Wrath found him."

"Where? What happened? When—"

"That's not why I'm calling you—for the third time." There was a *shht* and then an exhale, and Shuli could just picture the Brother lighting up one of his hand-rolleds. "You need to answer your fucking phone."

Next to him, the sheets started moving, and he nearly jabbed his hand under his pillow for the knife he kept there—until he recognized the dark hair, the breast, the naked hip.

Shit, lucky for her there was a glow from the bathroom or she woulda woken up dead. And fucking hell, the tail end of the night was coming back to him now. He'd gotten shitfaced, done a couple of lines of coke at Marhalle's, and ended up bringing home—

The woman looked at him with unfocused dark eyes. "Well, helllllo."

Closing his eyes, he said into his phone, "Sorry. I think I passed out for a while there."

Which explained why he didn't get any of the texts that had no doubt been sent about L.W.

"We want you at the Audience House in an hour."

"Okay, I'll see you—"

The call ended, and he stared at the screen. Ah, right. There had actually been seven missed reach-out-and-touches, as well as those group texts. It was a wonder the Brotherhood hadn't shown up here with their black daggers out and a coffin as a chaser the second the sun went bye-bye.

"Where are you going?" the woman asked as she reached through the sheets.

As her hand found his dick with the same accuracy his had grabbed his phone, he swung his legs out and put his feet on the carpeted floor.

"I gotta go." He cleared his throat. "My butler will take you home."

"Do you always wake up in a bad mood?"

Well, considering he was about to be killed for not doing a job he didn't want because a selfish royal fuck had fucked him off in the middle of the war—yeah, he was a little cranky.

"You know, I have ways of cheering a man up."

The sinuous way she rolled over and swept that glossy hair back over her shoulder had no doubt been a successful play many a time.

"My butler will pay you." And then, because he wasn't a total shit, he eased back down and kissed her pouty lips. "Thanks for all the fun."

"Keep me in mind."

"Yeah, I'll do that."

As he stood up, he swallowed a curse while he hit the summoning button under the lip of the bedside table. Then he limped over toward the loo with the full confidence that his bedroom would be empty when he came out: Willhis, his head *doggen*, would make sure she used one of the guest rooms to straighten herself before he escorted her down to the car and took her wherever she wanted to go.

And no, she would never know she'd been with a vampire.

Shutting himself in his black agate bathroom, he didn't make it over to the shower to start the water. His battered feet required an immediate interview, so he sat down on the padded stool in front of the double sinks and cocked one leg up.

The bloody blisters were concentrated on the back of the heel and the side of the big toe. He could feel that the same was true for the other foot, and as a twin set of heartbeats started to thump, he closed his eyes.

So many alleys. So many streets.

After Qhuinn had gone full confrontation with him in that alley outside of Bathe, Shuli had been taken off rotation and told to go home. But like that was going to happen. He'd walked the field for hours looking for his cocksucking roommate, to the point where he'd been a fucking zombie by the time his best friend, Nate, had found him and forced him into a car.

Even now, he wasn't sure whether he'd been looking for L.W. to save his own life—or just so he could punch the heir to the throne in the nads.

Then again, the two were not mutually exclusive.

And that was how he'd ended up at Marhalle's. If he'd stayed home and waited around? And L.W. had been walked through his door, all nonchalant-dick-in-his-hand?

Talk about waking up dead.

Marhalle, on the other hand, had given him exactly what he needed, right down to the escort: A brunette who had looked as different from Lyric as possible.

He didn't trust himself to fuck a blonde at this point. Why spin the wheel of shame and risk landing on such more-than-likelies as Impotence, Premature Ejaculation, or—worst of all—Crying Jag.

Putting his foot down on the heated floor, he checked the other one—which turned out to be in worse shape—and then forced himself up to the vertical. As he initiated forward momentum, the distance to the shower seemed to get longer and longer, but hey, at least he had plenty of time to enjoy the view of all his gold faucets and the gold-and-black monogrammed rug.

Oh, and also the black agate tub that had illumination running through it, the veins of white and gold crisscrossing like some kind of magical map to be deciphered.

He used the thing as his nightlight.

Over at the spacious shower alcove, which was the size of a garage and lit up thanks to a motion detector, he hit the water, and when things were warm enough, he stepped into the eight-headed spray—

"*Fuck.*"

All that raw skin on his tootsies screamed as the H_2O ran over his feet, and he gritted his teeth as he let his head fall back. Like the tub, the black agate walls and ceiling of the shower room glowed through that subtle veining, and he felt like he was up in the sky and there were ribbons of clouds all around him.

Was he still stoned, too? He couldn't remember whether he'd smoked a bowl before he'd crashed with the Absolutely Not Lyric escort.

Sweeping his hands back through his dripping hair, the shed water hit his ass with a slap that felt a lot like a cosmic spank. Was it about the sex worker? Or about all his unrequited?

The universe was going to have to be a little more specific if it was trying to teach him something.

God, he'd been watching Lyric from afar for so long now, he couldn't remember a time when he'd not snuck glances at her, or pretended to be cool when she'd hugged him as a greeting or a goodbye—or hidden behind his cool, rich fuckboy cloak of don't-care. When he'd seen that video last night, he'd been reminded that life didn't last forever, and what the fuck was he waiting for? Maybe he should finally say something.

Yeah, well, the punchline to that stupid idea was that his lifestyle—the drinking, the drugs, the prostitutes—might well be why she wrote him off. And his Sisyphean boomerang on that was that he was self-medicating everything he felt the instant she walked into any room.

Plus, God, Rhamp would kill him.

Then again, that male was going to have to get the fuck in line. The Black Dagger Brotherhood was already first on that list—

Shit, they might actually bury him tonight . . .

As his reality sunk into his parboiled brain, Shuli realized he'd hit a brick wall and there was a kind of peace that came with the impact—maybe because of an existential head injury, but at this point, he wasn't going to bother teasing out if this clarity was courtesy of destiny giving him CTE.

Bottom line, he had one hour to find that female and talk to her.

Before Lassiter only knew what was going to be done to him.

◆   ◆   ◆

When the sky was finally dark enough, L.W. left the mansion, making sure to lock up behind himself. He was stiff as fuck after sleeping on the floor in front of the hearth, and he'd been a block of ice when he'd finally woken up, the embers of the fire having long drifted into their ashy deaths, the warmth gone, gone, gone.

Outside, he looked up over his shoulder. Atop the gargoyle'd roof's slate peaks, the moon was peeking at him, like it was afraid of his mood and hiding in the forest of old iron lightning rods.

He told his brain to remember this sight, the silvery illumination broken up by those spiked diverters of bad weather strikes, the shapes of the purposely hideous creatures guarding the stone manse like something out of a fantasy novel.

Every time he left this place, he felt like it was a goodbye.

And some night, that was going to be true.

Closing his lids, he dematerialized and traveled in a scatter of molecules to the south, his destination one that he'd visited many times in his mind, and sometimes with his body. When he re-formed, it was in more knee-deep snow and in the shadows of a row of bare-branched trees. As he glanced across the drift-blanketed lawn to the well-lit, well-cared-for Colonial house, he shook his head.

There were footprints marring the snowpack. A lot of them. All his.

Fucking creeper, he thought as he followed his own trail.

Especially given that Safe Place was where females and their young were supposed to take shelter from dangerous males.

Not that he would ever hurt Bitty. Or anybody else in there.

Closing in from the side, he ignored the first level and all the people milling around there, and instead focused on the window that was smack-dab in the lineup on the second floor. The four small panes were all dark, but he fixed that by shutting his eyes again and imagining the profile that he'd come to see.

He'd never been any kind of artist, but his memory drew a picture of Bitty's bent head as she focused on her computer, her concentration so complete, it was as if she were responsible for the well-being of the whole world through that monitor. Her chestnut brown hair, recently highlighted with red sections, fell forward so her beautiful face was partially obscured, and her slender neck was a temptation even from a distance.

He'd never been inside the house, and he couldn't go in there now to find her in another room—or even just verify she was at work. Males weren't allowed to go in.

But she'd come out to him before.

Lifting his lids, he was stupidly disappointed that the female hadn't magically appeared, and he strained his eyes like he could force the image in his mind to become a reality in the flesh. Shit didn't work like that, though, and the panic that some night he wouldn't be able to see her choked him—

Movement drew his attention to the first floor, to one of the windows of the parlor . . . a female entering into view.

"There you are," he whispered.

An exhale of relief left his lips on a cloud that drifted toward the house, as if his very breath were called by her as well.

Tonight, Bitty was wearing a pale blue sweater, and her newly tinted hair looked great against the color. She was carrying a tray of cookies, and as she bent down to offer some to a female holding a swaddled young, her lips were moving as she chatted—and then there was that smile. Gentle and kind.

Your anger is your downfall . . . Unless you can forgive fate, you are going to destroy all of us.

The warning she'd spoken to him—as if it were a message from some kind of divine source—had been something he'd outright rejected. But no longer, not after last night. A hard truth had dawned on him as he'd woken up, and the shit was impossible to ignore: When he'd broken loose from Shuli in the field, it had supposedly been in the noble quest to win the war against the species and take out Lash by any means necessary.

Except that had only been his surface motivation.

Rage had been his real driver. The undeniable, furious energy that burned in his veins and his gut, that made him take risks—that made him utterly indifferent to the fact that a worthy male might well be killed because L.W. was flaking off his *ahstrux nohtrum*—was actually why he'd bolted.

The truth he'd woken up to tonight? He would have left anyway. Even if he'd thought Shuli would be put in a grave . . . he would still have deserted the guy.

So yeah, Bitty was right. That kind of shit was dangerous to people. That kind of shit was dangerous to *her*.

Opposites attracted? Fuck that. He was a curse waiting to happen—

Abruptly, Bitty looked to the window, and her brows tightened as if she had sensed his presence somehow.

L.W. swore under his breath and backed away.

Even as he hit reverse, however, his eyes clung to her, noting everything about the freeze frame of her standing there, in the glow of that room, everybody else who came and went around her disappearing, as if she were a brilliant light that blinded him.

She certainly hurt his eyes.

L.W. watched her for as long as he could, forcing himself to focus through the pain that had nothing to do with his sight . . . and everything to do with his soul.

Bitty was his female.

And after last night, when he'd proved those words of hers were not a caution, but statement of fact, he could never claim her.

CHAPTER SIXTEEN

I t's not much. But it's warm and dry, and it has running water."

As Lyric stepped into a studio apartment that was bare as a college dorm room before it was moved into, her heart was pounding like she'd run up the stairs instead of taken an elevator to the fourth floor.

"You're very neat," she remarked. And then wanted to smack herself in the head. "I mean—"

"When you don't have much, it's easy to be clean."

"Yes, it is." OMG, what was she saying. "Ah, how long have you been here?"

"A year."

She looked over her shoulder. Dev was back by the door, at a coat-rack that had been mounted on the white wall, and as he hung up the jacket she'd returned to him on the only vacant peg, she let her eyes go wherever they wanted on him—and what do you know, it was straight to his absolutely perfect—

"Ass?" he said as he turned around, his expression confused.

"I'm sorry?" Except then she did a two plus two on things. Had she really said that out loud? "Ass-tounding, I mean."

"That I've been here for a year?" He raised a brow. "You're a woman with a deep appreciation for the calendar, then."

No, it was ass-tounding that she was allowed out of the house without a minder. Because clearly, she was insane. And also, this wasn't her, this was not something she did, going to a male's—a *man's*—place alone, because . . .

Well, she wanted to have sex with the guy.

"Can we start over?" She unwrapped her scarf and took off the puffy jacket. Then glanced around for somewhere to put her things. "I was commenting on how neat everything was, and you were apologizing for things being not much."

His eyes grew hooded. "And then I hung the jacket up . . . and you looked at my ass. Did it pass inspection?"

"Oh, my God." She put her heated face in her hands. "Have I mentioned I'm terrible at this?"

The chuckle that came back at her was a low rumble. "I'm just giving you a hard time. And don't feel bad. I suck at . . . whatever this is, too."

"And yes, your ass is spectacular," she muttered.

Now he laughed, good and properly, and she drank the sight of him in as the man arched back on his solid hips, his muscular legs flexing in their second-skin running tights, the hard cut of his chin raised.

So his throat was exposed.

The tingling in her fangs was sudden and strong, and as a blast of heat went through her body, the hunger to bite and suck and have him inside her was nearly overwhelming—

He righted his head. And then stilled as their eyes met.

Over day, she had been able to remember his face, but now that she was staring at it again in person? His rugged features and his dark hair and his arching brows were hitting her anew.

"Sorry," she said as she walked—anywhere.

Oh, look. A window with a blackout drape. Annnnnnnd here was another one. The apartment was a standard studio, with a galley kitchen running down one wall, and a door on the far side of the bed that had to be the bathroom. The furnishings probably came with the place, she decided, as he didn't seem like a man who would bother to think about decor, and yet everything matched, was neither too big nor too small, and worked off a pale pinewood and white accent vibe.

"Lyric." When she stopped and turned back to him, he shook his head. "Don't apologize for the way you just stared at me. Ever."

"You don't know what I'm thinking," she said in a low voice.

"I don't care. I want that. Whatever it is."

Her fangs throbbed as they descended in the dental equivalent of a round of applause, and as she measured the span of his chest, the power in his legs, and the thick bulges of his biceps, she imagined herself stretched out on top of him, feeding from his vein.

She was pretty sure he could defend himself against her if she lost control and bit him.

But not completely sure.

And oh, yeah, the news flash that vampires were alive and well in Caldwell would be one hell of an icebreaker.

"You know, maybe I shouldn't have come after all," she whispered.

He shook his head again on his way over to her. When they were nearly chest to breast, she had to tilt her head to keep meeting his eyes, and she was relieved by how much bigger than her he was—and that he worked construction as a job, so none of it was fat.

There *had* to be a good chance he'd be able to keep her from killing him—

Guilt over everything she wasn't talking about made her take a step back. "I'm sorry."

"Whatever it is, you're forgiven."

"Are you always so reckless?" She tacked on, "Running into the street to arm-wrestle a billboard . . . being here alone with me."

She expected some kind of he-man put-down at that, but only got a raised brow. And then his shrug was offhand, even as the statement that followed was not: "I'm not afraid of anything or anyone."

So much confidence, and going by the size of him, she could well imagine he hadn't yet met anybody he couldn't beat.

Yet.

In the silence that followed, he took her parka and scarf and laid them out on top of the dresser.

"Now, about the food." He went over to his shallow countertop where a tray with many bowls had been set. "My neighbor is determined to put me on a bulking diet."

Lyric glanced at the door that led out into the hall and told herself to turn it into an exit. Except she didn't really want to leave. She'd said she wanted to do something important.

And this felt . . . important.

He got some plates out of the cupboard. "So I was surprised to see you out there. And not just because I didn't give you my address."

"Do you think I'm a stalker?"

His eyes flashed over his shoulder, and she couldn't read his expression. "Are you?"

"No, my *granmah*—my grandmother . . . told me to come over here tonight."

"Did she." He pivoted back to the food. "Why?"

Lyric opened her mouth. Closed it. "She thought it was unfair to keep your coat."

"So, do you like Lebanese food?"

Oh, that was right, she'd been so flustered, she hadn't answered earlier. "Ah, actually, I've never had it before."

"Come over and take a look at Mrs. Aoun's best efforts. She's appointed herself my honorary grandmother." When she hesitated, he drawled, "I don't bite, you know."

Well, that makes one of us, she thought.

But she went over to him and— "Oh, wow. That smells amazing."

Dev started to peel the saran wrap off of the serving dishes. "She told me what it all was, but I think I'm just going to call it delicious."

"For sure."

The next thing she knew, they were sitting across from each other at his little two-top, full plates in front of them, cutlery ready to do the duty, a pair of mismatched beers uncapped.

"Cheers," he said as he lifted his bottle.

She did the same with the one he'd given her. "Cheers."

She didn't try the Michelob, but the food—which they'd sent for a couple of carousel rides around in his microwave—was warm and tasty and fragrant, and the silence was . . .

Not comfortable. Not at all.

Every move he made was like a fishing lure for her instinct to feed, and she told herself she was going to leave as soon as she was done eating. God knew, she was still going to be hungry—

"So your grandmother told you to come find me and give me back my jacket?" He wiped his mouth with a paper towel. "That's a bold directive from an older woman, but maybe I underestimate the elder generation."

"She's dying," Lyric blurted.

As his fork paused on the way to his mouth, she sat back in defeat. "Look, I can't get even close to light and flirtatious tonight—"

"Who said I'm looking for that." He followed through with his bite, and finished chewing before tacking on, "Although I got to be honest, I'm not looking for anything."

"That's okay." She told herself this was good. Just a short fling. A one-night, something-sexual to take the edge off. "I'm not either."

"I don't think that's true." He shook his head slowly. "You definitely came here in search of something."

As she flushed, he forked up some more of the absolutely gorgeous meat. "What's happening with your grandmother?"

"Old age." Lyric thought about falling asleep in that flowered bedroom, and had to wonder if it had been the last time. "She's not ill in the disease sense—and that makes it harder in a way. She's mentally still with us, but her body has just decided . . ."

"That it's her time."

"Yes." She mostly kept the wobble out of her voice. "None of us want her to go, and I don't think she's ready, either. Whoa. Sorry, this is getting way too heavy—"

"Let me guess. She told you to come here and live a little while you can."

Lyric searched his hard, compelling face. "Exactly."

"Well." He wiped his mouth again. "At the risk of overpromising, you've come to the right place. For a certain . . . kind of living."

"Have I?" Lyric said in a husky way.

His eyes dropped to her mouth, and then went lower, to the V of her flannel shirt. As his lids dropped down, she knew he was imagining her naked. Maybe on her back on his bed. Maybe as he hovered over her, in between her legs.

"Oh, yeah," he replied in a deep voice. "Most definitely."

◆   ◆   ◆

Dev was very sure that the food was as good as the last three times Mrs. Aoun had forced dinner on him, but he couldn't say he was tasting anything much. The woman across the table from him was his sole focus, and if there was a way to look past or through her, he wasn't interested in knowing it.

After she left tonight? *That* was when he was going to start searching for ways to forget her—and hey, in a way, he was paying that graft forward. If they fucked? Then he'd get her out of his system easier. No problem.

And on her part? No doubt she just wanted to live a little on the wild side, the classic pretty, rich princess slumming it with a manual laborer storyline. Perfect compatibility right there.

Both of them were scratching itches, and neither was personal.

"So this was really good," she deflected as she put her fork down and pushed her plate off a little.

"Glad it's not just me." He put his last bite in his mouth. "About the food, that is. Good to know."

"Mm-hmm." She frowned. "You don't have a grandmother alive to cook for you?"

"No. And Mrs. Aoun doesn't have anyone to feed, either."

"Another case of destiny."

"Guess so." Rising to his feet, he took both their plates over to the sink. "I'm luckier than she is, though. I get all these eats."

"I don't know." She glanced over to his pulled drapes, and seemed to stare at them like there was a view showing in all those black folds. "My grandmother isn't happy unless she's in her kitchen and folks are coming over. Modern life thinks that's something that should be shamed or avoided at all costs—you know, the traditional gender role thing. But she takes great pride in what she provides, and her table is a hub for all kinds of people."

Leaning back against the counter, he crossed his arms over his chest. "I don't have dessert to offer you. Sorry."

Those blue and green eyes shifted in his direction, and he didn't bother to hide what was showing on his face. The transition from eating to fucking was only going to be as awkward as they made it, and on his side, he wasn't feeling awkward at all. He was ready to go.

"Aren't you hot?" she said softly. "In that windbreaker?"

"Nothing under it. I get hot when I run."

"Then . . ." The blonde cleared her throat. "Maybe you should take it off."

Dev shifted his weight so he was standing up, took the hem, and got to pulling the thing up and over his head. As his chest was revealed to her, he totally approved of the way her stare lingered on his pecs and his abs, but she stayed where she was. Fine. To give her time to consider exactly where they were going with all this, he walked over to the coatrack and forced the lightweight Gore-Tex onto an overstuffed peg of outerwear. As he turned around, he was well aware of everything that was showing at the front of his running tights, but there was no reason to hide the thickening.

He was prepared to give it to her if she wanted it.

And going by the way that gaze traveled down to the juncture of his thighs?

"I'm gonna be real with you," he said. "You can leave now. But if you don't go, I'm coming over there and picking you up. And guess where you're headed after that."

"Where," she breathed.

"Under me." He pointed to his bed. "Over there."

When her hands tangled and twisted in her lap, he wondered if he wasn't pushing her too hard. Maybe this was just a game of tease and retreat, and if that was the case, cool. Might be better in the long run for him anyway.

But then she really did need to go because he had some business he had to take care of. At least if he ever wanted to sit down again.

As she cleared her throat, he was ready for a bullshit excuse about her having to get home to let a dog out. Feed a cat. Go check on that grandmother of hers—

"Then you better come get me."

She barely got the words out before Dev stalked over and made good on his promise. He didn't even give her a chance to stand up. He shoved the table away from her, the screech as feet scraped across the parquet floor loud as a scream. Swooping down, he put an arm around her shoulders and hooked the other under her knees. Her weight barely registered as he lifted her.

Their eyes locked.

"Yes," she said as she focused on his lips. "I'm sure."

A shaft of something way too complicated went through the center of his chest. Fortunately, she cut that shit off by pressing a proper kiss on him—like she was sealing the deal.

Righto. Houston, we have contact.

When he got to the bed, he laid her out, and didn't take it slow. He stretched his body over hers, yet kept his torso up off of her breasts, his hips off her pelvis, and his legs not touching hers.

She knew what he was looking for, and answered his plank by splitting her thighs and making plenty of room for him.

Inch by inch, he lowered himself down starting with his chest, and underneath him, she arched to greet him, her hands finding the small of his back and riding up the muscles that fanned out from his spine. She hissed when his erection finally pressed into exactly where he wanted to penetrate, and he could have sworn he could feel her heat.

Oh, and yeah, her breasts were nice and high against his pecs, and her chin rose so her mouth was on offer.

Tilting his head, he hovered just above her lips. "You can still go," he growled. "Now."

By way of reply, she lifted her head so there was just a hair's width between their mouths. "If you keep saying that, I'm going to think you don't want me to stay—"

He cut that shit off by rolling his pelvis, the hard, hard length of him pushing against her core, stroking her sex through her jeans. As she gasped, he closed the distance, sealing his mouth to hers, and when she moaned, he swallowed the desperate sound. The more he kissed her, entering her with his tongue, he could feel her loosen up and go with it, her fingers tangling in his hair, urging him to keep it up, go even harder.

Take all of her.

Everything about her was so vivid that he had to close his eyes, as if to cut the glare. Bad idea. Not seeing the corner of the pillow she was on or the blank wall behind the cheap headboard or anything about where he was in familiar surroundings . . . meant his only grounding in the void was her.

Shit got way too intense, way too fast. From those soft lips to the way her body fit against him to how his blood started to pound . . .

Dev pulled back sharply and popped his lids wide.

This was just supposed to be fucking, he told himself. This was biology, not romance, for fuck's sake—

Her mismatched, luminous, punch-in-the-gut eyes opened. And the worry that came over her face was accompanied by her loosening the grip she'd taken on the hair at his nape.

"Is something wrong?" she whispered.

Shaking his head, he intended to lie to her. Tell her that he was a good guy just making super sure she was cool with them banging. Maybe murmur some bullshit that she was just so beautiful, and a great kisser, and yada, yada, yada—which was all true, but not what he was thinking about.

"There's a lot you don't know about me," he said grimly.

Her eyes searched his face. "The same is true on my side."

"I know." Then he added, "We're strangers."

And see? he told his conscience. Tit for tat with the withholding, s'all good. The seesaw of secrets was even, so he needed to stop being a little bitch.

"Let's just be here," he said roughly. "And then we go our separate ways."

She stroked his face, her fingertips lingering on his jaw. "Yes, that's all we need to do."

He told himself to be relieved as he lowered his mouth once again, but somehow, that shit didn't really stick—

A cell phone ringing was like a bomb going off, both of them jerking their heads to the dresser where he'd put her parka and scarf.

Who is calling her, he wondered.

He probably should thank them.

CHAPTER SEVENTEEN

L.W. arrived at his sire's Audience House, re-forming around the back by the kitchen entrance. Everything was plowed and shoveled on the property, not just at the main building, but over at Four Toys HQ, Vishous's satellite barn of IT brainiacs. It had been a long time since he'd been out here—had it been fall? maybe the end of summer—and he measured all the snow.

Goddamn, he'd hated coming to this place.

It was a reminder of the lie he'd been expected to carry on his own wherever he went for thirty fucking years. He'd been the only one of his generation to know the truth, that his father had died and been replaced with a chimera. And while he'd been on the sidelines, watching all the other young yuck it up with their pops, he'd been expected to keep his mourning to himself.

Couldn't fuck the ruse. And the real biter of it all? The whole thing had been to save the throne for him: Rahvyn had projected an image of the great Blind King in front of the civilians, L.W.'s *mahmen* made all the decisions as Queen, and everybody had held the reins with the expectation that he'd drop his ass in Daddy's old chair when he was mature enough.

No one had asked him what he'd wanted, and he'd grown up in the stew of grief that had been projected onto him, the Brothers, the fighters, and their mates always looking at him like he was some kind of antidote to his father's death.

Not as him as his own person.

He'd been over being a holy grail to catch their metaphorical tears as soon as he'd been aware of his purpose in their lives. But everywhere he went, there it was, as unrelenting as the color of his hair and his eyes and the bone structure of his face—which, given what had shown up the other week, back from the dead, was also because he was a "dead" ringer for the one they'd all lost.

Put like that, going after Lash was a way of *ahvenging* himself.

And he was running out of time.

Jacking his leathers up, he did a quick double-check under his jacket. Both his guns were holstered at his ribs, his steel daggers were across his chest, and his waist belt was locked on with another set of nine millimeters as well as a lineup of ammo across the small of his back. With the inventory over, he approached that back door, the one that was always mounted with a seasonal wreath to hide the camera lens.

At the moment, the thing was made of evergreen sprigs and red and green ribbons.

As the lock sprung the second his shitkickers hit the welcome mat, he wasn't surprised they knew he was here, and the same thing happened at each of the two inner portals, the bolts clearing for him without him having to make any calls or even speak a word for the mics to pick up.

No doubt they had known where he'd spent the day, too—

The kitchen was bustling, *doggen* in chef's whites making pastries for the audiences that were going to start up in the next hour or so—

"Your Highness—"

"Oh! Your—"

"—Highness."

All three females stopped what they were doing—one even dropped the egg she'd been about to crack over a bowl—and with a fluster, they whipped off their caps and bowed to him.

The deference was another thing he hated.

It was a mirror that showed him too much for the fraud he was.

"'Scuse me," he muttered.

Getting the hell out of there, he pushed through a flap door and walked down one of the common corridors. He probably would have been given access to the central, secured core of the building, where the Brothers gathered before things started for the night or took breaks between audiences, but he wasn't in a big hurry to run into any of those males. After fucking everybody off last night and going rogue, he could just imagine they'd stab him, but for his—

"—Highness!"

Saxton, the King's solicitor, bent down low. "Are you expected? Your father isn't here quite yet—"

"Not expected, no. Just need to see him."

The dapper male was all tweeded out, his ascot in place, his brown, navy blue, and cream checked suit jacket tailored so perfectly it was as if he'd been born with it on and the thing had grown along with him. As usual, his thick blond hair was swooped to the side, and with his perfect skin and nails, the guy looked like he was ready to ride off on a fox hunt.

Or at least a magazine shoot of one.

"Allow me to show you into the Audience Room, then."

"I'll wait. In the waiting room."

There was a pause. "I think it would be best if you—"

"Wait in the waiting area like everybody else who's here to see him."

Another long moment. And then the solicitor bowed once again. As Saxton straightened, he was pushing at his red ascot, his gold pinkie ring flashing. But he wasn't going to say what he was thinking.

"As you wish, sire."

When L.W. nodded briskly toward the front of the house, Saxton flushed. Still, the guy started off and led the way. Protocol was that members of the First Family always went first, and L.W. hated that deference, too.

There were all kinds of offices on the left-hand side of the corridor, and as he passed the open doorways, people looked up—and did double takes. Which was just ridiculous. His sire was the King, not him.

Rounding the final corner, he passed the front entrance and went into a cozy room that had comfortable sofas and chairs already accommodating the first rounds of civilians. Additionally, the receptionist was at her desk, bowed over a printer behind her chair that appeared not to be working.

The collective gasp brought her head up. And then she gasped, too.

Motherfucker.

Even though he wanted to scream, L.W. lifted a lame-ass hand because he didn't care to reveal how much of a total, unrelenting asshole he was—

On a oner, all of the civilians and the receptionist with the busted HP Laser-whatever-it was burst up to their feet and bent down like they were checking out their legs for signs of amputation. Then their faces lifted to him in their still-jacked stances, the adoration shining like half a dozen heat lamps pointed at him.

Now he knew what the fry station at McD's felt like.

"Perhaps the Audience Room would be best," Saxton said quietly.

"Yeah."

L.W. backed out and turned away as fast as he could. Still, he heard the hushed whispers in his wake, the excited voices and buzzy cadence to the conversation making his skin crawl. It wasn't until he was shown into his father's sanctuary of sucking up that he realized why he was so particularly bitched.

In spite of it making no goddamn sense, he'd assumed with the actual Wrath back, all that shit would stop happening. But that was dumbass and a half. As far as they knew, their King had never left, and they'd treated L.W. with deference all along.

"Would you like anything to eat?" Saxton asked from over by the doors. "The *doggen* would be most happy to serve you."

He couldn't remember the last thing he'd eaten, or the last proper meal he'd had. "I'm good. Thanks."

Shouldn't he be hungry? he thought as the male bowed and backed out.

As things were shut quietly, L.W. closed his eyes. He didn't want to waste sight on the purposely welcoming room with its fireplace already crackling and the pair of armchairs all ready for the ass kissing. He had quite enough memories of the place, from when Rahvyn had been parking it in the position of power—

The door opened behind him, and he knew who it was before he turned around or caught any scent.

Pulling a pivot, he popped his lids.

Wrath, son of Wrath, sire of Wrath, walked in with his service dog like he owned the place, but hey, he did. And with the force of his presence, the great male could no doubt have waltzed into the White House in D.C. and kick out the humans' president with just a glare. Towering in height, built like the fighter he was bred to be, he was dressed in his uniform, a black muscle shirt and black leathers. There were no weapons on him, and the only markings that showed on his skin were the tattoos of his lineage that ran up his thick forearms. The long black hair falling from a widow's peak was just like L.W.'s own, and behind those black wraparounds . . . were eyes that were the same.

"Give us a minute."

The King spoke and Tohrment, who was at his heel, backed out immediately, taking whichever other Brothers had also come with him. Annnnnnnnnnnd that was how shit ran. One look, one word, and people hopped.

L.W. waited as things were shut, and braced for the explosion—

"How you doin', son."

That was it. No screaming. No yelling. The guy just walked on past, his golden retriever by his side, the harness handle connecting them like a molecular tie. When the King got to the set of armchairs, he took the one on the left.

Interesting. Rahvyn had always sat on the other side.

Not that it mattered.

"Well?" came the prompt.

As he faced his sire, the Blind King's wraparounds were orientated straight ahead, those carved arms overflowing the chair, the legs splaying out, the shitkickers making him look like he was prepared to stomp out any disagreement by anyone about anything.

"I fucked off Shuli last night." L.W. crossed his arms over his chest. "We were in the field and he wanted to divert to a club."

"So I hear. To check on Lyric."

"She was fine. It was a waste of time. But I don't want him getting into trouble. I didn't give him a choice."

Those slashing black brows dropped below the shades. "How so."

"I ghosted him. And then I turned off my phone."

There was a long pause, and he had the clear impression that his pops was calling on an epic load of self-control. Either that or the male's jaw was doing chin-ups at his ears just for shits and giggles.

"That was fucking stupid," came the gritted response. "On so many levels. You may have survived the night—*alone*, in the goddamn field—but now we gotta contend with the Shuli shit. The punishment for an *abstrux nohtrum* if he fails to perform his duty is clear. I can have the male killed. Right now."

"You won't do that, though."

A cold wave blew out across the room to him, and the words that followed made his balls tighten. "Won't I."

"No," he said in the same tone. "It would be unfair. If Shuli fucked me off, that's one thing, but that's not what happened. And as for killing me instead, you'd have to tell your mate you offed her only son. Pretty sure that'll leave you sleeping on the couch for a couple hundred years."

The armchair creaked as his father leaned forward, plugging his elbows on his knees. For a split second, L.W. considered taking a step back. Even though the male was supposed to be blind, you'd swear those eyes were not just focused on you . . . they were burning a hole through your flesh and bone.

"You have all the answers, then."

"No, I just know that you're not going to kill an innocent male." L.W. focused on the black diamond that sat on the middle finger of that right hand. "And if anyone calls you on not ordering the hit, you're the King, right? You'll just change the rules to suit yourself or maybe bury the naysayers. That's the way it works, isn't it."

There was a long silence, and he could tell the dog was uneasy with the vibe in the room. George moved his body closer to his master's feet, and he kept his muzzle lowered like he didn't want to chance being in the line of fire.

That imperial head shook slowly, the hard face showing no emotion at all. "You don't have any idea how anything works."

The rage that was never far below L.W.'s surface flared up. "How would you know what I think or what I know. We're strangers, you and me. Linked by biology, nothing more."

More with the jaw shit, like Wrath was chewing his own molars to stubs. "Look, I realize the last three decades were hard—"

"You don't know shit about what life has been like here—"

"Do you think I was on a *fucking* vacation." That autocratic voice cracked like a whip, and then the King rose to his feet. "You think I *chose* what fucking happened?"

Oh, so we're going to do this, huh. Fucking fine.

L.W. jerked forward on his hips. "I know you weren't supposed to go out that night. But you did, and you fucked everybody by making the choice that suited you."

The laughter was low and nasty. "Just like what you did to Shuli last night. Guess that biology runs real deep, doesn't it."

As L.W. locked his own set of teeth, he deliberately unhinged his chin.

"I'm out of here." He wheeled around. "I've said what I need to say—"

"If this happens again, I'm taking you off rotation. You're out in the field with Shuli or you can stay the fuck home."

L.W. glared over his shoulder. "I'm not a teenager you can ground. And I'm not on your rotation anymore—I quit."

That expression got so dark it had its own gravitational pull. "Why are you so fucking determined to fight everything."

"There's a war going on out there. It's what we all need to do."

"Not if you're fighting the wrong people."

L.W. went over to the door, and when he hit the knob, the thing refused to turn. "Let me out."

"You're breaking your *mahmen's* heart, you know that."

He looked back across the Audience Room. "Naw, that was your job. All I had to do was watch her suffer and hate you for it for all these years."

He tried the knob again.

Before he could holler something about broken hinges and flying wood, his father growled, "I might have hurt her by accident, but you're doing it on purpose now. Be as angry with me as you want. She doesn't deserve it, though. She never did."

L.W. yanked at the knob. Then he lowered his head and told himself to shut his fucking mouth—

"I grew up in the cold shadow of your throne. There was no time for anybody or anything else, other than worshipping the ghost of you."

"Don't blame her for what she had to do—and she was keeping the power structure in place for you. She never knew I was coming back. Everything was done to give you the chance to lead—"

"I didn't *ask* for that fucking favor." He pulled at the door again and then sent another glare back toward the fireplace and the armchairs. "And bull*shit* she did it for me. All that crap about ruling was the only way to be close to you. She sacrificed all that time and energy for herself and the memory of her dead fucking *hellren*, her one true love. It had *nothing* to do with me. None of it."

"Yes, it did—"

"You weren't here! So quit with the recap of all the years you were gone." He jabbed a finger at the center of his own chest. "*I* was here, *I* lived through it, all the Brothers dragging themselves around, my *mahmen* weeping herself to sleep every day—for thirty fucking *years* it was a goddamn wake around here. And now you're back, and everybody's soooo happy. Well, *I'm* not, because I don't need you in my life and I remember all too clearly what everybody seems to have forgotten. *You* made a decision and *you* fucked us all. The fact that you've returned doesn't change that math."

He thought of the moment he'd seen his father actually standing in the study at the mansion. The great male, back from the dead.

There had been a spontaneous embrace between them. But it had been the lost and scared child who'd hugged the hero he'd needed to believe his father had been.

Not the grown-ass adult who knew better.

"Now, *I'm* telling *you*," he snapped. "If you don't order them to open this *fucking* door, I'm going to break it down."

"So much hate in you," Wrath said roughly. "And you're missing the point."

"Really? Tell me what I got wrong, *Dad*."

"I didn't set that bomb, son. Lash did."

L.W. finally felt the door give way. As he stepped out, he tossed over his shoulder, "Don't worry. I hate him, too."

CHAPTER EIGHTEEN

O f course it was her goddamned phone.

Laying under Dev, on the verge of the kind of pleasure that made you believe in magic, Lyric squeezed her eyes shut in frustration. But then she remembered all the reasons someone could be trying to call her.

And one in particular.

"I think it's me," she mumbled as she scooted out from under the human man who hovered over her with every promise of multiple orgasms that she'd ever heard about.

Her legs were like rubber, and her balance was wonky on the way over to her parka, and she couldn't decide whether the interruption was a good thing or not. Pro? It slowed things down from warp speed to what might be more reasonable. Con? Well, duh. It slowed things down.

At the dresser, she fumbled through her pockets—how were there so many?—and then she dropped the phone, but caught the slippery weight just before it hit the floor. As she turned the cell over, she frowned.

Shuli?

Why was he calling her? His party invitations were always on text.

Bumping the guy to voicemail with relief, she put the phone back and the—

Holy. Shit.

The man stretched out on that bed was like a Greek god who'd come down to earth. Gym-created muscles were all well and good, but there was something primordial about a body that had been carved from hard work. Dev was an absolute specimen, from his broad shoulders and heavy arms, to his six-pack . . . to his bulging thighs that strained those poor running tights.

She wondered just how far Nike had gone testing the tensile strength of all that nylon.

And then there was the erection he did nothing to hide. As with the contours of his legs, every detail of his arousal was visible from the long shaft to the blunt and curving head.

"You have to go?" he murmured. "Or did you put your coat on because you think it's cold in here?"

Lyric glanced down at herself. Huh. Guess some part of her had made a decision.

Looking back up, she found that his eyes were hooded with banked heat and that the dark waves of his hair were all messed up—because her hands had been in them. With his parted lips, he was the picture of a male who'd been interrupted at the wrong time.

But he didn't seem frustrated or angry.

No, that was her job. The frustration, that was.

"I . . ." She pulled her hair back and tied the length in a loose knot. "I don't know."

Dev nodded and started to sit up—Jesus, talk about a show. If he was all hard angles lying down, the rippling motion under his skin now was a show to watch—

"No." She put her hand out. "You just hang. I'll see myself to the door—" She glanced over her shoulder. "I mean, the exit. Downstairs."

Dev eased back against the pillows, stretching an arm behind his head. "Suit yourself."

Oh, God, why the hell had she come here. She had all the dating chops of a nun, and meanwhile, Mr. Sexual with the humongous hard-on over on the bed was just business-as-usual, like women came and went all the time for him.

And could he maybe drag a blanket over that baseball bat of his? Having that thing out on display reminded her of the time she'd tried to give up chocolate and had seen M&M's everywhere.

Then again, he'd make a tent even with all that spandex—*fuck*.

Focusing on her parka, she went to zip things—

When she glanced up, he was right next to her. Neat trick, given that human men supposedly didn't dematerialize.

She let her hands drop. "I'm sorry."

"What are you apologizing for."

"I . . ." Lyric shrugged—and decided to fuck it and be honest. "I really want to have sex with you. Except I'm just not sophisticated enough to walk away a couple of hours from now all, 'Hey, that's cool. See ya.' If I stay, I'm going to regret it. Not because it didn't feel good, but because I'm just doing a different version of the shit I decided to get away from after last night."

"And what shit would that be?"

There was a beat of silence.

"Pretending to be someone I'm not."

"Okay, I'll walk you out," he said evenly.

As a sinking feeling set up shop in the center of her chest, she thought, holy crap, how ridiculous. It was the height of insanity to feel let down because he so smoothly respected the boundary she'd set. What did she want? Some kind of tug and pull just to prove he wanted her?

She made a casual motion with her hand. "You don't have to."

"I know."

As he grabbed his windbreaker and pulled it back over his head, she snuck a final glimpse at those abs. Then he was opening the door and holding it wide.

"Ladies first."

Zipping up her coat, she shuffled past him, and looked down the hall. There were a dozen other doors, the elevator in the middle, and an open staircase over on the right. Heading for the steps, she waited for him to lock up. He didn't.

"So this is a safe building?" she murmured as she put her hand on the balustrade and started the descent.

"Safe is relative. But no, I'm not worried about someone going through my things."

Lyric made the half circle at the platform between floors. God, she was running out of time to talk to him, and all this silence was a waste—but as far as mood killers went, she'd just dropped the intimacy H-bomb of all time back there. Meanwhile, she could feel him behind her, his bigger body moving lockstep with the rhythm she set on the stairs, his heavier footfalls echoing around them. When they got to the lobby, she started to scramble for words and almost wished there were a reason for them to keep going, into the basement.

But "goodbye" was the only one she needed, wasn't it.

Dev did the duty with an inner door and then the outer one that didn't have a lock on it so that the mail carrier could reach the boxes in the vestibule. Finally, they were outside, the cold feeling so much colder somehow.

"Are you Ubering again?" he asked as he looked up and down the street.

"I—ah, yes, I am."

To prove the point she was independent, she front and centered her phone.

"Let's go back and stand in the lobby, then. While you call for one."

Lyric opened her mouth. But she wasn't sure how to lie her way out of the fact that she was tired and had just been planning to dematerialize. The species divide was not that big when they'd been eating or talking—or kissing. Just like last night, though, humans did not ghost away to other destinations.

Backtracking into the lobby, she went to work on her phone. The cell service wasn't great, only two bars, and she had to install the damn app.

Which was what happened when you'd never had to call an Uber before.

"Something wrong?" he asked as she fiddled with her phone.

And that was when she smelled it.

Glancing up from the little screen of her Samsung, she drew in a slow, deep breath through her nose—not that she needed the confirmation. The sickly sweet smell, of baby powder and dead flesh, was utterly unmistakable.

There was a *lesser* in the building. Close by.

And the thing was going to know exactly what she was.

"I have to go." She backed away to the solid door. "And I want you to head upstairs. Now—"

"What's wrong?"

"I . . . can't—" She shot back to the exit. "Goodbye, Dev. And lock your door, for once. *Please.*"

Dev's brows tightened. Then he shrugged. "Fine. Take care of yourself."

He turned away and started for the stairs, moving slower than she wanted. But at least it was so much faster than him standing still.

Blasting out past the mailboxes, she hit the night air again and kept on going down the steps to the snowy sidewalk. She told herself that as a human, Dev wouldn't be of any interest to a slayer, not unless they wanted to try to recruit him. But he didn't seem like the kind of lost, disaffected soul the Lessening Society went after.

Oh, God, what if they scented her on him?

"This isn't the damn field," she muttered. "What is it doing here . . ."

The street Dev's building was on wasn't some deserted, decaying stretch of bad zip code. It was a going concern, with all the buildings occupied, lights on in so many windows, cars passing by, even a couple of bundled-up pedestrians across the block hustling for their SUV.

But damn it, the war was everywhere.

All the time.

CHAPTER NINETEEN

L
ess than thirty minutes after Shuli arrived at the Audience House, he stepped back out of its cottagey front door in a stunned stupor. The meeting with the King hadn't lasted long, and though he was grateful he hadn't been run through with a black dagger on the spot, he was downright fucking flabbergasted that L.W. had shown up here first and come clean about the situation.

What the fuck?

In any event, the King had declined to go the pink slip/coffin route. He'd just grimly told Shuli to do his best to stick with his son—who, apparently, was no longer going to be on the schedule.

And that was it. Meeting over.

So yeah, here he was now, standing out in the cold in a suit and cashmere overcoat, more than a little shell-shocked—

As a pair of vampires re-formed in front of him, the well-dressed male and female jumped back in surprise.

"Sorry," he said. "I'm just leaving—"

"Shuli?"

He frowned and focused properly on the male. It took a couple of blinks for the face to place—then again, he'd been drunk on Dom Pérignon every time he'd ever hung out with the guy.

"Mitchus?"

"Yes! How have you been, old dog?"

The pair of them embraced, and Shuli looked over the male's shoulder. The female on the periphery was beautiful in the restrained way of the *glymera*, every hair in place, the pearls and sweater set peeking through a stylish caramel-colored mink coat. She was young, going by her open expression and her frozen smile, but she could have been five hundred years old for her matching pumps and handbag.

As Shuli eased back, he pounded Mitchus on the shoulder of his fine coat. "Are you here for any particular reason, my guy?"

"I'll bet you can't guess." The male motioned with a directorial hand. "May I present the lovely Mistress Perighrine, my intended. We're here for our blessing."

The female floated over and extended a glove-covered hand. "How do you do?"

And that was when Shuli scented it. Pregnant . . . Mistress Perighrine was with young.

Ah, so that was why the male had disappeared from the scene. And it was interesting that Mitchus was going through with the mating. There were only two kinds of females in the aristocracy, the virtuous ones you claimed before family and the *glymera*, who were virgins, and the ruined sort you slept with and enjoyed.

You never showed up in front of your King with the latters, looking for down-the-aisle a-okays.

"The pleasure is mine," Shuli murmured.

He touched the tips of her fingers with his own, then placed his palm over his heart and bowed. As their eye contact was broken, a series of images flipped through his mind, all of them of Mitchus fucking various human and vampire women, usually in pairs.

And usually in Shuli's guest room on the first floor. The one L.W. supposedly lived in now.

Come to think of it, though . . . that shit had stopped months ago. Maybe the guy had met the One.

"So when's the date?" Shuli asked as he straightened.

"Next year." Mitchus smiled, showing even white teeth, his fangs just slightly elongated. "You're on the guest list, of course."

Then the male stepped in and put his arm around his female's waist.

Wow. Talk about your turnarounds.

Except then Shuli thought of the call he'd made to Lyric, the one that had gone unanswered, the one he'd made just before coming over here.

Sometimes a good female could turn you around. Or fuck your shit up.

"Thanks." He cleared his throat. "I'll be there with bells on."

"Great." Mitchus inclined his head. "See you then."

"Looking forward to it."

The happy couple waltzed up to the front door and, ever the gentle-male, Mitchus opened things for his female. As she walked past him, he glanced back at Shuli and gave a final, gallant wave.

And then they were gone, the heavy reinforced door that was made up to look like something cheerful easing shut in their wake. Frankly, he was surprised that the pair had come here. So many of the aristocracy thought a common audience was beneath them. Mitchus's family had always been sticklers for propriety, though. Guess the knock to the ego was worth the royal rubber stamp, although how they'd accepted that pregnancy and still given their own blessing was a thing.

But whatever. Not his business, on so many levels.

He was never getting mated.

Closing his eyes, it was a hot minute before he could dematerialize—and then he was spiriting off, flying in a scatter of molecules. It didn't take him long to get home, and as he re-formed in front of his modern mansion, he surveyed the white, low-slung exterior with tired eyes. The shit was like a bunker in the snowy landscape, just one more bank in the bunch, and he knew he couldn't stay long.

He had to somehow find L.W.

And not just because it was his job. He'd come to a decision about—

His front door opened, and the shape that appeared between the jambs was way too enormous to be Willhis.

Also, his butler had never favored black leather with a chaser of weapons.

Shuli exhaled a curse as he started up his shoveled walkway. "I thought you wanted to avoid me like the plague."

L.W. shrugged and stirred his Cup Noodles. "My clothes are here."

As Shuli hopped up the steps and caught a whiff of chicken stock, the male didn't budge—so he shoved L.W. out of the way. Which, yeah, only happened because the fucker allowed himself to get moved, but hey, you had to take your victories where you found them. And then Shuli stalled out in his foyer because there was no reason to have this throw down happen any farther into the house.

Willhis hated conflict, and he didn't want to upset his *doggen*.

"Just take your shit and go." Shuli indicated the general direction of the wing L.W. had been camping out in. "Your pops gave me a pass on this bullshit job, told me to do my best. And I've just decided that my best is telling you to fuck off and do whatever it is you're going to do. You want to go solo, you got it."

As L.W. leaned back against the arch into the library, he was like a stain against all the white walls, and damn if the sonofabitch didn't look like some kind of brutalist sculpture come to life. But what do you know, there was already enough abstract art in the place.

"So . . ." Shuli walked over to the archway of the guest wing. "There ya go."

He swooped both hands forward. Like His Royal Cocksucking Highness didn't know where he'd been crashing during the days since the pair of them had been *Love Match*'d up.

When L.W. just kept standing there, eating those goddamned plastic noodles, Shuli frowned. "You're kidding me."

"What."

"You came to apologize?" he said in disbelief. "Is that what this is? You're . . . apologizing?"

Those black brows went down so hard, it was like they were trying to relocate to his nostrils.

"Wow." Shuli drew a hand through his hair. "You're full of surprises tonight, aren't you."

Those pale green eyes shifted away to the yellow-and-black Jackson Pollock that hung over a Biedermeier console table. And then the silence stretched out, big as the horizon. With the white marble floors and the white staircase and all the unadorned white everywhere, it was like they were still outside.

"You really suck at this whole 'sorry' thing, FYI," Shuli remarked.

"I don't do it often." The fighter tilted the cup and drank some of the broth.

When there was no tack onto that, no but-when-I-do-I-mean-it shit, it wasn't really a shocker. "That I believe."

Even more quiet. At which point Shuli closed his eyes and let his head fall back on his spine. "You could at least say the word. Or how about a synonym for it—hey, I'd even take something that rhymes. Worry. Quarry."

"Furry."

"That doesn't rhyme."

"Yeah, it does—"

"No. It doesn't. That only shares three letters—"

"It totally rhymes—"

"Then you're pronouncing 'sorry' as 'Surrey'—or 'furry' like 'fawrry,' like you're four fucking years old and missing a couple of teeth."

The front door opened, and without skipping a beat, they both spun toward it and pulled out guns. Or rather, L.W. pulled a Smith & Wesson and Shuli shoved his hand uselessly under his arm because of course he hadn't gone to see the King with any weapons on him.

The good news, though? It wasn't a *lesser* they had to take out or some human robber they could decide whether to kill or play mind games with.

Lyric's twin, Rhamp, came right into the house. The guy was

dressed to be out in the field, his dark hair pulled back in man bun territory, a fresh pair of shitkickers on, the scent of firearms and honed steel preceding him. All of which was business as usual. What was not normal? His laconic attitude was nowhere in sight.

In fact, he looked like his nuts were in a vise.

"Thank fuck you two are together," the guy said roughly. "I need you both to come with me. Don't ask any questions, and no, I don't want to talk about it after, either."

L.W. and Shuli glanced at each other.

"Gimme a minute to change and get my guns," Shuli said as he hit the stairs at a dead run.

CHAPTER TWENTY

As the wind whipped around and the cold was a pickpocket with deft hands, Lyric waited in the alley next to Bathe, right by the emergency exit. No way any *lessers* would come near such a busy place. After all, there was only one rule in the war between the vampires and the Lessening Society: Leave humans out of it. The lower the profile, the better, especially in these modern times with all the surveillance downtown.

Looking to her left, she trained her eyes along the darkened alley. The lane ran all the way through to the far side at the rear of the club, and the glow of Jefferson Street traffic back there and the hot spots that lit up that thoroughfare were enough to make shadows out of all the pedestrians looking for fun and games.

Meanwhile, in the other direction, she glanced out to what she'd come to think of as Dev's and her intersection. Everything had started there—

"Allhan!" As she blurted the name, she started fumbling to get her cell. "Oh, crap. I forgot about you—"

One by one, three males re-formed around her in a semi-circle: Her twin brother was the first to arrive. Then L.W., and finally Shuli. None of them were in clubbing clothes, not that L.W. ever downshifted from the togs of war.

"Thank Lassiter," she said under her breath as she shoved the phone back into its zippered pocket.

Jumping forward, she hugged her brother. "Thank you so much for coming—and you guys as well."

"Like we wouldn't." Rhamp set her back with a grim curse. "Now, what the fuck is going on? You saw a *lesser*? Around here?"

As the males started glaring into the shadows, she shook her head. "No, it's a couple of blocks away. More like a quarter of a mile, actually. I was . . . well, I smelled one—"

"What are you doing out here alone?" Rhamp demanded. "Does anybody know you're here?"

"Well, you do now." She waved away his questions. "Not important. I want you guys—can you just go . . . listen, I'm just asking you to—"

"Kill it," L.W. said. As if they were talking about a cockroach she'd found under the sink.

"Yes." Her throat closed up as she remembered the stench—or maybe that was her fear for Dev taking over. "I mean, I can't do that—"

"No—"

"—you—"

"—can't!"

The guys all said the same thing at once. Which was kind of galling. There were females who fought in the war. Payne and Xhex, and Paradise and Novo, were every bit as deadly as the Brothers, and then there were the human women who had been turned by the Omega's son into slayers. But now was not the time to squabble about gender equality in the proverbial workplace.

"I can take you right over to the building. Let's go—"

Rhamp caught her arm as she turned away toward Market. "You're going to tell us the address and we'll take it from there. You go home."

She glanced at the other two. L.W. had a gun already out, and he was withdrawing a dagger from his chest holster. Next to him, Shuli had both hands at his hips, resting on the butts of the pair of autoloaders belted around his waist.

"What's the addy," Rhamp prompted. "And you're absolutely not coming with us, so we can fuck around here and argue about common sense, or we can get to work—which was why you called us."

Cursing under her breath, she muttered, "It's on Twenty-third and Lincoln. The redbrick, seven-story apartment building. I smelled the thing as I was leaving, like the slayer was in the basement? You'll see the open staircase as soon as you go into the lobby."

"What the hell were you doing over there?" her brother asked.

Lyric did her level best to keep her voice, well, level. "Visiting a friend."

"What friend." That frown got even deeper. "Are you seeing somebody?"

Linking her arms over her chest, she narrowed her eyes at her twin. "None of your business."

"It sure as hell is when you call me for help with a fucking slayer."

Next to her brother, L.W. arched a brow. Shuli, on the other hand, looked away sharply like he didn't want anything to do with the heat.

"Go home," Rhamp gritted. "And don't talk to the dads about this. Maybe you got the scent wrong. There's so many humans in this part of town, we don't find them here."

"I *know* what I smelled."

"We'll see about that."

Rhamp was muttering to himself as he closed his eyes and dematerialized. As L.W. took off as well, she reached out and snagged Shuli's arm.

"Hey, did you mean to call me about forty-five minutes ago?"

There wasn't even a pause. The guy shook his head and stepped back. "Butt dial. Sorry."

◆   ◆   ◆

Qhuinn went back to the Brotherhood's training center an hour after he'd had First Meal out at his in-laws' house with Blay. His partner on the schedule for the night was Rhage, and the pair of them re-formed on the plowed lane that dropped down to the steel doors of the facility's parking garage. As they descended, they lifted a wave at the security cameras set into the concrete side wall.

Off to the right, there was a much smaller steel entry for pedestrians, and the instant they were in range, the dead bolts were sprung—thank you, V. After that, they were in a narrow cement hallway that was a mini version of the center's interior main artery. As always, cameras lined the ceiling, and so did little pinholes that could be triggered to release a flush of neurotoxins.

Qhuinn wasn't a pussy, but he was always glad when he got out of the murder-tube.

"You okay, my brother?" Rhage asked from the rear.

"Oh, yeah, just fine." Considering he was still going to fucking lose his mind between what almost happened to the younger Lyric, and what was definitely happening to the elder Lyric.

They came up to the second door and waited for the *thunk!* sound of the bolt being thrown. And waited. And . . . waited.

Qhuinn looked up to the camera over the entry and waved his hand.

As a waft of grape floated over his shoulder, he glanced behind himself. Rhage had put a Tootsie Pop in his mouth and was in the process of tucking the wadded purple wrapper into his leathers.

"You're not okay," the brother said around the lollipop. "You know, my Mary always maintains that talking helps—"

"Why aren't they opening this for us?" Qhuinn glanced up at the perfectly spaced pattern of holes directly above their heads. "It shouldn't take this long."

Had communications been cut? A power outage at Four Toys— and then the emergency generators didn't come on? Was something wrong—

What if someone tripped and fell on the button that discharged the neurotoxin? What if—

He reached forward and pumped the handle. Got nowhere. Shifted his weight back and forth, raised his arm, and peeled back the leather sleeve of his fighting jacket—except, come on, he didn't have a watch to look at.

Back with the stupid fucking holes—

"Oh, my God," Rhage said, pointing at him with his lollipop. "You've got that thing, don't you."

An overactive adrenal system? Yeah, sure. Who didn't after all these decades in the war—

"Trypophobia."

Qhuinn refocused on the brother. "What."

"Fear of holes." Rhage nodded up at the ceiling. "I mean, you know that there is no way V or any of his people would trigger any of the defensive systems on us. But you keep looking up there like you're expecting something bad to happen, and you do it every time I've been in here with you. Like all the way back to the install—"

"I don't know what you're talking about."

He trained his stare resolutely on the steel door.

This lasted a nanosecond and his peepers were back at the pinholes.

"Don't feel bad," Rhage remarked. "I got arachibutyrophobia."

Qhuinn had to glance at the guy again. "That something Doc Jane needs to give you a penicillin shot for?"

Rhage laughed in an easy and relaxed kind of way—which Qhuinn frickin' envied. "No, that's fear of getting peanut butter stuck to the roof of your mouth. Mary and I been working on it. I choked on a PB and J a couple of months ago and that's when it started—"

Clunk.

As the lock released, Qhuinn hit that bar like he was giving the damn thing chest compressions in a hospital code. The relief that came with stepping through into the parking area, with all its space in every direction, was like breathing clean air after you'd held your breath from a bad smell. And as for the irrational fears shit? He didn't know from whatever Peter-Pan-ophobia Rhage was going on about, but if he had to diagnose one for himself, he'd say it was garden variety claustro and fuck all the holes—

"Really," he muttered at his choice of words.

"Huh?" Rhage tilted his head like a big, beautiful dog. "Or you talking to yourself?"

They came up to the main entrance into the training center, and sure, now the lock turned immediately again.

"You gotta trust me when I tell you, you don't want to know." He opened things and glanced down the wide corridor to where Xcor and Tohr were standing. "And no, it doesn't have to do with food, peanut butter or otherwise."

"Roger that," Hollywood said amicably.

Passing by the lineup of classrooms, they stopped when they got to the patient rooms. Tohr was on his phone, texting something, but Xcor stepped up with the greeting.

"Dad—"

"Dad—"

He and Xcor clapped palms and then shoulders, and then Rhage joined in the hello'ing. As those two stepped back, Qhuinn nodded at the red can of high-test Coke in Xcor's hand.

"That kind of night already?"

"You know it."

The leader of the Band of Bastards was dressed for war, but he had to smother a yawn. Which was a surprise. The stocky male was strong as a bull, and on a typical night, he was the first to get out into the field to hunt. Not this evening. He seemed drained and distracted—and that was proof that he was worried about the Lyric(s) situation, too.

It had always been the way, the four of them concerned about the young and all the things that affected them.

Xcor took a draw on the can. "So to take our minds off it all, Layla and I binge-watched a show about veterinarians set in the Scottish Highlands at the turn of the twentieth century all day long."

Yup, they hadn't been able to sleep, either. "Not your usual gig."

"Too right. I started watching just to be pleasant."

"And you didn't pass out from boredom?"

Rhage nodded as he crunched down on his Tootsie Pop. "For real."

"Worse." Xcor took another long drink. "I got sucked in. I ended up with crumpled Kleenex all over the bed. And I do *not* cry."

Qhuinn had to laugh. "Softie for animals, huh."

"I joined PETA at three in the afternoon, and by six, I was ready to adopt all the dogs in Caldwell that didn't have a home. I am *never* watching television ever again."

As Rhage's phone rang, he turned away to answer. "Hey, Mary, you okay?"

In a lower voice, Qhuinn said, "How's Layla doing?"

"Not good." Xcor shook his head, his deformed upper lip flattening. "She keeps playing that video of the billboard over and over. Verily, Lyric's been so good to us, FaceTiming last night, coming home from her grandparents' right after sunset—she and Layla spent a little together—but I don't know. Sometimes the reminder of how important someone is becomes just as traumatic as the near miss."

"Maybe I can talk to her?"

"Yes, please." Xcor, with his Old Country manners, bowed. "Anything to ease my *shellan*."

Tohr put his phone away and came forward. "Hey, thanks for coming—and being willing to sit guard. Syphon and Syn just left."

"No problem." Qhuinn nodded at the door to the patient room. "Any change in the male?"

"He's breathing on his own, but not really conscious. Doc Jane's in the lab with Ehlena, if anything acute happens."

"Mind if I go in and see him?"

"Doc Jane says keep it at five minutes, no longer." Tohr lifted up his phone. "And if you get anything out of him, I'll come back from the field immediately. This is the most important thing on our docket tonight."

"Roger that."

With things settled, Tohrment and Xcor said their goodbyes and headed back down toward the dreaded hall of tiny little holes. If Qhuinn remembered the schedule correctly, Tohr was on at the Audience House and Xcor was downtown in the field. The two, as half-brothers, were never paired up, just like Blay and Qhuinn, and John Matthew and Xhex, as mated couples, were likewise kept apart. The same was true for V and Payne as brother and sister, and Z and Phury.

No doubt Xcor had come here to release his two soldiers from their over-day duties guarding the captive. Though the Band of Bastards had sworn their allegiance to Wrath long ago, they still had their own chain of command, and Tohr never questioned it, in spite of the fact that he was the King's right-hand male, and technically called all the shots over all the fighters.

"I'll stay out here." Rhage leaned against the concrete wall as he tossed his stick in a wastepaper basket. "Let me know if you need anything."

Qhuinn nodded and opened the door into the hospital room. Slipping inside, the heart rate monitor seemed too loud, and so did the whirring sounds from all the machinery around the head of the bed. The male they'd found in that hidden room at Whestmorel's was full of tubing and the color of a corpse, his skin gray and stretched over the bones of what had probably once been an attractive face. The bruising around his wrists, neck, and torso had settled into a series of dark purple blotches, and there were a couple of lines of neat stitches on his shoulder and under one arm. With the covers set just below his diaphragm, it wasn't possible to assess the lower body's damage.

But he wasn't a medical guy, anyway.

Going around the foot of the bed, Qhuinn sat in the chair that had been pulled up on the far side. Of course he thought of his brother. How could he not. Just like with Luchas, all they had was the aftermath of whatever had been done to this male and it was anybody's guess whether the aristocrat was going to live.

Oh, who the fuck was he kidding. If you had to say that, the answer was—

The eye closest to Qhuinn opened a little, a crack appearing between the matted lashes. Then there was a little gasp and both hands tightened into claws.

Qhuinn jerked forward, but made sure he kept his voice soft and even. "You're in the custody of Wrath, son of Wrath, sire of Wrath. What's your name."

When he didn't get an answer, he wasn't surprised. "You want to tell me your name? What's your name."

If they could get one, it would help the ID process. V had already run a search on the species databases, just in case anybody had reported a brother, son, uncle, father missing. So far, nothing. Then again, the male's entire bloodline could be in on Whestmorel's treason, with him the only holdout. Fucking aristocracy—

A rasp cut through the whirring of all the monitoring machinery.

"What did you say?" Qhuinn got up and leaned over the bed. "What's your name."

When there was no response, he decided he'd imagined whatever it'd been, and he glanced at the machines behind the bed. No alarms going off, so he assumed the big vitals were all doing okay—

"Geeeeorge," the male wheezed.

And then everything went haywire, the monitors flashing, a loud beeping ringing out at scream level.

Qhuinn looked at the heart rate, the peaks and valleys going irregular before spacing out farther and farther apart . . .

. . . until they stopped altogether.

CHAPTER TWENTY-ONE

The hell she was going home like a good little girl.

Lyric gave the males a good minute or so to ghost down to Dev's building. Then she closed her eyes and dematerialized as well. When she re-formed, it was on the snowpacked roof of a walk-up kitty-corner behind his address, and she kept herself hidden by staying behind an exhaust chimney for the heating system.

From her vantage point, she could see a back parking lot, and all kinds of windows with drapes pulled or blinds down. Counting up from the bottom, she focused on the fourth floor, and tried to orientate herself. Dev had a corner flat—but at which end? Or did his studio face front? She'd never looked, because his blackouts cut the view.

Crap, she was all turned around. Meanwhile, her heartbeat was loud in her ears, and as the wind whistled past her head, she braced herself for . . .

Nothing happened.

Impatiently brushing a strand of hair out of her eyes, she stared down at the shallow area with the cars squeezed in between piles of dirty, packed snow. The security lights that shined from the roof were so bright, there weren't a lot of shadows or places she couldn't visualize.

"Oh, God, Dev . . ."

What if things had gone haywire after she'd left and he'd been attacked on the way back to his apartment?

She waited a little longer, then stepped out from behind the industrial-sized duct. Going over to the edge of the roof, she counted the snow-streaked cars to give her mind something to do. Then she went back to all the windows on the fourth level.

And kind of expected to see flashes of gunfire and hear the screams of humans escaping a melee.

Still nothing.

But come on, what did she expect? For those three fighters to chase a couple of the undead out into that parking area, stab the bastards back to their maker, and then flash her the thumbs-up so they could all forget about this?

Well, put like that, the answer was . . . yes. Yes, she did.

Instead, this was the real world.

On that note, she closed her eyes and did the best she could to calm herself so she could change positions. When she was finally able to dematerialize, it was just across the lot to the roof of Dev's building. The wind was even stronger, as things were considerably taller than the walk-up, and as her body got bumped back and forth in the gusts, she thought about all the things that could get swept away and go airborne.

There was so much more ductwork and venting here, as well as a kiosk-like build-out in the center of everything—which she guessed was the top of the access stairwell. No security lights and no cameras, at least not that she could see. There was plenty of ambient light, though, probably even for humans—and they clearly came up here in the better weather, going by the grouping of lawn chairs weighted down with snow.

Oh, wait. There were some paths of footprints. Maybe because workmen had had to come up recently?

Annnnnnnnnnnnnd now what.

Heading for the ledge, she wanted to brace her hands on the lip as she leaned over, but she didn't have her mittens and it was all ice and snow.

The yawning drop to the sidewalk made her stomach flip-flop, but at least she got herself orientated. She was looking over the front of the building now, the cleared steps of the entry and its twin lampposts directly beneath her.

Crossing the whole of the expanse, she checked the back exit. How had her brother and the fighters gotten in? Then again, as this was a human building, they could have just willed the locks to turn. Or if they'd wanted to be sneaky, they could have traveled through the glass of any window or the seams in a loose door—probably not the ductwork. Even though there would be no steel mesh to keep vampires out, it was way too dangerous to—

Someone came out of the back door.

Lyric's heart stopped in her chest and she inhaled deeply through her nose. Which was stupid and maybe proved her brother's point that she had no business being here: There was no chance of catching a scent at this height.

Oh . . . shit. Whoever it was had very white hair—was it an old person? Or a slayer?

She leaned farther out—

Her boot slipped, her balance tipped, and she careened toward the void.

Just as she started to go into free-fall, a blare of light spilled out from the roof access door. The fact that she turned to look at the illumination was what brought her body back to rights, the treads of her waterproof trail shoes catching hold in the snow just before she toppled over the ledge.

Except maybe it would have been better to free-fall.

A large figure cut a shadow through the glare coming out of the stairwell, and she had an instant regret. She had no weapons, no training, and if this was the slayer she'd sent her brother to kill—

Whatever it was turned its head toward her. And that's when she heard an all-too-familiar voice—and not her brother's or L.W.'s or Shuli's.

"Lyric? What are you doing out here?"

Oh, *fuck.*

Dev.

◆   ◆   ◆

Getting into the apartment building had been the work of a moment, and Shuli was glad that at least the entry had been no-drama. The other two had waited for him to arrive around back, and then even before they'd gotten a plan together, someone had come out of the rear door— not that they couldn't have opened the thing, but hey, easy peasy thanks to the unwitting welcoming party. The basement had been clean—both from a housekeeping perspective and because it was *lesser*-free—so they'd found the open stairwell and gone up to the lobby on the first floor.

Nothing.

No baby-powder bullshit. No sounds of any struggle. No guns discharging anywhere.

"Up," Rhamp said softly.

L.W. and Shuli nodded, and they silently ascended in formation, with Lyric's brother in front.

At every level . . . nothing.

Well, no *lessers.* There were a lot of humans behind the numbered doors—which was a big change from the walk-ups and buildings Shuli usually swept through: The real estate in the field was always vacated and crumbling. Here, you had voices, televisions, food smells. And on the whole, he never had any problems with those rats without tails, at least not until they were inducted into the Lessening Society—hell, he got very close to countless women on a very regular basis.

At the moment, though? He found himself hating everybody in the building.

Okay, not all of them, he corrected as they continued upward. Just the man Lyric was clearly seeing.

Holy fuck. It had been plain as the expression on her face she was involved with someone—and it was also very obvious that whoever it was, she wasn't saying anything about him.

Had to be a human.

As Shuli stepped off onto the fourth floor, his eyes scanned the hall. Which one of the doors was his? Probably better not knowing—given how protective Rhamp was of his sister, if they found the fucker, things were going to get real messy, real quick, and not because of anything to do with a slayer.

Hell, Shuli was feeling a little fangy himself.

Make that a lot fang-ish, even though he had no right.

They kept going on the ascent, saying nothing, communicating through eye contact, not that there was much to talk about.

When they got to the top floor—lucky number seven—they stopped and listened. Tested the air for scents. Looked around—

A sudden creak and thump shot his head to the left.

Next to the stairwell, a door marked "Roof Access" was closing next to him, and he flared his nostrils. No scent of *lesser*.

Meanwhile, Rhamp leaned over the stairwell banister and looked all the way down to where they'd started their march. L.W. was the one who wandered, stalking halfway down the hall.

After glancing around, Shuli reached out and quietly cranked the door's knob. There was a dead bolt mounted on the jamb, but as he pulled things open just a little, he saw that the slug had been removed from its internals, and the hole it was supposed to plug into was stuffed with what looked like paper.

Flaring his nostrils, he leaned into the chilly staircase, and caught sight of the door at the top bouncing closed. Thanks to thermodynamics, the heat from the hall wafted upward, greedy for its liberation into the cold, so he got nothing.

If it had been a slayer who'd passed by here in the hall to get the door? They would have left plenty of nasty-scented molecules lingering in the air. The half-life on that shit was a good two weeks.

"Guess she was wrong," Shuli muttered as he eased back and shut things.

"Or it left." Rhamp shrugged as he straightened and turned away from the drop. "We could stake out, but I'm supposed to be in the field with John Matthew. A position here would be hard to account for."

L.W. was still walking away from them, looking at the closed doors of all the apartments like he was playing rock, paper, scissors with each one—and the rock was his shitkicker.

"I agree we need to just move on." Shuli shook his head. "His Royal Fuck-Shit-Up'ness is going to want to be west of here, in a zip code that has a much, much lower median income and a far higher likelihood of crossing paths with something that smells like a human grandma."

Plus he really wanted to get the fuck out of here. The idea Lyric was with somebody else made him want to get shitfaced on absinthe and fucked by someone with dark hair again—

He and Rhamp jerked around to the stairwell at the same time.

The scent they were looking for. Finally.

Lyric had not been mistaken.

"L.W.," Shuli hissed as he took out one of his nines and kept it down at his thigh. "We got a party to go to."

The heir to the throne might be big as a bus, but he could move like a sprinter when he wanted to. The asshole was instantly front and center—and even took the lead down the stairs as they started to track the stink. The three of them kept against the wall, moving silently, and at the floor below, they paused, even though the scent was still drifting up through the core of the building.

L.W. glanced back and met Shuli's eyes. Then Rhamp's.

When the heir nodded, they moved as a single unit. Down. Turn. Down. Turn—

They ran into two humans on the third landing, a couple on their way out, scarves wrapped tight on their necks, gloves being drawn onto hands. Rhamp, who was bringing up the rear, did the duty, brushing their memories clear and inserting the ironclad conviction that it was too cold for them to go anywhere. Home was better.

Or something like that. Whatever thought he put in their brains, they instantly backtracked and disappeared.

Now was not the time for kibitzers.

As Shuli arrived at the lobby, he dipped into the vestibule. No smell, so he shook his head sharply.

The slayer had to be in the cellar.

When L.W. pointed to the secondary fire stairs at the far end, Rhamp nodded and jogged off, his shitkickers quiet over the carpeting, his weapons making a sweet chiming sound under his jacket that only fellow vampires would hear.

Before L.W. could continue the descent from their position, Shuli latched on to the male's sleeve. Those pale green eyes swung around, and the two of them just stood there.

Time slowed down as the scent of the enemy wrapped around them, binding them together—and Shuli reached up to his face and put his forefinger under his eye. With a swipe, he removed the foundation he used to cover the teardrop that had been inked onto his skin.

Unlike the King's son, the tiny outline was the only tattoo he had—and he had a thought, as they were suspended on the precipice of yet another engagement with the enemy, that as much as he hated the job he'd been force-fed . . .

He was going to take the shit seriously.

Especially after tonight. It wasn't the audience with the King and the sparing of his ass that shined a light on his intention. It was the dumb shit with Lyric, the fantasy that he had to let go. She was out living her life, and he needed to get real and find a better purpose than mooning after that female.

As he had no other potential motivators, it might as well be keeping L.W. alive—and that was a noble calling: There were plenty of people engaging in the war, plenty of fighters and Brothers killing *lessers* and trying to get to Lash.

But there was only one who was supposed to watch out for the heir.

And whether L.W. liked it or not, they were stuck with each other.

"Doing his best" was going to be a lot more than a throwaway excuse from now on, goddamn it.

"Let me go first," Shuli said in a low voice.

L.W.'s expression screwed down into the frustrated anger that was as much a part of the male as his frickin' heartbeat.

And Shuli just shook his head at the guy. "Please. I'm not important. You are, and we don't know what's down there. Let me die as the target, and you can clean up."

The curse that came back at him wasn't a surprise. "Come on. Why the hell are you doing this—"

"Because I don't have anything else in life, you dumb shit." Shuli stepped around the other fighter. "And being remembered for trying to save you ain't a bad way to go out. You can put it on my gravestone."

On that note, he started his descent, and he was light on the balls of his boots, twinkle-toeing toward the well-lit hallway below. With every step, the stench of the undead got stronger—and so did his conviction.

No one knew how much longer they had left. So he might as well do something worthy while he was counting down the hours.

And what do you know.

When he hit the half landing, he glanced up over his shoulder. L.W. was where he'd left the heir to the throne, poised between standing on that top step and the rush his body was momentarily going to fall into.

For once, that harsh face wasn't sporting aggression.

There was a sadness revealed that surely the male would have denied if he'd been called out on it. But everyone had their own demons.

Even fighters who fought with everybody.

Maybe them especially.

CHAPTER TWENTY-TWO

U p on the roof, Lyric stared across at Dev—and pulled the kind of blank that there was no recovering from: No thoughts in her head, body frozen, breath exhaling in a rush. She couldn't have looked guiltier if she'd jimmied the lock of his apartment and waltzed right in.

The fact she'd shown up back here—on the roof no less—after her no-one-night-stands speech made her look like a deluded stalker.

And it wasn't like she could defend herself with the ol' you-have-an-infestation-of-the-undead-in-your-building yarn.

"What's going on here?" Dev walked over to where she stood at the ledge. "What are you doing?"

He'd changed out of his running tights—into loose sweatpants that added bulk to his lower body—but he'd kept his windbreaker on, the folds flapping in the wind. Had he bothered to put a shirt on?

Like that was any of her business . . .

"Are you okay?" he asked with a frown. As if he were thinking they might be entering 911 land.

"My scarf," she blurted.

He glanced around. Then both his eyebrows lifted. "I'm sorry? Your scarf is up here?"

"Um, no. Sorry." She starting doing jazz hands for some reason, so she shoved her fists into her parka's pockets. "I think I left my scarf in your apartment. I don't have your number, I couldn't get in through the front door, and I thought—"

"How did you get up here?"

She looked over her shoulder—

Directly below, her brother, L.W., and Shuli filed out of the basement door the white-haired figure had left from. And their weapons were out, the guns glinting subtly.

Instantly, her eyes panic-scanned the parking lot—and landed on a car whose brake lights came on. Next, steam petered out of its tailpipe.

Shit.

Whipping her head back around, she tried to remember what Dev had asked her?

Out of the corner of her eye, she caught sight of a pair of curved metal arms swooping over the ledge. "Fire escape."

Feeling like an utter ass, she pointed at them and then headed in that direction. "I thought maybe I could get down into the building and . . . find your apartment. My grandmother made that scarf." Which was not a lie. "It's . . . priceless to me, and I was all flustered. I get it, I look like a total lunatic here, but I didn't know what else to do and I wasn't thinking clearly—but I need that scarf back. And I'm really sorry."

There was a pause. Then he said, "I found it on my dresser. I was wondering how to get it back to you."

"Oh, thank you—"

As she all but lunged toward the door he'd come out of, he caught her arm. "You mind if I have a smoke first—"

Pop! Pop! Pop-pop!

The gunfire was muffled, but unmistakable if you knew what it was, and Lyric found herself bracing as if she were the target. As Dev's head ripped around to the sound, she wanted to curse. Courtesy of her adrenaline load, she couldn't concentrate enough to get into his mind and manipulate his thoughts.

Except then he just remarked, "That's close by."

And went back to where she'd been standing, like he wanted a bird's-eye view of the action.

Lyric shuffled her body in front of his. "Let's go inside. It's not safe here—"

"Whoever it is, they're not shooting at us." He took out a pack of Camels. "They can't even see us if we can't see them—"

When he went to step around her, she waltzed with him, trading places again. "Stray bullets kill. You don't have to be in the shootout to get hurt."

Dev put his hands on her arms, picked her up so her feet dangled, and set her out of his way. "I'm going to go see what's happening. In case I need to call the police—"

"Oh, please don't do that," she whispered.

As he leaned over the ledge, she racked her brain about what to say to get him inside. What if there were more slayers in the building, what if—

The metal-on-metal crunch of a vehicle hitting something immovable echoed up to them. Below in the parking lot, the car that had been started had reversed out of its spot and shot backwards with a good dose of velocity—and then its brakes either hadn't grabbed or hadn't been pumped: The shitty Toyota was butted into the receiving dock of the office building that faced out on the far side of the block.

Three figures were closing in on the vehicle, their arms out straight, guns trained on whoever was behind the wheel.

Whatever was behind it.

And that was when she caught sight of what was coming down the alley from the east side: Another knot of figures—at least two of which had hair so white the stuff glowed even in the darkness. The lot of slayers was traveling fast, like they'd been called to the scene, and as her brother and his friends didn't look in that direction, she knew that they were upwind of the flank of backup *lessers*.

Without thinking, Lyric put two fingers from each hand into her mouth, pressed her tongue into them, and blew as hard as she could.

The whistle rang out, loud and clear over all the city's night noises.

It was the warning signal she and her brother had always used as young, when they were getting into trouble and one of them was playing scout—

Instantly, her brother looked up toward the roof, and she didn't need to worry about whether she'd have to point at the threat and pray he saw her.

The route his eyes traveled to get to her intersected the approach of the *lessers*.

Rhamp started shooting, the discharges suppressed when it came to sound, the flashes from the end of that muzzle dampened as well. Instantly, L.W. trained his own gun in that direction as he backed up his friend, but Shuli stayed locked on the Toyota. He advanced on the driver's side door and emptied what had to be an entire magazine into the car, safety glass shattering, the bursts of illumination highlighting the deployed front airbags that had exploded out of the dashboard—

The stray bullet came out of nowhere on a ricochet, pinging off the ledge right next to her.

"Get down!"

Dev tackled her off to the side, but somehow managed to roll them over in midair so that they landed with him on the bottom. As she hit his chest, all his breath exploded out of his lungs on a curse.

Which pretty much said it all, didn't it.

◆   ◆   ◆

Down at the parking lot level, Shuli swapped out his magazine for a new one and turned his attention away from the Toyota so he could join in the fun and games with the new additions to the party: Somehow, Rhamp had sensed that backups were coming down the cross street, and thank fuck for his instincts.

Otherwise, they would have been ambushed.

Pulling his own trigger, he cursed as the flank of *lessers* broke ranks and scattered into shadows, corners, and doorways. This was bad, this was fucking bad. They were engaging the enemy and discharging guns in full view of every fucking tenant with a rear-facing apartment—and already there were only about a dozen drapes getting pulled back, the outlines of all kinds of humans with all sorts of cell phones poking their heads into their windows to see what the commotion was about.

As he himself ducked for cover behind the car he'd shot up, Rhamp and L.W. joined him around on the driver's side—

The moaning was loud enough for them to hear, soft enough so nobody else could. Popping his head up over the door, Shuli punched the safety glass out and got a gander at the *lesser* behind the wheel. The bastard was leaking like a sieve, black blood dripping all over the place, but as with the night before, it was far from "dead"—

Annnnnnnnd that was when an entire church choir of cop sirens started to ring out, all of which were close by—way too close by.

"Stab the *lesser*," Rhamp snapped. "We gotta disappear him before we—"

"Fuck that," L.W. cut in. "I'm taking him with us—"

"Fuck *you*. Are you out of your mind—"

"He might have information—"

The robocop cars were approaching from all directions, the speed of their response frustratingly efficient going by how the noise was ramping up. But hey, at least it cut off the conversation about taking a hostage for interrogation—something Shuli was not about to let happen with all the eyeballs around them.

Whipping out one of his steel daggers, he leaned into the car, and got a quick close-up of the leaking mess that was already trying to escape by crawling for the passenger-side door. Trading grips on his hilt because of the angle, he called on all the strength in his left arm to get that fucking blade into the sternum—

Happy Fourth of July in January.

The burst of light was bright enough to blind him, but the complication was the burst of energy. He caught the *whoof!* of incineration right against his chest, and it was powerful enough to blow him out of the car. His landing was a flat-on-the-back kind, his breath knocked from his lungs—

Just as the robocops arrived on scene.

Funny, he thought. He couldn't hear the sirens anymore. The ringing in his ears was so—

"You're injured," someone said from all the way across the city. Or maybe the whole ass state of New York.

Were they talking to him?

"We gotta move him." L.W. bent over him, and patted around like he was trying to find Shuli's torso. "*Now*."

Wasn't his chest still attached?

"I'm fine," he mumbled as he forced himself to his feet. "Let's go—"

Rhamp shook his head. "Lyric's here. I can't leave without her—"

"This is the Caldwell Police Department," a calm, robotic voice chimed in. "Please drop your weapons and put your hands over your heads. Any further gunfire will put you at risk of lethal counteractions. Please drop your weapons and—"

As all kinds of robocops exited their vehicles, Shuli struggled to make his mouth work. "Lyric's at home, she went—"

"She whistled." Rhamp nodded toward the roof. "Up there. The tipoff signal was hers."

Trying to blink his fuzzy sight clear, Shuli noted that a fourth cop car was tooling down the alley those *lessers* had come from, its headlights turning everything to noontime. A quick survey of the environs and there were no retreating figures with granny hair—so the slayers had already disappeared back into the night.

"—put your hands over your heads," the robocops continued as they advanced their position.

"Go get her, then," L.W. said. "I've got Shuli."

Annnnnnnnnnnnnnnd that was when the fucker took out a hand cannon.

The gun was four times the size of a forty-five, and appeared to have old-fashioned revolver action. "Go, Rhamp."

At which point, the guy started working out his forefinger.

Boom! Boom! Boom—

L.W. was just shooting and making noise to get the cop-bots to take cover, something they were programmed to do, and God love Rhamp. Even though you had to calm yourself to dematerialize, the fighter somehow pulled off that trick in spite of the chaos—and it was just as he disappeared that Shuli looked down and smelled his own blood. No time for an exam—and he didn't need one to know he wasn't going to be able to dematerialize.

For a split second, he played carousel in his head for options. Most were grim, with only one that held any chance of getting him out of this shitstorm alive. But hey, that was where life landed you sometimes.

A lot of the times, recently.

While L.W. kept the cops off, Shuli dragged himself into the Toyota and squeezed behind the wheel. The engine was somehow still running, even though there was all kinds of lead in the damn thing. At least it was facing in the right direction—assuming he wanted to play bowling ball with the CPD's city surveillance and rescue resources.

"Go!" he barked at L.W.

The guy glanced at him as Shuli stomped on the brake and put the engine in drive with a punch of his finger.

And that's when the heir to the throne lost his damn mind.

L.W. drew his arm back, shattered the rest of the backseat window with one blow, and dove into the rear end.

"*Now* go!" he shot back.

Shuli hit the accelerator and swung the car around in a tight circle, the deflated airbag flapping, his free hand struggling for a grip because the steering wheel was greased up with black blood. As the headlights pulled a parabola, they eyeballed an immediate problem. Two patrol cars were parked side by side in the middle of his intended escape route. The robots that went with them were temporarily taking cover behind the vehicles, but that was going to change quick.

There was one piece of good news.

The lights also illuminated Rhamp—who, instead of heading up, up, and away to wherever he thought his sister was, had taken a position around the corner of the restaurant at the end of the block. Behind those cops.

The male flashed three fingers.

Then he pulled the pin of a grenade out with his teeth, and tossed that thing like the trunks of those squad cars had bull's-eyes on them.

As L.W. started discharging bullets the size of bowling balls out the back window of the Toyota, Shuli began the countdown: "One one thousand, two one thousand, three one thousand—"

He shoved his shitkicker all the way into the gas pedal, and bless the Camry or whatever the fuck it was, but somehow those front tires found the only patch of clear asphalt in the goddamn city. They shot forward just as the grenade's explosion parted the way, the shock wave lifting both patrol vehicles onto their outer tires, the fireball a curtain of heat that licked at the Toyota as the shit box tore the flames in half.

As soon as they were out the other side, the sirens of more approaching law enforcement bloomed even over the wind that barged through the car's interior—and the fact that the chemical-scented smoke didn't clear out of the cockpit meant the shit wasn't from the grenade, but because something in the engine had sprung a critical leak.

He glanced up into the rearview. On the far side of L.W.'s bulk, he caught a quick glimpse of the pair of burning cop cars flopping back down onto their all fours. And what do you know, the other cop-bots who'd fallen into pursuit got tangled in that bottleneck of their comrades.

But there were incoming ones about to Tokyo drift around the corner up ahead—and they were going to fill in the gaps, unfortunately.

"Hold on to something," he hollered.

No countdown to three this time. He stomped on the brakes, wrenched the bloody wheel to the right, and hit the R button on the dash. Hitting the gas and cranking around to see out the back, he shot them in reverse into an alley that was so narrow, sparks flew from the side mirrors streaking down the brick flanks of the tight-squeeze buildings—

"Dumpster!" L.W. hollered over the breeze. "Twenty-five feet and closing."

Shuli shoved his shitkicker onto the brake again, and looked out across the hood. Blue lights were flickering all over the street he'd gotten off of—and they were going to come up to the alley in a matter of seconds.

"Dematerialize," he shouted as the car shimmied between the brick walls until it came to a halt on the ice. "I'll find somewhere to hide—"

He grabbed for the door handle and—

Thunk!

Great. There was no opening the doors.

"L.W., you gotta—" When he didn't get any response, he twisted back around.

Naturally, L.W. was ignoring him as the male reloaded his guns, slamming magazines into both his nines.

"Dematerialize, motherfucker! I'll figure something out—"

Ignoring the protests—as usual—L.W. started squeezing through the rear window frame. "Follow me."

Shuli looked down to the head of the alley again—and saw speeding patrol cars pass by, going in the direction of the scene. Where, for sure, they'd get to the bottleneck, back up, and figure out the alley escape soon enough.

"You gotta go—"

When had L.W. ever listened to anybody, though? As soon as the fighter managed to extrude himself out of the Toyota's ass, he wheeled around and leaned back in. With impatience, he motioned to Shuli.

"Gimme your hand."

Shuli followed the command partially because he was surprised the guy wasn't fucking him off. And then it was a case of—

"Ow! Fuck! Slow down—"

Now he knew what birth was like.

That was all he thought of as he was pulled out on a oner, his body scraping between the front seats, bumping over the backseat, squeezing through the window frame, and landing on the trunk.

The next thing he knew, he was up on L.W.'s shoulders, and they were on the move. Which was about as comfortable as having a sledge-hammer massage.

"Didn't we just do this last week," he muttered with exhaustion as the big fella took off at a run.

And jumped up onto the top of the mega-trashbin.

CHAPTER TWENTY-THREE

As the shooting intensified down below, Lyric tried to count the bullet discharges, but why bother? She didn't know who was pulling what trigger—and it wasn't like she knew how many bullets were in a magazine, anyway. What she was sure of was that beneath her, the pump of Dev's breath was slow and steady, and the warmth from his body was spreading into her own in spite of the cold—and all her fear.

What if her brother or the other two were killed? Injured seriously? Captured? It would be all her fault. She'd sent her brother and—

"Come on," Dev said urgently.

Except then her hearing registered a change in the noise chaos. Still distant shouting and all kinds of sirens, but a pause in the shooting.

"Inside," he ordered as he shuffled them upright. "While we can—"

She raced right back for where they'd been standing. Except just as she got to the ledge, he grabbed her by the waist and swung her around.

"Are you crazy?" He started to carry her off. "That's a full-blown turf war out there—"

As if to prove his point, there was an abrupt flash of light down below that was so great, it lit up everything behind the building—and then there was a series of loud booms, like someone had upgraded their weapon, big-time. Wrenching around in his hold, she caught a glimpse of a showdown at the far side of the parking area.

The crashed car. Cops getting closer. A couple of figures, not that she could make them out—

Her view was cut off, and the next thing she knew, she was in a stairway, with Dev closing the door and leaning back against it.

He was breathing hard. So was she.

Outside, the fighting sounds dimmed, and not just because they'd found a little shelter. She could tell the battle was moving away, going to the west, toward the river.

"Fun, fun," he muttered as he took out a pack of cigarettes.

He shook out one of them, put it in his mouth, and flicked a Bic. Just as he was touching the flame to the tip, he did a double take.

"Sorry." He frowned. "You mind if I smoke this?"

She had so many bigger problems than that. "No."

Pushing her hair out of her face, she fumbled for her phone. But like she could ring her brother? Like he could answer?

"The cops are already here," he said on the exhale. "Who are you calling?"

She looked down at the cell. "I . . . don't know."

And if she reached out to the Brotherhood? How was she going to explain how she knew what was happening? Besides, it was protocol, asking for backup—she'd overheard her brother talking about it loads of times. One of them, down there, for sure already had.

"I have to go," she blurted.

This was a total fucking mess.

"What about your scarf?"

"Huh?" She glanced up at him blankly. "Oh, yes. Right—"

Her phone went off and she ripped it up to her ear. "Oh, thank God, Rhamp—where are you? Are you okay?"

There was a loud rushing noise coming over the connection, like the wind was swirling around him, but her brother's voice came through loud and clear: "Where the hell are you?"

"I'm—" She glanced at Dev. He was taking a draw on the cigarette and regarding her with a remote look. "Are you okay?"

"Where the fuck—"

"You're okay, though?"

"I'm on the roof of a fucking apartment building, the one that I'm pretty fucking sure you whistled down from."

She looked to the door, focusing on it over Dev's shoulder. "What about the others?" she said tightly.

"*Where are you.*"

Dev's eyes met her own, and he continued to be totally calm. To the point where she wondered what kind of life he led. It didn't take a genius to catch the drift of the one side of the conversation he was hearing, and yet there was no shock on his face.

"I'm safe," she said quietly. "I'll be home soon."

"You were supposed to be home *now*—"

She hung up the phone. Put it back in her pocket. "Let's go get my scarf."

Taking his hand, Lyric made quick work of the descent, and dragged him behind herself. At the bottom of the shallow steps, she pushed through a door, and then continued piloting them down the open stairwell. When she got to the landing with the little "4th Floor" sign next to it, she hit the hallway and beelined for Dev's apartment.

Even though she had no right, she let herself in—and didn't need to mentally spring the lock because of course he hadn't thrown the bolt. After she closed them in together, a quick glance confirmed the blackout drapes were still closed, and—

Her eyes shot to his messy bed. Then she breathed in deeply through her nose. The scent in the studio was intoxicating, the tips of her fangs tingling in response.

So he'd . . . taken care of himself after she'd left.

With a curse, she rubbed her eyes, then put her palms to her windblown cheeks. Now was not the time to be thinking about that stuff.

"Good thing I don't care about breaking rules."

Lyric jumped, and turned to him. He was leaning back against the door, taking a drag on his cigarette.

"I'm sorry?" she mumbled.

"No smoking in the building." He exhaled a steady stream. "But I don't think anybody's going to be worried about a little nicotine cloud smoke in the air tonight. Do you?"

"No," she replied grimly. "I don't."

Unable to stay still, she paced around, going from the refrigerator to the bed and back. When she started to feel too hot, she undid her parka.

"Look," he said, "I don't need to know what you're involved in."

Stopping, she glanced over. He had the pack of Camels in his palm along with the lighter, like he was thinking about going for a second the moment he finished what he was currently smoking. Not because he was stressed, though. He was still cucumber calm over there.

"In fact," he continued, "I'm a firm believer in not sticking my nose into other people's business. And if it makes you feel better to play pretense with that scarf or my jacket or my phone or whatever, that's fine with me, too. You don't owe me anything, and that includes your truth."

She searched his face. There was no reserve, no artifice in his strong features, and his eyes were not avoiding hers—and that was when she discovered that she couldn't do what was expected of her in this situation. She couldn't wipe his short-term memories, which was absolutely the thing to do when a human knew too much or got too close.

But getting into his mind and stealing his thoughts? Well, that was robbery.

"I'm sorry," she repeated hoarsely. "God, I keep saying that, don't I."

"You don't have to apologize." He shrugged. "Hell, less than twenty-four hours ago, we didn't even know each other existed. Why would you feel guilty about anything when it comes to me?"

Lyric felt herself go totally still. And even though there was a warning voice ricocheting through her head like a stray bullet, she heard herself say:

"You're the first male I've noticed in a very, very long time."

Okay, that was a half-truth. He was the first male she'd ever *really* noticed. For all the attractive fighters she was around on a regular basis, and all the aristocrats who hung out with Shuli, and even the two she'd dated for a while, there had never been much resonance to any of them.

"I don't know why you're different," she said in a low voice. "And I don't even care."

Dev glanced down at the cigarettes in his hand. Then he put them in his pocket and walked over to his bed. At the little table that held his lamp and charging station, he pulled out the drawer and riffled around. Straightening, he didn't close things up, but went into his bathroom. There were other sounds of him moving things around.

When he came back out, he had a pen in his hand, and he walked straight by her. Unspooling a paper towel from its roll, he bent over the counter where the serving dishes of their meal were still sitting out.

After he finished writing something, he put the pen down and approached her. "This doesn't have to be a one-night-stand thing. If you don't want it to be."

When she opened her mouth, he shook his head sharply. "Nope. Don't answer now. Go home and think about it. And if you decide you want more than tonight . . ."

He took her hand and pressed a folded-up square into it. "Here's my number. You call me and we'll have dinner tomorrow evening. Like a proper date, without all kinds of naked happening and no gunfire in the background."

She looked down at the wedge of paper towel. "How are you like this."

"Like what?"

"After everything tonight . . ." Her eyes lifted to his. "Most guys would have run in the opposite direction when I stopped the sex. And they never would have gotten to the . . ."

"The shooting part?"

"Yeah. How are you not asking questions."

His eyes grew remote. "You don't want to know."

"Yes," she said urgently. "I do."

It was a while before he answered, and when he did, his voice was so deep, it was nearly inaudible.

"No, you don't." He went over to his dresser. "And don't forget your scarf."

CHAPTER TWENTY-FOUR

estination. They needed a fucking destination with adequate cover, sufficient camouflage, and medical supplies.

On the far side of the dumpster, L.W. jogged through the frozen slush with the aristocrat on his shoulders, trying to triangulate their position relative to the Brotherhood's secret garage. If he could get over there? He had the code to access the bulletproof interior, and he could pull the rip cord on an evac for Shuli.

The male was hanging on, going by the breathing on L.W.'s biceps, but he was losing blood stuck-pig style—

Down at the end of the alley, a *lesser* dropped into their path from a fire escape, like something from *Spider-Man 22.*

As the thing lifted its arm and a gun flashed, L.W. tried to get to one of his autoloaders—

The discharge of a bullet was loud as a clap of lightning in his ear, and for a split second, he thought someone was behind them. But then it came again—

Shuli was shooting, and his aim was good, the slayer ducking and returning fire before jumping into an inset doorway—

L.W. flattened against the wall of the building on the left, and decided Shuli'd been right. They had just done this last week. Then again, they'd done this last month, too. And the month before that.

Just not necessarily together.

"Nice shootin', Tex," he muttered to the aristocrat as he wondered when more backup slayers were going to arrive.

"You're not . . . going to leave me, are you."

Not a question. Resignation. And because L.W. liked making people miserable, he said, loud and clear: "Nope."

The guy coughed weakly. "You hate me, remember?"

"Yeah, I do. Always."

Shit, no cover. No doorway like the slayer had. He looked up. Under his arm. All around. It was dark as a colon in the damn alley because the buildings that formed it had no windows, no security lights, no—

"Fire escape." As Shuli swapped out magazines, he pointed with his nine. "Right there. Go—"

"That's gonna get us nowhere—"

Ping! Ping! Ping—

Fireflies flared all around them as the *lesser* discharged a variety of shots that ricocheted off the bricks—

"Fuck!" L.W. crumpled sure as if someone had baseball'd his lower leg. "Goddamn—"

He did what he could to give Shuli a soft landing, but there was no helping the poor sonofabitch. Like a load of manure dumped by a wheelbarrow, the guy spilled out all over the ground—

Despite being seriously injured, Shuli flipped onto his belly, shoved his elbows into the ice, and went classic sniper position as he let his trigger finger go autoloader-aerobic. The barrage of return fire cut the crap with that slayer, so certainly the thing had been hit—but the reprieve was only going to be a temporary kind of thing.

And motherfucker, the cops were just two blocks over. They'd surely heard the fresh gunfire, and there'd been enough of it to track. This place was going to be swarming with plug-in policemen in the blink of an eye.

L.W. craned his neck around. There was no going back where they came from. Not unless they wanted to dance with the CPD patrol cars who'd revved by just as the dumpster had appeared—and as soon as those cop-bots figured out they were in pursuit of absolutely nothing, they were going to be pulling one-eighties.

Okay, they were totally trapped.

As he tried to put some weight on his left leg, his brain stem went opera-singer with pain. "*Fuck.*"

"How bad are you?" Shuli asked as he reloaded again—with hands that shook.

"I'm just great—"

"Can you fucking walk?"

He gave it another shot with putting his shitkicker in the snow and pushing on it a little—and had to lock his molars to keep from yelling.

"No—"

The slayer started shooting again, and as bullets pinged around, L.W. glanced back at the dumpster. He couldn't get himself there to take cover, much less Shuli—

The high-pitched whine of a motorcycle going fast at a low gear rang out off in the distance, so loud, you could hear it over the continuing gunfire. L.W. grabbed Shuli's leather jacket and used his good leg to push against a tread-hold and drag them farther back while staying against the wall. As flecks of brick hit his face and speckled his chest, he knew that shit was about to get so much worse, assuming that bike came with a *lesser*.

Snagging his cell phone, he fumbled with the damn thing. He had so much blood on both of his hands, he couldn't enter the code. Shoving the phone in his own face, he blinked because suddenly there was a brilliant light on them—

Even more bullets now, to the point where he had to hunker down and protect his head and internal organs. At least the bike had slowed its roll, though—

"Don't shoot me!"

Huh . . . ?

L.W. couldn't see a thing, but he'd know that voice anywhere. "Rhamp—"

"Oh, fuck. You're injured, too. I'm calling for backup—"

"I can dematerialize. Take Shuli—"

Shuli's voice was nothing but a weak mumble: "Take L.W.—"

"Shut up—"

"Shut up—"

As he and Rhamp barked the same two syllables at the aristocrat, he was reminded why he loved Lyric's twin. Only a male with balls as big as church bells would steal a bike, and penetrate an active shooter situation in a blind alley when there were more CPD bots around than human gawkers at this point.

Plus the fucker moved fast. With a lithe surge, Rhamp dismounted, grabbed Shuli, and somehow managed to get them both back on the Harley. Which clearly had been "borrowed."

"You good?" the guy demanded at L.W.

"Yeah. I'm good."

"So dematerialize."

"Go!"

When Rhamp just shook his head, L.W. started cursing, and then realized that was not going to calm his ass down. Closing his eyes, he took a deep breath and ordered his heart rate to slow—

Someone was talking on a bullhorn. A cop-bot, for certain.

Even more sirens now. Some shouting—

He tried to focus himself inward. But instead, the sweet smell of the gas-powered engine on the bike got louder in his nose. And so did the scent of *lesser* blood—and the vampire variety, too.

He took another deep breath. His ass was cold, his leg thumping, and there was a bad-news sense of wetness under his thigh.

Come on, he ordered himself. After all the tattooing he'd had done on his skin, he was good with pain. He liked it, actually. So that wasn't the problem. Something else was—

His eyes popped open. "Goddamn you, Shuli."

The guy, who was at half-mast over the bike's gas tank, lifted his head enough so they could meet eyes. "What . . . ?"

L.W. glared at Rhamp. "Until that aristocratic fuckboy is out of here, I'm not going to be able to go ghost."

"Jesus Christ, you two," Rhamp muttered. "Will you *please* decide whether you hate each other or not—"

"You want to save us both? Then get him the hell out of this alley."

There was a moment of indecision on the other fighter's part. Except then, on the far side of the dumpster and the Toyota, a patrol car stopped. Reversed a little. And turned into the alley, its headlights streaming all the way down the chute.

To the point where if it hadn't been for the dumpster's bulk, they would have been spotlit like a bunch of criminals.

"Go," he spat.

Rhamp cursed and hit the gas, kicking up a shower of ice that sparkled in the beams of the patrol car. In the aftermath of the departure, L.W. slumped against the wedge of dirty, bloody snow under him. Turning his head, he looked down at where the cop-bot was advancing through the alley toward the busted-out Toyota.

He glanced in the other direction and saw the slayer in the doorway was still moving. Fuck. The bastards could be pumped full of lead, but unless you stabbed them in the heart, they stuck around in whatever shape you left them in. They could literally be on the verge of a leaked-out "death" for a century.

L.W. knew what had to be done. But he didn't have the energy.

He'd lost a lot of blood himself—

Summoning the very last dregs of his strength, he dragged his body up off the icy ground—and as he lurched toward the *lesser*, he made sure he stuck to the center shadow cut by that hulking trash bin. Just as the cop-bots swarmed over the Toyota, he came to that doorway.

What a waste, he thought as the undead's head moved so it could look up at him.

He could have interrogated it.

Under other circumstances.

Falling to his knees, he took a deep breath. And another. While he drew out his steel dagger.

"You're . . . going . . . to . . . die . . ." it said.

The words were a hushed curse that wafted up at him along with the stench of that rancid oil in the slayer's veins. And the laughter that came next was nasty and self-satisfied, like it had called for help.

"No shit, Sherlock," L.W. muttered as he lifted his weapon over his shoulder. "I'm mortal—"

Three more *lessers* appeared at the end of the alley, about twenty yards from him, forty yards from the dumpster, and nearly fifty from the cops and the Toyota.

"And fuck you," he snarled to everybody in the whole city.

As a vicious anger overtook him, something strange happened: A sudden tunnel vision shrank the world to just himself—which he supposed a lot of people would say was his S.O.P. And then he pictured his sire in that Audience Room, the two of them yelling at each other.

He took one last breath.

And stabbed the slayer.

The blast of illumination and the *pop!* drew the attention he knew they would. The cops instantly started clambering over the dumpster, ordering all kinds of weapons-down, hands-up, in their automated voices. The good news? The *lessers* at the end of the alley took one look at those uniforms and melted into the shadows.

Which just left him, his puddle of blood, and some of the many guns that had been used to shoot at the fine, electric members of the Caldwell Police Department.

Except before they could get to him, he shut his lids, exhaled . . . and pictured the one thing that could give him any peace.

Just as the police came barreling down at him, he disappeared into thin air.

Thanks to the image of Bitty's beautiful profile.

CHAPTER TWENTY-FIVE

About twenty miles north and east of where shit was going down with the CPD, Vishous was sitting at his glass desk in his glass office at Four Toys HQ. Drumming the gloved fingers of his cursed hand, he stared off into space as his most recent hand-rolled cigarette burned to a stub. In the background, ancient D12 bumped, but he didn't hear anything except the bass stride.

Stabbing his coffin nail into a nub, he lit up another one and got to his feet. As soon as he stepped out of his office and looked down the modern barn's spanned central space, heads popped up over the monitors along the rows of his team's workstations.

All typing stopped.

When he put his palm up in a no-not-you way, the work immediately recommenced.

The males and females had been cherry-picked from hundreds of applications, and he had to say, they'd never let him down. The two dozen or so IT experts monitored about a hundred properties as well as countless databases of civilians. They also aided in the investigations of crimes, kept up with the human world, and were available for special projects at the drop of a hat.

This was a 24/7 operation, with people coming in at sundown and staying for forty-eight-hour shifts. Down on the lower level, there were plenty of sleeping quarters, a kitchen that the *doggen* kept stocked with prepared meals, and a gym. And in a move hearkening back to the good ol' days of the human tech boom, you were allowed to bring your dog to work if it behaved itself, with the servant staff more than willing to take them out during the daylight hours as required.

It had taken a lot of thought, facility construction, and hiring to put this living organism of an IT department together, and he took great satisfaction in the service they provided the Brotherhood, the King, and the species at large.

Not that he was feeling good about tonight.

That shit didn't have anything to do with his people, though.

Rounding the corner of his office, he stared over at the desk that had been set right against the barn's back wall. There were even more monitors on its surface than the other workstations, and the dark-haired, underdeveloped male who was bent over one of three keyboards and comparing four different tables of data at the same time was probably smarter than Vishous himself.

Take out the "probably."

When there was no response to his presence, he cleared his throat—something that should have been unnecessary given his exhale of Turkish smoke.

Allhan glanced over his shoulder in surprise and took out one of his earbuds. "Nothing of value yet."

V lowered his voice. "You eat tonight, son?"

As a blank look softened those dark brows, V was pretty sure it was a "no." Besides, that long, lean face was longer and leaner, and paler, too.

"I think so?"

Crooking his finger, V shook his head. "Come with me."

Allhan glanced with panic at his screens. "But I haven't found George. Or Gheorge. Or Georghe. Or Georghes—"

"Now."

Like he'd been called to attention in a military school, Allhan ditched the keyboard and scrambled to his feet, his gray SUNY Caldwell t-shirt waving like a flag from his bony shoulders, his loose jeans flapping around his stickpin legs. His shoes were black Crocs that had more scuffs on them than a dance floor, and his socks were mismatched. Dark green and light blue.

"Yes, sir." The kid took his other earbud out and started forward with an earnestness that was heartbreaking. "What did I do?"

Vishous took a drag on his hand-rolled and wished he'd never met the young male. "Nothing. You're good. I just want you to come with me."

One of the two stairwells down to the lower level was next to the back side of V's office, and as he opened things and stood aside, Allhan jangled by him and hit the steps like his arms and legs were only loosely attached to his torso. As V followed, he had no fucking clue how he'd gone from a hard-ass Dom to a . . . dad.

Was that what he was, though? Except goddamn it, what else would someone call it. He was constantly worried about whether some pre-trans had put a fork in their mouth. Whether Allhan had slept. If he was feeling okay, was he sick, did he need more clothes, or less time in front of those monitors . . .

Oh, and that was just the little shit. The big one was stark terror over a biological process that was as unstoppable and untreatable as time itself.

Or death, for that matter.

FFS, whether Allhan made it through the transition was totally out of V's control—and he knew this terrible reality was keeping Jane up during the day, too.

As Allhan bottomed out in the break area, the kid seemed lost, like he'd never seen the tables and the buffet line before.

"I'll go with you," V said.

Walking around the kid, he went over to the food that was on offer. Tonight it was pizza, sandwiches, salad—

"Good evening, sires," the *doggen* cook said as he came out from the kitchen. "How may I serve you? Any special requests?"

"I think we're going to see what appeals," V replied. "Thanks."

As the cook waited patiently, Allhan wandered by the platters that were under the warmers. Official lunch break time for the B team was coming up in about eight minutes, so everything was fresh and fully stocked—but it was like the kid was looking at roadkill.

"Do you happen to have any white rice and gingerroot?" V said softly to the cook.

The *doggen* bowed low. "Yes, sire. Right away."

"Yo, Al, let's sit down over here." V pointed to one of the tables that was away from the others. "They're going to bring you something."

"Yes, sir."

The kid went right away and sat down, facing the wall. Putting his hands together, he placed them in his lap, and lowered his head like he was in some kind of church.

As V sat down across the way, he scrambled his brain for what the hell to say. Sixteen fucking languages, and he had no clue how to make small talk.

No interest, except when he was around Allhan.

As the silence between them stretched out, he pinched his hand-rolled out and reflected on how he'd always had some latent masochistic tendencies. Maybe that explained why he was putting himself in this position with the kid.

"Don't stress if you can't find that name," he said.

Allhan's eyes lifted. "I'll find it."

"Sure you will. But if you don't, it's not—"

"I'll find it."

As things got quiet again, V stroked his goatee and decided he might as well tackle the obstacle in the room. "Listen, Al. I think it's time to choose."

"Choose what?"

The *doggen* chef swooped in with a plate of sauced white rice, a fork, and a napkin. "For you, master."

Allhan looked up, but kept his eyes on the cloth buttons down the front of the cook's white uniform. "Thank you," came a small voice.

The servant's face grew gentle. "Anything you wish, I shall make for you."

The *doggen* bowed and headed back to his station. As the kid started to eat, V imagined where Allhan would be without him and Jane taking him in. Fucking hell, V'd seen a lot of depravity in his life, but the idea that Allhan's parents had abandoned him? Just fucked the kid off without any money or clothes, no place to live, a pretrans about to go through the change with no one to help him? He'd literally shown up at Safe Place six months ago because he'd heard about it online in one of the private groups for the species. He'd been dehydrated and starved, and his shoes had been worn through because he'd walked all the way across town.

After having waited like a dog for a week for his parents to come back for him, outside on the doorstep of the house they'd been renting.

They'd locked him out when they'd left, and he'd been too polite to break in because he hadn't wanted them to be in trouble if he damaged the landlord's doors and windows. Fortunately, as a pretrans, he could still handle daylight, and he'd literally just sat there by himself.

Thank fuck he'd had a phone that still worked—

"This is good."

V refocused on that too-lean, too-pale face. "It'll settle your stomach."

"Did your father give it to you when you were nearing the change?"

V thought back to his youth in the war camp. His sire, the Bloodletter, had set up fights for him. And when he'd won, he'd had to fuck the loser in front of everybody.

Oh wait, that had been after his transition.

"Yeah," he said roughly. "He did. Handy, huh."

"You must have had really good parents."

An image came to him of his *mahmen* in her black robe, a diminutive, disagreeable entity who didn't allow anyone to question the great Scribe Virgin. Ever.

"The best," he muttered.

Refusing to go down the rabbit hole of his past, he let Allhan get through half of what was on the plate before repeating, "So, yeah, it's time to choose."

"For what?"

V narrowed his eyes on the plate that was getting mercifully cleaner by the moment. "You're too smart to play dumb."

Allhan took a deep breath and sat back. "I don't like to think about the change."

"I know." V rubbed the center of his own chest. "But we have to be practical. Is there anybody you want to be there with you—"

"You."

The answer was shy, but the speed with which it came out of that mouth was a kicker. And fuck him very much, V was absolutely, positively not blinking faster all of a sudden.

"I'll be there. Wherever, whenever it happens."

I'm not going to drop you like trash on the curb and drive away like I stole something. Not like those fucks you won't tell us anything about.

The kid had steadfastly refused to give his parents' names or tell where they'd all been staying. What little history they had on him had come out as the social workers had counseled Allhan over the first couple of months he'd stayed at Luchas House. The little peeks of his backstory with the abandonment had breached his silence only occasionally. For the most part, he'd stayed quiet.

He was still like that.

V cleared his throat and went for another hand-rolled. But he wasn't going to smoke down here. It was just something for him to fiddle with. "There are Chosen who can come to you. Their blood is very pure. It will help make sure you . . . do well."

"So that's what you meant." The kid pushed the plate away, with only a little rice left on it. "By choosing. A Chosen."

As always, so factual, so literal. And like Allhan knew anybody or had any friends he could call on to feed from? Besides, V had just been trying to give the kid some decision over any part of his life. He sure as shit hadn't picked getting left behind and being at the mercy of others.

"One's already arranged. Sahsa is her name."

"Will she have me, though?" Allhan wiped his mouth with a paper napkin carefully. "I know you would make the King order them to give me their vein, but I don't—that isn't right."

V opened his mouth. Shut it. Like he should be surprised the kid knew him so well, though?

"They would be honored to provide the service to you."

Allhan shook his head. "You're just saying that."

"No, I'm not. That's what they're there for. They serve the blood needs of brothers who can't feed from their mates, and injured fighters as well. And they also help during transitions."

Allhan met V's eyes fully for once—and it was such a surprise, Vishous found himself sitting back in his chair.

"For truth?" came the suspicious prompt.

V nodded once. "I swear on my *shellan's* life."

Allhan released a long breath. "Okay, then."

From over at the stairwell, the sounds of approaching voices and footfalls spilled into the cafeteria before the team entered, and you could just watch Allhan shut down, the locking of his features and body so complete, it was like he'd turned to stone where he sat.

"You done?" But V was already getting to his feet. "And I'm getting you some milk to go."

Allhan nearly knocked his chair over as he scrambled to the vertical, and even though his hands were shaking—and it made the *doggen* uncomfortable because they preferred to bus the tables—the kid picked up his plate and carried it over to leave at the buffet's serving window. The chef came out of the flap door immediately, but the kid was already wheeling away, his head down, his cheeks red like he'd been out in the cold.

V snagged a carton of milk from the drinks refrigerator and headed by the males and females who'd come down. No one stopped him to ask work-related questions. They all knew if he was with Allhan, he was going to bump them for however long the kid needed him. That was just the way shit was.

Back on the stairwell, it pained him to see how slow Allhan went on the ascent. It was clear his bones and joints were aching, but he never complained. Never asked for so much as a Tylenol. He just trudged upward, like he'd been long used to enduring.

When they stepped out into the first level, the kid went dutifully to his desk, sitting down again and going right back into those tables of names.

As V watched all that erstwhile concentration, he thought of how they never would have learned that Allhan was a computer genius if Luchas House's common room Dell hadn't ended up with a virus. Before anyone could call Four Toys HQ, Allhan had it fixed—and he'd created an additional security overlay outside the commercial one that had been installed by the staff.

V had been pissed that protocol had been broken and they hadn't waited for someone from his team to get there, but when he'd seen what the kid had done, he'd been impressed.

A week later, he'd given Allhan a workstation. A week after that, he'd moved the kid over here, to this corner. A month after that, he'd issued an invite for Last Meal at his and Doc Jane's quarters at the Wheel. And then another. And another. A shortage of beds at Luchas House had resulted in some couch surfing with them.

And that arrangement had quickly become permanent. To the point where neither he nor Jane could imagine their home without—

"Can I ask you something?" Allhan said softly as his eyes stayed on the screens.

"Anything."

There was a period of silence. "Is . . . um, Lyric okay?"

Say what— "Lyric? Yeah, sure. Why—oh, from last night."

Allhan nodded. And that was when a blush rode up the guy's throat and lit his face on fire.

Holy shit—

"What." Allhan's whole body turned to V. "You said she was okay—"

V cursed and waved off the worry. "No, no. It's good. I'm just surprised, true."

"About?"

The kid was so guileless as he stared back, V didn't know how the hell to answer that one. "She's fine. Uninjured and doing well after that billboard thing."

And then it suddenly made sense . . . last night, the video that had been sent around to everybody. It had been from Allhan's phone. V hadn't thought much of it at the time. He'd just assumed some of the partyer crowd had taken pity on the kid and issued an invite they'd no doubt felt forced to by conscience.

Except she'd had a work thing down there at Bathe, hadn't she. Layla and Xcor had been talking about it the night before.

"You went to see her at the club, didn't you," V murmured. "And you were recording the line who'd showed up to see her."

"I didn't go to see her exactly." Allhan stared down at his thin hands. "I just was worried she was alone with all those humans—which was stupid, wasn't it. I mean, look at me. What could I ever do to save any-body?"

V shook his head. "Never apologize for wanting to protect some-one."

"I wasn't who saved her." Allhan turned back to the monitors and tapped one of the screens. "That's why I'm going to find that name. I'm good at this kind of stuff. I can help the King, and you. This I can do be-cause physical strength doesn't matter here."

V's one and only thought was that he needed some Goose. Right now. He was just *not* cut out for this parental shit—

He went over and knelt down, swiveling the kid's chair around. "Allhan, I want you to know something—"

"I'm sorry, for whatever I did wrong—"

"Stop apologizing for everything." Fucking hell, he'd never wished that he was Tohr before. But that guy would know how to put— "You don't need to earn your place with me, okay? And you're not going to do anything that gets it taken away, either."

"This is my job—"

"You're safe. You're welcome to stay with me and Jane, for however long you want—and we hope it's a long time." Now V tapped the monitors. "*This*, and this job, isn't you. It's what you do. And it's not connected to being with us. You *don't* have to earn your bed or the roof over your head."

Allhan seemed to cave in on himself. "But why else would I have them."

V hesitated. "Because me and Jane, we like having you around. It's a good feeling for us, looking after you."

There was a long pause. Then Allhan brushed his eyes, and spoke in a low voice. "There's a plot against the King, right. I've heard you talking about it."

"Yeah, there is. But the Brotherhood is going to handle it—"

"And George, or whatever the name is, might help you find Whestmorel."

"Maybe, we don't know. But that's not on you."

Shit, he shouldn't have given the kid the assignment. The trouble was, Allhan was the best bloodhound they had—

"I want that male dead." Allhan's eyes swung up, and they were harder than stone. "If he's threatening the King, then he's threatening you, because you will go out and fight to protect Wrath, son of Wrath, sire of Wrath. I'm doing this work . . . because it's the only way I can think of to help you."

V closed his lids for a split second. Then he reached out and put his gloved hand on the kid's shoulder.

"Thanks," he said roughly.

"No," Allhan returned in a small voice. "Thank *you*. For everything."

CHAPTER TWENTY-SIX

L .W. had meant to send himself away from the alley, the fighting, the cop-bots.

And he'd managed to do that. The problem? No clue where he'd ended up.

And when he'd returned to his corporeal form, he'd also meant to be up on his feet, but he failed at that. He was flat on his back—and not like in a hospital bed, or even the bed he used at Shuli's. This mattress was ice cold, as if he was outside—

He turned his head. The blurry structure next to him was certainly a big house, and there were all kinds of lights glowing everywhere inside. But it was not Shuli's white, building-blocks mansion.

Bringing up his hand, he—

Why was his whole arm covered in snow?

Craning his neck, he looked down his body. There was snow on top of him, and as the wind gusted, more of it blew over onto his legs and torso, further dusting his leather jacket—and getting into it. Alarm bells started ringing in his head. How long had he been out here? He'd intended to go to the Brotherhood's garage downtown to be triaged— which was what you were supposed to do for injuries in the field. That was where Rhamp would have taken Shuli.

Where the fuck was he?

And how many hours had he been here?

Forcing his eyes to focus, he . . . got nowhere with that.

Shouldn't he be cold?

As his addled mind struggled to assess his body temperature, he let his head fall back into the snow, and as it lolled into an uncomfortable position he realized he had a far more pressing problem.

The first tip was the subtle whirring sound.

The second was the shifting all around the house: Shutters. Coming down because daylight was like a freight train gunning for Caldwell.

Phone. He needed to get his phone—

Good plan, but he didn't have gloves on and his fingers were stiff as claws.

"Help . . ." he croaked out. "Heeelp . . ."

His voice was so weak it didn't carry over the wind, and all he could do was watch as the glow through all those windows was gradually reduced.

Until it was gone.

The utter darkness was a shock, even though it shouldn't have been, and he looked up at the night sky. Clouds had rolled in, and he felt cheated that he couldn't see the stars or the moon—which was probably proof that he wasn't thinking right. He needed to get to that house, somehow, not worry about what his last sight was.

Forcing himself to roll over, he threw out his dagger hand and shoved his frozen fingers into the snowpack like they were a grappling hook. Using what felt like the last of his strength, he tried to pull his body forward, but he just brought snow to himself—and the same was true when he tried with his left reach.

He wasn't a fucking quitter, though.

So he paddled uselessly for a while, packing the shit around his head and shoulders.

Time for a breather.

Turning his head to the side again, he laid his cheek down on the snow, his breath whiffling the flakes—

The light of dawn arrived faster than he expected and he closed his lids. His vision was so bad, it didn't really matter if they were open, and glaring to the east sure as hell wasn't going to stop the sun from rising and doing what it was going to do to him: Up in smoke. He was gonna be up in smoke.

Not dissimilar to those fucking *lessers*—

Wrath.

The sound of his name was such a surprise, his eyes opened again. For some reason, the sun's brilliant, blinding light seemed to be right next to him, and this was confusing on so many levels. But also, why would the great glowing ball of death be saying his—

Worry not, son of the King. I shall send her. But in return, you must tell them the truth.

Okay, not the sun as it turned out. And what the fuck was this? "Tell . . . who," he wheezed.

All of them.

Lifting his head, he glared at the apparition. "Don't know . . . what you're talking about."

A wave of such intense cold came at him, he felt his heart stop, sure as if he were being freeze-fried on the spot.

You are your father's son, and that is a curse upon my species.

Justlikethat, the light was gone, and all he could do was shake his head. He supposed it was so like him to fight with a savior showing up at just the right time—then again, it was undoubtedly just a hallucination—

Another light now, far dimmer. The actual sun popping up over the horizon this time?

"Oh, my God! Oh, my God! Heeeeeeelp!"

Okay, now *that* was how you yelled for assistance.

And as L.W. drew in a breath, the scent that he woke up to on so many days courtesy of his dreams ran through his nose and went directly into his blood.

"Bitty . . ."

"Help! Yes, help—we need to move him! But gimme your belt— your belt!"

There was a moment of pause, and then a searing pain in his right thigh.

"Lift his leg up higher—I need . . . to get . . . this around his—"

"*Fuck.*"

"I'm sorry." Bitty's voice came close to his ear. "I need to get the tourniquet on. You're bleeding out."

L.W. tried to focus on her face, he truly did. When he couldn't manage that, he had to be satisfied with memory playing a patch job on all that he couldn't bring out of the darkness. She was wearing red, he knew that—oh. No, that was his blood on her sweater.

"Hold on," she said. "We're going to bring you inside—"

"Can't. No males allowed—"

"When it's life or death, it's allowed. Now, hang on."

That leg of his proved to be a fucking nightmare, especially as they rolled him over onto his back, and someone propped his injured leg up at what felt like a seven-thousand-and-eighty-degree angle. Then there was tugging, tugging, tugging—followed by a pinch that went right through his whole body. When shit settled, the constriction was set very high up his thigh, right under his groin.

Helluva way for her to learn his anatomy, huh.

And after that? The single worst transport of his life.

There were all kinds of people around him now, hands biting into his arms, his legs, his shoulders, his ribs. It was like piranha snacking on him, and that was before they started walking him across the lawn.

And up the porch stairs.

He knew exactly when they got him inside. Light. Warmth. The smell of chocolate chip cookies.

Bitty's voice barked out, "Call Doc Jane—"

She was right next to his head again, and for a female who was usually so quiet, she was giving orders tonight.

Especially as she announced, "He needs to feed—"

L.W.'s eyes popped open. "No, I'm good—"

The scent of her blood, delicious and enticing, burrowed into his nose, and in spite of the condition he was in—cold as a block of ice, probably hypoxic, definitely in clinical shock—he could feel himself getting aroused as his fangs dropped down from his upper jaw.

Bitty came into sharp relief, his panic giving his eyes the extra charge they needed to get with the fucking program: She was removing her wrist from her lips, her bright red blood running free from the twin puncture wounds she'd made in her own flesh.

A growl started to rumble through him.

And instantly, he projected into the future. What it would be like for her. How he would ruin her life, not just with what he did, but who he was, and what he brought along with him.

With a soul-deep conviction, L.W. knew if he took her vein right here, right now, there was no going back, for either of them. Yeah, they'd almost shared a kiss during that one date they'd gone on. But this feeding shit was . . .

Bad news. For her.

Between one blink and the next, he saw his *mahmen*, curled on her side on a twin bed in an empty room, crying with her hand locked over her mouth so she could be quiet enough not to wake him. And it wasn't just the one memory. There were so many that they ran together, like a painting that had been sluiced with water.

She was going to be that female. On a bed. Curled up around herself.

Either because he was killed in the field. Or . . . because he did something out there so heinous, so extreme, she couldn't reconcile his hatred and his actions with the male she thought she loved. If he took her vein now? If he learned her taste? He wasn't going to be able to stop the bonding that was already happening on his side and save her from the car crash collision that was coming her way.

Better to quit this now—

"No," he said as she brought her scored wrist forward.

With a fumbling, frostbitten hand, he pushed her arm away. "Anyone . . . but her."

For all his eyes' sloppy efforts, they didn't spare him now. He was able to see with heart-wrenching clarity the shock, and then the hurt, transform the urgency in her face into a horrified shame. And the sight of how he'd hurt her was burned into him, a brand on his soul.

"No," he repeated hoarsely. "Not you."

Bitty fell back. Then looked down at her wrist.

As she brought the wound she'd made for him to her mouth to seal it closed, there was a sudden hush that came over everybody. That didn't last, however. Another wrist was pressed against his lips, and biology took over when his freedom of choice would have denied the swallowing.

He drank, even though the deepest part of him was revolted.

More fuel for the rage, though.

Except it wasn't like he needed it.

CHAPTER TWENTY-SEVEN

O
h, you're home! I thought you were going to stay out at your grandparents'?"

As Lyric entered her *mahmen*'s living quarters at the Wheel, the happiness she was greeted with made her feel like absolute shit. The Chosen Layla was at the kitchen table, her blond hair tied in a bun, her white robing the traditional dress of her station that she wore still because, as she said, "it's more comfortable than PJs." In front of her, all of her beading trays were lined up, a colorful display of Lucite boxes that glowed like a rainbow, and she had a half-made bracelet in her hands, a mug of hot chocolate at her elbow, and her favorite jazz music threading through the warm air.

It was such a common scene, something Lyric had walked in on for as long as she could remember. Her *mahmen* made the jewelry to support Safe Place and Luchas House, and Layla's Baubles was a very successful store on Etsy. God only knew how much money she'd been able to donate over the years—and all from this bright, cheerful kitchen, sitting under a flowered light fixture.

As Lyric's eyes stung, she felt like she hadn't seen any of it for years.

And that included her fair-haired *mahmen*. Which was nuts. They'd spent time together here just hours ago.

"I . . ." Lyric cleared her throat. "I just wanted to come back here."

Layla frowned. "What's wrong."

The female didn't wait for an answer. She ditched the string of beads and scrambled around the table, her skirting flowing out behind her. "Do you need Doc Jane because of the accident last night—"

"No, no. Nothing like that."

Trying to hold herself together, Lyric took her *mahmen*'s hands and drew her back to the table. "Ah . . . so what are you working on tonight?"

Pointedly pulling a chair out, she sat herself down and made like she was looking over all the little squares of those glass beads. In reality, she was trying to give her eyes time to air-dry the tears that had flooded into them.

There was a creak as her *mahmen* settled back into her chair. "Talk to me, daughter mine."

Lyric reached out and stirred some iridescent beads in their little container. When she'd been a young, the tiny donuts had delighted her, especially as the collection had always included every color imaginable, from the softest of lavenders and the brightest of reds, to the deepest of blues and the crispest yellows. And everything in between.

She cleared her throat and picked up a single crystal bead. "You know . . . when I was little, I used to think you had the power to splinter rainbows. I was convinced that somehow, you were able to go out during stormy days and find them, and these were what was left over. Fragments from your magic."

Layla put her hand across the table, a beckoning gesture. "Something's going on. A *mahmen* knows these things."

Letting the bead drop back with its lot, Lyric replayed all kinds of clips from what she had decided was a night from hell. And considering the billboard bullshit from the evening before was her standard . . . that was really saying something.

Her *mahmen* might have intuition, but with everything else that was going on, there was no reason to verify that hunch so graphically.

"It's really okay. I'm just . . . a little off."

The hell it was okay. She'd roped her brother into something that had turned into a royal mess—literally, because L.W. had been involved—and then against her better judgment, she was getting totally obsessed with a human she couldn't really be with.

Not truly. Not deeply . . . honestly.

God, she really wanted off this drama carousel.

"What was it like," she abruptly heard herself ask. "Back when you were up in the Sanctuary with the Scribe Virgin."

Layla's perfectly beautiful face registered surprise. "I—well, ah . . . why do you ask?"

"I don't know." Lyric played with some red beads. "I've been thinking a lot about life lately. I've made the decision that I'm not going to do the social media thing anymore."

"Why? You've enjoyed it so much."

"It's fake. Nothing but pretend. I can't . . . I can't keep going between my *granmahmen*'s deathbed and a makeup chair so I can look good for pictures I don't care about." She shrugged. "And you know . . . sometimes I think it would be easier if I had a higher calling. Transcribing the history of the species, being so close to the creator of us all . . . must have been such a sacred duty."

Her *mahmen*'s brows drew together again and she seemed to retreat into herself. "It was rather heartbreaking, in truth."

"Because you couldn't live your own life?"

"No." Those pale eyes lifted. "Because we couldn't help. We could only sit on the sidelines and watch."

Lyric immediately returned to being up on that roof, hearing the shooting and the sirens. "Yes . . . that would be terrible."

"It was." Layla seemed to shake herself back to the present, picking up the bracelet she'd been working on. "That's why I do this. I can make a difference for people who need help and support."

"That's what I want to do."

"And you have so many years ahead of you." Layla smiled with reassurance. "There are many avenues to work for the species—"

"What if I wanted to fight?"

"*No.*"

They both turned around. Xcor had come into the kitchen, and the expression on his face was like someone had suggested he invite a squadron of slayers to sit at his table.

Lyric frowned at the male. "Payne and Xhex fight—"

"They're different." He marched forward, peeling off his leather jacket as if he meant to show all of his weapons. "And I don't want any more talk about this—"

"Why are they different?" Lyric knew in her heart the reasons why, but pride made her want to defend herself in some way. "They had to train. They had to learn. No one comes out of the womb knowing how to—"

"I'm not talking about this. Not tonight—"

Layla spoke up. "Okay, let's just all take a—"

"Well, I am." Lyric stood up. "And there's nothing you or anybody else can do to stop me from—"

"You know what I did tonight?" He tilted forward on his hips, his distorted upper lip lifting off his fangs. "You want to know why I'm home early? I got to carry the bruised, dead body of a torture victim to the incinerator at the training center and burn the remains. He was found in a hidden room at a traitor's mansion and we have no idea who he is or if he had any family. He'd been left for dead, tied to a chair in the abandoned house. He died in spite of everything Doc Jane did to try to save him, but we might well have had to kill him anyway depending on his involvement in the plot against our King."

Lyric lowered her gaze to all the pretty beads on the table, and the bracelet that was in process.

"You want to deal with *that?* You want to look at that—smell it? And that's before you add in getting shot at, killed, or worse, taken in for questioning by the Lessening Society. Oh, and Lash is inducting women now. Do you want to be the first female vampire to—"

"Enough!"

As Layla slammed her palms into the table, all of the boxes of beads bounced, the colors mixing as shimmers of light fell back down.

There was a moment of tense silence as *shellan* and *hellren* stared across at each other. Then Xcor cursed and headed for the sink. From the drying rack, he took a glass and filled it with water. Tilting his head back, he drank the whole thing slowly, before rinsing it out and putting it back where it had been.

Pivoting around, he said in a more even tone, "I apologize. It's been a long night, and frankly, this is probably why I need to take some time off. But I don't want you involved in the war. One son is more than enough, I can't take a daughter, too—"

The door that led in from the Wheel's outer ring opened and Rhamp walked in. He was covered in red and black blood, stank of *lesser*, gunpowder, and gasoline, and had a foot drag that suggested he'd been injured.

"What happened to you?" Xcor demanded.

As Layla jumped up, Rhamp glared at Lyric. "Ask her. Or the human she's sleeping with—if she'll tell you who the hell he is. And no, I'm not interested in talking about tonight."

With that, he went down the hall to his room, and shut the door with a resounding clap.

✦   ✦   ✦

Out in the countryside, Qhuinn re-formed on the front stoop of his in-laws' house. As he reached for the door, he hesitated—and thought about all the times when he hadn't done that. For so many years, he'd just walked right in, happy to be there, looking forward to seeing the people inside . . . beyond ready for the food, whatever it was.

He took a deep breath. Then another—

Pushing things open, he pinned a smile on his face. The shit didn't last as he walked in. You could smell the medical-grade cleaner, the astringent not even a little covered up by the fake lemon scent that floated along with it.

Ehlena or the other home nurse must have just left.

He closed things quietly. Rocke's study was immediately to the left, and as he glanced in, his nape sounded a warning. The office chair was swiveled away from the desk, and a pen without its cap on had been dropped in the middle of a page.

"Oh, fuck . . ."

As he strode forward, the formal living room to the right was also vacant, but it was always that way, the fancier furniture arranged with throw pillows that had tassels, the dark green and gold drapes made not of linen or cotton but a nice, weighty velvet. Even though it was an outlier in the midst of all the comfy-cozy, the color scheme still went with the rest of the house, though, and he'd seen the elder Lyric standing on the thick carpeting and slowly turning 'round and 'round. Like she couldn't believe she had such a beautiful room in her house.

The renovation and furnishing had been an anniversary gift from Blay and Qhuinn about ten years back, a tack-on when Lyric and Rocke had been redoing their kitchen and family room. He and his mate spent too much money on it, something that both his in-laws had always reminded him of, but they would have dumped four times the cost into the decorations just to give Lyric that shy happiness.

As Qhuinn followed a rising sense of alarm to the back of the house, he braced himself for whatever was waiting for him. Although surely he would have gotten a phone call if—

The hall gave way to the open area that faced the pond and the gazebo, and Blay was over at the sink, an anemic stream of water piddling into a coffee mug, the male's eyes focused on the middle ground in front of him like he wasn't seeing anything. There was another mug upside down on the rack, dripping, and an open bag of Pepperidge Farm mint Milanos at his elbow.

Blay looked utterly exhausted, and that red hair was clean, but uncharacteristically messy—it was also longer than usual because he hadn't been able to get to the barber *doggen* back at the Wheel. How long had he been sleeping out here for . . . the last week? Ten days? The calendar had been a blur lately.

"How you doing?" Qhuinn asked as he approached.

Blay jumped in surprise. Then cleared his throat. Twice. And seemed to take extra, extra care with the sponge on the rim of that mug.

The silence that followed was a reminder that, however hard a night Qhuinn had been thinking he'd had . . . it was nothing compared to what was going on under this roof.

He went over and they kissed briefly. Then he stepped back to give the guy some space.

"Ah, so, Simone just left." Blay shut off the water by putting the heel of his hand on the faucet arm. "She's really good with *Mahmen*. So patient. So unhurried, even though she must have been coming to the end of a long shift."

Pulling out one of the stools at the counter, Qhuinn moved slowly. Blay seemed like he was going to startle at the slightest unexpected anything.

"She's really good, yeah."

"I gave my father a grocery list." Blay nodded at the door that led out into the garage. "He said he needed something to occupy himself with. Neither one of us has felt like eating tonight, but it was the only thing I could think of that seemed even remotely appropriate. You want some coffee?"

Those familiar eyes were imploring as they looked up, like he was also begging for something, anything, to do.

"That would be great."

"And if you happen to be hungry, I can make you some—" He went over and opened the refrigerator. "Well, there's not much, but I can do eggs and toast?"

"I don't have much of an appetite, either. But I could use a coffee."

Blay went right to work, heading to the Keurig on the other counter and taking a fresh mug from the cupboard above even though he'd just washed the other two. In a little wicker basket, there was an assortment of K-Cups to choose from, but Qhuinn didn't need to point out that he liked the Dunkin' dark roast the best. His mate knew all of his preferences.

With the machine set, there was a burbling and the scent of the coffee bloomed. Then came the little bit of sugar and the tinkling as the common stirring spoon did a couple of circles before it was tapped on the rim and put back down on a spotted paper towel.

Blay came back over, rounding the island and offering the steaming mug.

As things changed hands, Qhuinn murmured, "This is delicious. Thanks."

"You haven't tasted it yet."

"Don't have to. You make mine perfect—"

With a quick surge, Blay leaned and pressed his lips to Qhuinn's properly. "I've missed you," he said in a voice that cracked.

Qhuinn reached up and cupped the male's nape, keeping them close as he kissed his *hellren* back in a way that lingered. When they eased apart a little, he nodded.

"I've missed you, too."

Talk about understatements. A couple of real kisses and his balls were aching for a release, his fangs descending, his arousal instantaneous behind the zipper of his leathers. But it wasn't just sex for him. He also wanted to fall asleep with the male against his chest, like they usually did—and wake up with the same closeness. Their apartment back at the Wheel was cold and lonely, no matter how much he turned up the heat and how many movies or TV series he played in the background while he tried to get a little rest.

FFS, it was like he was turning into Lassiter, the way he'd been binge-watching ancient shows like *The Office* and *Schitt's Creek*.

But here was the thing. He wasn't bringing any of that shit up. He knew Blay felt the same absences he did. The guy was just missing all that at the same time he was watching his *mahmen* die by inches. Plus there were things to talk about—like, whether their daughter was dating a human, and what that meant for her.

News traveled fast in the family.

And oh, God, he just didn't have the energy to worry about that right now.

Blay went back over to the Keurig and took the used pod out of the top. "Simone says we don't have much time."

Qhuinn took a sip of the coffee. And yup, it was absolutely perfect. "What does that mean?"

"Days, maybe. She's sleeping more and more."

"Do you want me to step off the schedule and stay here with—"

"No, don't do that. I know . . . you'll always come if I call. When . . . I call. But with what's going on with Wrath? The Brotherhood needs you."

"You need me, too."

"And I have you."

As a mixture of relief and guilt hit him, Qhuinn closed his eyes briefly. Work, even with all its chaos and danger—maybe especially because of all that—had been a kind of salvation. Granted, it was a double-edged sword, as part of his mind was always back here. But the shit recalibrated him, and made it so he was better able to deal with what was happening to the elder Lyric.

"Do you think we should call the twins?" he asked his mate. "Have them come today?"

Blay tossed the K-Cup in the recycling and walked across to the bank of windowpanes that looked out over the backyard.

"No." The male took a deep breath. "I don't really want them here when she dies. I know—I mean, it makes no sense to treat them like they're too young to understand—and as we come to the end, if they ask to stay, of course, they're welcome to. But I don't want them to remember her in her last moments. What if it's not . . . what if we can't control her pain? Or her breathing gets bad and she struggles?"

"Well, I think we should talk it over with them. But at least they have been visiting a lot, so important time's been spent. Especially on Lyric's end."

"She and her *granmahmen* have always been so close." Blay frowned. "I worry about her."

Qhuinn took another draw of the mug, and thought about the frantic way their daughter had run into his arms the night before in that club. Although the show of emotion was more than reasonable given what had almost happened, he'd sensed an undercurrent of stress that was all new.

Their shiny, happy daughter wasn't shiny or happy these nights and days, and he wasn't sure how much was what was going on here . . . and how much was stuff parents didn't always know about.

"Me, too," he said grimly. "I worry, too."

CHAPTER TWENTY-EIGHT

Dev woke up the following evening on a moan. He was on his back, one arm over his head, the other twisting a wedge of blanket up in a fist. Down at his hips, shit was thick and demanding, and tendrils of the dream he was coming out of tantalized.

Something to do with that stairwell to the rooftop and Lyric straddling him, as he held himself in place on the steps.

Closing his eyes, he went right back into the fantasy, seeing her blond hair flowing over her shoulders, her parka open, her turtleneck shoved up over her breasts, her bra pushed under them, her nipples peaked hard—

Another moan rumbled up through his chest—

His alarm went off, the sound of a barking dog shooting through all the sexy and blowing it apart to hell and gone. As his eyes popped open, he slapped his hand around the little table and sent the cell phone flying.

"Mother*fucker . . .*"

Sweeping his legs free of the covers, he planted his feet and yanked the blanket aside. Of course, as things dragged across his lap, he hissed through his locked teeth at the friction. And then as he stood up, shit was positively obscene, his erection sticking straight out in front of him like a divining rod—

Bending down for the phone, the true north stayed its course.

As he silenced the alarm, he heard people moving around upstairs, voices in the hall, a siren outside. Life, happening all around him.

Going into his texts, his heart started to pound, but he ignored—

Nope, Lyric's initial text was still there. She really did want to meet him for dinner.

After verifying she hadn't changed her mind, and that his affirming response had been seen, he closed out his phone and put it facedown on the bedside table.

Not too late to change this, he reminded himself. *You can still pull out.*

With a grim resignation, he headed to the bathroom, and as the door was partially closed, he swung his hips and pushed it open with his cock—

Payback was a bitch.

The contact shot was a bolt of lightning into his balls and he sagged against the doorjamb, the wood creaking as his weight hit it. When he went forward again, it was directly to the shower. No chance of going the bladder route, and he didn't wait for the water to warm up. He stepped under the blast of spray, and led with his dumb handle.

Another plan backfire. He'd wanted to punish himself, but the stinging impacts that tickled his proverbial ivory just made the thing throb more.

Turning his back to the spray, he grabbed his shaft with his left hand, braced his other palm against the tiled wall, and dropped his head into his biceps. The stroking was goddamn delicious, especially as he closed his eyes and imagined it was a different palm against his cock—Lyric's—and she was setting a rhythm that was hard and fast.

Naked. He pictured her naked and with him, her nipples dripping with water—

Annnnnd that was what did it. He didn't even have to get to the part where he got down on his knees and licked those drips off the tips of her breasts. He came so hard, he had to bite down on a knot of muscle to keep from yelling loud enough to scare the neighbors—and as soon as the orgasm started to fade? Another ramped right up.

Not his usual thing. But did he even have one?

As he kept working his erection, he told himself—when he could think—that he was doing everybody in Caldwell a public service. He'd been pent up ever since Lyric had left last night, and he had a feeling that seeing her again, even if it was just across the table in a restaurant, was going to sharpen his libido to a blade.

So this was a good idea. Take himself down a notch or two. Chill himself out.

When he finally released his grip, he also let his biceps go.

"Great," he muttered as he washed off the spots of blood where he'd broken his own skin.

Shampoo. Conditioner. Soap.

And then he got out before there were any other great ideas from down below.

Getting dressed took a little more time than usual. He had two uniforms: going to work and sitting around. Neither of which was quite right, but it wasn't like he could accessorize them up. In the end, he went with "going to work," and picked the best versions of blue jeans, Hanes t-shirt, and pullover he had. Pathetic, really.

He just wasn't used to having anybody to dress for.

On that note, he grabbed his cell phone, put it into his windbreaker, and was opening his door when he stopped and looked back.

Dev closed things up. Returned to his bed. Shoved his hand deep between the mattress and the box spring.

The Beretta he took out was loaded and in its tuck holster with the safety on. He put the nine millimeter through a checkup, then stowed it inside the waistband of his jeans, with the holder arm tucked under his belt. Going back to the bathroom, he stood in front of the sink, but had to step away some so that he could see his torso in the mirror.

Yeah, you couldn't see anything—

Shit. His hair.

He started to go through the drawers, but that was a waste of time. He didn't have a comb or a brush, and well, that checked out. He kept his hair cut short just so he didn't need anything to run through it.

Overdue for his bimonthly trim. Great.

Dipping his palm under the sink faucet, he got some water, put it on the top part, and passed his hand over the dark growth.

"Whatever."

Back at the door, he went to step out. And had to pull up short as his neighbor appeared in her apron.

"Dinner." The old woman wiped her hands on a red dish towel. "In ten minutes."

"Thank you, Mrs. Aoun. But I can't tonight."

She set fists on her ample hips, her expression like he'd cursed in church. "Where are you going."

"I—ah, I have a date."

Instantly, her attitude shifted, her forehead wrinkling as her gray brows shot up. "You have a girl?"

"Woman. And we're just having dinner together."

"What's her name."

"Lyric."

"She nice? You know her family?"

"She's—yeah, she's very nice. I don't know her family, no. This is our first date—well, actually, we shared your dinner last night."

As well as the shit up on the roof. But in case his neighbor had missed it, he wasn't bringing up the drama.

Down with the brows. "She like my food."

"Oh, yeah, she loved it. Particularly the fattoush."

"Ah. Good." Mrs. Aoun turned back to her door. "You will tell me how it goes when you get back here."

Dev opened his mouth. Closed it. "Mrs. Aoun?"

"Yes."

"I'll tell you about it tomorrow."

There was a grumble of disapproval on that, but the old woman was nodding as she closed herself back in. Dev waited a second. Then he went over to her door.

Rapping with his knuckles, he said, "Ma'am? Throw your dead bolt for me. Please."

There was a pause. And then shuffling.

The door opened and the tiny old thing stuck her forefinger in his face. Okay . . . his sternum, because that was as far as she could reach.

"You a good boy."

Then she shut things back up with a clap—and that bolt was engaged with a *chunk*. As he went over to the staircase, he was shaking his head. How the hell had he ended up going out with some blonde for dinner and worrying about some geriatric's locks. He'd lived here for—

Dev paused with his boot hovering over the first step. This was a really bad idea, he thought.

He could still turn back.

Then again, he could still turn back on his way to the restaurant.

The trip down and out of his building was a solitary one, and he tried to find good luck in that. As he hit the snowy sidewalk, he hung a right, and put his hands into the windbreaker. The gusts coming over from the river were cold and bitter, as if the weather had taken a personal interest in driving the citizenry of Caldwell into their homes and locking them down, and he decided that was another sign this wasn't as stupid as he thought it was.

Then again, maybe it was a sign he should have stayed home.

Whatever.

While he traced the path he usually took to work, he looked up to the tops of the buildings he passed. No billboards. And he also didn't run into any other damsels in distress.

Good thing, as he was retired from that line of work. Permanently.

A couple of blocks on, he passed the construction site. The place was lit up like a stadium, and the muffled sounds of machines running made him check his phone. Second shift had just started. The fuckers had four more hours before lunch, and he didn't envy them.

No doubt Bob had been surprised Dev hadn't showed, but probably relieved, too. Petey with the mouth was no doubt even more happy, and you had to wonder if he'd resumed flapping his lips. Or maybe the lesson not to pick on other people had stuck. Either way, none of it was Dev's problem. He'd tendered resignation through the Wabash business office, and his former foreman would no doubt hear about things on Monday, if not sooner.

The restaurant was another two blocks to the south, and as he came up to the glow of that nightclub's blue and green sign, he double-checked his gun was in place and entered the alley. There was absolutely no one else out walking, just a couple of cars traveling on the salted roads, and you never knew who you were going to meet.

He was not into complications tonight. He'd had enough already.

As he arrived at the front entrance of the Italian joint, condensation blurred the view of the interior, but there was no mistaking who was sitting at the table in the window.

Like he wouldn't recognize that fall of blond hair anywhere.

Unfortunately.

Lyric was facing away from him, her profile as if drawn in pastels, all those long, flaxen waves falling down over her shoulders. She was in some kind of a dark blue sweater, and that scarf, the one she'd maintained her dying grandmother had knitted, was around her neck.

"You can still leave," he said into the icy night.

As his breath drifted off, a waiter approached and she looked up at the man. There was some communication between the two as glasses of water were put down—and then it happened. The man in the white shirt and black apron nodded like he was going to go, except he paused as she resumed staring straight ahead of herself.

The bastard was looking at her, kind of awestruck—

Dev's body moved before he decided to go inside, and he might have pushed that door open with a little more force than necessary.

And what do you know, the way Lyric's face lit up as she saw him guaranteed that waiter was going to live to see his next birthday—as did the way the guy took one glance at Dev and backed off quickly.

Fuck, he did not need to start getting possessive over here—

"Hi," she said.

Lowering himself down across the table from her, he felt himself smile, even with all the shit in his head. "Hey."

✦   ✦   ✦

Okay, Lyric was the first to admit that the brain was capable of dreaming up all kinds of romantic bullcrap.

Particularly when you were lying awake during the day, curled up into your pillow, your family a mess, your career floundering, your purpose in life evaporated . . . and yet you had a man who had just texted you back that yes, he would meet you for dinner at Roberto's at seven p.m.

All of that was arguably the breeding ground for delusions of sexual attraction, but, good golly Miss Molly, as Lyric stared at the face she had been busy recasting for the last however many million hours, she could confidently say that the real thing was so much better.

Dev in person was next-level—and she laughed a little. Then almost knocked her water glass over when she went to pick the thing up.

"Sorry." She took her hands back and put them in her lap. "I, ah— how are you?"

For God's sake, did she have to sound like someone on a customer service line? In that tone of voice, she might as well ask for his social security number next.

"Good." His smile faded. Then he glanced around. "Nice place."

"It is, isn't it."

Even though she'd gotten here fifteen minutes early, she brought fresh eyes to the restaurant's narrow interior and limited number of tables. The uniformed waitstaff brought a little formality to the otherwise casual place, and the countless maps of Italy that hung on the exposed brick walls, from all different eras and in all different frames, made her feel like they were in a lowbrow museum. Overhead, opera music rose and fell, and the smells coming out of the flap door in the back were pure heaven.

There was only one other couple in the place, and they had to be in their sixties, the pair of them each with reading glasses on their noses as they went through their menus.

Dev cleared his throat. Then went for his water glass like a total pro, even bringing it to his mouth and swallowing without a drop spilled.

She was about to comment on it—like he'd mastered some kind of complex skill—but fortunately caught the words before they left her mouth. As she racked her brain for something, anything, to say, she focused on his hands. They were such strong hands, with blunt fingers, and all those calluses.

They had felt good on her waist, and she wondered what they'd be like on her skin—

"Listen," he said in a low voice. "I've got to be honest."

Her stare shot up toward his face, but she couldn't make it any farther than his Adam's apple. The tension rolling off him was palpable, and as a cold, hollow feeling struck her chest, she braced herself, noting he hadn't taken his windbreaker off.

Closing her eyes, she nodded. "It's okay—"

"I haven't been able to stop thinking about you."

Blink. Blink. *Blink.* "You . . . haven't?"

"Why do you sound so surprised." He laughed with an edge as he shrugged out of his jacket. "I can't believe I'm the first man to say that to you."

She refocused on her water glass because the fluttering feeling in her chest had probably translated into something rather walleyed-ish on her puss.

"That's true," she whispered. "But you're the first man I've cared about hearing it from."

Everything seemed to dim down around them, especially as he extended his arm and laid his hand on the table. Except just as she was about to reach across, the waiter, a tall, lanky young man with a ponytail, approached again.

"Hi, can I get you all some drinks?"

Dev took his palm back. "I'll take a beer."

"Sure, I'll bring you the menu—"

"Just a beer. Doesn't have to be special."

That seemed to confuse the kid. "Do you want a seasonal lager? Or a draft—"

"Fermented hops. Cold. In a glass—but only because this looks like the kind of place where you can't have it in a bottle."

"Oh. Okay." The waiter looked in her direction. "And you?"

Lyric smiled. "A ginger ale."

"Right away."

When they were alone again, she was the one who extended her palm this time. "Hi."

Dev chuckled and took her hand in his. "Hi."

"I thought about you, too."

"Did you," he drawled, his smile slow and sexual. "Good."

The door opened and cold rushed in along with a quartet of bundled-up people. As their laughter spilled throughout the place, the sound barely registered.

It was amazing how you could be alone in a public place.

"Not much for drinking?" he remarked.

It was hard to translate his words, what with her mind going in all kinds of NSFW directions. But then the syllables arranged themselves properly.

"No, I don't drink."

He glanced out into the restaurant like he was looking for someone. "You want me to change my order? I can change—"

"Oh, no. It's fine. I just don't like the taste—as lame as that sounds."

"Now that you mention it, you didn't drink the beer I gave you last night. I would have gotten you water."

The waiter came over with two golden long-stems, one of which had ice. "I'll get your menus."

"Thank you," Lyric murmured. And then as they just stared into each other's eyes, she flushed. "So . . ."

"Hard to make conversation without the soundtrack of bullets, huh." As she recoiled, he put his free palm up. "Too soon?"

"Ah—no. No, I—"

"That was a bad joke. Sorry."

Well, she thought, it would have been funnier if her brother was willing to talk to her. Or if all of her parents would have stopped looking at her like she was someone they didn't recognize.

But come on, casually dating a human shouldn't be that big a deal. And all of them had dealt with their own kinds of unconventionals in their relationships.

The arrival of the menus cut that avenue of thinking off, and that was not a bad thing. The conversation also got easier as they started to talk about food choices: what they liked, didn't like, hated, would eat until they passed out.

After they put their order in, Dev sat back and regarded her in that way he did . . . like there was absolutely no one else on the entire planet. He'd been right. She did get told she was beautiful by males. But that was usually as their eyes were going down her body.

Dev's were right on her own—

In the back of her mind, something registered, some kind of . . . not an alarm bell, no. It was something else that—

"So tell me more about your work?" he prompted.

Snapping out of it, she forced a laugh. "Well, I'm about to be out of work."

"Career transition?"

"You might say." She took a sip of the ginger ale. "I have one more commitment I have to honor, and then I'm through with the influencer business."

"Oh?"

Lyric tucked some of her hair behind her ear. "Yeah, my manager's roped me into that Resolve2Evolve convention—yes, the billboard that almost killed me. You're remembering it correctly. Kind of ironic, all things considered."

His eyes narrowed. "What are you going to do there?"

"Not stand under any big signs, first off. And it's not my scene, trust me. All that self-help stuff, I think, is largely just spoon-fed platitudes." Although considering the state of her own life, should she really be so judgy?

"My manager—former manager—Marcia set it up before I could tell her I was dissolving my online persona and then couldn't get me out of it."

He took a long draw on his beer. "Is that what the convention's about? Improving yourself?"

"From what I understand. With some beauty tips thrown in along with all the avaricious inspiration, I'm quite sure. Have you never heard of R2E before? The woman who's the face of it is everywhere, all around the country, doing press and social media. It's a huge event. They're taking over the whole Caldwell Convention Center. A thousand people, maybe more."

She was babbling, really, at this point. But she could sense him withdrawing, and that made her want to paddle forward. Which was lame, yes, she knew.

"Sounds . . . interesting." He took another draw from his beer. "When is it?"

"Tomorrow night."

"I've never been to anything like that before."

Now she laughed. "Well, get your surprised face on, but you're not exactly their target audience."

"You don't say."

Lyric frowned. Then leaned into the table. "Hey, do you want to come with me?" As his brows lifted, she blurted, "I mean, it could be a second date. And we could tell everybody you're my bodyguard. You could look at it as a social experiment."

What the hell was coming out of her mouth—

"I think that would make it our third date," he murmured. "Or fourth if you count what happened on the roof."

God, she hoped the flush she could feel on her face wasn't obvious. But as if showing up here and meeting her had magically erased all that gunfire stuff?

"So the whole billboard thing was more than an introduction?" she said roughly.

CHAPTER TWENTY-NINE

Well. That was fun."

As Shuli carefully shifted his legs out of the back of the blacked-out Mercedes, he planted his monogrammed slippers on his shoveled walkway like he had a pressure bomb under each heel. He was beyond ready for some shut-eye in his own bed, but goddamn that was a long way to the door.

Looking up to the front of the vehicle, he said, "Thank you, Fritz. I can get myself out."

From the wheel, the Brotherhood's butler glanced with worry over his shoulder and bowed. "Oh, master. Are you sure?"

"You have other things to be concerned with."

He nodded meaningfully at L.W., who was sitting beside him and staring off into space. Like the guy wasn't even aware they'd pulled up to the house.

"Yes." The elderly butler inclined his head again. "Do be well, master."

It was hard to ignore the *doggen's* vaguely panicked expression. Especially as it was backed up by absolutely no words. But the butler would never be so forward as to comment on someone's decision to discharge himself from the training center's medical center AMA.

No matter how stupid it was.

"Yeah, stay there, Fritz," came the hoarse order from the other side of the bench seat. "I'll take care of myself."

Well, what do you know, it was aliiiiiive. L.W. had been quiet the whole ride in, a brooding, mostly-not-leaking-anymore bag of badass in a set of hospital scrubs who had clearly been humbled by his femoral artery problem from the night before. Pretty pathetic, really, but hey, Shuli was in bad shape, too—just better dressed. Willhis had brought him his red satin robe-and-PJ set. Along with the slippers.

"Oh, master, you are getting out now?" Fritz unlatched his seatbelt in a panic as that other rear door was opened. "I thought perhaps you were returning home to the Wheel—"

"I live here. Besides, if he's getting out, I am, too."

That old face got even more wrinkled as the butler regarded the heir to the throne with eyes that were downright alarmed. "Sire, of course. But may I at least help you to the door?"

"No, you can't."

Leaving the pair of them to fight it out, Shuli extricated himself from the sedan's backseat, and pinned a smile on his face through the pain—because he hoped, as his whole body protested the vertical, that he didn't give away too much and trigger a medical review. Meanwhile, on the far side of the Mercedes, L.W. had the black Nike duffle bag with their weapons up on one shoulder, and the pair of crutches that had been forced on him under his armpits.

Meanwhile, Fritz was hyperventilating in the front seat. Except there wasn't much he could do with that kind of direct command.

And after L.W. had hobbled around the rear of the car, he lined up with Shuli at the base of the shoveled walkway. They even waved with the same hand, in coordination. That Mercedes stayed right where it was, though, a curl of steam lifting from its tailpipe, the calling card of the gas-powered engine drifting off.

Undoubtedly, the butler was in a terrible internal debate, trapped by his need to serve—especially when it came to L.W.—and the lack of invitation to help. And this was causing a full body paralysis.

As time ticked by, Shuli just stayed where he was, like one of those repair shop inflatables. L.W. was the same, standing there like an idiot in the cold, waving his hand with an expression as if someone were driving nails into the soles of his feet.

Finally, the lights flared redder, the engine was engaged, and forward motion occurred.

They waited until Fritz had gone all the way down the private lane and taken a corner at the iron gate before dropping their arms with a couple of curses. It was as they turned around that the reason the *doggen* had departed became obvious.

Willhis was barreling down the snow path like he was worried they were going to both go into cardiac arrest if he didn't show up with canapés, *stat*.

"Master! Sire!" The butler paddled to a halt, his spit-shined patent leather shoes having all the traction of twin ice cubes. "Allow me!"

As the duffle and its load of leather and weapons was pulled off the heir's shoulder, Shuli was goddamn grateful when his *doggen* had the sense to offer him an arm. Ordinarily, he would have tough-guy'd it and marched on his own, but not after the last twenty-four hours. He loop-di-looped himself right around all the steady freddy, and together as a threesome, they started the shuffle up what was absolutely, positively the longest walkway that had ever existed.

L.W. took the lead, making better time with his crutches, and for some reason, maybe the painkillers in Shuli's system, the dark figure the fighter cut against the stark, white house seemed like something out of a gritty noir comic book: All stark visual cuts, the "stately Wayne Manor" bullshit updated for a new audience, no longer Gothic-roofed and many-storied but as if the Guggenheim had decided to go private residence.

With all the money his parents had left him following their untimely deaths, he could afford to live anywhere, and he'd deliberately picked this place because it was not like the traditional mansion he'd grown up in. Everything was different. Every piece of furniture, all the art and rugs. The staff, too.

Fresh start.

And now he had a roommate.

"Yay," he muttered into the cold.

Willhis had left the door wide, and L.W. hobbled right in, heading across all the polished while marble to the hallway that branched off to his wing of the house. As he disappeared down to his rooms, Shuli remembered when the whole *ahstrux nohtrum* shit had first gone down. It had been a relief to give the guy a whole section of the floor plan—in the hopes that the two wouldn't run into each other very much.

There had also been a traitorous sense of security, having the fucker under his roof during the day and when they were home at night. Not that he would have admitted it to anybody, especially His Royal High Horse-ness. The reality was, though, Caldwell was getting more dangerous by the minute now, and L.W. was a cantankerous sonofabitch, but no one could argue with his fighting abilities.

After what had been done to Shuli's parents, he didn't sleep all that well—

Nope, he was not going there.

Willhis stopped. "Master? You're not going where?"

Shit, he'd said that out loud. "Sorry, ignore me."

Once he was over the threshold, he dropped the *doggen*'s arm and measured the floating staircase that went up to the second floor. As he tilted his head back and counted the steps, the ache over his hip sharpened to an outright pain.

"Perhaps master would like to use the elevator?"

"You're so right, Willhis."

"May I bring you aught?"

"I already ate at the clinic, but thanks." He took the duffle from the butler and started walking down to the Otis. "You might want to bring some food and drink into L.W.'s room. Just make it like breakfast stuff with a carafe of fresh coffee? Knock to announce your presence, but don't ask for permission to come in, and like, leave the tray on the bureau and walk out. Don't ask him anything. He'll just tell you to fuck off."

"Oh, yes, master. I shall do that right away—"

Shuli stopped in front of the elevator doors and pushed the summoning button. "One other thing. He's supposed to be on pain meds, but he's not going to take them."

"Should I prepare a pill schedule in the event he forgets?"

"No, he left the stuff back at the clinic. I want you to bring him a bottle of Jim Beam. He'll drink it so he passes out."

"But of course." Willhis bowed low. "And for you, master?"

"Oh, I took everything they wanted to give me and I got backups in this duffle bag." As a *bing!* sounded out, he put his hand forward. "Thank you, though."

"My pleasure, master. I shall attend to our guest immediately."

He swung the duffle into the elevator, where it landed with a *thump.* "He's not a guest. He's our roommate."

Stepping in, Shuli hit the button and watched the door close on his butler's worried face. During the ride up, he propped himself against the mirrored wall and hung on to the chrome balustrade. There was a bump to announce the arrival, and the doors opened. No reason to pretend to be a tough guy now.

He let the bag drag along on the thick white carpet.

The second floor had all kinds of bedroom suites opening off both sides of the white-on-white-on-white hallway. The primary suite was all the way down at the end, and as he continued to haul his sorry ass and the bag along, he wondered: (1) why he didn't live in a smaller house; and (2) why he didn't take advantage of any of the other cribs.

It was like when you hit a tennis ball off the rim of your racket. You paid for that part, even if it wasn't the sweet spot in the middle.

Or something like that.

"What was the question," he mumbled.

In a stunning optical illusion—one that echoed the shit with the snowy walkway—the corridor seemed to get longer the farther he went. It also felt like he was getting shorter, for some reason.

When he finally got to his door, he went to open it with his mind. Failed. Had to do things the old-fashioned way and turn the knob.

His inner sanctum of white-on-white-on-white reminded him of a cloud, and when he'd hit the blanco so hard with the decorator, he'd told himself it was to set off the Rothkos he was collecting. Give them a backdrop to really show off on.

As he kicked the heavy panel closed now . . . he just thought it showed a lack of commitment. Like he'd moved his things in, but he hadn't moved himself in.

"Fine. Okay, that's great."

He left the duffle just inside the door, and congratulated himself for the stellar thinking that had made him take a shower before he'd left the clinic: He'd used the chair they provided and the grips on the wall, and that nozzle thingy.

So all he had to do was shuffle across to the king-sized bed and fall face-first onto the fluffy-as-Wonder-Bread duvet. As the thing puffed around him, pressing gently into his wounded body, he turned his head to the side, exhaled, and closed his eyes.

It was so quiet here. No beeping machines. No footsteps of people moving around the clinic. No hushed voices—

Knock.

"I'm good, Willhis."

Knock-knock.

"I'm all good, Willhis!"

He heard the click of the door opening, and started wrenching around with a struggle. Though he wanted to curse, he held back. The *doggen* did not deserve to be on the receiving end of his frustration at the entire world.

Okay, the shit was mostly about Lyric. And that human—

Not the butler or another member of the staff.

L.W. stood there in the doorway, balanced on one crutch, still in those hospital scrubs. On his big body, it was like he was wearing a miniature set of them, his ankles showing, his tattooed lower abdomen, too. The shit was also super tight across his chest.

"What's doing?" Shuli asked.

"Mind if I come in."

Not exactly a question. But it sure as hell was closer to one than the guy usually got. "Yeah, sure."

The heir to the throne closed the door and hesitated.

"Okay, you need to tell me what the fuck is going on." Shuli tapped his temple. "'Cuz my mind's going in a lot of bad places, the longer you stand there looking like you have bad news to drop and no idea how to start the fucking conversation."

Although considering *all* the fun they'd been having together lately, what could possibly make shit worse. Yes, the Brotherhood had accepted the story that they'd run into *lessers* and chased them behind that apartment building, but the lie they'd taken up to protect Lyric wasn't sitting well.

Even though, really, Shuli would have done anything for that female.

L.W. limped in farther, stopping to look at the Rothko above a bureau. "I've been thinking."

"So that's why I smelled wood burning all day long," Shuli muttered.

The fighter glanced over his shoulder. "I've never understood that expression."

"Me neither." Shuli shoved himself backwards, until he could lean against his pillows. "Human vernacular is a playground of nonsense. We can discuss clams that are happy, being on cloud nine, and that whole over-the-moon thing later."

When L.W. just started limping from painting to painting, Shuli exhaled the flare of pain that had come with the repositioning, and waited. He'd never seen the male so tense.

"Whatever it is," he found himself saying, "we'll handle it."

He couldn't believe the temerity of the statement. The son of the great Blind King didn't need help from anybody when he had Wrath in his corner. But clearly this shit was private.

The kind of private that people picked and chose who they shared it with.

"I've been a real asshole lately."

Shuli lifted his brows. "Lately? Try your whole life."

L.W. glared across the room. "Not when I was a young. I was good then. I was . . . a good kid."

Shuli inclined his head in acknowledgment. "I wouldn't know. But I take it you do."

That proud, regal head turned back to a yellow and orange canvas. "It wasn't until I hit my transition that I . . . changed."

"Which is what's supposed to happen."

There was a long silence. Then L.W. seemed to talk to himself. "It wasn't that bad, really. Right after. For, like, years, I was okay. I think the compensations started without my even being aware of them."

The male moved on to the next painting, the one to the left of the white marble hearth that had never had a fire in it. Never would.

He hated the smell of hardwood burning, and then there was the mess.

"Lately, though . . ."

L.W. shook his head as he walked around to the twinsie canvas on the other side.

"I haven't been able to keep things right," he concluded as he turned to face Shuli. "You remember when you told me not to fuck around with Bitty? That she was too good for me."

"I don't remember phrasing it like that."

"That was what you meant."

"Not really. You're the King's son—from a bloodline perspective, you can't get any better than your station."

"I'm not talking about family trees. You said she deserved better, and you meant it."

A strange feeling of foreboding came over Shuli, tightening the back of his neck. "What the fuck are we talking about here. Are you . . . do we have a psychological issue here. Like, a real one."

The kind that made people you thought you knew turn out to be the sort of monsters that true crime enthusiasts talked about for generations.

Shuli measured L.W.'s upper body. Even if that leg wound slowed the guy down a little, it went without saying who was going to win if the fucker had a psychotic break right here, right now.

He eyed the duffle bag where the weapons were. He had a nine in the little table next to him, but there was no reaching for it without a big show of movement—and that was before you added in the injury to his own side.

L.W. took a long, slow inhale. "I can smell your fear."

Okay, so there was no way to respond to that—

"I just . . . can't see it properly."

Shuli got real fucking still. "What are you talking about."

The heir to the throne was silent for what felt like forever. And then he said in a low voice:

"I'm going blind."

CHAPTER THIRTY

As Dev and Lyric emerged from Roberto's, she was all up in her head, wondering if he was going to bring up the what-next, whether she was going to do it, if they were going to go back to his place and finish what they'd started. Or ... maybe just take it a little further—

"This was great." He turned and faced her. "And not the food."

"You didn't like your Bolognese?"

As he laughed, she watched his face, seeing the crinkling at the sides of his eyes, something she'd come to look for when he smiled. It made him seem younger, somehow, even though for a human he was only in his late twenties. Had she asked him his age? She didn't remember. And P.S., check them out, being all regular-people, regular-problems: Date commentary, lingering in the glow of an Italian eatery's sign, hesitating to go forward, not wanting to leave.

Big difference from the night before—and for that matter, the night before that.

"I liked you." His hand came up and brushed a strand of her hair that had caught the wind. "But the food was good, too."

"Yes," she whispered.

Was that an answer to the question he hadn't asked? Hell yeah, it was. Except as their pause turned into an actual silence, she wondered once again whether a brush-off was coming—

"I wish I could take you back to my place."

"Oh." She shook her head to clear it. "I mean, sure. That's . . . fine. I get it—"

"It's not because I don't want to be with you. I'm actually moving."

"You are?" She tried to tamper down a shock that resonated way too much. "From Caldwell?"

No, North Dakota, you idiot, she thought.

"I don't know where I'll end up."

She waited for him to say more. "Oh. Okay."

But come on, where did she think this was all going? He didn't know what she really was, she didn't know who he really was—and now that she looked back on it, the talk over their table had all been very superficial. He'd never once asked about her family or her life, and she'd been relieved because what could she share other than mother, father, father, father, and brother? And even that buried the lead, as the saying went.

Come to think of it . . . what the hell *had* they talked about? She couldn't remember now—no, wait. That wasn't completely true. She'd asked him on a third date and he hadn't said yes. He'd just changed the subject to whatever she was going to order, or something equally banal. As disappointment crested, she decided that she needed to be real here. They hadn't been thoughtfully set up by friends, or met over a shared interest. They had . . . collided.

"This was a goodbye dinner, then." And then she forced a smile. "Or maybe a see-you-later without it really being meant."

His eyes traced her face. "I shouldn't be doing this with you. It's not . . . fair."

"Are you married?" She put her hands up. "I should have asked this last night—"

"No, I'm not. Marriage is for a different kind of man than me."

"Oh."

Out on the street, a couple of cars crunched by them, the light down at the intersection having turned green. As the wind strengthened, she shivered.

"Where do you live," he said after a moment. Like he really didn't want to know.

"Why did you waste the time meeting me here."

"You're cold. Where's your car—"

"Answer me," she shot back.

Dev put his hands in the pockets of his jeans, and stretched his chest forward like he was realigning his back. Then his eyes traveled around, focusing over the top of her head.

"Why did you waste our time," she repeated.

"Because no matter how much I tried to talk myself out of it, I couldn't not see you." He lowered his stare to her face. "I can't get you out of my mind."

Lyric opened her mouth. Closed it. And that was when his eyes dropped lower . . . and stayed on her lips.

"So what do we do now," she murmured.

Dev stepped in closer to her, his arm moving around her waist. As he tilted her backwards, she put her hands up to his shoulders.

"You tell me," he said.

✦   ✦   ✦

"Who else have you told," Shuli breathed.

Across his bedroom, L.W. kept going, moving to the flat wall by the bathroom door. He stopped in front of yet another painting.

"Rothko," he murmured.

Shuli frowned. "You know the artist?"

"Of course. And don't sound so surprised."

"I just thought between polishing your ego and judging people, you didn't have a lot of time for art history."

"You are such an asshole." Except the tone was mild. "And you have a lot of net worth on these walls. Downstairs, too. That Pollock in the foyer is my favorite."

"My parents collected European Old Masters. I do not."

L.W. glanced over. "Parental problems, too, huh."

Shuli was not touching that one. "Who else have you told about your eyes."

"Nobody."

Rubbing the back of his neck, Shuli measured the male in a new way. The heir to the throne was still monstrously strong, even injured and with that crutch, definitely not the kind of thing anyone would want to meet in a dark alley. But shit.

He shook his head. "Jesus. Are you sure?"

"Yeah, it's been coming over the last year. And I'm only telling you—"

"Because you want me to make sure you don't get killed out in the field."

"No, to explain why I've been acting like I have." L.W. came over to the foot of the bed. "I don't know how much time I have left to really fight. I want to get to Lash while I still have all my faculties and kill him."

"Don't you mean 'destroy'?" Shuli fiddled with the sleeves of his red satin robe, and thought, hey, at least he wasn't thinking about how much his body hurt now. "And for what it's worth, I don't know if the evil monster can be killed."

"If that sire of his, the Omega, could be eradicated, he can, too. They're made of the same shit. That's why I'm looking for a location. That's why I'm out there every hour I can be. I've got to find him before it's too late."

Shuli wagged his forefinger like a librarian. "You're going to get yourself killed if you keep this up. Especially if you can't—"

"I can see well enough. For now."

And then the two of them just stared at each other.

"You lie," Shuli said after a moment.

"About what."

"You're not trying to explain your behavior. You want me to be your accomplice."

When eye contact and silence were all he got in return, he laughed in a short burst. "Wow."

"You're my *ahstrux nohtrum*. You're along for the ride."

"I'm supposed to keep you alive, not be your Robin on some suicide mission."

"This is not a suicide mission." L.W. shifted the crutch in front of him and bounced the gray tip on the white carpet like he was pointing to things written on a board. "We're trained to fight, killing slayers is our directive, and taking out the head of the Lessening Society is possible in pursuit of that goal. We just need to find out where Lash is, figure out how to get at him—and blow him the fuck up."

"Payback for what he did to your father." Shuli considered the motivation. "You know, the last time I saw you with the King, I got the impression you didn't like him very much. Strange calling—revenge for a sire you can't stand."

"I don't want him to stop me."

"That's why you hate him? Because you're afraid he's going to take your toy away?" Shuli shook his head. "I don't buy it, but that's your business. And I will tell you you're wrong about all this."

"Who cares? My personal convictions and your opinion are irrelevant to what I'm going to do."

"Nah, this is not about that fee-fee bullshit."

"Huh?" L.W. frowned. "Fee-fee—"

"Feelings. Emotion." Shuli batted the air with his hand. "But I digress, you big, dumb, royal asshole. What you're wrong about is my part in your grand plan. This is a suicide mission for *me*, not you. Did you hear what the Brothers were talking about down at the clinic over-day? There's a plot against your father."

"Yeah, I heard."

"They're going to kill that Whestmorel guy. Soon as they find him."

L.W. shrugged on the side that didn't have the crutch. "As they should."

"So what do you think is going to happen to me if I aid and abet the heir to the throne on an undisclosed, rogue mission to get to Lash. That's treason against the throne because your ass is next in that fancy chair, you dark, brooding idiot. The King and the Black Dagger

Brotherhood will absolutely kill me, and that's true whether you succeed or fail."

"They spared you last night."

"They are not going to cut me *any* slack on this one." Shuli shook his head again. "You fucked me off in the field then, I had no control over that. What you're talking about requires my full participation."

"No one needs to know."

"How the *fuck* do you think that's going to work."

"Because I'm not saying shit, and neither are you."

Shuli looked around his room, at all the paintings he'd bought with his dead parents' money just to spite them. He wasn't sure he even liked the blotchy fucking canvases from an artistic point of view. He'd bought them because they were a fuck-you to those two aristocrats. The truth was, if his brother hadn't overdosed a year before they'd died, Shuli would have been out on the street without a dime. As it was, the "spare" got the goods by default. Probably because they were so grief-stricken, they forgot about revising their wills.

So yeah, he understood complications with parents.

"Tell me you need my help," he said in a low voice.

When nothing came back at him, he cocked a brow. "You ask a male to put his life on the line for you, you can damn well make the request properly. And I'm not too proud to admit that I'm a little bit hurt."

L.W. rolled his eyes. "About what."

"That the only reason you're coming to me is because your eyes are failing and it's dawned on you that you might not be able to go it alone. Oh, and P.S., I rubbed my fucking feet raw trying to find you two nights ago. Blisters all over them. If I were a human, I'd be crippled."

"I'll buy you orthotics."

"And Band-Aids."

"Deal."

Except then L.W. lowered his chin and stared out from under his brows. "What's your answer, aristocrat."

"What's the question, prince."

L.W.'s voice went low and so level, it was all but dead. "Don't fucking toy with me."

"So no's not an option, then." Shuli rose up off his pillows. "You going to kill me if I don't play ball, huh? Make it look like an accident in the field tomorrow night? Whoops, good ol' Shuli got caught in friendly cross fire. How sad. Or maybe it's more like you slaughter me and my *doggen* here and now, and pretend a *lesser* did it. Probably better, the latter. If you give me too much time, I might just have to go to the King with your bright idea."

"Guess we'll find out, aristocrat. What's your answer."

"Tell me you need me," Shuli shot back.

L.W.'s upper lip lifted from his fangs. "It's the other way around. You have no purpose, no calling, no reason to get up at night. You're a fuckboy, trust fund junkie who can't hide his boredom at the very parties he throws to distract himself from his zero existence. The money you have is inherited, not earned, and you buy your friends with it because it gives you control over them and that way you don't have to worry about them seeing the real you and judging you for being so fucking useless. You even have to pay for sex because you're in love with a female who wouldn't have you if you put a gun to her head on account of—unlike the suck-ups who drink your liquor and snort your coke—her knowing that underneath your thin skin there's nothing worth fighting for or falling in love with."

Shuli swallowed through a thick throat. Then he said roughly, "And you're the one asking me to commit treason with you. So, sorry, your epic, shit-talking soliloquy was nice and all, but you're not exactly looking like a genius here if you're choosing me and that's your opinion of your partner—*Little* Wrath."

"Fuck you," came the growl.

Cupping his ear, Shuli turned his head and motioned toward himself with his free hand. And then he just sat there.

There was an eternity of silence. Until, finally . . .

"I need you," the heir to the throne gritted out.

CHAPTER THIRTY-ONE

Lyric had never used either of the downtown apartments before. She and her brother had each been given one a while ago—a couple of years ago now—in recognition that they were both out of the change and probably should be living lives separate from parental proximity. Except neither she nor Rhamp had moved out of their rooms at the Wheel. Why bother, really. Rhamp used Shuli's for his private endeavors, and otherwise slept where he always had. For her, she liked being in the community underground location. There was always someone to talk to, something to do, something to learn.

And she'd certainly not needed a place to go for—

"The Commodore?" Dev said as they rounded the corner.

The remark was a casual one, neither here nor there particularly, but she knew that the high-rise was the most luxurious in the city, the Caldwell equivalent of NYC's the Dakota.

Well, if the latter were modern. And had been through a $100 million renovation about five years ago.

She glanced up at his profile. "It's just a one-bedroom unit. Nothing fancy."

"How long have you lived here?"

"I don't—I mean, I live with my parents." She paused, expecting him to ask . . . something, anything. "And my brother."

As he made some kind of *hmm* sound, she wanted him to say something more, but again, that was so ridiculous. There were too many limits on what she could tell him—and anyway, if this was a real "dating"-type deal, details about families eventually led to inquiries about introductions.

And given that Rhamp wasn't even speaking to her at the moment, the fact that her next-of-kin's were all vampires was actually the secondary problem.

Oh, and Dev was moving, anyway. So . . . yeah.

Together, they walked up the building-wide steps that ascended to the refurbished marble entry. The Commodore looked more like a governmental office building with its concrete collar of steps that rose to the glass necklace of its entries, but there was only so much you could do to spice up twenty-five layers of windows rising out of the urban ground.

They mounted the half dozen snow-cleared levels, and as he put his hand on her elbow, she was reminded of his manners. And the mother who had died who he hadn't liked. What was it about physical attraction that made you want to get into the mind of the other person? she wondered. Then again, with how intensely she was feeling, she did want to understand him, as if in doing so she could understand her own powerful response.

Although on that note, given the number of inquiries he hadn't made of her, clearly she was on a one-sided quest in this relationship.

Situationship, rather.

As they entered the lobby, they stomped their soles off on the matting and their footfalls echoed all around. The security guy at the desk gave them a wave, and as they both returned it, she wondered if she was going to be asked for ID because it had been so long since she'd been here.

Except the security system no doubt had facial recognition software.

Over at the bank of elevators, Dev punched the button, and they waited together. In the reflection of the polished steel doors, she looked at the pair of them. He was calmly perusing the lobby they'd just gone through, his body relaxed as he wandered around with his eyes. God, how she envied him, especially as she watched herself jump as the arrival *bing!* went off.

"What floor?" he asked as he got in by the rows of glowing buttons.

"Fourteen."

"You got it."

There was a subtle bump, and then up, up, up, and away they went. When the next *bing!* came, she felt like it had taken a second and a half, but that was distraction for you.

"Here we are," she murmured as she stepped out.

While she walked along the corridor, she kept an eye on the numbers by each door. They went down . . . until she got all the way toward the end. Then frowned.

"Oh, wait. Sorry, it's back there. Sorry, I'm all turned around."

"No problem."

Lyric doubled back, taking them past the elevators again and down halfway to the other end. "Here we are."

The copper key went in fine, but she held her breath, wondering if she had the right—

The bolting mechanism turned just fine, and she opened things up. The scent of fresh lemon greeted her nose, and she was surprised. She couldn't remember the last time she'd been in here, and yet it had clearly been cleaned recently. Fritz and his staff were just amazing.

The interior was dark, and she tried to be discreet patting around and searching for a wall switch. She ended up wandering out past the half bath and the entry into the kitchen, and wondered whether she shouldn't just will things on and call it motion detection. Crap, she couldn't remember if there were lamps or maybe it was track lighting—

Thank God. A switch. "I'll just turn this on."

Click.

As illumination bloomed, she looked over her shoulder. Dev had hung back, and while he leaned against the wall, his hooded eyes were on her.

"You don't have to do this," he said as he nodded over his shoulder at the door they'd come through. "I can leave now that you're safely home."

She glanced around. The place was like a hotel room, in the anonymous sense of the words. Neat, tidy, with functional furniture in the right places. The color scheme of gray, cream, and white was clearly intended to calm the weary mind, and the view of the western horizon showing the twin bridges and the city's twinkling other side was beautiful, but cold.

She met his eyes in the reflection from those windows, and all she could think of was that he was leaving Caldwell.

"No." Turning around, she went over to him. "You're going to stay."

Reaching up to his windbreaker, she trailed her hands down the pads of his chest. Even through the layers, she could feel the heat coming off of him, and when she got to the lower hem, she didn't hesitate. She lifted the folds up his torso.

He was hardening already.

It was obvious at the front of those jeans.

And seeing that . . . no, she wasn't stopping this time. The thing was, this wasn't a one-night stand. She'd been looking for magic, and even with all the shadows between them, she'd found some with him. Sure, they would only have right now, but she was going to remember him for a very, very long time.

Besides, hadn't the last couple of nights—hell, the last month with her *granmahmen*—proved that there were no guarantees about anything? Even if they tried to date, who knew what would happen.

"You are so going to stay," she repeated.

In response, Dev nodded and put his arms over his head, letting her do the work as she shucked the jacket off of him. Tossing the thing on the nearest armchair, she immediately put her hands back where they'd been, on his pecs. They were warm, and his muscles flexed under her palms like her touch was resonating through his body.

Lyric did not look at the strong column of his throat. She focused on his mouth, especially as she leaned into him.

"I can see how much you want to kiss me," she breathed.

His hands slipped into her own coat and peeled it off her shoulders. "Yeah. It's bad."

"Good."

She had no idea where he threw what he removed from her, and she didn't care as he dropped his head. With his mouth just an inch above her own, she ran her hands up his back. The muscles along his spine rippled as he put his arms around her, and God, she loved the power in him. The hardness of him. So very different from herself.

With an easy shift, he picked her up and carried her to the sofa.

Laying her out on the soft cushions, he knelt beside her. "How far do you want this to go?"

"I don't know. I'm not thinking too much ahead right now."

"Good."

Dev loomed over her, and then melded their mouths. With a moan, she arched into him as he kissed her, his lips stroking, seducing, none of that hard, hot passion from before—as if he was giving her a little time to consider what they were doing. And she had a feeling he was also giving her physical space because she could scent his arousal: He was ready to mount her and orgasm inside of her already, the mating instinct clearly not so different in humans.

But he was holding his body back, keeping things in check . . .

Even as he started to explore. With tantalizing deliberation, his touch drifted across her stomach, and she felt a tugging as he pulled the bottom of her blue sweater up from the slacks she'd worn. Then came a little skin-on-skin, his warm, calloused palm moving over her belly, going around to her ribs . . . moving up to right below the cup of her bra. Meanwhile, his tongue licked into her, and when she felt a moan rise up in her throat, she didn't hold back.

His chuckle was very self-satisfied, the vibration on her mouth making her wonder what it was going to feel like when he was at her breasts—

On a quick shift, Lyric sat up and ripped the sweater off herself. Underneath, she had a button-down shirt on, and as she lay back down, Dev's eyes raked over the next layer he was clearly going to take off her.

"Yes," she whispered, answering the question in his hot stare.

Easing back on his heels, he went to work on the fastenings of her shirt, starting with the one at the bottom first. Then the next. And the next . . . the next. His eyes were hooded and volcanic as he looked at what he was revealing, inch by inch, the two halves of the shirt falling free as if the damn thing was complicit.

As he got to the last button, the one right in front of her bra, he growled, "It's gonna be hard to put the brakes on if this goes much further."

"Let me help you with that."

Lyric reached up and unfastened the final one.

He hissed as she pulled the shirt away from herself, and then without missing a beat, she freed the clasp of her bra. As the cups snapped back and her bare breasts hit the cooler air, she felt her nipples tighten.

Dev's jaw worked as he stared at her, the muscles in his thick neck flexing. "*Fuck . . .*"

"We're not stopping," she said with a boldness that would have shocked her the night before.

As he rose up fully on his knees, he towered over her, and she speared her fingers into the hair at his nape, pulling him down so that his mouth was on her sternum. He took things from there, kissing his way over to one of her nipples, brushing his lips over the peak before sucking her into his mouth. The subtle pull made her cry out again, one knee coming up on the sofa cushions, her pelvis rolling with hunger.

Lifting her head, she looked down at him, the sight of his lips on her flesh and the hollow of his cheek moving as he worked her, shooting pleasure directly into her core. And as if he knew exactly what she was hungry for, one of his hands traveled down to skate her hip and stroke the outside of her thigh.

And then the inside of it.

With shaking urgency, she went for the belt around her waist, and she was rough with the gold H buckle, tearing at it so that she could get at the button and the zipper of her pants—and when she made a fumbling mess with all that, he took things over with admirable aplomb. The second the slacks were opened, his fingers slid inside, all the way inside, the confines pressing him tight against her—

She cried out his name as he stroked over her panties, the silky folds going into her own folds, the heat redoubling, the raw lust threatening her self-control as the friction ramped everything to a nuclear heat. Meanwhile, up top, he was working on her other breast now, and his free hand was in her hair.

"Come for me," he commanded.

Dev started stroking her in a rhythm and it was electric, the sensations overwhelming in the best way, her body jacking up off the couch as she worked her hips against him. The wet sucking on her breast, the tightened grip on her hair, the slippery heat between her legs—

The pleasure snapped deep inside her core, and as the release tackled her, it was the *best* thing she had ever felt.

Talk about magic. And she only wanted more.

Slapping a grip on his wrist, she held him in place as she closed her legs on him. "Again . . ."

✦   ✦   ✦

Holy . . .

Fuck.

Dev had lectured himself all the way over here to take it slow, and let her go. Take it slow, let her go. Take it—

Yeah, that was not how shit was going down.

As her husky demand for more hit the airwaves, a flush of pure erotic drive went all the way through him, and he knew he was in trouble. His plan had been to get her on the sofa—because it kept his body away from her—and give her some pleasure because she was beautiful and he could sense her nervousness. As long as he focused on her and what she was feeling, and limited contact with his dumb handle, he figured he had a good chance at keeping himself controlled. And things had been going well—at least at the shirt-part start of it all.

But fuck him all the way back to the Stone Age, the instant she'd released that bra of hers, and he'd seen for real what he'd only imagined? Then tasted her, rolling her nipple around under his tongue, feeling her arch into him?

And add in . . . what he was doing to her now?

Well, things had taken on a momentum of their own.

Glancing down past her breasts, the image of his wrist disappearing into her open pants, coupled with the feel of her slick heat on his fingers through what had to be silk? How could he slow things down.

He was about to come himself—and that was even before she orgasmed against his hand and wanted—

"More," she groaned as she speared into his hair and held him to her breast.

"You want it," he said against her skin. "I'll give it to you."

Dev straightened, and she protested as his lips left her nipple and he retracted his hand, but when he stroked down her legs and stretched them out on the couch, her hazy, sexy eyes clung to him. Looping a hold into her waistband, he slowly pulled her pants down.

Boots.

She had short-stack boots on.

Shifting to her feet, he made fast work of her laces, and then the treads were off along with her jeans and her socks—

"Jesus, even your feet are perfect."

He started at her ankles, sweeping his palms up the insides of her legs. When he got to her knees, he parted them—annnnnd had to take a little breather. The sight of her pink silk panties wedged into her core undid him to such an extent, he had to pause to lower his head and think of . . .

Well, anything else than what he was about to do.

Too bad he didn't actually know a goddamn thing about golf.

"What's wrong," she whispered.

"You're . . . I can't even think."

"Then take a page out of my book—and don't. Just feel."

Dev felt a sound rise out of his chest and vibrate up his throat. As whatever the fuck it was breached his lips, he was very sure he'd never heard anything like it come out of him before.

"Oh, I'm feeling something," he muttered.

Stretching her leg up, he urged the other out to the side so her foot slipped off the sofa and landed on the nice wall-to-wall carpeting. As he went down, he reminded himself that good things come to those who wait—so he did what he could to linger with his lips on the inside of her thigh, only inching upward while every part of him just wanted to dive right in on her. Bringing his hands to the lace piping on the panties' top edge, he started to pull them—

With a smooth move, Lyric sat up and shoved the things down at the same time, yanking the undies under her ass.

He groaned as she lay back down, that shirt of hers still on her shoulders but fallen completely free of her breasts, her bra cups down by her sides, now her panties halfway to her knees.

And hey, he could help with that last one. He took them the rest of the way.

And then just stared at the glistening core of her.

There was absolutely no going back. He spread her wide and led with his tongue, licking upward—

As she cried out, her spine jacked up and her breasts splayed out, her nipples taut and beautiful as the flesh bounced. With her blond hair falling to the floor, and her lithe body undulating with sexual need, she was the single most compelling thing he'd ever seen—and then there was the knowledge that he had done this to her. She wanted . . . *him*.

The feeling was more than mutual, he thought as he went in her sex again.

She was hot and wet, and he made her wetter as he worshipped her exactly where she deserved to be treated so well. And he knew she was getting close to another orgasm by the way she panted and strained, her hands gripping the cushions under her, one of the throw pillows flipping off the arm of the couch.

He watched it all, looking over her belly, and between her breasts that moved to the beat of her rapid breaths. He couldn't see anything of her face. She had her head craned back, only the graceful rise of her chin showing, but her throat was as gorgeous as the rest of her.

Dev kept going, even after she came for him, right against his fucking face.

He loved the taste of her.

And the sounds she made.

Actually, he could do all of this for an eternity . . .

CHAPTER THIRTY-TWO

The aristocrat Whestmorel stood facing a wintery lake view, his back to the roaring fire in the hearth across his safe house's study, his feet in monogrammed slippers, a glass of bourbon in his hand. Courtesy of the darkened room, he could readily see out across the vista he had come to love. Though he was a city male at heart, and very fond of the things that urban living could provide such as good food, good company, and opportunities for acquisition and financial appreciation, there was something to be said for the seclusion and privacy of wilderness.

Especially when you were being hunted by the Black Dagger Brotherhood.

The floor-to-ceiling windows before him were coated on their exteriors so no one could see inside his Adirondack retreat, and the panes were also thick enough to withstand a bullet. Well, mostly thick enough. During the installation of this expanse of glass, the contractor had referred to things as "bullet-resistant," not "bulletproof," and one had to admit that the latter was in fact far more desirable. At the time, however, he had been more concerned with climate control for his bourbon collection than protecting his body from lead projectiles.

His ambitions had not been so clearly formed two years ago.

Lifting his rocks glass to his lips, he took a sip. The Pappy 25-Year was always a little oaky for him, but it was rare and it was an indulgence.

He liked indulgences.

This remote house on the shores of a lake where property values were very high and the head count of neighbors very low was another indulgence—although at its conception, the spec project had been a luxury meant for someone else. In the planning stages, the multi-layer, terraced stack, mounted on the side of a mountain, had been just another way to make money. However, as the site had been judiciously cleared to retain the tree canopy, and the shape of the home had started to come to fruition, he had begun to see a bit of himself in the construction.

And then very much of himself in its layout, flow, and especially, this view over the currently frozen water that stretched out as far as one could see to the south and the north.

In fact, a male with ambition could see the whole future from this spot—

A knock sounded at the door.

"Yes," he said without turning around. "What is it."

Conrahd Mainscowl the Elder entered. The male was like a sword in so many ways, tall, thin, and angular, with prematurely silver hair that was always precisely in place, and a wicked tongue that was sharp with wit and intelligence. He had proven to be quite an asset to the cause, although one did not fully trust him. In this work of treason, one should indeed take no single person fully into confidence—and that truism was especially apt with somebody as shrewd as Conrahd.

"I believe we may have a problem," came the announcement.

Conrahd strode over to the display of rare bottles on the teak bar and helped himself to a serving of Woodford Family Reserve. Which proved he had perfect manners: Having been invited to partake at his discretion, he nonetheless knew that to pour the Pappy would have been an overstep.

Whestmorel pivoted on his velvet slipper and went over to the twinning sofas by the hearth. Lowering himself into a sit on the herringbone cushions, he crossed his legs at the knee and pulled the edge of his satin robe over.

"You mean other than this interminable delay?" He propped his elbow on the Hermès blanket that had been folded over the arm.

"That cannot be helped."

"It can indeed, although that is another discussion." Whestmorel finished off the Pappy in his glass. "Do tell."

Conrahd came around and took a seat across the glass table with its display of crystal pinecones and leaves. "Thermon is proving a difficulty."

Whestmorel pictured the dark-haired aristocrat. Of all the allies he might have expected trouble from, the gentlemale was not on his list. Not like Conrahd was.

"What about him."

"He is considering breaking the sequestration."

Putting his glass on the Vuitton trunk that had been turned into a side table, Whestmorel arched a brow. "Is he now. For what reason."

"He will not say. But I caught him with a burner phone, and when I asked him what he was doing, he stated that there were family goings-on."

"Did you monitor his email."

"Yes. His *shellan* reached out to him."

"And has he contacted anybody else."

"No, only her, and he gave me the phone. Her number was the only one he called." Conrahd lifted his squat glass toward the windows. "And no, he spoke unto her out of doors, so we have no audio recording of the approximately eighteen-minute call. I did confirm via video monitoring where he stepped outside to converse with her. He went to the clearing with the view, and used the phone there. The trail cameras picked his movements up."

"When did this occur."

"Last evening."

Whestmorel looked to the flames, watching the oranges and yellows dance. Ironic, how something so beautiful could be so deadly.

"Why am I only finding this out the now."

"We had no reason to check the security feeds, as no alarms had sounded because we are permitted to go outside to smoke. His affect was off, however, and out of an abundance of caution, I decided to investigate."

Closing his lids briefly, Whestmorel kept his tone level. "Bring him to me, will you. That's a good lad."

Conrahd nodded at his bourbon. "May I please leave this here for a moment?"

"Please do."

"Thank you."

Whestmorel watched the male stand up and return to the doorway, his stride elegant and even, his hand-tailored dark suit fitting him perfectly, even as he walked.

"Conrahd." He waited as the male glanced back. "You have very good manners."

"And I do not break rules."

We shall see on that, Whestmorel thought as his newest right-hand male departed.

Poor Jenshen hadn't worked out, after all. And had had to be dealt with.

Getting to his feet, Whestmorel went over to the glossy black slab of granite that had been propped up on two curated, hardwood trunk slices. On his rustic desk were a laptop, three cell phones, a charging pad, and a Montblanc pen. Picking up the latter, he turned the torpedo over and over in his hands, admiring the workmanship, from the precise lines of the white star on the crown of the cap, to the gold bar of the pocket clip, to the absolutely smooth circumference of its body. He had many more down in Caldwell, but he'd had to leave them behind.

So much in that house of his he missed, although he reminded himself that his separation from the property was only temporary.

The Brotherhood would of course have taken possession by now. When he returned unto that mansion triumphant, however, he would reclaim it all.

And if they divested his collections? He would buy anew.

One could not afford to be sentimental in matters of material objects when one sought to rule by overthrowing a leader such as Wrath, son of Wrath, sire of Wrath.

Unscrewing the fountain pen's top, Whestmorel regarded the gold nib. The etching in the metal was so finely done, a reminder that discipline created beautiful things.

He looked up.

Conrahd led the way forth into the room, his suit jacket open, his hand sweeping down his red silk tie as if its unrest irritated him. Behind him, Thermon, in a navy blue blazer and gray flannel slacks, walked with his head down. But the male had never been stupid. That was why he had been chosen from the many who were otherwise qualified by virtue of their bloodlines, finances, and abilities.

"Ah, my friend," Whestmorel murmured as the pair entered. "Would you care for a drink."

"No, I would not." Thermon dipped his torso in a bow, revealing the other character value that had recommended him: There had always been a deference to character that bordered on the subservient. "But I thank you for the kindness."

And then they all just stood there.

There was no way there would be an invitation to sit. And the fact that Thermon didn't broach the subject of a chair was appropriate. Yet perhaps he had been a bad choice from the beginning, for all his apparent virtues.

Whestmorel smiled coldly. "There were certain expectations that were placed upon the members of this innermost consortium. When you all came here, unto my safe house, you agreed to the conditions prior to moving in."

"Forgive me." The male glanced up, his pale eyes worried. "There has been a . . . complication within my bloodline. I am simply trying to—"

"We all agreed that we were leaving our families behind." Whestmorel indicated Conrahd. "He has departed his *shellan* and young son. Why are you different?"

"I am not breaking our covenant—"

"You already have." Whestmorel walked over to the view. "You have potentially compromised all of us by—"

"I used a burner phone—"

"You were to have *no* phone," he snapped at the reflection of the male. Then he calmed himself. "And we all could make excuses or allowances for those we've left behind. But that was the temporary sacrifice we agreed to make, knowing that in our success, our families would vest once again."

An image of his "daughter" came to mind, the female who had been raised as his own, but who was in fact another male's. She had possessed beauty and intelligence, and he had permitted her a claim to his blood-line for a while. But she was not his, not really, and thus he had cut her out as this next phase began—and he felt nothing for her departure from his life.

One had to be clear about these things.

And clear about with whom one consorted.

"I saw no one," Thermon protested. "I communicated—"

"With your *shellan*."

"To whom I have been mated these many, many years." Thermon appeared exhausted with the line of questioning. "I have violated nothing, and if you wish to interrogate her—"

"You do not want me to do that."

The male's eyes widened. "Surely you would not harm a female."

"Surely you would not be so stupid as to procure a cell phone and call out from my property to a female who the Black Dagger Brother-hood could well be monitoring."

"They know naught of my involvement."

"And you have decided this based upon what information." Whest-morel put a hand up. "Do not waste my time answering that. We must assume we are compromised."

"Is there naught I can say in my defense?" Thermon looked over at Conrahd with entreaty and got absolutely nowhere in his search for a backup. "Shall you just send me out from here after I have been such a loyal supporter of yours for how long the now? Mine was our first dona-tion. I brought the others in."

"Only to violate the very rules that ensure our safety here. Again, I submit to you, how do you know the Brothers did not get to your mate?

You do not." Whestmorel narrowed his stare. "What, pray tell, was the subject of discussion."

"My son, he seeks to mate a female who has proven to be unworthy of him."

"Unworthy how."

"She has found herself pregnant." Thermon cleared his throat. "We understand that she went unto her needing, and demanded that he service her. Worse, it appears as if he is following through with the engagement we had previously approved of. My *shellan* sought my urgent help as they were going for the blessing from the King last night."

A wash of fury went through Whestmorel, but he banked the emotion. "And did they go unto Wrath?"

"Now do you understand why I called her—"

"*Did they see Wrath.*"

Thermon seemed shocked by the tone. Which suggested he was stupid, rather than merely malleable. "That was their plan, but I was counseling her as to how to stop them. You cannot seriously be worried they went unto the Audience House? The pair of them believe I am in the Old Country, as I often travel back to our ancestral estate there. There is no reason to worry they said anything."

When Whestmorel did not respond, the male threw up his hands. "Verily, you are paranoid—"

Whestmorel shot over to the male, moving so fast, there was a possibility he dematerialized for a second. Putting his face into Thermon's, he said, "I am trying to kill the great Blind King. Paranoia is a virtue when one is standing in my shoes."

As he eased back, Thermon released a defeated exhale. "So where does that leave us. Shall I go pack my bags—"

The male gasped and grabbed for his neck.

As a clicking sound registered between them and those eyes bulged with shock, the collar of the gentlemale's white shirt bloomed with bright red.

"Worry not," Whestmorel said levelly as he retracted the Montblanc's pen nib out of the male's jugular vein. "We shall pack and dispose of them for you."

Thermon slapped both hands over the wound in his neck, his blood pulsing through his fingers. He lasted only a moment longer on the vertical before he fell to his knees.

"Help me, will you?" Whestmorel inquired of Conrahd, who instantly approached. "No, not him. Let us roll up the edge of this carpeting so it does not stain. I am very fond of this weave and it was specially made for this room."

Whestmorel kicked Thermon's torso, which caused the male to fall back in a sprawl. "Come. The carpet, please."

He picked up Thermon's ankles and dragged him a couple of feet over to where the varnished oak flooring was exposed, and Conrahd was right upon the rug, the aristocrat promptly taking a corner and walking backwards, pulling half the expanse over until it was folded in on itself and well away from the growing red pool.

After which, he and his second-in-command just stood over the slowly writhing male, that navy blue cashmere blazer smudging everything to hell and gone on the varnished floor.

"How inconvenient," Whestmorel muttered.

Then again, neither of them had ever cleaned up so much as the condensation ring from a cocktail glass. This much blood?

Thankfully, he'd brought his most-trusted butler with him.

"What do you wish to do with the body?" Conrahd inquired.

"That is what the sun is for." Whestmorel knelt and grabbed the dying male's right hand. "In the meantime, you have other things to be concerned with."

"Worry not, I shall present you with what you require."

Grabbing the gold signet ring on Thermon's middle finger, he pulled the representation of lineage off quite readily. Thanks to the blood.

As he pocketed the heavy weight, he glared up at the other male. "Best you do that. For your own sake."

There was a pause. Then Conrahd, in his rather inscrutable way, bowed.

And took his leave.

CHAPTER THIRTY-THREE

In her one-bedroom apartment's living area, Lyric collapsed back against the sofa. Everything was spinning, and her entire body was flushed, and she couldn't tell whether she was back on planet Earth or still on a trip to the center of the universe. Lifting her head, she opened her lids—

The absolutely magnificent man between her legs swept a hand down his mouth and sat back on his heels. Dev's dark hair was mussed, his lips parted as he breathed hard, his eyes glowing with heat. Yet as their stares met, he didn't come closer or keep going.

"What about you," she asked in a husky voice.

To make her intention absolutely clear, she would have made a move on him, but her body weighed so much it had its own gravitational pull—which had evidently claimed the sofa. And whatever apartment was underneath them. Maybe the whole building and the entire city block the Commodore was on.

"Nah, I'm good . . ." Dev's voice was so deep and low, it was nearly inaudible. "Seeing you like this . . . is all I need."

"I'm not so sure about that." Her eyes drifted down to the enormous bulge in his jeans. "In fact . . . I think that's a lie."

Dropping his head, he seemed to battle for control, his hands curling into fists, the muscles of his arms flexing against the long sleeves of his pullover.

"I want you," she purred. "All of you—"

"You don't know what you're saying—"

"I've never been more sure of anything in my life." Lyric shook her head, and was able to speak with the kind of surety she hadn't had the night before. "I'm not looking past this moment. And neither should you."

"It's not that simple."

"So talk to me, Dev." She pulled her shirt together, and sat up. "Help me understand why it isn't."

"I have to go." He looked at the windows behind the couch like he was thinking about jumping out of them. "I just . . . have to go."

A shaft of pain penetrated her sternum, but she was not going to beg him. "Okay. So leave."

When he didn't move, she leaned forward so that they were face to face. "I don't know what's got you locked up, but whatever it is, it's on your side of things, not mine."

"I'm not looking for . . . this." Dev rubbed his hair, his palm sweeping back and forth like he was trying to polish the thoughts in his head. "This . . . cannot happen. Between you and me."

In the silence that followed, she became even more resolute. "Well, I'm not asking for more than right here and now."

"And that's my problem," he said harshly.

"What is."

"I'm afraid if I have you, I'll never be free of you."

As his words registered, she thought . . . *Well, hell.* For all the reasons he was right about them not having any kind of future, she was suddenly flushed at the idea that he could want her that much.

"You can always walk out the door afterward." She wanted to touch his face, but resisted. "You're free to go now, too."

"Just because you leave someone doesn't mean you can forget about them," he countered bitterly.

"Who hurt you, Dev. Tell me."

Instead of answering her, he got to his feet, and from his great height, he stared down at her for the longest time. She could sense the retreat in him, and wondered where in his mind he had gone. It was a dark place, wherever it was, given the stark lines of his expression.

"I want to go to that convention with you," he said grimly. "Unless you want to end this right here."

Lyric recoiled a little. Then again, he had a habit of surprising her, didn't he.

"All right." She cleared her throat. "Meet me at the loading dock of the convention center tomorrow night at six p.m. It's around in the back, and I've been told there's only one."

"I'll be there."

Dev nodded briskly, like that was that, and as he turned away, she was reminded of being out in the middle of Market Street the night before last, picking up his helmet.

This evening, she was not going after the man.

Staying where she was, she listened to him walk down to the door. There was a clicking sound and then the subtle creak as things were opened and closed behind him.

The deflation in the aftermath was real, and so was the chill that shot through her skin and into her bones. Except what did Mary always say? Don't take other people personally.

"Easy advice," she muttered. "Until you're sexually frustrated even after you've had three orgasms."

Or was it four.

Getting up, she went down to the exit he'd put to use and locked things up. Then she walked through to the bedroom, where she paused for a moment to mourn all the perfectly pressed sheets and pristine duvet. In the bathroom, she was somewhat surprised to find the toiletries she usually used at home stocked in the drawers and the shower, down to her brand of toothpaste.

There were even changes of clothes in her size, as well as underwear, and shoes, in the walk-in closet.

Fritz Perlmutter was *not* paid enough, no matter how much he earned.

The impulse for a shower turned out to be a good one. Standing under the spray, she closed her eyes and pulled herself together—and when she failed, at least she had clean hair and a rosy glow.

It wasn't until she was toweling off that she decided where to go, and after she dressed and blew out her hair, she returned to the sofa. The throw pillow that she'd shoved off the arm was hard to put back in place. In doing so, it was like she was erasing what had happened from her timeline.

Still, she was never again going to look at this couch without re-membering what had happened on it.

God, she hoped that wasn't true for all couches, everywhere.

Sitting down, but keeping her back stick straight, she settled her hands in her lap and closed her eyes. She wasn't exactly sure how this was supposed to work, or even if she would be granted an audience in the Sanctuary by Lassiter the fallen angel. Compared to all the things going on in the vampire world, her little corner of chaos was nothing. But you were supposed to be able to ask for spiritual guidance if you needed it, right?

Breathe in. Breathe out. Breathe in . . . breathe out . . .

Was it like dematerializing? she wondered. Or something else?

As the drift of the heating system crossed her face, she heard voices out in the hall and the *ding* of the elevator. Somewhere above, someone was playing music on a very good sound system, the thumps subtle but not muddled—

At first, she thought the spinning was an effect of the HVAC system blowing air, but then she realized it was actually her, even as she didn't shift her position—

❖   ❖   ❖

The next thing Lyric knew, the breeze on her forehead and cheeks dis-appeared and so did the sensations of the cushions beneath her and her bare feet on the carpeted floor. Abruptly, she felt like she was floating, but it was no float she'd ever felt before, her weightless body suspended on what surely was a molecular level in . . .

She opened her eyes and gasped.

Stretching out before her, a rolling green lawn rose to various Greco-Roman temples and structures, and in the distance, a shimmering pool glowed like an aquamarine jewel. Clutches of colorful tulips popped up here and there, like bouquets ready for picking, and at the horizon, a solid forest of trees was a friendly boundary, no shadows lurking anywhere.

She glanced over her shoulder with a sense of awe and wonder. A marble colonnade was beside her, and from its airy confines, she heard the chirping of songbirds and the tinkling fall of a fountain. There was also another temple, this time with a set of closed cathedral-like doors—and she had the sense that that building was quite large, even though she couldn't see how far back it went.

As she tilted her head up, the sky above was like nothing she had ever seen before, a dense, blue cover preventing her from seeing anything beyond it . . . except she had a feeling there was nothing to see there.

"Dearest . . . Lassiter," she whispered.

The Sanctuary was indeed on its own plane of existence, one that she recognized instinctually as being outside the reach of time and entropy, and as she stood on the hallowed ground, she knew without a doubt that the lore of the species was all true. Vampires had come to be when the *mahmen* of the race had exercised her single act of creation, and her brother, the Omega, had been so consumed by jealousy of the grace she'd been granted that he had resolved to kill her precious young. Thus the Lessening Society had come into being, and the war commenced.

And even though the Scribe Virgin was now gone and the Omega also eradicated, others had taken their places . . . and so it was all a direct line right up to what had happened last night, when her brother, the heir to the throne, and their best friend had been out behind an apartment building, fighting slayers in the midst of humans.

Proof that time was infinite for history. Mortals were the ones just passing through for brief periods, embers flaring only momentarily before going dark.

As she massaged the sad center of her chest, she glanced around at all the temples. She could see no people, sense no movement.

It was like a stage set for Claymation.

Annnnnnnnnnnd now what, she wondered—

At first, she thought she was hearing things. And then she realized she was. Off in the distance, there was some kind of music playing. Not a band, no. More like . . . a cheap, tinny speaker?

She waited around for a minute, then figured what the hell.

Taking a step forward, and another, and another—she had to stop. The weightlessness and the lack of any breeze whatsoever, coupled with the perfect seventy-degree temperature, made her feel like she was walking through bathwater. And you would have thought that was perfection.

Instead she felt carsick.

Forcing herself to keep going, she eventually got used to it, and all that Italian food stopped rolling around in her gut. The landscape's beauty helped. It was so bucolic, so peaceful, assuming you could get used to feeling like you were about to float off the undulating ground.

It was as she ascended a rise that the music became clear enough to decipher, and as she placed the beats and the lyrics, all she could think of was . . . yeah, wow, that was an oldie. And the only reason she knew what the song was was because—

Up on the plateau, two rainbow-striped plastic folding sun loungers had been set up side by side. Between them was a little table on which were an old-fashioned portable radio with the antenna angled out to the side, a pair of pineapples that, given the pink umbrellas, had tropical drinks in them, and a bowl of guacamole.

Madonna's "Like a Virgin" floated over on the non-breeze.

Lassiter, the fallen angel who had succeeded the Scribe Virgin as the spiritual head of the species, was stretched out on the chair on the left. His blond-and-black hair was up on the top of his head and tied in a pink scrunchie, and he was wearing a coordinated set of pink, yellow, and bright green Tommy Bahama swimming trunks.

Naturally, his sunglasses were twin pink flamingos whose cocked legs poked into the angel's cheeks as he smiled.

"Hi!" He indicated the vacant chair with the bag of Tostitos he was about to open. "Join me in a nosh?"

Lyric blinked. A couple of times. But here was the thing. The tension in her drifted off as she approached, all the chaos in her mind settling, the tightness in her shoulders and neck gone as if it had never been. She'd been expecting some kind of formal audience, with Lassiter in ceremonial robes—and, like, maybe an ancient tome tucked under his arm. This was . . .

Well, exactly what the male was like.

Lyric sat down as the angel popped the bag open, and as he tilted the Scoops! to her, she reached in for some and then went for the dip just to do something with her hands.

"So their standards are slipping." He took out a chip. "Does this look like a scoop to you?"

He turned the disk around, examining it from all angles. "This is flat. Maaaaybe slightly concave. If it says 'scoop' on the label, you expect scoops. All scoops. Not these Frisbee things thrown in every four or five of them. How'my going to guac this. Come on, Frito-Lay, do better."

Having no idea how to respond, Lyric eased what she'd filled into her mouth and bit down—"Mmmmm."

"Good, right? Should we add queso? I feel like we need queso."

With a pop and a curl of smoke, the table got bigger, and a bowl over a little tea light appeared.

"Perfect." The angel picked up his pineapple and took a draw from the straw. "Just fruit juice, mind you. I don't drink while driving, so to speak. And actually, that's a lie. I don't drink at all, I'm high on life. Cheers!"

Figuring in for a penny, in for a pound—or in for the chips-and-dip, in for a sip—Lyric palmed up the scratchy exterior of the one left for her and brought the straw to her lips.

"Oh . . . my God."

"Right?" Lassiter took his flamingos off and gave her a wink. "Only the best up here."

As the Madonna song switched to another pop-ish melody about walking like an Egyptian, she looked out over the lawn and wondered who tended to it. There didn't seem to be any lines associated with mowing—

"It is as it is."

She came back to attention. "I'm sorry?"

"The lawn. The flowers. The trees and the buildings. All of this is as it is. In this respect, the Sanctuary is like destiny. There is nothing to attend to because the immutable requires no gardening."

Lyric glanced down into her pineapple. "Then why do we have free will."

"To keep things interesting," Lassiter said with a smile. "And to give the illusion that people have some control over their nights and days. Otherwise they'd just give up and bed rot—not that that isn't appealing and appropriate from time to time."

"So is everything . . ."

"Meant to be?" The angel shrugged. "Does the answer to that really matter? It's not going to change your experiences."

"So . . . do you already know why I'm here?"

"I've been expecting you. But why don't you tell me what's going on."

As she stared into her own soul, Lyric shook her head. "I don't know why I came."

Okay, that wasn't true. She just couldn't seem to find the words for anything.

"Talk it out." Lassiter reached to the far side of his chair and brought up a reflective half circle. "It can be helpful to just hear our own voices sometimes."

Settling the shiny expanse across his bare chest, he eased back in the chair and closed his eyes, as if there were a sun to bathe under.

"G'on, then. Tell me what's on your mind."

Lyric stared out over the lawn that was so even in color and blade that it was like a carpet. Then she focused on the temple that was all closed up, the one that was just off the white colonnade where she'd heard the birds and the falling water.

"Is that the Temple of the Sequestered Scribes?"

"Yuppers. That's the one."

"I've heard there's also a library here, and the books on the shelves contain all the history of the species . . . every vampire soul and whatever they went through is listed on those pages."

"You've got it right. And the seeing bowls with their water levels are still at the transcribing stations that feed all of those pages."

"Why haven't you kept it up? Is it because the Primale freed the Chosen?"

Lassiter shrugged. "It's just not my style. Plus, there's another way."

"What other way?"

"It's a secret." With his eyes closed, he made a *shhhh!* with his fore-finger over his mouth. "But that's my business, as I'm in charge now and each one of us will do things in our own way."

"Each one . . . wait, how long do you think you'll stay here?"

"Until it's my time to turn this over to someone else."

A strange alarm struck in the center of her chest. "You're supposed to be permanent."

"Come on, girl." He popped his lids and looked at her. "There's noth-ing permanent in the universe, and even immortals have lives that pass. It's called eras. But you came here to talk about you, not my existential employment."

"I'm afraid I'm wasting my life," she blurted. "I was thinking maybe if I had a higher calling, something sacred to do, it might make me feel . . ."

"Like you matter?" The angel cracked a that's-cute half smile. "Come on. You have four parents who love you, a brother who would die to keep you safe, and more protective uncles than this place has tulips."

Okay, the part about Rhamp stung, it really did.

"But I need to do something that matters or all this is a waste." She motioned over herself. "I know I need to make a change, but I just can't see how to get out of this neutral. I've been running in circles having my picture taken, talking to strangers. Meanwhile, everybody else around me is doing something . . . that matters."

"So you've come up here, thinking I might put you to work in the library shuffling books around? Or maybe taking notes on other people? And you think that will make you feel better?"

"Is there something else I could help with? My *mahmen* contributed up here. I could follow in her footsteps."

Lassiter put aside his under-the-chin tanner and sat up. Now, when he looked at her, he was all business, the jokey-jokey gone, his eyes grave.

"To devote your life in service to this place is a great fantasy, but the reality is you're here to avoid confronting the things you need to deal with down below. A sacred duty is a calling, not something manufactured to hide behind when shit's not going your way."

Images of Dev played across her mind's eye—especially what he'd looked like as he'd walked out of the apartment. And then she pictured Marcia, barking out orders with phones up to her ears. The chaser? Rhamp down on the street, fighting off *lessers* while she watched from that roof.

Lyric lowered her head. "You're right. You're right, I know . . . you're right."

"Oh, my God, I love that movie!"

"I'm sorry?"

"*When Harry Met Sally.*" Lassiter slapped his bare knees as he grinned. "Carrie Fisher as Marie. It's a classic."

"Oh. I'll have to watch it sometime."

"It's a love story."

"Just what I'm looking to avoid at the moment," she muttered as she refocused on the scribing temple with its closed, ornate doors.

The angel reached out and took one of her hands. "If you want to live a different kind of life, then make it happen. Purpose is like clay, Lyric. Mold it with your choices and your efforts. Sculpt the hours and the nights and the months and the years you have . . . to create what you want. You have the strength and the determination. And listen, I gotta tell you—you are not someone who needs to record the lives of others. That's not who you are, and you know it."

"I'm so tired." Her voice cracked. "I'm so . . . lost. How am I this young, but feel so ancient."

"Well, you know how they say that every friend was once a stranger?" When she nodded, he continued, "The same is true for the new 'you' you're becoming. It takes work to develop any relationship and that's tiring. Once you get to know who you really are, though, you'll feel like all this confusion was just part of learning your landscape. You'll be glad you persevered."

"You sound so sure." She exhaled with defeat. Then realized, of all the people she could have said that to, he was the one person who was in a position to be clear about life advice.

"That's 'cuz I am." Lassiter leaned in and lowered his voice, like he was sharing a secret. "I'm like Farmers."

She blinked in confusion. "I'm sorry, what?"

"I know a thing or two . . . 'cuz I've seen a thing or two." He squeezed her hand. "Trust me, Lyric. You are going to do extraordinary things."

"How can you be sure," she murmured to herself.

"Do I have to prove it to you?" the angel said in an odd tone. "Well, then, I guess I gotta. Because your true purpose is coming for you, sooner than you think, and you're going to have to be ready."

Frowning, she sat forward on her lounger. "What do you mean—"

Lassiter rose to his full height, and the sheer presence of him was like the ringing of a gong, something that went through her with a vibration: No ceremonial robes, no great hall, no gaggle of sycophantic attendants. And yet the profound nature of the audience suddenly reso-nated through her and left waves of awe in its place.

His voice abruptly warped in her ear. "You're going to resolve to evolve. It's your destiny."

With that, the landscape began to rotate around her.

Or rather . . . she was the one set into a violent spin. And as she was sucked away, her last vision of the angel was one where his gossamer wings extended out over his shoulders and his hair was down and flowing, and his body was hung with gold.

The grim expression on his face terrified her.

It really did.

CHAPTER THIRTY-FOUR

Back in Caldwell, in the rural outskirts far from the city's gritty center, Qhuinn walked through the various security doors at the rear of the Audience House. When he got to the one with the little pinpricks in the ceiling—that were just like the teeny fuckers at the training center—he refused to look up. Goddamn Rhage. The queasy tension as he stood under them was worse now than before whatever the hell he had had a name.

Tinyholephobia. Or whatever the fuck the brother'd called it.

As the last door opened and he burst into the kitchen, all he smelled was fresh baked goods, and his stomach came to attention. He didn't know what it was, but he couldn't eat when he was out at Blay's parents' house anymore.

Ah, fuck that. He knew why. Food there made him think of his *mahmen*-in-law—

The instant his presence registered on the cooking staff, all kinds of *doggen* chefs turned to him.

"Sire, may we get you aught—"

"—may we do for you—"

"—anything, at all?"

Faced with such earnest pleading, he glanced over at some pastries that were fresh out of the oven and frosted to perfection.

"Actually, yeah, please." He nodded in their direction. "I'd like the whole nine yards, if it isn't too much trouble, but in the meantime, mind if I take one of those?"

"Oh, sire, indeed!" The silver platter of Danish was brought over to him like it was life support. "Take them all—"

"Just one, thanks." He picked a cherry—though he did have to admit the lemons looked very tempting. "I have to watch my girlish figure."

Over at the stove, a *doggen* already had a pan out. "Would you care for scrambled eggs and toast with bacon?"

"And coffee, of course," another one said by the industrial-sized pot.

"That all sounds perfect." He took a bite of the Danish and holy shit it was good. "I have to be in on a meeting in the—"

"We shall bring it to you directly!" A travel mug was put in his hand. "With just a little sugar."

Qhuinn glanced around at all of their hopeful, happy faces. "Thank you," he said roughly. "This is going to hit the spot."

They all but gave him a round of applause for gracing them with his presence, while the only thing he'd done was add to their duties. Amazing.

Shaking his head and munching along, he stepped into the vacant central core of the building. The fact that no one was in the lockdown area gave him the opportunity to pull his shit together. His work really *was* his salvation, and after a day spent staring at Blay as the male stared at the black-and-white picture on the baby monitor out in the family room, he was ready to think about anything other than when someone was going to die.

Well, treasonous plots aside, that was—

The panel that permitted access to the Audience Room opened and V stuck his head in. "You good to go?" the brother with the goatee asked in a quiet voice.

Qhuinn snapped to attention. "I'm not late." He jacked up his wrist and double-checked his watch. "I have two minutes—"

"Didn't say you were late." The brother exhaled a stream of smoke and immediately took another drag of his hand-rolled. "I asked if you're okay."

"Right as rain." He toasted V with his travel mug full of wakie-wakie. "Glad to be here."

"You sure about that? You're only on the schedule because you asked to be and—"

"I'm here"—he indicated himself with the mug—"so Blay doesn't feel as bad not being on the schedule himself, and anything that makes him feel less shitty is what I need to be doing right now."

V stepped to the side and held the door open, his diamond eyes grave. "You let me know if you need to pull out, true."

All he could do was nod at that. And the choked-up shit got worse as he went into the Audience Room. All of the Brotherhood was there, and the Band of Bastards had also squeezed into the space.

Every single eyeball trained in his direction as he entered, and fuck him very much, but they each knew him too well: Even though he took an exaggerated pull off the traveler, and swallowed the last of the cherry Danish in spite of the burn on his tongue, there was no hiding how fucking awful he felt.

No one else asked him how he was, however. Which was exactly what he needed.

No chinks in this armor tonight. Nope—

"Qhuinn," the King said from up at his armchair. "What's going on at your mate's parents'."

Ohhhh, great. But he wasn't about to duck a direct question from his King.

He had to clear his throat. "She's still with us."

That autocratic head nodded, the long black hair shifting over Wrath's shoulder as the male leaned down to stroke his dog's boxy blond head. "You'll keep us informed. Do any of you need anything?"

If that wasn't a loaded question, he didn't know what was—because the honest answer was, they needed the elder Lyric to pass, for her sake and for their own. When she did, there was going to be a new hell to get used to, but at least they would have the peace that came with her no longer trapped in that bed, wishing she could be doing the things she used to.

"No, thanks." He cleared his throat, and got nowhere with the lump in it. "Lyric's comfortable, and we're just waiting for the inevitable. Not much to be done."

"You sure you want to be here tonight?"

"Blay knows where to find me and wants me here. He's well aware of what's at stake because I've updated him on everything."

The guy had insisted on talking about Whestmorel as dawn had arrived, as a matter of fact. Helluva change in subject from what was going down with his *mahmen*, but hey. Beggars, choosers, and all that bullcrap.

"He's a male of worth," Wrath said. "And so are you."

There was a growl of approval that vibrated through the room, and Qhuinn resolutely stared at the travel mug until that passed.

As things quieted, Wrath nodded again, with obvious respect. Then he looked in V's direction. "Now, you were saying."

The brother stabbed out his cigarette on the tread of his shitkicker and put the butt in his back pocket. "Nothing. The 'George' lead went nowhere—and if Allhan can't find anything on it, no one can."

"And nobody's come forward with a missing *hellren*, sire, or son."

"No."

"Sonofabitch." The smile that stretched the King's hard mouth was cold as the wind that prowled around outside. "My guess is that Whestmorel and his crew are sequestering, and they've told their families to wait it out—which is why there is no report of a missing male. That poor bastard we found fucked up somehow, so they couldn't take him with them to whatever safe house they're in because they no longer trusted him, and they sure as fuck couldn't let him go. They left him alive in there to send a message to any others who might have doubts—"

The knocking that interrupted things was loud and insistent, and everybody had the same reaction. Guns were unholstered, unsafety'd, and brought up to be trained on the door that opened out into the civilian corridor—while at the same moment, Qhuinn, Rhage, and Phury closed ranks around Wrath to form a shield with their bodies. Meanwhile, as the King bent down and picked up his golden, the rest of the Brotherhood and the Band of Bastards formed a second circle, an outer rim of aggression, between the ruler and the door.

With the defensive positions set, Vishous checked the security feeds on his phone, his brows drawing tightly together and distorting the tattoos at the corner of his eye. "What the hell—"

Pounding now, on the door. "Hello! Help!"

Per protocol, the trapdoor beneath Wrath's chair sprung. As the lowering began, Qhuinn and the other two stepped in tighter on the descending platform.

"Help! We need help!" came the muffled cry on the far side.

◆   ◆   ◆

The next thing Lyric knew, she was back in her physical form, and the first sensation that properly registered—beyond the fact that she had weight on her bones again and pressure on her feet—was the cold. The bitter, biting cold.

She rubbed her eyes and looked around in confusion. She was outside in the snow, standing in front of an enormous, double-sided barn door, and for a moment, she couldn't place where—

The left half of the panels opened and someone all but ran her over as they burst out in a full-on bolt.

"Hey!" she barked as she got spun around.

The male, who was only in a t-shirt and blue jeans, just kept going, gunning for the back of the—

Audience House. She was at the Audience House, and standing in front of Four Toys Headquarters, the seat of all the security monitoring and IT—

Shouting voices from inside urged her up to the open doorway, and she frowned as she looked inside. The workstations laden with computer monitors and equipment were all vacated, people having jumped up out of their chairs or knocked them over as they clambered for something deeper inside the building.

Lyric hesitated on the threshold, intimidated by all the important work that was done here. Vishous was in charge of the security and monitoring of the King, the Brotherhood, and all their properties, but also so much more. This was definitely not her place to hang around—

One of her feet stretched forward without her willing it to do so, and the other followed right behind. The next thing she knew she was walking down the center aisle between all the desks, wondering what in the hell she was doing here—

Abruptly, her body cut through the lineup and zeroed in on the far corner. That was when she saw the drama. There was a group of males and females clustered around something on the floor, all the way against the barn's rear wall—

A scent in the air speared into her nose. And then her brain made the kinds of connections that scared her into a scramble.

Allhan. The transition had finally hit him.

"Let me do it!" she called out. "I carry the blood of a Chosen in my veins! I will feed him!"

As she skidded to a halt, faces lifted and stared at her in shock and wonder. On the other side of them, Allhan was sprawled on the floor under his desk, all the color drained out of his face, his frail body contorted in pain. His eyes were bloodshot and wild as they rolled around, his hands curled up so that as he dragged them over the floorboards, the scratching sound competed with his heaving breaths.

"Move!" she barked.

Without hesitation, she grabbed the shoulder of the nearest person and all but threw him out of her way. The others broke apart in response, and she fell down beside the male whose transition had hit him like a freight train.

Scoring her wrist, she put her face into his own. "Drink. Now—"

As her blood welled and started to drip on his vintage Prince concert t-shirt, his stare swung around to her, and there was a sudden fear in his eyes. "No—"

"*Yes.*" Tears made her vision wavy. "You will drink now—"

"No," he said in a hoarse voice. "I can't do that to you—"

"If you want to live, you will take my vein—"

Twisted by a fresh spasm of pain, he writhed on the floor, his leg kicking out, one arm knocking into the footing of the desk with a horrible, cracking impact.

"No," he moaned as he turned his face away from her wrist. "Can't do that to you—"

With her other hand, she moved him back to her. "For me, then." She stared into his eyes. "Do it *for* me, Allhan."

In the periphery, she was vaguely aware that other people had rushed up on them, but again, she ignored all that.

"Allhan," she said urgently. "I want you to drink for me. Do this, take my vein—I am begging you, do this for me."

His myopic stare locked on her own.

"Yes, Allhan. *Please.*"

This time, when she brought her wrist to his mouth, a single drop of blood landed on his lower lip, glistening and vitally red, and she watched as it slipped into his mouth—

The groan of hunger that came out of him rose up to the rafters. And then he lifted his head—

The seal was sloppy. At first.

But as he started to take draws, it improved, the suction set properly. Shoving her other arm under his head, she shifted him into her lap. As her hair fell forward, she impatiently tried to get it out of her face—

A hand in a black glove drew the weight back and held the blond waves out of the way.

Looking over, she recoiled at who was next to them.

The Brother Vishous was kneeling beside her, his diamond eyes with the navy blue rims staring at her with an expression she had never seen before. And behind him, looming tall and strong, was her father Qhuinn, whose lips were moving.

Even though her hearing wasn't working right, she knew her sire was speaking to her, encouraging her.

Praising her.

She glanced back down at Allhan. He was breathing harder now, his nostrils flaring, as a flush bloomed in his face. His body was still moving with restless abandon, but she witnessed the strength come to him—

With a hoarse exhale, he cried out in fresh pain and twisted on the floor, his limbs straightening all at once, his fingers splaying. As he jerked and spasmed, she locked a hold on his head and pushed her wrist against his lips to keep them in place.

"Don't stop," she said. Then more loudly, "Allhan, you have to drink, no matter what happens. It's too soon for you to stop—"

He did as he was told, and she prayed she was right. She was just remembering what it had been like for her several years ago, the racking agony, the gnawing, horrible hunger, the sense that she was surely going to die. And oh, God, she knew what was coming next, and it was terrible.

"Drink, drink, drink . . ." She repeated the entreaty over and over again as minutes passed.

The first of the bones breaking occurred in his right leg, the snap of his femur loud in the tense silence. As curses from the assembled rippled through the beats between the male's tortured breaths, his sneaker changed position on the floor—and not because he'd straightened his knee any farther.

The growth was starting.

"We have to get his jeans off or his skin will tear," someone said.

Vishous. It was Vishous.

"Everybody down to the break room," he continued. "Monitor protocol on laptops and phones. *Now!*"

The males and females who worked at the facility immediately dispersed, and she was aware of Fritz coming in with blankets and pillows, juice and bread.

The latter were for her. If she needed to eat something.

With her father's help, Allhan was repositioned out from under the desk, and his clothes removed, a blanket laid over him for modesty's sake. Meanwhile, pillows were wedged under her arm to help support her—

The next broken bone was the other femur, and then his shoulder popped out of alignment.

Allhan screamed at that point, and she had to squeeze her eyes closed.

What if my blood isn't strong enough, was all she could think of.

CHAPTER THIRTY-FIVE

Exactly what the hell time was it, Qhuinn wondered, hours later.

As he emerged from the break room's stairwell and stepped out on the main floor of V's facility, he had a coffee in his hand and a—oh, look, it was another Danish. He'd had no idea what he'd ended up taking out of the display of food down there, but evidently, his subconscious had been front and center enough to remember that the cherry from earlier last evening had been fucking amazing.

He shoved the pastry into his mouth and sipped on the mug as he glanced out at the empty workstations. The place had been totally vacated about an hour ago, everybody except the Brotherhood—who remained downstairs—sent home for the day through the escape tunnel to keep things quiet. And now? The silence was interrupted only by random beeps and whirs from all the unmanned computers.

Refocusing on what mattered, he stared at the tableau next to Allhan's desk. The male was under a mismatch of blankets, his body four times the size it had been, his face drawn in new lines that were pretty fucking handsome as it turned out. The best news, though, was that the kid was breathing, and a lot of his pain was in the rear view.

Right by his head, as she had been all night, Lyric was practically asleep on her proverbial feet. But her eyes, though they were half-mast, did not leave the male she had so heroically helped.

He was alive only because of her.

Qhuinn still couldn't believe how it had all gone down, the knocking that had interrupted the meeting with the King, everybody pulling guns on the IT specialist who'd rushed over on foot, a stammering, fucked-up mess as he'd said the same name over and over again.

Allhan.

No one had seen Vishous run that fast, and for once, the brother hadn't been texting out various commands on his phone for whatever he needed. Too frantic. As the Brotherhood had piled into the barn, V had crashed through the workstations, knocking over monitors on his way.

And then Qhuinn had done a little OMGing of his own.

The last thing he'd expected was to find his daughter on her knees, her wrist scored, her voice so commanding as she ordered Allhan to take her vein.

She had taken control of the dire situation all on her own, and as Vishous had stared down at her in utter, dumbfounded shock, Qhuinn had felt an echo of that himself. There were a lot of things that he associated with Lyric. Kindness, elegance, beauty, warmth, loyalty.

But assertiveness was just not something intrinsic to her nature.

Coming back to the present, he glanced at V, who hadn't moved from the young male, either. In spite of the stress, the brother had not smoked even one cigarette since the change started. Though vampires did not get cancer, Allhan's new lungs needed a little time to fully mature.

So it was either nicotine withdrawal or all the adrenaline ebbing off that was making those normally steady hands shake so badly.

Doc Jane had come by the second things had gotten rolling, to check vitals and worry over Allhan. She was momentarily back at the clinic now to pick up some pain meds. It was tricky, though. Too much and you could slow respiration, she'd said. Sometimes, suffering just had to be borne—

"When will he be out of the woods?" Lyric asked in a rough voice.

Qhuinn opened his mouth to answer, but V got there first—as he should have. The brother was not only a medic, he was, for all intents and purposes, the abandoned male's father.

"We're getting there." V passed his gloved hand down his face, then smoothed his goatee. "You saved his life."

"Oh, I don't know about that—"

"I do." V offered his dagger hand. "I owe you, true."

Lyric stared down at the palm that was in front of her as if she'd never seen one before. "Oh, you don't have to—"

"I owe you a debt for saving his life. Period."

Tentatively reaching out, she shook his hand. "That's really not necessary."

As was his way, her uncle V didn't argue with her—but not because he wasn't into confrontation. The fucker loved conflict. No, he'd stated his point and that was that. Lyric's opinion on the matter was irrelevant.

When she looked up Qhuinn's way, as if she couldn't believe what was happening, he smiled as his chest swelled. There were few greater things in life than when your kid impressed someone important. It made you feel like you hadn't fucked them up, after all. And also that you had done a very, very good thing in bringing them into the world.

Qhuinn went over and knelt down next to her. Glancing at the raw wound on her wrist, he felt a spike of concern. "Do you need anything?"

Smothering a yawn, she shook her head. "No, thank you. I'm just a little tired."

"You should go crash," V said. "You need a rest—"

"I'm not leaving," she shot back, "until he stands up on his own and walks out of here."

As V chuckled with respect, Qhuinn had to ask: "How did you know? To come here when you did?"

Her blue and her green irises, identical to his own, shifted away, and she hesitated.

"I, ah . . . I'd come to apologize, actually." Lyric cleared her throat. "The night that billboard fell, he'd come to visit me at Bathe. He was very sweet to do that—but this woman who I'd hired was rude to him and he left in a hurry. I chased after him, right into the middle of Market Street, where I . . . well, you know what happened. So, yes, I came here because I wanted to thank him and make that apology happen—"

"Not . . . necessary . . ."

They all focused on Allhan. The male had come around and was staring at Lyric. "It's . . . all right."

Qhuinn watched as his daughter leaned down and stroked some of the dark hair off the male's sweated brow.

"No, it's not." Her smile was gentle. "But something tells me, nobody's ever writing you off again. I can't wait to see what you think of your new body."

"For . . . truth?"

Lyric nodded and took his hand. "I think you're going to like what you see, my friend. I really do."

"Thank you . . ."

"You'd have done the same for me. In a heartbeat."

As the two continued to talk softly, Qhuinn looked over at V. The brother glanced up at the same time, and as their eyes met, it was weird. They'd bonded a lot over the years, what with the fighting and the stress and the camaraderie that just happened among the members of the Brotherhood.

The sudden connection that linked them now, though, was something different.

His kid had been good to V's, and that was an even deeper level, wasn't it.

◆   ◆   ◆

From Shuli's recline in his own bed, he put his hand out to his side table and picked up his vintage rose-gold AP Royal Oak. As he looked at the dial, he groaned.

"What's the matter," L.W. said next to him. "Not drunk enough to sleep?"

He glanced across his mountain of pillows. The heir to the throne was stretched out next to him on the enormous king-sized mattress. The pair of them had been propped against his headboard and watching movies since they'd decided to pair up and commit their own kind of treason.

Nothing like some felony-level insurrection to bring two guys closer.

The current viewing selection—the old-school, evergreen favorite *Aliens*—was playing quietly, Sigourney Weaver locking into a giant cargo mover that was like a transformer suit.

"You still awake, too, sunshine?" He pushed himself up a little higher. "I could have sworn you were snoring—or was that just your trademark dark, brooding menace escaping out of your nose instead of every pore."

"Oh, fuck off," the male said with exhaustion.

The good news? Sleep or no sleep, they were both on the mend. One of the many advantages for vampires over humans was the healing. If they'd been among those rats without tails, they'd have been hung up recovering from their wounds for weeks.

Instead, they could probably go out into the field as they were. It wouldn't be smart, but—

"We're going to have to bring someone else in on this." Shuli went back to looking at the TV, which dropped down out of the ceiling. "And shut up. We can't go this alone, and you know it. We need one more person."

When there was no reply, he rolled his eyes, figuring His Royal High Horse had devolved into his characteristic *grrrrrr*. Except Shuli knew he was right. He was going to require some help in the field, especially if L.W.'s vision problems were worse than the guy was saying.

Or worse than he thought—

"Okay."

Slowly turning his head again, Shuli cocked a brow. "I'm sorry— I didn't hear you."

The guy shrugged and glared at the TV.

Shuli cupped his ear. "Hello?"

"Fineyoureright. Now fuck off."

He chuckled and took a long, deep, satisfying stretch. "You know something, I don't want to get kinky, but goddamn, that's a real turn-on. You can whisper that in my ear anytime you want."

"You are so fucking weird."

"I'm good with that, too." He got serious. "It can't be Nate, though. He's mated. I trust him with my life, but he has too much to lose now."

There was only a heartbeat of silence:

"Rhamp."

"Rhamp."

Like there was any kind of question?

Shuli went for his phone to hit the guy up—and found that all kinds of texts had come in on all kinds of group chats. His heart dropped. Lots of notifications were never a good thing. Opening things up, he—

The scrolling was fast. The impact was a punch in the gut.

Lyric . . . had fed Allhan and seen him through his change.

"What is it?" L.W. demanded.

"Ah, nothing." He tried to focus on the little screen. "Nothing—hey, Allhan's through his transition safely. Good news, right?"

"Obviously," L.W. said on a dry note. Then, with suspicion, "You okay over there?"

"Oh, yeah. I like the guy. Really glad Lyric could help him out. I mean, her blood's so pure, and all. Would have been my choice—for him. For Allhan. To be given the best chance. So, yup. Rhamp."

Right. What was the question—

He all-thumb'd his way through a text to the guy and then put the phone facedown between him and his partner in crime.

Immediately, he picked the thing back up. "You hungry?"

He didn't wait for an affirmative, just started texting Willhis. One thing he did like about His Royal Disapproval was that the guy would eat anything. French fries. French cuisine. Sushi. Italian. Whatever was good.

"Yeah. Whatever you like."

Bingo, Shuli thought as he kept going with the order. Just because it gave him something, anything, to focus on.

When he got a text back, he reported, "Rhamp's coming over now."

When he got a grunt in return, he let that stand, and tried not to think about Lyric and Allhan and feeding and . . . everything. That went nowhere—big surprise—so he reached into the bedstand's drawer and took out a hand-rolled red smoke. He had to futz around some more for his gold lighter, and when he finally got the thing, he kicked up a little flame and—

"You got two of those?" L.W. asked.

He passed the lit roll over and got another for himself. "There's an ashtray in the drawer on your side, too."

The knock on the door came as L.W. was fishing around in the side table next to him, the cursing something you could have added a beat to and thrown on Spotify.

"Come in!" Shuli called out around the f-bombs. "And for crissakes, use mine. God, what are you, blind—"

As L.W. shot a glare his way, he exhaled a stream of red smoke. "Shit, sorry. I didn't mean—"

"That's *not* funny—"

"You think I don't know that, asshole—"

Over at the door, Rhamp walked in wearing head-to-toe Adidas because clearly, he was feeling some bumps and bruises from the night before, too. With a Dos Equis in one hand and some kind of egg roll in the other, he looked like was at the frat version of a cocktail party.

He stopped as soon as he was across the threshold. "Well. Ain't this cozy."

"Close the door behind you." Shuli motioned. "And we're about to eat. You want some?"

The guy lifted up his beer. "Willhis got me on the way in, but yeah, I'm good for more food." That shrewd stare narrowed. "Wait a minute, what's going on. The last time I saw you guys shoulder to shoulder was never."

"Shut the door," L.W. commanded. "We gotta talk to you."

Rhamp looked at the heir to the throne. Looked back at Shuli.

Then he took three steps backwards and elbowed things closed. In a low, even voice, he said, "So it's like that, is it."

"You're going to want to sit down for this," Shuli murmured as he indicated the end of the bed with his hand-rolled. "And it goes without saying that this is not for anybody else's ears."

"Great," Rhamp muttered as he took a swig of his beer. "More fun with the two of you is *just* what I'm looking for."

CHAPTER THIRTY-SIX

The following evening, when Dev arrived at the Caldwell Convention Center, he was running on no sleep, but was as hyper-aware as someone behind the wheel of an Audi on auto-launch. Standing outside the front of the glass and steel building that spanned two whole city blocks, he stared at the computerized banner that arched across the entrances before him.

Resolve2Evolve. A New You on Your Terms.

The title and tagline were followed by the dates and times of each of the three days of sessions.

And then off to the right, taking up an entire quarter of the expanse, was the picture of a dark-haired woman who was beautiful as a model, but who had grave eyes that suggested an old soul with weighty knowledge to share.

Staring at the image, he felt an elemental response, deep in his bones, and goddamn it, he wanted to know why—*why*—this was all happening now—

An image of Lyric came to mind, and he thought about the social media bullshit she'd quit because she hadn't wanted to be just a facade. She'd wanted . . . reality. Not some created illusion sold to other people as something it wasn't.

Dev reached up and touched his own face, feeling the smooth cheek and jaw he'd shaved just a half hour ago.

Masks, whether worn casually, with intention, or as a defense, were a lie that was lived. And if you did it for too long? You forgot who the fuck you were.

Even if that had been your point, all along—

Dev was knocked into by someone bumping his left arm.

"Oh! Sorry!" A bubbly young woman dressed entirely in purple smiled at him. "My fault!"

As she kept going, she was one of what had to be hundreds of just-like-her: All around him, women were streaming into the banks of glass doors, in groups, by themselves, in pairs. A lot of them were in various shades of purple, and some had even dyed their hair along the grape spectrum.

Falling into the flow—as one helluva this-thing-is-not-like-the-others—he eventually found himself in an open-air lobby that was so large, it had horizons, the brightly lit concession stands on either end like rising suns. Escalators went up and down to a second story, and there were bathrooms every ten yards, it seemed. Filling the space were long lines before all kinds of tables, purple branded tote bags being given to women who were presenting IDs and tickets on their electronic wallets.

The din of female voices was like being in an echo chamber of birds.

With his head already starting to pound, he hit the nearest escalator and rode up to the second level along with a lineup of buzzing, chattering, fizzy women.

Getting off along with them, he hung back as the stream of attendees zeroed in on sets of double doors that opened into a ballroom-sized event space congested with hundreds of ten-top circular tables. Standing like sentries to a temple, staffers in purple logo'd shirts checked phones for etickets, and then ushered people in.

The brunette woman's face and the R2E logo were everywhere, all around, on banners than hung from the steel rafters, and step and repeats for photo ops, and signage on every flat surface and all the load-bearing concrete pylons in between.

Heading over to the entries to the event, Dev stared across the sea of tables to the stage down at the far end. Purple walls, purple draping, and screens reflecting all that purple, which would soon magnify the speaker's face.

Like anybody might have forgotten the damn thing.

"I do not want to be here," he muttered.

A woman popped in front of him and grabbed his forearm with the zeal of an acolyte. "Oh, the tenets apply to all of us, men included. You're more than welcome!"

Then she wrapped a purple boa around his neck and kept right on going.

Had he really thought he could avoid this forever, Dev thought as he ditched the feathers.

No, he'd just been hoping he could. But ever since that billboard had caught that freakish wind, this collision course he'd been determined to dodge had been locked and loaded. And if not for Lyric?

He wouldn't fucking be here at all.

It was only by keeping the memory of her front and center in his mind that he was able to continue. But he didn't go into the ballroom. He skirted the event space altogether, and went around the corner.

There were a couple of cops—live ones, not the robots—blocking the head of a corridor that paralleled the lateral wall of the ballroom to a fire door with a red glowing EXIT sign over it. Halfway down, a group of people, not in purple but in professional suits and slacks, were clustered around a doorway that was attended by another pair of cops.

The steel panel under that red sign opened.

And there she was.

The face of Resolve2Evolve, the focus of all the attention . . . the reason everybody had come to this convention center, was in the house.

Except it was all a lie. That was no woman.

That wasn't even a human.

It was a demon who had convinced all these women that she was not only one of them, but a messenger of their emotional and mental health—and as she stepped out under the galaxy of the ceiling lights far, far above her, he had to admit she glowed.

She was even more beautiful than in the pictures, downright resplendent in the flesh, that long dark hair curling naturally and bouncing with shine, that visage full of health and possessing one-in-a-million perfect features, that body wrapped in a purple dress that accentuated the hips, waist, and bust that needed no help whatsoever.

He could practically smell the Poison by Dior from here.

Valentina Disserte—the name she was going by now, no longer the Devina she'd once been—was talking to the people who were coming in behind her, and as she strode forward in high heels, the marching band of advisers who accompanied her were clearly going to merge with the ones who were already in place and waiting. Meanwhile, her red lips smiled easily as she spoke, and her eyes slanted this way and that, managing to be both authoritative and flirtatious. Motioning with her hands, her red-tipped fingers splayed and closed, to emphasize whatever points she was making.

No jewelry. No watch. No phone, no handbag, no car keys.

He had to guess that the people around her were her living, breathing purse—

All at once, she stopped, and as she halted, she put her palm up to silence her entourage. In the beats that followed, everything around her went absolutely statue, sure as if she were the breath and the heartbeat of an organism.

That perfectly beautiful face turned and those dark, flashing eyes looked down the hall.

Toward him.

Ah, but he kept himself hidden from the demon, as he had been doing for how long now? And as she searched for him, he thought of Lyric.

He did not want to be here. But he was not leaving.

"Hello, Mother," he said softly.

✦   ✦   ✦

When Lyric materialized in the shadows next to the Caldwell Convention Center's loading dock, she felt scattered. Everyone had assured her Allhan was way out of the woods, but she just couldn't seem to shake off the stages of his transition, the violence of it, the pain. He did seem stable, though, and when she'd finally said goodbye to him after they'd moved him down to a bedroom suite, she'd told herself his destiny was in someone else's hands now.

Other than her own.

But she had done something important. Something that had changed the lives of everybody around her. If Allhan had died, Vishous and Jane would have never been the same, and if they had been taken by that tragedy, the entire Brotherhood, and all the fighters, and all the mates, would have likewise suffered.

One life, but so many ripples, the connections transferred from person to person, invisible strings that were stronger than any rope.

And she had saved them all.

As a renewed flush of feeling went through her, the warmth wasn't arrogance. She wasn't proud of herself, or mistaken that she was in some way Lassiter's existential mini-me. But she was grateful, especially to that angel.

He had indeed given her an opportunity to prove what he'd said about her.

"And now, I am here," she said into the cold night.

Exhaling, her breath drifted off over her shoulder as she smoothed her hair. She'd taken a super-hot shower at home, and changed into black satin pencil slacks and a borrowed black leather top that had a deep V for a neckline and straight shoulderless sleeves. As she started for the door she was supposed to enter, she was able to walk under a shallow roof, sparing her thigh-high boots the icy assault that had killed her Louboutins.

Then she waited.

As the frigid air seeped into her, she fiddled with the low neckline of the top. And then pulled the right sleeve down farther. The bite wound on her wrist had healed a lot, but there was still a red orbit around the faded twin punctures. To make sure no one noticed, she'd covered everything up with the foundation she used on her face—

A car entered the rear lot, the headlights swinging around. The way it parked grille in, three feet from the entry—despite the fact that there was no designated space there—instantly told her it was Marcia, even if she hadn't recognized the Audi.

The woman got out with her two cell phones going, yet another variation on her black-suited uniform making an appearance.

But the soon-to-be ex-manager was not the priority.

Lyric took out her cell phone to check the screen. Then she glanced around. Rechecked the screen—

"Well. Look at you."

Lyric jerked her head up. Marcia had ended the calls and was standing right in front of her.

"Are you sure you want out of this business?" The woman motioned with the phones, up and down. "Because this is another level."

Lyric looked over Marcia's head into the parking lot. Which was stupid. Like a human could just materialize out of thin air? Dev would come in a car or on foot. And she'd confirmed there was, in fact, only one loading dock.

She cleared her throat. "Have you—ah, have you seen anybody around here?"

Marcia's head set on a swivel. "Who are we looking for?"

"Ah, no one." She glanced down at her phone again. "Really, it's fine."

"Let's do this then." Marcia went over and rapped on the dented metal door impatiently. "I just called Valentina's personal assistant. She should be here in a sec."

There was no handle to pump or knob to turn, and that was probably a good thing. As Marcia all but jogged in place from frustration, she was liable to break off anything that—

The panel swung wide, and a harried woman in a bright purple R2E shirt motioned for them to come in. With a walkie-talking in one hand and a lanyard with a laminated ID around her neck, she was clearly deep in the nuts and bolts of the conference.

As Marcia stepped up with the demands, Lyric glanced over her shoulder. And then had no choice but to enter an industrial hallway that had a concrete floor and all kinds of exposed ductwork and pipes.

"Oh, wow," the woman said to Lyric as that steel door slammed shut. "You look amazing. And hi, I'm Jenny."

"Hi, Jenny, *doesn't* she just shine?" Marcia pulled an old school Vanna White as her affect of emphasizing words came back with a *vengeance*. "She's an *absolute* star."

"She is! I'm so happy to meet you, and thanks for coming. Valentina is really excited you're here."

Lyric shook the hand that was extended, but her attention was on the closed door. She kept thinking she was going to hear a knock or her phone was going to vibrate. But . . . nothing.

"I'm excited to be here," she said with a forced smile.

"Now, there's been a slight change in plan. Valentina really wanted to meet you beforehand for the footage with you, but we're going to need to get all that after the intro address? It won't take long and I'm sure you don't mind. An opportunity to hear her speak is a special thing. Great!"

Lyric opened her mouth. Shut it.

"I think that's a *fabulous* idea," Marcia chimed in. "We'd *love* to be included—up in the *front* row, of course."

"Of course! We'll just head this way," the staffer said as she set off to the left. Then she glanced back at Marcia. "She has quite the following."

"It's *so* hard to get *penetration* these days." Marcia shook her head gravely, like she was commenting on an asteroid heading for earth. "But Lyric's *engagement* is through the *roof*. You can have people with more followers, but *her* audience *engages*."

"Yes, we saw the statistics you sent over . . ."

Lyric followed the two down the corridor, letting them talk shop. She told herself her silence was because she had to be careful about foot placement—with the pinpoint heels of her boots, if she hit her stride wrong, she was going to land on her ass. But that was so not it.

So not it.

Jenny escorted them through a maze of high-ceilinged, roughed-in corridors, and every time they came up to a door, Lyric prayed they'd go through it and get on some carpeting. And all along the way, she turned her hand over and looked at her phone so many times the motion became a nervous tic.

"And here we are just outside the lobby." Jenny finally paused by a set of double doors. "Registration is wrapping up, although a few attendees remain in line. Still, I'd like us to go through here to get to the greenroom because it's a super long walk otherwise, and in those boots?"

When the rush of words stopped, Lyric just stood there—until Marcia elbowed her and she clicked back into place. "Oh, of course, this is fine."

"Wow." Jenny put her hand to her chest, tangling her fingers in the lanyard. "You are *so* easy to deal with."

As Marcia nodded with approval, the staffer opened the door, and—

The cacophony was incredible. So many voices, so much movement, so many perfumes and bath lotions, shampoos and hairsprays. The convention center's lobby was the size of a football field with sets of escalators that ran up to the second level, and holy crap, if this massive crowd was only "a few" of the attendees? How many people were—

"Five thousand," Jenny answered cheerfully. "And we're hosting them over all three days."

Okay, there was also a lot of purple, all different shades represented, and not only because of the branded convention bags that hung off shoulders: The clothes were purple, the hair was purple, there were people flashing purple tattoos of the R2E logo.

Jenny indicated to go forward. "This way—"

"Oh, my God, are you Lyric?"

"Wait, Lyric—of Lyrically Dressed!"

"—Lyric!"

"Holy shit, it's—"

Instantly, a tight knot of people formed around her, separating her from Jenny and Marcia, and that was just the start of it all. More flooded over, the cell phones coming out, someone jumping in for a selfie, camera phones blinking their flashes.

Maybe it was the blood loss from the night before, maybe it was the fact that she hadn't eaten much, maybe it was the strobing lights and her name being called, but things started spinning.

Lassiter? Calling her up for another chat?

If she heard more Madonna, she knew the answer to that—

As panic closed in and she frantically looked for Marcia, she saw nothing but a tidal wave of women dressed in purple. And then she got jostled, someone putting their arm around her waist and holding up a cell phone, another grabbing her arm and trying to pull her away. Meanwhile, more and more people were coming up, the bodies pressing into her, shoving her back against the wall, trapping her.

With a sickening dread, she felt like she couldn't breathe, and as anxiety swelled, she became convinced there was no escape, ever: Her mind just shattered into discordant thoughts, and she started to hyperventilate.

Except all of a sudden, from out of nowhere, a looming presence cut through the crowd, forcing its way through—

And there he was.

Dev was inexplicably coming toward her, his huge shoulders and bulked muscles cutting through the purple onslaught, his strong arms pushing people away until he was right in front of her, his face all that she could see.

"Sorry I'm late," he said levelly. "And don't worry about a thing, I've got you."

CHAPTER THIRTY-SEVEN

W e have one. I have gotten what you requested."

As Conrahd spoke the words, Whestmorel punched the stop button on his treadmill. Through his heavy respiration, he asked, "Where."

When the word came out hoarsely, he told himself the breathlessness was the running.

"In the caretaker's building. It is well in hand for whenever you want it."

Whestmorel grabbed a monogrammed towel and dismounted the machine. In the mirrors that surrounded the workout room, he dabbed at the perspiration on his face and checked his dark hair, making sure it still laid flat. He was also checking in with his reflection, to make sure this was not a dream.

"We go now," he ordered.

His exercise facility was above the safe house's garages, and after they proceeded to the end of the room, he sprung the lock to the exterior set of stairs with a code. The outdoor temperature was frigid, and the sweat on his skin beneath his Nike training togs froze upon his shoulders, chest, and arms. He cared not.

On the descent to the snowy ground, he was dogged by a sudden, ringing worry. Though he would talk to no one about this, he had always been trepidatious at the next stage of his plan. If things were dangerous with the King and the Black Dagger Brotherhood already involved, it was all going to get so much more intense.

As he brought Lash, the head of the Lessening Society, into the mix.

His heart rate did not slow down as they proceeded on a wooded path to the outbuilding. There were purposely no exterior lights to guide them, and infrared sensors were triggered all along the way, guards watching them from the security room in the safe house. Well-paid, ex-military human guards, whose loyalty could be trusted—up to a point: All they knew was that they were to shoot anybody who was not one of the males who were at the heart of the consortium.

And the butler, of course.

The men didn't know what was happening or who they worked for, and though Whestmorel had always disdained those rats without tails, the species divide was critical at this juncture.

On the approach, the outbuilding that was set into the rocky elevation had always been part of the site's master development, a space in which to house collectible boats and convertibles during the winter months.

Not what it was being used for tonight.

At the side door, he inputted another code, and he and Conrahd entered.

A blacked-out van was parked in the center of the open span, the banks of fluorescent lights on the ceiling raining down a peach-tinted light in the otherwise vacant, windowless interior.

"Where did they find it?" he queried as they continued forth.

"Downtown. Our scouts located the thing and secured it. Then they turned it over to our guards at the neutral location and they brought it on-site."

"And there were no questions asked?"

"With the money we're paying, the chain of custody is very, very secure. And to that point, its personal affects are bagged and in the passenger seat."

Whestmorel reached up to his sternum. The alert button that hung by a gold chain slid into his grip, though he did not trigger it.

"Open the doors," he commanded.

Conrahd stepped in and sprung the releases, the panels popping wide. That peachy illumination flowed in, but what was revealed was not the first registry upon the senses.

The smell.

Stench, was more like it.

Both he and Conrahd stumbled back on a recoil, the other male taking out his handkerchief and pressing the folds into his nose. The vicious stink was as if old, spoiled meat had been doused in baby powder, the sickly sweet combination spearing into the nose and contaminating the sinuses.

Whestmorel even tasted it in his mouth, and then down the back of his throat as he swallowed. But what foe would he be for the great Blind King if he could not withstand this proximity to the enemy?

Gathering himself, he forced his arms down and his mind to regulate. That was when the physical details sank in. The *lesser* was restrained and suspended from a rack that was bolted into the roof of the back compartment. With a black hood over its head and those chains at the ankles and the wrists and across the chest, there were no complaints about the presentation, and yet he still hesitated.

"Take the hood off," he commanded Conrahd.

There was a long pause. It wasn't until he glanced over with a glare that the male put the kerchief back inside his breast pocket and proceeded to awkwardly duck into the rear of the vehicle. At Whestmorel's request, they were alone, but now he was rethinking that, and not just because this historic moment perhaps should be witnessed by the others.

Clearing his throat, he rubbed his thumb over his alert button—

Eyes that gleamed with menace stared out at him. And the fact that there was no struggling, no cursing, no threats or even movement was somehow more threatening than any of the alternatives.

This was one deadly entity, Whestmorel concluded.

And then the physical details were a surprise: Dark hair that was long and unkempt. Irises were dark as well. Skin tone was Caucasian, but certainly not the pasty white he expected. Then again, a slayer who had been in the Lessening Society long enough for the paling to occur would probably be sufficiently trained and experienced not to get ambushed and kidnapped. On a side note, the clothes were stained and ratted, and not, he gathered, due to the abduction.

"Do you know what I am," he said to the thing.

The *lesser* sneered. "Yeah."

Whestmorel nodded. "I have a message to give your master. And you will be released as soon as I am confident it has been received."

The *lesser* frowned, as if that was the last thing it expected.

"You heard me correctly." Whestmorel glanced at Conrahd, who had expeditiously extracted himself out of the van. "You shall be but a messenger in my favor, nothing more—and once the communication has been delivered, you shall be freed unharmed. If the message is not received, and trust that we shall know, we will not hesitate to maim you such that you shall suffer in perpetuity, never being released by a stab through the heart."

As the brows lifted in surprise, Whestmorel flashed his fangs, a shot of aggression spurring on his sense of utter superiority.

"Or did you think we do not know how it all works," he drawled.

CHAPTER THIRTY-EIGHT

W e embrace who we truly are, and accept no other above ourselves."

As thousands of voices repeated the words in the purple-draped ballroom, Lyric looked around. She and Dev were seated up in the front, and she had to admit that, however much she had written off this whole convention, when you were in the room with Valentina Disserte addressing this adoring crowd . . .

There was a sense that the woman was making a difference.

Up on the dais, Valentina strode with grace and confidence, long, shapely legs terminating in black stilettoes covering the distance easily. "We understand that any piece of ourselves that we receive from someone else's praise can be taken from us."

The crowd repeated the words, and a few of them got to their feet—which led to a rush of women standing and putting their hands up.

"We further understand that any piece of ourselves that might be removed from us by someone else's criticism is rejected as unnecessary to our core being."

The Marco Polo aping continued, the words that were spoken trailing across the screens mounted all around the room, as well as the top of the purple backdrop of the main stage, the chorus repeating what the choir leader laid out.

"We take up the space we claim, and we stand alone, for we are our own foundation, and therefore all we build is owned by ourselves and no one else."

Even more people stood up. And more.

Until everyone in the event space was on their feet and leaning forward, eyes rapt on the stage, on the woman in purple.

Lyric glanced over at Dev. He was sitting back in his chair, having watched the whole thing with an absolute patience that impressed the hell out of her. She could only imagine what her brother or Shuli would be like in this situation, rolling their eyes or laughing under their breath in places.

Not Dev. He just stared at the woman and seemed to be listening to what she was saying.

Maybe the message would help the two of them. Somehow—

Oh, what the hell was she thinking with that. Truthfully, she hadn't been surprised when she'd arrived and he wasn't waiting for her around back. No, the surprise had been when he'd appeared at just the right moment.

Saving her again.

"—next three days, a journey of self-discovery and affirmation! Give yourselves a round of applause!"

As applause erupted, Lyric felt compelled to get to her feet and clap as well. Meanwhile, a convention photographer swooped in on the side and took a number of pictures, most of them looking up from a wide angle so that he could capture Valentina Disserte and the adoring audience in the one-shot.

So now what, Lyric wondered.

Off to the side, on the wings of the great room, Marcia was waiting with the rest of the event staff, no doubt mining the convention and the larger national tour schedule for opportunities with her other clients. This was actually a good thing—made it less of a waste of time for her.

When the photographer backed off, Lyric leaned down to Dev,

who'd remained in his chair. "Sorry about all this. I really did think it was going to be an in-and-out."

He shrugged, his eyes still on the stage. "It's okay. I'm here for the ride."

Just before she went to straighten, he turned to her—and their mouths came close together. As her breath caught, she stammered, "Ah . . . thanks. For understanding."

"S'all good—"

Jenny, the assistant, appeared by the table. "Come with me, you guys. We need to get you backstage before the crush after dismissal."

"Oh, sure." Lyric swept her hair over her shoulder. "Of course—"

Dev stood up, dropping his napkin next to the dessert plate he hadn't touched. She hadn't eaten anything that had been presented, either. But like they'd come here for the food?

"Let's go," Jenny said. "Quick, quick, quick."

As Valentina stepped out of sight with a final wave to the crowd, Jenny hurried things along the lineup of packed tables and then around the corner, to a split in the waterfall of purple bunting that was guarded by uniformed cops. The two men nodded and let Jenny lead the way into a backstage area filled with sound boards, even more staffers, and all kinds of cords, lighting equipment, and extra chairs. There was so much activity, people buzzing around and—

Marcia jumped in front of Lyric. "Wasn't she *wonderful!*" Then she looked at Dev. "Aren't *you* glad you decided to play *savior* in the middle of the *street?* Not everybody *gets* this kind of *access.*"

With her pitchy voice and jazz hands, the woman helped Jenny herd them over to a build-out that had a purple door set in the center of a lot of black felted panels. The sign that hung front and center read "Valentina," and another set of police officers were standing outside.

Jenny greeted the uniforms, and then the door was opening.

What wafted out was some kind of perfume with a grape-scented undertone. And then Lyric saw the woman herself across the gold and black reception room.

Okay . . . wow.

One thing that had become clear after a couple of years with the social media peddling set was that what you saw online wasn't necessarily what you got in person. Filters, plastic surgery, camera angles, and lighting made a huge difference. Except Valentina was even more resplendent in person. There was just an aura around the woman that made it seem as if she were in a spotlight that followed her—and what do you know, Lyric wasn't alone in the starstruck. A ring of adoring people surrounded Valentina, and the interesting thing was, she actually seemed to see them all. As opposed to most influencers, who tended to skate over others with their eyes and affect, R2E's leader seemed to truly connect—

The crowd abruptly parted and the woman of the hour looked over.

It was the oddest thing. A sudden stillness overtook Valentina's animation as she stared at Lyric and then Dev, her head slowly tilting to the side as she considered them—after which she seemed to snap out of whatever it was to come forward.

"Lyric, of Lyrically Dressed." The smile was broad and welcoming. And now she looked at Dev. "And . . . you know, I could swear I've seen you somewhere before."

"Oh, you *have*," Marcia chimed in. "From the *news*. He saved her life in the *middle* of Market Street the other night. Hi, I'm *Marcia*, Lyric's rep."

As the manager shoved out her hand, there was a perfunctory shake. Then again, the self-promotion was a little much.

Valentina smiled at Dev. "You saved her life. How noble of you."

Lyric glanced over at him. He was staring at Valentina, rather like she was an exotic bird at a zoo. He probably thought she was insanely beautiful—because hello, she was—and didn't that come with an unwarranted sting of jealousy.

"And you!" Valentina pivoted back to Lyric. "I am so sorry I couldn't meet you beforehand. My schedule is not my own. Thank you for coming backstage now."

"You are very inspirational." Lyric laughed in a short burst. "Okay, I suppose that's a stupid comment."

"It's not." The woman grew serious. "It's my goal, the reason I do everything, so I truly appreciate you saying that. All I want to do is reach women, and give them the support I wish I'd had earlier in my life. We need our power most when we feel lost or we're at a crossroads, and that is when it can elude us. What I do is try to help the individual see that everything they need is right here."

She pointed a red-tipped finger at her own sternum, and it was so strange. Everything seemed to fade away, the noise, the other people, their very location. In this respect, the moment was not unlike being up in the Sanctuary, a weightlessness creating a buoyancy in Lyric's bones—

It just was so true. It was just . . . exactly what Lyric had been struggling with.

"You're right," she said hoarsely. Then she laughed again to cover up her emotions. "You know, I kind of feel like this was meant to be."

"Meeting me?"

"Yes."

"You're at a transition in your life?" Valentina reached out and put her hand on Lyric's shoulder. "Tell me. What's going on."

A sizzle of energy passed between them, the earnest compassion coming with a charge that made it feel of vital importance.

The stuff of destiny.

"I want . . ."

She thought of Allhan, and the way Uncle Vishous had looked at her with respect, the kind that was fully adult, shared between equals. She wanted to be *seen* like that again, by the ones who mattered. She did not want to be on the roof while others—

"Fight."

As the word was spoken on a loud-and-clear, Lyric came back to attention. "I'm . . . sorry?"

"You must learn to fight," the woman said in a voice that didn't carry. "You have been beautiful all your life, but that's not who you are meant to be. *Fight.*"

The moment stretched out between them.

Until it reached some terminal point of elasticity and snapped back into place.

Valentina laughed easily as she removed her hand. "I just have that instinct about you. And I'm never wrong about these things. You might say . . . I have a second sight. Is it time for some postable pictures now?"

The question was posed with a casual inflection, but it was an order nonetheless, and people responded as such, rushing forward even though they ultimately didn't do anything. It was only the photographer who'd been working the main event who was needed, and as soon as he appeared, Valentina stepped in close.

The woman looked over. "Do you have a brother?"

Lyric's brows popped. "Yes—yes, I do."

"You know, sometimes those of shared blood can be tremendous resources." Valentina gave her a little squeeze. "Of course, that's not always the case. But, I don't know, something tells me he might be able to help you—smile."

The flashbulb went off a number of times in a row, leaving bald spots in her vision.

"And now," the beautiful woman said, "if you don't mind, I'd love you to go with Jenny. There are a number of VIPs with big followings who'd just die to get your picture with them? It'll be good for you because they'll cross-promote your brand and socials."

In a daze, Lyric nodded. And then remembered. "Oh, but what about—"

"Your friend can stay here. It's no problem whatsoever."

CHAPTER THIRTY-NINE

As Lyric was led off, Dev stayed right where he was. Funny, he hadn't had any kind of concrete plan coming here, just vague ideas that were noble in theory, utterly ridiculous in practice. Listening to that speech had been time well spent, however. As the words had drifted around and fed and watered the assembled acolytes, he had clarified things.

So yes, he knew what he wanted now.

"Would you like to wait in my dressing room?" the demon asked him with a wide, winning smile. "It's very loud in here. Come on, I'll show you the way."

Even though the door with the gold star on it was only about ten feet away.

"Give us a minute." As Devina—oops, sorry, *Valentina*—spoke to her staff and reps, she took his arm in a light grip. "I have to take care of our guest and get him settled."

Aware that jealous eyes were locking on him, Dev allowed himself to be steered through that special door, and then, for the first time in a decade . . .

He was alone with his mother.

As she closed them in, she leaned back against the panel.

When there was only silence, he went for a wander over to the dressing table. A mirror, with rows of lights running up both sides, was perched over a tabletop scattered with compacts, wands, pencils, and potions. He picked up a perfume bottle.

Poison. By Dior.

"I know it's you," she said in a soft voice. "I can't see you . . . but a mother knows."

Pivoting back around, he held up the fragrance. "I didn't know you could still get this."

"There is nothing I can't get."

He laughed with a hard edge as he put the bottle down. "That is *not* true."

"Anything material, that is—" Her voice broke. "Will you not let me see you properly? It has been . . . so long."

"What about all your hangers-on out there. Don't you need to get back to them?"

"They can wait. Forever."

When he turned around, he released the lock on his essence—and he had to admit, she was a good actress. The demon let out a choked gasp and slapped a hand over her mouth. As tears flooded those gorgeous black eyes, she rushed forward—

Dev shoved his palm out. "Give it a rest. I know who you are, so just like the bullshit you're peddling to all those humans isn't necessary or interesting in the slightest, neither is any kind of sloppy reunion here."

"Must you be so cruel."

Now he laughed honestly. "Coming from you? That's rich. And spare me the acting. Let's get real, *Mom*."

Her face tightened into a mask. But her voice remained level. "Why did you bring a vampire here."

"You were the one to invite her, not me."

"Curious company you're keeping. Is it true you saved her life in the middle of a street?"

"From you, no less. It was your billboard that went flying off the top of that building—"

"What would your father think, you consorting with the enemy like that."

Dev cocked a brow. "Oh, you think I'm with him?"

"You didn't answer my question."

"I haven't seen him, either." He frowned as the tension in her eased. "Yeah, don't worry, I don't like him any more than I like you. The acrimony is totally equal. Your ego can stay intact."

"That's not why I asked."

"Isn't it."

"No." She shook her head sharply, her luscious hair catching the flat artificial light and gleaming as if the sun were behind her. "I don't want you anywhere near your father. Ever."

"Careful, Mom. Your territoriality is showing."

"It's got nothing to do with that. He's evil, and I love you. And I don't want you hurt by him."

"*He's evil?*"

Valentina—Devina—whatever the fuck she was calling herself—paced around, her outrageously tall stilettos making a soft pattern of noise on the short-napped purple carpet.

"I'm not who I used to be. I'm not who you used to know." She stopped and stared at the closed door as if seeing through it, seeing all the humans who had gathered around her. "You may think that what I do on the stage is an act. It's not."

When he didn't respond, the demon glanced over her shoulder. "I mean every word—"

Dev clapped slowly a couple of times. And then dropped his arms. "You want your Oscar now? Or should we wait until later."

Those gleaming black eyes stared across at him for the longest time. "There's such darkness in you."

"Have you checked out our family tree? You think I'm going to show up as the goddamn Easter Bunny?"

"Why did you come here." She turned fully around, and smoothed her purple dress. "Tell me. Whatever it is, I'll do it. I'll give it to you. Name it."

Dev's brows slowly lowered. Then he laughed. "Damn, you're good. I'll give you that—"

"What can I do for you."

When she just kept looking across at him, going nowhere, patient to wait as if she didn't have anything else in the world to do, he felt the strangest pull at the center of his chest. Oh, but he wasn't stupid. His mother had the superficial charm of a sociopath, and the follow-through of an atomic bomb—

A vibration went through the still air, causing a distortion similar to heat waves rising off asphalt, and then . . .

Dev gasped. It was gone. All the beauty, all the artifice, all the masking. Instead of a gorgeous, sexy woman in a purple dress and black heels . . .

His mother was a twisted, ugly creature, with skin like the bark of an old tree, a deformed face where the nostrils and the eyes were on the same level, and claw-like hands to match toes-in hoofed feet. No more with the lovely locks of mahogany and copper, there were only sprigs of spiky gray tufts on the top of her head, and she didn't have any ears.

She was . . . indescribably ugly. To a degree he never would have guessed at.

"I lie to them," she said in a guttural distortion laced with sadness, "because it serves my need to help. To speak. To move them. If they saw who I really am, they would run from me for all the good reasons in their world. Devlin, I have stopped pretending I am someone I am not. I am not who you once knew."

All he could do was stand there and refresh, again and again, the hideous vision before him . . . the monster who had mated with pure evil and brought him into existence.

She never, ever would have displayed this true nature of hers before.

"I am what I am, Devlin. I know that now, and having accepted my truth, I'm not interested in hurting anything anymore. It's impossible to hate others when I no longer hate myself."

"What happened," he demanded roughly. "Why . . ."

"I lost you. That's what happened."

A single, glistening tear appeared in the corner of her fleshy eye, and seeped over the uneven, mottled skin of her sunken cheek.

"So I ask you again. What can I do for you? I know you didn't come here for yourself—you've avoided me for a decade now and I can't imagine you want to be here. It's that vampire, isn't it. She's touched you somewhere deep, and she's the reason you came. So say your purpose out loud for the both of us. Something tells me you need to hear it, too."

When he spoke, he released the feelings he'd been repressing since the moment he'd looked into a vampire's eyes in the middle of a cold, snowy street.

"I want you to tell him to stop it."

The demon cocked her head, the bones cracking in her neck. "The war."

"Yeah, the war. I want you to tell that asshole you mated with to stop going after vampires. Stop hurting them, stop killing them. Tell him to slaughter humans if he needs prey. Fuck knows there's more of them around, and if he wins, he can rule the world. That'll give him something to do for a couple of years."

His mother's disgusting stare searched his face.

And then in a soft voice, she whispered, "You love that female, don't you."

It was a long while before he could respond.

"No," he lied. "Of course not."

◆   ◆   ◆

Back behind the event stage, Lyric was running on autopilot, smiling when she was supposed to, posing next to people, having the same near-miss-billboard conversation over and over again. She was impatient to get back to Dev and leave for so many reasons. What got her through was the bone-deep conviction that this was her last event.

The end finally came as she turned in place, ready for the next—and there was no one else in the loose line that had formed.

Marcia stepped up and shook her head. "You're an absolute pro at this. Are you sure you want to quit—"

"Do you know where Dev is?" She craned a glance over all the heads, toward the door of the private dressing room. "I'm going to go find him."

"Listen, I'm serious." The manager stepped in front of Lyric. "When you rethink all this, call me. The next level is waiting for you—but don't wait too long. You have to strike when the iron is hot, and that's not forever."

"Thanks, Marcia." As she tried to look through the woman, she knew it was rude, but a sudden weird feeling was making her agitated. "Take care of yourself."

Weeding through the tangle of staff, she got to the starred door of the—

It opened just before she could knock or go for the handle.

And for a third time, there Dev was, stepping out and closing things up behind himself.

"Oh, thank God." Sagging, she could have hugged the man. "Have you always had perfect timing?"

He stared down at her for a moment. And then in a rough voice, he said, "Are you ready to go?"

"I was ready to leave as soon as I got here," she muttered under her breath.

"Then let's not waste any more time."

With him in the lead, they made their way toward an exit sign, and then it was a case of concrete steps down, down, down. As their footfalls echoed upward into the stairwell, she appreciated how he waited for her on the landings, their progress steady, just rushed enough without risking a slip-and-fall. When they got to the bottom, he went over to a fire door.

But it was there that he hesitated.

Turning toward her, Dev seemed to retreat even as he stayed right in front of her, his eyes going remote, his jaw tightening. Except then he reached out and stroked her face, lingering with his hand on her shoulder.

"Lyric . . ."

"What is it?" She frowned. "Is something wrong?"

When he nodded, her stomach dropped. And when he didn't go on, she said, "Just out with it. Whatever it is—"

"Can we go back to your place?" He lowered his head. "But I have to be real with you. Talking isn't what's on my mind."

Exhaling with relief, she stepped into his body. "I couldn't stop thinking of you, all day long."

His smile was slow and sexy. But it didn't change that dark light in his stare.

"Isn't that my line." He lowered his mouth, almost to her own. Yet he didn't close the distance. "Lyric, there are things I need to tell you . . ."

"Well, talking isn't on my mind, either—"

"I'm sorry."

She had to laugh in a short burst. "And that would be my line. Dev, there is time for . . . whatever it is, later. The night is young, and I'm very hungry right now."

He said something, but she couldn't catch it—because whatever he'd spoken was against her lips. And God, the feel of his mouth on hers as his arms wrapped around her and pulled her close, her breasts meeting his pecs. Then his tongue licked inside of her, and she slid her hands up his back to hold on tighter. When she couldn't reach his shoulders, she went down to his waist and urged him even farther, until there were no spaces between his hard angles and her soft contours.

It was so good. It was exactly what she'd thought about while she couldn't sleep, and during the quiet moments when she'd been alone.

But there was also a pep talk in the back of her mind, a reminder to go slow, take it easy, wait until they were back at her apartment because this wasn't a private place—all of which was excellent advice. Too bad she was raw in a way she wasn't used to, in a way she'd never been.

Slipping her palm between them, she gave in to her lust, finding the juncture of his thighs—

"*Fuck*," he growled.

Stroking him, she felt the length and thickness of his erection grow—and later, she would wonder what the hell had gotten into her. At the moment? She was feeling reckless, on the verge of life decisions that would change everything—and she wanted to be bold.

So she lowered her other hand, and went for his belt.

"What are you doing," he groaned.

"What do you think I'm doing." She dropped down onto her knees and arched her back, aware of exactly what she was showing him as the tight leather top pushed her breasts up even higher. "I told you I've been thinking about you all day long."

As Dev's hungry eyes went to everything her push-up bra and the low V neck had on display, she worked the strap free of its buckle. Then she tugged his jeans' top button from its slot. Before she hit the zipper, she extended her tongue and ran it along the ridge that was straining at the denim—

"Oh, God . . ." He fell back against the fire door with a clang, bracing his hands against the jambs.

When Dev bit down on his lower lip and she looked at his flat-tipped canines, she was jolted back to reality and reminded of everything that divided them, but she couldn't worry about all that. Not right now. Not when this could be one of their last chances.

He was leaving: She had looked into his eyes just now, while he'd stroked her face, and known all of his doubts and also his restless need to flee. He was going to ghost her after tonight, and even though it would make the pain harder to bear, she wanted to know what he was like.

Inside of her.

But also any way she could.

"I want to taste you, Dev," she said in a low voice. "I want you to come in my—"

Somewhere up above, a door into the stairwell opened and voices percolated around.

Dev yanked her upright, and held her against him. As he put his forefinger to his lips in a *shhh*, she tilted back and looked up the lattice-work of metal balustrades. She couldn't see much, but it was clearly a male voice and a female one. And they were talking urgently, going back and forth—

Lyric squeezed her palm in between their bodies once again, finding his arousal—

As he gasped, she clapped a hand over his mouth. Then she whispered, "Shhhh."

His eyes flared as she started to stroke him. Then she slowly sank back down at the same time she unzipped things.

"What are you doing," he hissed.

After she *shhh*'d him again, she finished with the unfastening and peeled the two halves of his fly apart—and his erection exploded out at her.

God bless commando, she thought as she regarded his incredible girth.

Overhead, she could still hear the voices, but the words—though decipherable under other circumstances—blended into meaningless syllables as she extend her tongue and, without touching him with her hands, started to lick up his underside.

All of Dev's teeth showed as his upper lip peeled open and his hands strained on the door jambs. As his head fell back, it banged on the door—

Instantly, the voices stopped.

Shhhh, Lyric pantomimed again—before she returned for another lick. In response, his erection spasmed up from its proud, straight jut-out and banged down on her tongue. And then it was enough with the teasing.

Just as the man and the woman started talking again, she slipped a grip around his girth—and Dev groaned, but held the sound in his chest. At least until she opened her mouth and sucked the head of him in.

Then it came out as a squeak that made her grin around his arousal.

Meanwhile, his whole body bucked, his hips shoving forward, his weight sinking into his thighs as his knees bent. It was at that point that the argument upstairs concluded on a door slamming with a metal clap that reached even Lyric's distracted ears.

She paused and looked up, Dev's erection stretching her lips wide.

Up on the higher floor, there was a curse. And then the door slammed a second time.

Which was her cue to really go to work.

Staring up his bowed body, she met Dev's eyes as he looked down at her. The sucking and the stroking fell into an immediate rhythm, and the flush that lit up his face glowed red as he strained and pumped with her.

She knew when he was getting close because he leaned down, as if to try to get her back on her feet.

Lyric shook her head with him in her mouth.

"I'm going to fucking—" The news flash ended on a strangled sound.

And then his pelvis punched forward, twice.

She swallowed everything he had to give her. But didn't let him go.

It was a good move. Dev was ready for more as soon as he finished. And so was she.

CHAPTER FORTY

N oodle legs.

Holy fucking shit, as Dev walked along the snow-covered urban sidewalk, he had seriously loose legs, to the point where he was amazed he was not only upright, but throwing out fairly even strides. Beside him, on the other hand, Lyric was having absolutely no problems with the ambulation—

He stole another glance at her.

She was fucking resplendent in the wind, her blond hair loose in the cold gusts, his windbreaker protecting her from the tundra temperature, her cheeks flushed from the chill. Or all that exertion back in the stairwell.

Dear Lord, from her damn exertion.

As they hit the straightaway back to her place at the Commodore, he kept replaying what she'd done to him, and what do you know. His dumb handle was beyond ready for more of her attention. Just the memory of her lowering herself onto her knees in front of him was enough to bring back the blood flow—and the fact that she had done it to him in that stairwell? With all those people in the convention center? She'd surprised the hell out of him.

Between her lips, and that leather top with her breasts almost spilling out—

"Whoops!"

As she grabbed for his arm, he snatched her from a free-fall, swinging her off her totally impractical thigh-high boots.

Not that he didn't appreciate the boots. Fuck him very much, he wanted her to straddle him, wearing nothing but the frickin' boots.

Lyric's laughter was free and light in the winter night, and as he settled her against his chest with an arm behind her knees and another around the small of her back, he knew two things: He didn't ever want to let her go; and he was going to have to do just that.

"We should have taken an Uber," he said roughly as he started walking again.

"It's not that far. Only, what—like eight blocks?"

"On ice. Those boots of yours are deadly."

Lyric extended one leg out. "You don't like them, huh."

"Oh . . . I like them." He rather *liked* the idea of her making him kiss them. While he was on his hands and knees. "Just not outside in January in Caldwell."

"You can put me down, you know."

"I'm good. If you are."

Lyric smoothed some of his hair back. Then she laid her head on his shoulder. As he continued on, he cherished the feel of her against him, the use of his muscles to keep her up off the ground, the way his body inflated with purpose.

His sire really had been part vampire, hadn't he.

All Dev's life, he'd taken after his mother's side of things, no fangs, no drinking blood, no transition, and no night-only shit. But there was something primal happening, right under his skin, as he carried Lyric to that apartment she didn't really live in . . . something that felt ancient and important.

Not that she could ever take his blood.

"What else were you going to talk to me about," she asked. "Back at the stairwell."

"Before or after the incredible blow job."

Lyric's laughter vibrated into him, and he would have closed his eyes just so he could track every nuance of it if he could have. But he didn't need both of them on their asses.

Up ahead, the vertical lettering on the side of the high-rise glowed like a false moon: COMMODORE. Of course she would have an apartment in a place like that—a place where she could take humans if she was going to be with them—

A sudden urge to snarl cut off that line of thinking.

But come on. Like she hadn't had lovers before? And maybe there were other reasons for her to have a crash pad in the midst of the other species: Like a pretend driver's license or social security number, it was another level of nothing-to-see-here.

Part of the necessary ruse.

"Dev? What do you need to tell me?"

He shook his head. "Sorry, I just . . ."

"It's okay." She cleared her throat. "Look, I know that you're not going to see me again after tonight—"

"That's not what I was going to tell you."

"It isn't?"

No, his revelation was going to lead to that, though. When she threw him out for being her mortal enemy.

All he could do was shake his head again, and take them across the street—jaywalking, of course, because there was no traffic—so they could go down the last block. As he surmounted the steps to the glass ring of doors, he felt like something was stabbing him in the chest, and the sensation got so much worse as he lowered her back down onto her own two feet while he leaned forward to get the door for her.

The warmth and light of the lobby should have been a welcome relief, but as they both waved at the security guard behind the front desk and headed for the elevators, the sense that he was sending her off into a world he could never be part of made him long for the darkness and the cold.

When they got to the buttons to summon the lift, he wanted to redirect them both to somewhere, anywhere, just to prolong things. How about another stairwell—

"Oh?" she drawled. "Would you like to walk up fourteen floors?"

If she was willing to unzip his jeans again? He'd go to the top of the fucking building—with a car on his shoulders.

"Sorry, guess I was thinking out loud." He punched the up button. "Although you've turned me on to fire doors. Who knew that was my kink."

"Safety first."

"Always—"

Bing!

As the doors opened, he extended his arm to make sure she got in safely, and then followed. He'd had some idea that he was going to leave her off at the glass doors. Then at the elevator. Now it looked like he was going to head all the way up to that apartment—

Lyric took one step and brought their bodies together.

She didn't say a thing. Her eyes did all the talking.

"I can't stay," he said hoarsely. "I . . . shouldn't. I know I keep going back and forth, but every time I'm with you, I forget my fucking mind."

Her disappointment was almost hidden. Almost.

"Okay," she whispered.

Stroking her hair back, he lingered on her shoulders and imagined what she looked like underneath his windbreaker.

"Lyric, I want to . . ."

"What," she prompted.

"I want to be with you tonight, but I have something I need to do first." When all she did was nod, he felt the distance of everything he wasn't telling her. "Here's the thing. I want to take care of you, I want to do the right thing."

The tension in her eased a little. "You do?"

"I do."

There was a bump and the doors opened. Extending his arm again to hold things back, he made sure she cleared the threshold before stepping out himself, and it seemed like the most natural thing in the world to put his arm around her and escort her down the hall.

When they got to her apartment, she took out a copper key and slipped it into the dead bolt. As she unlocked things, he liked that she didn't beg him to come in or try to seduce him into staying. Not his Lyric. She was above all that.

As she stepped through and turned around, he recognized the shadows in her beautiful eyes, and even though there were so many reasons to keep his mouth shut short of a goodbye, he wanted to ease her. Even though he couldn't.

"Don't think so much," he said quietly. "Bad for the soul."

"I'm not sure the great philosophers would agree with you."

"They're all dead. So what do they know." He dropped a kiss to her mouth. "Thank you for tonight. And no, I don't want to end us here. I keep trying to, but . . . the idea of never seeing you again feels all wrong."

Her hands drifted up to the pads of his chest. "It's the same for me."

His eyes roamed around her face and then he brushed his thumb over her lower lip. "You shouldn't worry . . . over what you're concerned about."

"Wouldn't that be nice advice to take."

As Lyric gave him a rueful look, he kissed her one more time and then eased back. "See you tomorrow night?"

"Yes," she said.

"It's a date, then."

He forced himself to turn away, and as he started to stride off, she called out, "What do you think I'm worried about?"

Dev paused at the elevators. As he looked down the hall at her, he knew in his gut he was going to remember the image of her standing in that doorway, her thigh-high boots all sex-symbol, his windbreaker more this-is-my-boyfriend's.

"I'll see you tomorrow night."

Bing! As the doors parted for him, she said, "Wait! Your wind-breaker!"

"Keep it," he tossed back as he got in and punched the L button.

◆   ◆   ◆

Lyric ran down the hall after Dev, but she didn't make it in time. The elevator closed and sealed up just as she skidded to a halt. She didn't even manage to catch one last glimpse of him.

Crossing her arms over her chest, she glanced at the hem of his jacket. Then she walked back to the apartment and shut herself in. As she leaned against the door, she had the eerie sense that he knew what she was, and had been trying to indirectly reassure her.

But she'd been so careful about not flashing her fangs, and it wasn't like he'd ever suggested they meet up during the day—something she was never going to be able to do. Even that *lesser* fight had been too distant for him to see anything that might be a tip-off something paranormal was going on.

And most humans had no clue vampires lived in their midst.

"I don't know," she muttered.

As she went down to the bedroom, there was a marked disappointment that he wasn't with her, that there were no naked things happening on the soft mattress—not that they would have made it all the way down here.

God, she wanted him so badly.

In the bathroom, she took her phone out of the back pocket of her tight pants and called up a text screen. When she was done sending the message to her brother, she extricated herself out of the thigh-high boots with care and did the same for the leather top.

It was like peeling a frickin' grape.

She made sure the shower was long, and very hot.

When she finally stepped out, she checked her phone and saw what Rhamp had sent back.

"Figures," she muttered. At least he hadn't bumped her.

Heading for the walk-in closet, she changed into yet another set of the clothes that were there, the turtleneck sweater and jeans cozy, the snow boots far, far more practical. As she hung up her influencer outfit and propped the thigh-highs in the corner, she lingered a moment. Then she folded up Dev's windbreaker, and hid it in the back of one of the built-in drawers. After that, she turned off the lights and went for the exit.

Along the way, she checked her phone a couple of times, hoping for something from Dev.

He didn't reach out, though.

All kinds of when-and-wheres about tomorrow night shot through her mind, but she had to leave them be. Not only did she not want to chase him, but she had something else to do that seemed vitally important—although she couldn't believe she'd have to go twenty-four hours before she could get in front of him again.

Instead of leaving by the door, she cracked one of the windows, closed her eyes . . . and tried to calm herself.

It was a while before she could dematerialize, but she wasn't surprised. When she re-formed, it was in front of a modern mansion that was lit up on the inside like some kind of display cabinet. Cars of various European extractions were parked in the drive, and the front door was wide open, in spite of the cold. The music was techno-swing, a new genre she hadn't gotten into, and she didn't need to be anywhere near the entrance to smell the red smoke, the liquor, the perfumes and colognes.

It was typical Shuli.

As she approached the cacophony, she marveled at how she'd been to the male's shindigs for years, and had always looked forward to them. She'd liked the excuse to get dressed up and do her OOTD posts—and then there was the gossip, and her friends, and the shenanigans that Rhamp and his buddies always got up to as the hours wore on and critical thinking became less and less critical. Besides, what else had she had to do with herself?

Now, though, as she entered the white-on-white foyer with all its contemporary art, she wondered why she'd wasted so much time, hanging around with the same people, as the same conversations and jokes were shared.

"Lyric!"

The sound of her name brought her head around. Mharta was heading for her, the female looking sleek and sexy as ever in a skintight pantsuit. Another blonde, but she was not at all like Lyric in her style, opting for sex, before fashion.

"Hey, girl." As they kissed on both cheeks, those judgy eyes went up and down Lyric's sweater and jeans as if the female were looking at a dead squirrel. "How'd the leather top work out?"

"Oh—sorry, great. Thank you for loaning it to me. I'm going to dry-clean before I return it."

"Not quite your usual shit, but I'll bet you were fabulous in it." The smile was patronizing, but not in a mean way. It was just how Mharta had always been. "I can see you've downshifted into comfy. How cute."

And of course, both c-words were curses.

"Do you know where my brother is?" Lyric rose up on her toes and tried to see through the heads.

"No, and I can't find L.W., either. They're probably together—or they blew this off?"

"Rhamp, miss a party? Come on. Besides, he texted me he's here."

And also not to bother him. But she wasn't hearing that.

"Well, I haven't seen him." The female frowned. "They better not have left without us."

"He got in touch with me only twenty minutes ago."

Mharta swung her stick straight blond hair over her shoulder, and it flowed down her back like a river. "Their loss. I'm going to leave—you want to go to Bathe with us?"

I'd rather lose a limb, Lyric thought.

"No, thanks. I'm going to try to find my brother."

"If you see him, tell him he and L.W. are on my shit list." Those red lips smiled easily. "But you know me, I'm a forgiver. Especially if it's L.W."

Mharta disappeared into the crowd of sophisticates, and Lyric kept going on her own way, squeezing between males in silk suits and females in haute couture. As she went along, she was reminded of how she'd always found Shuli's house to be stark and way too modern, especially when it came to his taste in art. Then again, if you were going to pack a couple hundred people into these rooms on a regular basis, you might as well leave enough free space to accommodate them.

After she made a circuit of the lower floor, she was about to give up when she glanced to the stairs. The velvet rope was in place, which meant that people were to stay on the first level.

Interesting.

Ducking underneath, she jogged up the white carpeted steps, then went down the hall to the primary bedroom suite. She could scent the red smoke waaay before she got to the door, and she hesitated before knocking. Knowing Shuli, she might be interrupting an orgy—

The panels opened, and her brother was on the other side, like he'd done that for her.

And she didn't like the look on his grim face.

It couldn't be their *granmahmen*. She would have gotten a call as well.

"Now's not a good time," Rhamp said gruffly. "I told you."

Looking past him, she saw Shuli and L.W. lying side by side on the big king-sized bed, the former in satin PJs, the latter in hospital scrubs. A drop-down TV the size of a living room rug was blocking most of the view of them, some gunfight banging through the surround sound and drowning out the music from the first floor.

Obviously, the pair of them were going nowhere, even with everything that was happening downstairs—

As soon as Shuli leaned to the side and looked around whatever they were watching, the male came to attention, rising off the pillows he'd been sprawled on. "Lyric . . ."

L.W. shifted down so he could see under the TV for only a split second. Then he shook his head and went back to whatever they had on.

"We can talk later," Rhamp said roughly.

Pushing him out of the way, she barged in. "What's going on here."

She'd known the three of them for far too long not to recognize the telltale signs they were planning something. Plus the tension was so high, the air in the suite was almost a solid.

"Care for a drink?" Shuli mumbled as he fell back into his recline. "I'd get you one, but I'm far too wasted to be able to stand. Rhamp—grab your sister whatever she wants?"

"She's not staying," her twin muttered as he took her by the arm. "Come on, I'll see you out—"

Lyric yanked her arm free. "The hell you will—"

He glanced at the others. "Sorry about this, I didn't think she'd show up—"

"Whoa, hold on," she snapped. "Like I'm your little sister and I'm bugging you while you do big boy things? Screw you, Rhamp."

"I'm not going to argue with you."

Crossing her arms over her chest, she lifted her chin. "How refreshing. This a new leaf? 'Cuz going by your expression, I'm thinking it's a resolution you're not going to be able to keep."

Her brother's head fell back in dramatic fashion. "Your timing is like your taste in lovers. Bad, as usual—"

"Fuck you—"

Rhamp kicked the door shut with a clap. "No, see, *you* called me for help the night before last, and my friends could have died—all because you wanted to make sure your human toy didn't get recruited and end up on the wrong side—"

"It's your *job* to hunt *lessers*—"

"To protect the species, Lyric," he shot back. "Not your little fuckboy—"

The volume on the TV got much, much louder, L.W.'s outstretched arm pointing a remote at the flat-screen. But the guy didn't otherwise interfere. Likewise, she had the sense that Shuli was content to just sit back and watch the drama. Or maybe "content" was the wrong word—he was looking sick to his stomach.

Goddamn it, the idea that they were both still so injured from the gunfight that they couldn't go out into the field or to a stupid party made her guilt so much more intense.

"—surprised you're not with him now," Rhamp was saying. "Or did he decide he needed his sleep. Like humans do."

She refocused on her brother. His eyes were spitting anger, and his black hair was all messed up, as if he'd pulled at it in frustration. His big fighter's body was dressed at the midpoint between casual and field-ready: There was still a lot of black, and she didn't doubt that there were plenty of weapons under his loose Adidas track suit, but there were no obvious daggers, no shitkickers.

He'd come for a party, yet he wasn't inebriated, and he sure as hell wasn't relaxed. She looked back at Shuli and L.W., and wondered what was going on between the three of them. As a twin, she'd always had a knack for knowing what her brother was thinking. Maybe not specifics . . . but she could sense his mood.

And this wasn't about their *granmahmen* or even about the fighting at Dev's. It wasn't even about Dev—that was just a distraction to piss her off and keep her from asking too many questions that were too close to the real issue.

"What's going on here," she repeated softly.

Rhamp's face went full mask and he took her arm. "Nothing that involves you. Now go—"

The fact that he was trying to process her like a problem brought the anger back. "Okay, fine, I'll get someone else to teach me how to shoot—"

Instantly the TV was muted, and as her brother spun her around, both L.W. and Shuli sat up on the bed and leaned around the TV again.

"What did you say?" Rhamp demanded.

"You heard me." Lyric made sure to meet those stares without flinching or apology. "I want to learn how to handle a gun."

"Why do you need to know how to shoot."

Lyric narrowed her eyes and thought of the woman in the purple dress. "I want to learn how to fight. In the war."

There was a pause, and then her brother threw his head back and laughed.

Okay, so maybe Valentina hadn't had a point about going to her brother.

"I'm serious!" And she was *not* going to demean herself by stamping her foot. But holy shit, she suddenly wanted to punch a wall. "Do you think I enjoyed being on the sidelines while you all got shot up behind that apartment building? I might have been able to help—"

Rhamp's head re-leveled with a snap. "No. Absolutely *no*. You're going to cut this shit out, right now. You are *not* the kind of person who can handle the field—"

"How do you know? When you guys started in the training program, I'll bet you had to learn a lot. And practice. Why can't it be the same for me?"

"Really." As the others stayed silent, her brother narrowed his stare at her. "After the way you've spent the last ten years? You have to *ask* that."

"There are females who can fight."

"And they're not Barbie, okay? They're not you."

As Lyric blanched at the dismissal, she opened her mouth to respond. Shut it. Tried again.

"I didn't know you had so little respect for me," she said in a voice that cracked. "Hell, I'm surprised you're not embarrassed to claim me as your sister."

Rhamp tossed up his hands. "I didn't mean it like that—"

"I think you did." As her eyes flooded with tears, she slashed at them angrily. "And I'm glad to know where I stand with you. I won't bother you again—"

Her phone went off at the same time her brother's did.

As they both took their cells out and Rhamp glanced at her with alarm, she knew this could only mean one thing.

She answered Qhuinn's call at the same time her brother answered Blay's.

"We're coming," she choked out before their sire even said a word. "Rhamp's here with me, and we're coming right now."

When she hung up, Rhamp stepped to her. "Are you okay to dematerialize or should I drive you."

His voice was the same, and so were the features of his face—and his height and muscularity, too. The offer to make sure she was okay was also right up his alley, and before, the gallantry had always seemed a reflection of his good character. Now?

For the first time in her life, she looked at her twin brother as if he were a stranger.

"You take care of yourself," she said. "I've got me."

On that note, she turned and headed for the door.

"Oh, come on, Lyric. Now is *not* the time—"

"I couldn't agree more," she muttered as she let herself out.

In the hall, she paused to collect herself. Then she headed for the guest suite next door so she could ghost away.

To her grandparents' house.

CHAPTER FORTY-ONE

Lash, son of the Omega, walked out into the city park on a meta-physical float, his footfalls so light over the undisturbed blanket of snow, he not only didn't break through the surface, he left no prints. In response to his presence, the wind shifted direction, rounding about and coming restlessly from the north to riffle through his long black robes, while overhead, he brought with him a dark cloud cover that shut down the moon and the stars.

Coming to a halt, he looked to the river first. The Hudson's current was sluggish and constricted by ice that was germinating from the shores. On the far side, the other half of Caldwell sparkled, the homes perched over the water like fallen galaxies. Turning to the south, he regarded the illuminated spears of Caldwell's Financial District that rose from the tangle of their asphalt root systems, as well as the arching twin bridges that kept the two parts of the metropolis tethered together.

The Northway that flowed in and out of the spaghetti junction of exits that fed downtown was dotted with headlights, taillights.

It had been a very, very long time since he'd stopped and looked around.

With a curse, he rubbed his pounding temples. His head was aching and he felt alarmingly weak within his physical form. Likewise, unease weaved through the evil core of him, the sense that things were moving behind the scenes and being arranged to his disfavor dogging his consciousness.

Something was changing for him. He just didn't know what.

The impending existential crisis had been coming for some time now, and try as he might, there was no putting his finger on any specifics. No matter how much he reflected, rested, tried to recharge, he couldn't shake the drain.

So when he'd received a call from one of his inductees, and heard an unfamiliar, haughty-accented voice over the connection, the out-of-the-blue had certainly seemed to be part of the ennui.

Or at the very least, a trail marker—

A figure appeared at the edge of the park, and Lash scented the air, picking up the vampire's subtle, sophisticated cologne. With keen eyes, he discerned the fine, fitted overcoat in the correct camel shade, and the maroon scarf knotted around the throat. Hair was dark and parted on the side, face was handsome in the way of good breeding, and the carriage of the torso was perfect.

Ah, yes, the aristocracy. Having grown up with them, he did appreciate the surface aspects of the *glymera*.

Especially given who he consorted with now.

Lash stayed where he was and let the male trudge over to him. All the while, he scanned the periphery. Nothing was lurking, and as he willed a boundary into place, he intended to keep it that way. The Brotherhood had its *mhis*; he had a version of the same.

"Whestmorel," he drawled.

"Lash, son of the Omega."

The bow he got was a nice touch, an indication of a loyalty split from Wrath, son of Wrath, sire of Wrath—in theory. He trusted no one and nothing, however, in this world and the next.

And on the note of the great Blind King, he still didn't know how that bomb had missed thirty years ago. But that was a rumination for another time.

"I was surprised to receive a call like yours." As the wind continued to weave through his long black robes, Lash was glad he'd changed out of his fighting attire. No reason to spook the male. "Most aristocrats prefer to leave the heavy lifting to others."

He talked to put Whestmorel at ease. The more relaxed a target was, the easier it was to get into their mind and soul. Interestingly, however, his probing was blocked.

Someone had been practicing their own mental control.

"I have something to give you," the aristocrat said. Without any tone of superiority.

The calm steadiness was a surprise. Lash was used to people quaking before him—then again, if someone was going to betray Wrath, they had better be able to keep a level head in front of an enemy.

"And what might that be," Lash murmured.

"I can tell you where Wrath's Audience House is. I can give you the nightly location of the King and the Black Dagger Brotherhood."

In response to the statement, a kindling occurred deep within him, and as he felt a surge of power, he thought, maybe he'd been coasting along for a while now. Maybe that was his problem.

"And let me guess," Lash said evenly. "You wish to exchange this information for assurances you will be put in power after I overthrow the throne for you."

That head inclined only once. "You will need someone to rule over the vampires on your behalf."

Lifting a brow, he very nearly pointed out that his goal was the eradication of the species. But when your enemy sought to betray his own, there was no reason to point out that he was betraying himself.

"Go on," Lash prompted.

"I cannot believe your ambitions lie only with us. Do you not wish to take over the world? Why rule just vampires in Caldwell, when you could dominate Earth—and indeed, to do that, you will need many armies, not merely your own. With a piece of you in each slayer, how far can you go before you are weakened? If you have vampire fighters loyal to you, then you are far more powerful."

As his fangs descended, Lash's upper lip twitched. "You know little of which you speak, aristocrat."

"I know that all bank accounts have a zero point, and a fortune spread over too many heirs dwindles to nothing."

Of course it had to be put in terms of money.

Whestmorel arched his already high brows. "If you could have killed Wrath by now, you would have. If the Lessening Society could have eradicated the vampires, it would have. Generations of this war have endured because the approach has always been the same. You against all of us. But what if there was another way. What if instead of a perpetual seesaw that leads nowhere, there was a collective effort against humans instead—"

The aristocrat grabbed for the center of his chest and gasped for air. As his knees buckled and he strained for breath, he landed facefirst in the snow, his legs kicking at the ground cover in their no-doubt-handmade loafers.

Lash extended his palm and flipped the male onto his back with a surge of will. Crouching down, he locked eyes with his prey. "I could kill you right now."

"You . . . won't . . ." Whestmorel wheezed an inhale. "You need . . . me."

"You overestimate your necessity."

Straightening to his full height, Lash put his foot on the male's chest and leaned his weight forward. The suffering increased, which was satisfying—to a point.

But then that strange unease percolated up once again, and the next thing he knew, he was releasing not only that set of lungs, but the grip of his will around the male's cardiac muscle.

Whestmorel dragged in gallons of air, swallowing the oxygen and spitting it back out in clouds that reminded one of an old-fashioned Christmas choo-choo.

For a moment, Lash went into his own past and remembered growing up in what he had thought was his parents' mansion. There had always been a decorated tree in the drawing room standing in glittering elegance the second December arrived each year. The display had not been because the human holiday was being observed, but rather because it was just another beautiful decoration to be enjoyed.

And there had always been presents, of course.

Those had been much simpler times, before he had discovered his true sire, before he had taken over the Lessening Society from his father, the Omega, before . . . the last couple of decades when things had neither progressed nor regressed in terms of the war. And in other areas of his life.

If one wasn't going forward . . . wasn't that losing ground, in a manner of speaking?

Surviving was not victory. Not the kind that came with the mastery and control he had always craved.

"You must ask yourself . . ." The aristocrat coughed. "If you eradicate all vampires, how can you rule . . . over the dead . . ."

Lash looked out toward those skyscrapers, and then he let his stare roam over to the suburban sprawl that skirted the downtown. There was so much more that he could not see, so many homes, so many towns, so many cities.

Across the globe.

"If you kill all the vampires," Whestmorel rasped, "who will you govern. What . . . will you do . . . if you win."

"You don't know my plans, aristocrat."

He injected derision into his words, but that was just to hide the truth he abruptly found himself confronting. So involved had he been on the ground floor of the war—the recruitment, the inductions, the outfitting and arming, the to-and-fro of slayers being brought into the Society and then cast back out to him as the Brothers and their fighters sent them home—that he hadn't considered a broader strategy.

Yes, he thought. This was the reckoning he needed, and it was about so much more than the war.

Standing over the aristocrat who had spoon-fed him the very aspirations he should have germinated within himself, he reflected on the nature of fathers and sons. He had readily stepped into the role of his sire—and there had been a time when he had expected his own son to do the same.

The fact that the great Blind King always had his progeny right by his side, in lockstep, was just one more reason to hate the male. Lash's son, on the other hand, had fucked him off years ago.

What a disappointment Devlin had been, but that sonofabitch was too much like his mother.

Hell, for all Lash knew, the pair of them could be scheming to overthrow him right this very minute.

It was something he always worried about—

What if this emissary is actually their doing, he suddenly thought. *Or someone else's?*

"Who shall you rule," the aristocrat repeated. "And wouldn't you like to get to Wrath. Tonight."

As the tantalizing taunt rose up to him through the cold, blustery air, he tried anew to get into the male's mind. And when he failed, he narrowed his eyes.

What lurked behind this offer? Was this a chimera created by his ex, something to trip him up, a play to his lust for power? Was this a plant from Lassiter? Or the great Blind King?

Lash regarded the male who lay sprawled at his feet. The rage that boiled up was no news flash. Hatred had always defined him. Except he was older now, and much, much wiser.

Even as his emotions swirled, he retained self-control.

If he lost his composure, the veil of protection he'd put up here would slip, and fuck knew what was waiting for him on the periphery of this park.

The safest thing he could do was get out of here.

Glancing suspiciously over his shoulder, Lash couldn't remember a time when he had felt so destabilized. It was almost as if some kind of fulcrum was being established, and his energy was being drained because of it. He had been aware of this for a while, but as with all incremental changes, he'd been the frog getting boiled by inches.

Until now he was here, in this snowy city park, with his own resolutions crashing down on his head, along with a sense that there . . . was something else. Some other kind of alignment happening to his detriment—oh, fuck it. He was going in circles again, his mind on a loop that he couldn't get un-snared of.

This was happening a lot lately.

"I don't believe you," he heard himself say.

As he departed, he didn't kill the messenger. He wanted the male to go back to where he'd come from, and take with him the fact that the ruse hadn't been fallen for.

And there was a second reason to keep Whestmorel alive.

He knew how to get hold of the aristocrat.

If Lash was wrong, and this was an honest offer of treason, there would be time to reel it in. The most important thing right now was to find out exactly why his own energy was being drained, and deal with that first.

Then he could proceed.

With other things.

CHAPTER FORTY-TWO

Lyric arrived first to her grandparents' house, and the instant she walked through the front door, she could smell the death. As she breathed in, the surface scents were all the same, the floor cleaner, the Windex, the coffee, the shampoos, and that horrid medicinal tint, everything she was used to, but now there was a deeper undertow to the familiar, a musty calling card that, though she had never had it in her nose before, some ancient part of her was able to identify.

As she shot down to the kitchen, she stumbled to a halt. There were so many people in the house, clustered in the family room, gathered over the counter by the sink, seated at the table. Faces turned to her, and looked at her with love and sadness—yet she couldn't place them even though she had known each all of her life.

Smothering a cry, she wheeled toward the first-floor bedroom, her sloppy boot falls echoing the chaos in her mind. She had known this was coming. They all knew this was coming. So why was this such a shock—

The door was closed, but she didn't knock. She burst in, broke in, fell in—

Lyric pulled up short. Her *granmahmen* was lying back against the pillows, her eyes closed, her face drawn and nearly gray, the smocked front of her flannel nightgown showing only the frailest of breaths.

She was still alive. Barely.

Kneeling by her side on the bed, Rocke had one of her hands in both of his, his stricken visage pale and tearless, for undoubtedly he had no more tears to cry. And at the dying female's feet, Lyric's fathers were crouched together, Qhuinn holding Blay, who was just staring down—

Loud footsteps rushing in had Lyric glancing over her shoulder.

Rhamp all but mowed her over as he arrived, but she didn't have the energy to bicker about being shoved out of the way.

Especially as her twin stopped short like he'd forgotten how to move.

Blay looked up. "Hi, guys. Come on in."

As if they were young once more, they did as they were told, and shut the door quietly. But when they didn't approach the bed, Rocke smiled and motioned at them.

"Get closer, so that she knows you're both here. I have a feeling . . . I think she's aware of us. All of us."

Lyric took a step forward—and when Rhamp didn't follow, she hooked her arm through his and brought him along. At the bedside, there was space to sit a hip down, and she took advantage of it, opposite her grandfather.

"Hi, *Granmahmen*," she choked out. Then she looked at her dads. "What happened? What changed?"

Blay took a deep breath. "About fifteen minutes ago, her heart stopped while I was checking her oxygenation. It started again on its own. Then stopped a couple of minutes later . . . it's just time. Ehlena and Doc Jane said they could try and give her stimulants, but . . ."

Through the lump in her throat, Lyric addressed her namesake: "We're here, too, *Granmahmen*. Rhamp and I are here."

She expected her brother to chime in. When he didn't, she glanced at him. He hadn't sat down, but rather was hovering on the periphery, his eyes on the wall across the way, his body tense as a statue.

"Rhamp," she whispered. As he looked at her, she nodded at their *granmahmen*. "Rhamp's here, too," she said more loudly.

He shook his head and took a step back, his hand dragging down his face.

Lyric refocused on their *granmahmen* and saw more clearly what her frantic first glimpses had missed. The elder Lyric's mouth was slack and blue-tinted, her sunken eyes ever so slightly open but surely not seeing anything, her hollow chest barely inhaling . . . barely exhaling . . .

"I love you," Lyric said roughly as she stroked the thin white hair.

She thought back to just nights ago, when she had stretched out next to the female. Those moments had seemed important, then. Now? They were precious beyond any earthly wealth, for they were the last ones she was to have.

Sniffles percolated up, and she realized they were coming from her.

And then she looked at her *granmahmen's* free hand as it lay on the flowered quilt, so still, the purple veins and white bones showing through the paper-thin skin.

She looked at Rhamp. "You need to say goodbye—"

He shook his head once more.

"No," she intoned. "Come here. Sit with me. And talk to her."

Rhamp took yet another step back, and she thought of their youth. He was the one who had always protected her, even before his change, when he'd been small. And then after his transition, when he'd come through things, he'd been so big, big enough not just to fight, but to win against the enemy.

Whereas she had been . . . a Barbie.

She was still pissed at him for that crack. Except that wasn't what was on her mind now. The only thing she was remembering . . . was what he would do when they'd been young and the thunderstorms had come during the day, and the rumbling had been so loud and deep, that it had vibrated down even into the underground.

He had always turned to her then, and been the one to seek her comfort when he'd been scared.

For all his courage in the field, he was scared now.

"Rhamp," she said with force. "You're going to regret this for the rest of your life. Come and sit with me, and tell her you love her."

Extending her arm, she kept their eyes locked. "It's going to be okay. Come here, brother mine."

There was stillness all in the room, her fathers and grandfather watching them in silence. And she could positively feel the emotion weaving through the air that was tainted with the harbinger of death—

That's what he is frightened of, she thought. *The scent.*

"It's still her," she commanded. "Breathe through your mouth, not your nose. Forget the smell, and join me here. There's not much time left."

His Adam's apple—so prominent in his thick throat—undulated. And then he finally stepped forward.

Rearranging herself so there was room for him, she pulled him down beside her.

"We're all here," Lyric said as she stroked her *granmahmen*'s wrist.

The skin was dry and cool, too cool.

"Tell her," she prompted her brother.

It was a while before Rhamp responded, and as the moments ticked by, she got more and more anxious.

But then he cleared his throat, and in the voice of the young he hadn't been for so many years, Rhamp said, "I love you, Nana."

Lyric brushed a tear from her eye at the old name, the one he'd called their *granmahmen* because when he'd been young, he'd had a little speech impediment, and hadn't been able to handle the big word.

"Everyone's here, *Granmahmen*," she whispered as she took a deep breath. "We're all with you. It's okay . . . for you to go."

She braced herself for the last breath, just as everybody else did. And when that didn't come, she glanced around at the males surrounding the bed. They were all staring at the person who had kept them together, these many years.

"It's all right, *Granmahmen*," she repeated. "You can . . . go. It's okay."

The chest continued to haltingly go up and down.

Lyric frowned, and thought of how she and her *granmahmen* had always been the only females in the household here, and how the elder Lyric had always been in charge: Four strong males, who were loved so dearly by so many, three of whom fought for the species, were sustained—had always been sustained—by the female who had run everything.

And that was when Lyric realized . . .

"I'll take care of them," she said hoarsely. "*Granmahmen*, don't worry. I will take care of the family, of all of them, in your absence—"

A deep breath was sucked in. And then the exhale came, long and slow . . . ending on a quiet catch.

And with that very characteristic lack of fuss, with her message having been received, their matriarch was gone.

CHAPTER FORTY-THREE

A s soon as Shuli passed out, L.W. left the aristocrat's mansion. To avoid the fucking party, he snuck out the back, and to get off the property, he borrowed one of the Range Rovers in the four-car garage. The fucker had two of them—because of course he did. He had to make sure his butler could get out in style, and there were the other staff to think of.

Or maybe one was just for backup. Who the hell knew.

It had been a while since L.W. had been behind the wheel, and it sure as shit hadn't been during the winter. He supposed that was another reason to have Range Rovers. The traction was outstanding, even with all the ice.

His Samsung provided the route. All he had to do was sit back and steer—which wasn't as easy as it sounded. Part of that was because he'd had to borrow some of Shuli's duds, so everything was too tight: the track bottoms, the nylon shirt, the Vuitton parka.

Like LV made fucking parkas.

The thing that really irritated him? The guy's running shoes had fit him. He was taller than Shuli by almost a head. He should have been busting the Sauconys at the seams.

Maybe Shuli was packing more than just big guns in his leathers.

As L.W. drove along, working his way through stop signs, then stop-lights, his leg hurt like a bitch, and of course it had to be on his driving side. Then again, he hadn't expected to be making this trip—or for it to take this long.

Then again, Shuli's house was in the fancy part of town, and where he was headed was in the older part of the suburbs.

Still, as he arrived at his destination, he almost wished he had more distance to travel.

Hovering in front of the address, he didn't pull into the plowed driveway. He just stared out the passenger side window at the Colonial, looking at all the lights that glowed inside. Safe Place was like one of those snow globe houses, the kind that got the fall of flakes after you shook things up.

Picture perfect.

Pulling past the front walkway, he put Shuli's SUV in park, killed the engine, and took a deep breath. Then he popped the door open, got out, and shoved his fists in his pockets.

Shuli's pockets.

It was a strain on his slow-healing wound to get over the drifts, and stomping through the snow made his thigh ache. Still, he kept going, cutting a path around the front of the house to the side . . . to that win-dow he'd stood under before.

Bitty was at her desk.

She was right there, sitting in her chair, staring forward at her monitor.

For a moment, he felt bad, interrupting her work. But then he realized . . . she wasn't typing or moving a mouse around or talking on a phone. She didn't seem to be doing anything except focusing on what was in front of her.

She just sat there, her eyes unblinking, her body unmoving—

Her head lowered, as if she were looking at something in her lap. Or maybe she'd just closed her lids to take a breather.

Because she hadn't been sleeping.

Yeah, and whose fault was that, he thought.

"Leave her," he muttered. "Just fucking leave it—"

"May I help you—"

As L.W. turned to the female voice, he went for the gun he'd tuck-holstered on the track bottoms' waistband. But then stopped his hand from drawing. "Hello."

The social worker leaning out over the porch's balustrade abruptly straightened and bowed. "Oh, my God, I mean—your Highness."

He put his hand up. "That's not necessary—"

"I saw that someone had gone through the snow." She pointed out to the front lawn and the tracks he'd made. "I'm guessing you're here to see Bitty? Come around to the porch and she can meet you out here—"

"Listen, you don't have to bother her." He glanced up to the window. "She looks busy."

And he was looking like a stalker here.

"Not at all." The female put her hand to the base of her throat. "And may I just say . . . we're so glad you're back on your feet."

Before he could take another shot at dissuading her, the female disappeared out of sight.

Stepping back, he looked up once again.

Moments later, Bitty came to attention and glanced away from her computer. Then there was a long, long pause.

She lowered her head again. Then surged up to her feet, turned her back to the window, and arranged her hair.

I'm definitely a stalker, he thought as he limped over and stood by the side of the porch.

As the big door opened and light spilled out, he crossed his arms on his chest. Then he dropped them—

Bitty was impossibly beautiful as she stepped out and shut things behind her. Dressed in cream-colored corduroy pants and a red sweater, the new highlights in her hair really gleamed in the exterior lighting. But her face was strained as she turned to him, and she did not meet his eyes—and none of that was a surprise.

"So, you're looking better." She cleared her throat. "I'm glad you're all right."

"Yeah. Good as new."

"That's great."

"Yeah."

L.W. looked out to the Range Rover. "I, ah, I just wanted to thank you for helping me the other night—"

"That is not necessary." Now she looked at him. "Sabrina is the one you need to save the gratitude for. Do you want me to go get her? It's no trouble—"

"I'm here to see you."

"Well, she'd be thrilled to get a visit from the heir to the throne." She put her hand up to stop him from talking. "And I really think it's better if you lay your thanks at the foot of someone else."

"I'm sorry. Bitty. For what I did."

Her brow arched. "Why are you apologizing exactly."

"I hurt you. And I'm sorry—"

"You saved me from having a sore wrist. I should be thanking you." When he shook his head and cursed, she said, "Oh, listen, I don't know if you've heard, but Lyric and Rhamp's *granmahmen* died about ten minutes ago. Did you get the text?"

No, because he'd only been thinking about getting here.

He cursed under his breath. "I'm sorry to hear that."

"Standing in that snow, you're just sorry about all kinds of things, aren't you. Bummer. Well, I hope your night gets better."

As she turned away, he said, "You're right about me being angry. And how dangerous it is. I just don't want you to get rolled into . . . all my shit."

He kept quiet about what he and his boys were up to—and the fact that he had to was a reminder of how he was doing the proper thing with her. Even if it fucking *sucked*.

Bitty pivoted back around, and it was funny. He hadn't realized exactly how warmly she'd looked at him until now . . . when all that was gone.

"You don't owe me any explanations." She wrapped her arms around herself. "We almost kissed—once. I'm very sure you've done much more than that with a lot of females, so I'm not confused about where I stand with you—or rather, if I once was, you cleared that up. For this, I'm grateful. I really think clarity is good in life, don't you?"

The hardness in her was something he'd never seen before, and he blamed himself for changing her.

Yet another reason this was the right thing to do.

"Goodbye, Bitty."

She stared at him for a moment. Then she bowed to him. "Goodbye, Your Highness."

✦　　✦　　✦

Out in the city park by the Hudson, Whestmorel dragged himself through the snow in a lurching walk. The lifting of his feet and the shifting of his weight made his heart pound from effort, and the pain in his chest flared and receded with each slow step.

From time to time, he glanced around with trepidation.

He hadn't thought to bring a weapon. And in any event, he wasn't trained in them.

He wielded pens, not swords.

Yet no slayers set upon him. It was quite curious, actually. With the evil having repudiated him, one would think Lash would have eliminated that which had been rejected, either there on the spot while they'd met or the now, by sending slayers forth.

Yet he remained alone in the field.

The extent of his isolation seemed rather relative, given that there were cars on the Northway, and people living all around the downtown, but as he considered his circumstances, he felt as though he was in Antarctica. If only he could dematerialize, but his heart was not functioning right—

Up ahead, a car pulled over to the shoulder of the four-lane road that ran past the park's outer rim. As a figure stood up from behind the wheel—and waved—Whestmorel exhaled with a relief that he was going to need to keep to himself.

Lifting his hand in return, he tried to speed up, but his body just wouldn't allow it. Thus he continued his trudging.

Certain now of his evacuation, his mind was free to rehash the meeting. In the flesh, Lash had not disappointed. He had been fair and quite beauteous, the kind of male who would have turned many a head, and one had to approve of the accent. He had been taught to speak properly, and with good diction, clearly by members of the *glymera*.

Did that make the tales true, Whestmorel wondered. Had the evil once been one of them, raised among aristocrats?

Whom he had later gone back and slaughtered, the start of the raids that horrible night so long ago.

When the great Blind King had once again failed the species.

Except Whestmorel was confused. Surely one as powerful as the Omega's son would have seen not only the logic, but the opportunity, that had been presented to him. Instead, Lash had walked away.

Not the outcome one had wanted or anticipated.

Focusing on his car, Whestmorel continued to battle through the drifts—and the fact that Conrahd stayed with the sedan was irksome. But the male was not a butler, and in any event, what could be done to shorten the distance?

Still, as Whestmorel finally got within range, he gave into his dissatisfaction with everything and snapped, "Do come help me!"

Conrahd strode around the front grille, but hesitated at the nearly waist-high snowbank that curbed the thoroughfare. "You're almost to it. Nearly here. Allow me to get the door."

Well, wasn't he accommodating, Whestmorel thought bitterly.

The last ten feet felt like ten miles, and then mounting what had been plowed and frozen into place was the kind of obstacle course that tried the last of his patience. When he finally fell into the bucket seat on the passenger side, he closed his eyes and felt a sickening dizziness.

Conrahd did the duty with shutting him in, at least—what a male—and then came around and got behind the wheel.

"Rather good timing," the male muttered as he put them in gear and started off. "A cop-bot is approaching us."

Just what they needed.

Fumbling with the seatbelt, Whestmorel buckled himself in, and looked out the back. Indeed, a CPD unit was on their tail, and stayed that way as they took the nearest northbound ramp onto the highway. As the municipal vehicle eventually pared off, there was a spot of relief, but then the queasiness started.

Dearest Lassiter, he was sick to his stomach all of a sudden.

"So what happened," Conrahd demanded.

"We are in process." Whestmorel cracked his window, the cold air whistling in. "Get off at the next exit."

"I beg your pardon? We are well far from our—"

"*The next one.*"

Conrahd did as he was told—except then the medical predicament became clear: There was no going to Havers's clinic to get his heart checked out. What was he thinking? The healer's first phone call would be to the Black Dagger Brotherhood, as he and Havers had been acquainted since they were young, and there was no way there wasn't an alert out for him.

There was also no going to a human provider. All they needed was imaging of a six-chambered cardiac muscle to be set loose on humanity.

"Pull over," Whestmorel choked out.

Conrahd glanced across the console. "Whatever has gotten into you. You're making no sense—"

"Stop the car!"

Even before they came to a full halt on the highway's shoulder, Whestmorel opened his door and emptied the contents of his stomach into the briny slush. After he threw up a second time, he then endured a round of dry heaves. When he felt as though things had resolved, he unknotted his Hermès scarf, and wiped his mouth on the silk.

"Verily, are you all right—"

"Shut up." Collapsing back against the seat, he left the panel cracked so he could get some cold air. "Proceed back unto the safe house. Fast."

"I cannot until you close the—"

It took him two tries to get the latch mechanism to catch, and the nausea that had come upon him threatened to return as soon as forward momentum resumed. As he sank into the fine leather, a misery entered his system that he had not felt since . . .

Well, ever. Throughout the course of his life, he had enjoyed going from triumph to triumph, and bringing others along. The plot against Wrath was supposed to be in this same vein.

But how he felt now was . . . not enjoyable, at all.

He had males waiting to hear of yet another success, such that their sacrifices were bolstered, and the promise of the future—which he had spoken of, which he had vowed to lead them unto—would be closer to being made manifest.

Except at the moment, he felt very mortal. Very, very mortal. And as if he had not just failed them all, but sentenced the lot of them to death at the hands of the Black Dagger Brotherhood.

"What about the slayer, then?" Conrahd glanced across the interior. "We were going to go give the order to release him at the neutral holding location. That was the plan. You were going to meet with Lash, and then we were going to personally tell the guards to release the *lesser.*"

Yes, he'd meant to go there and free the thing himself because he would have been protected by its master. He had played the scene out in his mind's eye many times, before they'd even abducted that particular undead.

The performance was supposed to be so that Conrahd could see it happen and carry the details back to the others, evidence of Whestmorel's growing seat of power.

How naive he'd been. How ignorant. Riding on a wave of surety that had been not destiny or fate, but . . . mere ego.

As another wave of nausea hit him, Whestmorel returned to that moment, when he had stood before the master of all evil—and felt that crushing weight in his chest. He had been fine until he was not, and the next thing he had known was being down in the snow.

No breath that he could draw, nothing but the agony of a heart-seizing known unto him—

"No," he said roughly. "We do not go near that thing. Not now, not ever."

Conrahd stared over with disbelief. "We're just leaving it then? That location is secure, but there are limits. What if a human finds him?"

"Then the human will deal with it." He glared over at Conrahd. "Do not go back there. Do not go *anywhere* near that slayer."

The male frowned. "What happened in the park, Whestmorel."

"All is going according to plan," he said with exhaustion. "Worry not on that. Let us continue forth to the safe house. I will rest and we will reconvene at nightfall next."

"When are you going to take Lash unto the Audience House?"

As he groaned and closed his eyes, he was once again all too well aware of Conrahd's ambitions, and he found himself ruing his decision to go with one who was so competent: If he himself showed any further weakness the now, he was quite confident it would be exploited in favor of an insurrection.

"Just drive," he commanded. "I alone know the when of it, and it shall stay as such until I say differently."

With his nausea returning, he went to wipe his mouth—

There was a stain on the maroon silk of his scarf . . . a black stain. With a shaking hand, he touched his mouth, then dipped his fingertips to his tongue.

When he brought them out again, he gasped at the black oily sub-stance upon them.

"What is it," Conrahd demanded.

"Nothing," he muttered as he wiped his hand off. "Nothing a'tall."

CHAPTER FORTY-FOUR

The following evening, Lyric was back at the Wheel, sitting on her bed in a bathrobe with wet hair. As she stared off into space, she decided it had been the longest twelve hours of her life. Fifteen. Whatever.

And now she was here, in familiar pastel surroundings that looked strange, a hollow feeling where her heart needed to be, a headache spearing into her left eyebrow. The fact that every time she so much as blinked, all she saw was that final breath of her *granmahmen's?* That just made everything worse.

Putting her head in her hands, she replayed the immediate aftermath in her mind. After she left the bedroom, the first people she'd gone to had been her *mahmen* and Xcor. Her other parents had been waiting just outside the door, and the way the two of them had hugged her, hugged Rhamp, hugged Blay and Qhuinn, and her grandfather, had made her feel proud of her family. Always supporting each other, through good times and bad, both sets of parents steady and true.

And then there had been all her uncles and their mates, the fighters who came by, plus other members of the community, including Fritz.

The only people who had gone into the bedroom had been Doc Jane and Dr. Manello. The decision for cremation back at the training center had been made years ago, and though it had been hard watching the body be removed, there had been closure in that, too.

And then dawn had come.

With the guests departed and the shutters down, the eight of them had sat around and talked about the past, and shared food, and cried—

Seven.

Oh, God, there were only seven people in her family now.

And though she'd merely been grieving for half a day—well, if you didn't count the anticipation of all this that had been going on for weeks—she had learned one thing about this very specific kind of sorrow: Your brain struggled to adjust to the new normal. Even though intellectually, she was very well aware that a big part of her life had just died, she kept having to get used to it, over and over again. Like the seven, not eight. Like the fact that there were going to be no more Sunday night dinners.

And tonight was Sunday.

Or at least . . . not family dinners as she remembered them.

"Who's going to make lasagna for Father," she murmured.

Maybe she could learn how, although why hadn't she asked her *granmahmen* to teach her before—

As her phone went off with a text, she glanced over her shoulder at her bedside table.

Dev?

She'd turned off the preview function as soon as her brother had fixated on her dating someone human, so she had to get up and go to her phone. And as she did, she prayed like hell that man wasn't canceling their meet-up tonight. There was nothing more to be done about her *granmahmen* at the moment, and she had no interest in sitting around here with a frozen smile on her face as people continued to express their sincere condolences or look at her with that grave expression of banked sadness. It wasn't that she didn't love them all, she just felt suffocated by the emotions—

"Thank God," she murmured as she checked the time and texted him back.

Dev was complicated for sure. But not as complicated as the rest of her life—

Knock-knock.

Sending the text, she hid her phone in the pocket of her robe. "Come in?"

When Rhamp was the one who entered, she was surprised—and didn't have the energy to try to hide the reaction. She couldn't remember the last time he'd been in her room. Then again, this was hardly normal times.

Oh, and you know, he was right about one thing. There *was* a lot of pink in here—

Annnnnd he was shutting them in together. So this was clearly not just a quick check-in, how's-Dad, update kind of thing.

As Rhamp leaned back against the door and crossed his arms over his chest, she braced herself. "What's on your mind?"

There was a beat of silence. Then he cleared his throat. "I just wanted to thank you. For what you did last night at the bedside. I couldn't . . . I just froze. And if you hadn't reached out when you did? You're right. I would have regretted it for the rest of my life."

Wow, she thought. This was unexpected—

"And it dawned on me," he continued, "that you were much kinder to me in that moment than I've been to you in a long time. Especially recently."

His eyes roamed around her room with its silk-upholstered furniture and its canopied bed. Dressed in his black leather, he was like a Goth who'd gotten lost on his way to a graveyard and wandered into a dollhouse.

And was she really hearing him right? Was this an apology?

"You've been out in the field a lot, that can't be easy." She knotted her hair up and put it over her shoulder. "And I know that you've been worried about *Granmahmen.*"

"So have you."

"Well, it's true. But we've always handled things differently."

There was a long silence. "Can I be honest with you?"

"That depends," she replied hoarsely. "I'm a little raw right now, so if it's going to be hard to hear, I'd rather wait."

"I really don't want you to date a human." He put his hand up. "Not because they're intrinsically bad or we're intrinsically better. It's just I live in terror of you ever falling into the hands of a *lesser*, and to me, every one of them is a slayer just waiting to happen. I know it's not fair, and I clearly wasn't able to put that into words the other night, but that's where I'm at—and yes, I'll do my best to get over it. I have no right to put a stamp on them that says 'forbidden.'"

Lyric lifted her brows. "I . . ."

"And listen, if you want to learn how to shoot, I will absolutely teach you. But I'm going to want you to learn hand-to-hand as well." He took out his phone and nodded at it. "To that end, I took the liberty of talking to Xhex and Payne. They're willing to start training you anytime you're ready. I thought it was important for you to learn some basics from females, and then I can put together some sparring sessions with the guys. You need both. Best practices for females, and some experience with a full-grown male coming at you."

As her brother fell silent again, he put his phone away and crossed his arms once more over his big chest. Then he murmured, "I'm sorry, Lyric. For a lot."

"I . . . I don't know what to say. Other than thank you." When he flushed and nodded, she added, "This is also more than you've said to me in a very, very long time."

He frowned at that. "I've been kind of blinders on about everything lately."

"I understand. And I get your response to the human thing now a little better. I'm glad you explained yourself."

Rhamp nodded again.

When things went quiet, she assessed him as a male, not as her twin, the brother she'd never not known, never not been around.

"You remind me of L.W.," she murmured.

"How so."

"You're so angry—and I'm not picking a fight with you, honest." She put her palms up. "I'm just making an observation. He's like that, too."

As Rhamp rubbed his face, he looked older than her, much, much older. "Ever since I've gone out in the field, I've just seen . . . things I can't get out of my mind. Civilians who were tortured, the aftermaths of inductions—humans who have been hurt by humans. The night is not a kind place, and I take all of it home." He tapped the side of his head. "Everything's trapped up here. I don't sleep well, I worry about our dads out there fighting, I worry about what happens if the *lessers* find you or the grandparents. It's just . . . the only way I know how to handle it is to fight some more or get drunk."

He laughed in a short unhappy burst as he kept his eyes studiously away from her own. "Put like that, I probably need to go talk to Mary, huh."

"I think so, yes." She frowned. "Do you maybe resent me for not fighting?"

"That would be ridiculous. I don't want you anywhere near the field." He put a palm out. "I'm not saying I'll stop you, but . . . I do *not* want that for you."

"Emotions aren't logical. So do you get frustrated because I'm just skating along, while you're in the trenches?"

"I don't know," he said remotely.

Which was a "yes" he didn't want to admit to.

Lyric laughed a little. "I've been feeling frustrated at being on the sidelines, too. But I'm changing all that now."

Finally, those bright green eyes shifted over. "I don't want you to be like me, though. Don't lose that wonderful warmth you're known for. The world is a much, much better place with you in it. You light up every room you walk into, sis. And maybe I'm a little sexist, but I just wouldn't want you out in the field . . . turning into me. So be careful, if you decide to go there. It changes you, forever."

There was such exhaustion and sadness behind his words, the shadows in his eyes making him seem positively ancient.

Lyric got up before making a conscious decision to do so, and as she went across to her twin, he sighed like he was putting down a tremendous weight.

As they hugged, she couldn't remember the last time they had done that, either.

"I'm glad you came to talk to me," she whispered as tears tangled in her lashes.

"Me, too," he said.

They stayed like that for a long moment, and when they eased apart, she watched the emotion on her brother's face get shut down again.

"I thought you were off rotation tonight," she murmured.

"I'm just training this evening. I've got to do something with myself, you know?"

"Yes, I do."

He nodded and went for the door. Except he paused before he turned the handle.

"Listen, Lyric," he said, "if anything happens to me, I want you to know something—"

"Wait, *happens?*" She recoiled. "Like what happens?"

His eyes sought her own. "I want you to know that there is no one else I'd rather have as a sister. And that you're going to fill *Granmahmen's* shoes in this family perfectly. But you're also going to do it in your own way."

With that, he slipped out. Before she had a chance to say . . .

That she loved him, too.

CHAPTER FORTY-FIVE

Dev was waiting outside the Commodore, under the glow of its signage, when he got Lyric's text, and he read the message twice—because he was confused. They were supposed to meet here, so why had she gone to his place? Fucking hell, that apartment building was the last address he wanted her anywhere near.

Racing around the corner, he got into the shadows, closed his eyes, and dematerialized.

Something he was not in the regular habit of doing.

To avoid both his parents, he had shut out the black magic that threaded through his very cellular makeup—but there was a time and a place for the shit. And with his female waiting out in the cold, in an unsecured area? Where slayers had been gunned down a few nights ago? And where he knew there had been at least one inside the building, maybe a minion sent out by his father as a scout to his location?

For that matter, Dev was also worried he'd tipped off his presence when he'd revealed himself to dear old Mummy.

When he re-formed, it was in the alley next to his building, and as he ran out of the lane, he—

There Lyric was, standing on the stoop, huddling in the windbreaker he'd given her the night before, that knit scarf around her neck.

Her hair was tied back, and she was wearing blue jeans and those boots of hers that laced up to her ankles. No makeup, no frills, no fancy dress or shoes.

She was . . . more perfect than anything he'd ever seen before.

"Sorry I'm late," he said as he jogged forward. "Hey, you want to head to your place—"

He scented her tears before he saw them shimmer in her eyes, and the next thing he knew, he was pulling her into his arms and ushering her inside, out of the cold.

"I'm sorry." She sniffled and wiped her face. "I forgot we weren't supposed to meet here. It's been a long, long day . . . my *granmah*—mother died."

"Oh, shit. That's awful—"

"We knew it was time, yet it was a total shock." She put her hand over her heart. "But yeah, it's been a hard day."

"Do you want to go home? Does your family need you?"

"Oh, we spent all day together." She shook her head. "Can we just stay here? I don't want . . . I want to be away from my life for a minute. I just need a break."

Well, fuck. Guess they were staying. "Ah . . . sure. Yeah. Let's take the elevator."

The good news was that the doors opened as soon as he pushed the up arrow, and then they were inside the car. He hit his floor and immediately pulled her back into his arms.

He'd been planning on talking to her, laying everything out, telling her the whole goddamn truth even though for sure she wouldn't believe it at first. But with a death that recent? How in the hell was he going to drop more bombs on the female . . .

As the doors opened and they stepped out, he tried to seem casual as he put his arm around her waist and led her down to his apartment. In reality, he was on high alert to the point of raging paranoia. He felt marginally better after locking them in his place, and reminded himself that he had ways of protecting them both—

"Dev."

There was such an urgency in her voice that his heart skipped a beat. "What do you need."

Even though he knew. And maybe it made him perverse, he just really wanted to hear her say the words. Not because he needed the ego boost, but because he wanted to store them away in his memory for when she hated him.

"You," she said hoarsely. "I need . . . you tonight. I need to feel alive, and you make me that way because it's magic when you touch me. Please. I've been doing nothing but crying and reminiscing—and I can't be in the past right now. I can't . . . be with my memories right now."

She stepped into his body. "Make love to me, Dev. *Please*. I need your magic, and I need it now."

Fucking hell. Like he was going to say no, though?

Cradling her face in his hands, his eyes roamed her perfect face, from the flushed cheeks to the bloodshot, puffy eyes to her parted lips. Then he lowered his mouth to hers. The kiss started off slow and soft, but God . . . it didn't stay that way. The desperation was unleashed on both sides, everything she didn't want to think about igniting all that he wasn't talking about, the two of them burning together.

Burning for each other.

He ended up taking her over to his bed, and when she fell back, he went with her, covering her body with his own. Clothes melted away. Reservations melted away. Reality . . . melted away. And that was the way he wanted it, too.

Just for this one time. Before he told her who he really was. And if she would just give him a chance to explain, she might see him as something other than the parents he refused to be like.

"Lyric," he groaned.

Underneath him, she was glorious all naked and undone, her blond hair on his shitty pillow, her body all curves and length intertwined with his own. With raw lust, he kissed his way to her breasts, and heard her call out his name as he worked her nipples, his hands seeking the heat between her thighs—

She was beyond ready for him.

There were reasons to draw this out, until the anticipation cut like a knife and the release was all the sweeter for the pain of delay, but that was not tonight. That was not now.

Shoving his hand down to his hips, he angled himself and—

With a thrust, he—

Shorted his fucking brain out.

The sensations of sliding smoothly into her were too goddamn good, but it was more than just her tight, hot hold. It was her breasts against his bare chest, her mouth under his, the way she moaned his name—

Dev started pumping, and he meant to go slower, but there was going to be none of that. Linking a hold under her knee, he stretched her up and went even deeper. Faster. Harder. Until he felt her nails in his back and there was no way to keep kissing her and the headboard banged against the wall.

She took all of him.

And he did what he could to hold out so that she could orgasm first, but he really didn't care about baseball or golf or anything right now. In the end, his strokes grew shorter and even quicker, and as his balls tightened and his lungs burned, as she craned underneath him in spite of all his weight—

He started to ejaculate into her, just as she arched one last time herself.

Locking onto Lyric's lips, he felt the rhythmic contractions of her core as she milked his erection, drawing everything out of him . . .

Even his soul.

◆   ◆   ◆

There was a cleansing to the release.

Lyric didn't want to think in terms of using Dev—and that truly wasn't the point, hadn't been the point, of the sex. No, this raw, explosive collision had been inevitable ever since that snowy street and that stupid billboard, and she was so glad it was finally happening, his body penetrating hers, her arms around him and hanging on for dear life, her inner thighs wet from everything he was pumping into her.

But the reality was, the power of what he made her feel was so overwhelming that it lifted all the burdens she had been carrying. The worry. The sadness. The grief and the fear.

All of that upset would still be waiting for her. Just a little later, on the other side of the pleasure.

And this reprieve was what she needed to keep going.

When Dev finally came to a rest, he kept their bodies linked and lifted his head from her neck, brushing a strand of hair from her face.

"Hi," he said gruffly.

"Hi."

Sweeping her hands up his back, she felt some fresh welts— "Oh, no. I think I—"

"Yeah, there will be no complaints about any of that." He caressed her lips with his own. "You're welcome to use me as a scratching post anytime you want. But here, let me get off you so I don't—"

"No," she whispered. "I like the weight of you on me. And I like you inside me."

Both made her feel like she wasn't floating off the planet.

They kissed lazily for a little bit, and then she wasn't sure who started moving again first. Maybe it was him. Maybe it was just the friction of her shifting as she repositioned her hips. But as his arousal pushed into her, he then retreated—and sank into her again. And then he eased away—and came back.

The momentum now started, there was no stopping it, and that was exactly what she wanted.

As her head rolled back and forth on his pillow, she stared up at the ceiling above. Tears came to her eyes, and they were hot down her temples. It was so good to just feel . . . good.

And Dev's body was incredibly powerful as he started to pound into her again, and she only wanted him to go even harder—

As if he knew that, he pushed his torso up off her, the muscles of his chest flexing, his abdominals clenching and releasing as he dug into her in waves. Angling her pelvis, she linked her legs over his lower body and swept her hands down his ribs. He was a male animal, in the throes of mating, and she wanted to receive everything he had to give her. On a primordial level, this was just so right—

Another release snapped inside of her and she arched up, her breasts rising, her breath stopping, her eyes seeing stars.

Like, actual stars.

She'd always assumed that was something for novels and movies . . .

Dev continued to pump, a growl coming out of him, and then he pitched forward, his face once again in her hair, his exhale a roar in her ear, the scent and feel of him taking over everything—

Click.

Click.

He was still ejaculating into her when they both looked to his door. The handle was turning slowly, as if someone were quietly testing the lock.

She'd never seen a human move so fast.

One moment, he was on top of her and coming; the next, he was grabbing a gun out of his bedside table and pushing her off the far side of the mattress. She landed with a thump right next to where she happened to have thrown her clothes.

Scrambling to get dressed, she peeked over the bed.

Dev was naked and advancing toward the door like it was second nature to him, the gun up and steady, his stare fixated on the panel, his magnificent body carved with muscle and power.

And that was when she smelled it.

The sweet, sickly stench of a *lesser.*

Closing her eyes, she could only guess that the slayer had caught her own scent somehow—so she had brought the enemy right to his door. Literally.

"Dev."

He shook his head with a jerk. Then he glanced over his shoulder. "Dematerialize."

Lyric blinked. "*What.*"

"Now's not the time. I know what you are." He nodded toward the window. "Crack that and go."

A sudden, tingling awareness came over her, a warning that the reality she had thought she knew was *not* what had been going on—

All at once, a buffering hit the air around him, some kind of aura emanating out from his body before retreating.

Abruptly, he was fully clothed. And that was when it happened. As he glanced back at her, she met his eyes . . . and realized they were navy blue with a black rim, a color combination she had never seen before. For all the times she had looked at his face, for all the times they'd stared at each other, the color of his irises had never registered.

It was the one detail she had never seen about him, she suddenly realized.

And while she was grappling with that—and so much more—he said in a voice that cracked with regret, "I'm sorry, Lyric."

He sounded the same, maybe deeper somehow—and as she narrowed her eyes on him, her instincts screamed that he was . . . not human. Not human, at all. In fact, he was nothing she had ever encountered before, not vampire or Shadow, not even a *symphath*.

He had just hidden behind a mask of being human.

"Go."

Right behind her, the blackout drapes parted without anyone touching them, and the window sash lifted on its own. "Fuck, will you just *leave*—"

The door was kicked open, and the *lesser* on the far side locked on her, a smile on its pasty face, two guns up front and center, in its palms.

"Gotcha," it said.

Except then its pale eyes shifted over to Dev. Instantly, everything changed, the weapons lowering, an expression of confusion taking the place of all that satisfaction.

And then the words she'd never forget:

"Holy shit, your father's been looking for you."

CHAPTER FORTY-SIX

Some ten blocks away, Shuli was in full pursuit of the enemy, and his two boys were with him. They were very careful about the trail, though, because none of them were supposed to be in the field tonight.

Grief. Injury recovery. Yada, yada, yada.

Except they had work to do. This pair of *lessers* they'd tracked starting down on Twentieth Avenue had been on a slow walk—but for only a block or so. Before there could be any proper interception, the shorter of the slayers had checked his phone, said something that didn't carry, and things had suddenly sped up as the enemy had taken off at a quick jog to the north and west.

If the goal was to get one and work it over for intel, anything more than a solo *lesser* was complicated and unnecessarily dangerous. So the plan had been to try to split the pair up, with L.W. doing the abducting.

On the other hand, however, if the *lessers* had been called home to the master? Well, then wasn't that the lottery win they hadn't expected.

Of course, L.W., who had the impulse control of a handgun with no safety, just wanted to reach out and touch the targets. But this was the agreement the three of them had made: No hotdog bullshit. Logic over emotion, always—and they *always* stayed together.

And so they ran. Quietly.

As the rows of shitty walk-ups changed to better housing, and then stores, businesses, and restaurants, he had no fucking clue where they were headed. Until he caught an inkling. It was hard to pinpoint exactly when he realized where they *might* be going—except his brain just refused to work the coordinates because, really, what were the chances.

And then, as the *lessers* made the turn off Market, went down another couple of blocks, and linked up onto Lincoln . . .

Their targets passed right in front of the apartment building they'd all fought behind just the other night.

That was when he started to get worried.

A quick look at Rhamp's face, and he knew he wasn't the only one. L.W. didn't seem to care either way—at least until the slayer rounded the corner to the rear of the address and entered the parking area that was still marked with CPD evidence tags and yellow tape. Then even he seemed to catch on.

They pulled up short behind a pickup truck.

At that precise moment, up on the fourth floor, a set of drapes opened and a window sash lifted, without any visible hands moving things around. But the magician shit wasn't what he was worried about.

"Oh, fucking hell," he muttered as a figure stepped into view.

There was only one person in the world who had long blond hair like that—and then Lyric jumped back in alarm. As her arms raised over her head and shock distorted her face, he had a really bad fucking feeling about all this.

At that moment, Rhamp shot forward—

L.W. grabbed him and held him hard. "Let me go in—"

"She's my fucking sister—"

"And that's why I'm going in—"

The pair of them got right into it, aggressions misdirected. Meanwhile, Shuli stared upward and just froze in place. Every drive in him was screaming that he needed to get to Lyric, he needed to save her, and meanwhile, that pair of *lessers* they'd been tracking headed for the back door into the building—

Lyric screamed.

Instantly, the dam broke. L.W. up and dematerialized, and Rhamp—too distracted by emotion to be able to ghost out—leaped forward into a run and started shooting at the *lessers* up ahead. His suppressor killed most of the noise, but his aim was crap. As bullets pinged off all kinds of things, Shuli hauled his own ass and added some lead of his own.

He managed to drop one slayer, but the other hit that rear door with a key and a panic scramble.

Into the lowest level of the building it went.

As Rhamp rushed up on the downed *lesser*, the male had the presence of mind to palm one of his daggers, and do a dispatch on the move. Then even before the flash of light and burst of sound faded, the guy was at the back door—

Shuli yanked him away by jumping on him. "You don't know what's in there! We need to call for backup—"

"Lyric is in there," the fighter spat. "You remember, the female you're in love with. Get with the fucking program—"

Rhamp settled the argument by shooting the back lock and ripping open the steel panel. Left with no choice but to protect his buddy, Shuli jumped through the jambs and covered left, while Rhamp covered right.

The slayer who'd penetrated the entry was wounded, but still up on its feet: Little drops of foul-smelling black oil dotted the concrete floor, disappearing into the elevator.

Rhamp didn't even blink. He wheeled around and took the open stairwell.

Shuli followed again.

In perfect coordination, they hit the steps two at a time, bolting around each landing as they hit 'em. And Shuli told himself this was going to be fine. They'd dealt with shit like this before.

Really—

Fuck.

When they got to the fourth floor, there was no question which way to go. He could scent a *lesser*, but there were no drops of blood on the carpet. Didn't matter. Lyric was the point; they could get to the wounded slayer later. Clearly of the same mind, Rhamp took off running once again, and as he let out a whistle—

From out of nowhere, something stepped into their path.

A little old lady in an apron with a tray full of food.

Rhamp nearly mowed her over, and then, as a chaser, he pointed a gun at her head.

"Whoa, whoa, whoa—" Shuli barked.

Just as L.W., for reasons that couldn't be explained, came down the stairs from up above, even though he'd no doubt tried to dematerialize into the apartment itself.

Yeah, this was going just *great* for their first night out.

◆   ◆   ◆

As Lyric tried to process the words she'd just heard, she stared at the paled-out, snow-eyed *lesser* who'd shut them all in together. Going on some kind of reflex, she put her palms forward, but in her fucked-up head, she couldn't tell if she was trying to stop the slayer or Dev—or what had just been said.

Father.

Father?

And if she needed any confirmation that this was not a dream, this was in fact a terrible, living nightmare, it was the look that Dev gave her, his hooded, oddly colored eyes grave, his expression a tight mask—

It all happened so fast. Dev jumped on the *lesser*, grabbed it by the head, and jerked the skull around with such violence, the crack of the spinal cord was like an axe going through hardwood. Then he dropped the body off to the side and wheeled around to her.

Moving back until he was against the door, he fanned his hands as if he were holding out the whole world from them. Meanwhile, across the way, cold air entered the apartment, riffling the drapes, stealing all the warmth out of the space.

Or maybe the latter was the shock wave that was running through her body.

"I was going to tell you."

"Tell me what exactly." She couldn't breathe, she couldn't breathe, she couldn't— "Oh, God, that was why you weren't surprised about the fight behind this building. Or why I never had a car. Or why I had a shadow apartment. It was why you never bothered to ask me out during the day . . . or put out any questions about my life. You *knew* what I was."

"I'm sorry—"

A sudden surge of rage helped with the whole chills thing. "Oh, you can fuck off with that—"

"You lied, too." He shook his head sharply as a distant banging sounded out. "I didn't see you volunteering what you were or avoiding me because you thought I was human. I'll accept what I did was wrong, but don't pretend you weren't keeping your own secrets for your own reasons."

Lyric exhaled in a rush. "No, you're not going to put this back on me—"

"You told me you weren't looking for anything. So what were my obligations exactly."

She marched over to him. "You're the son of the Omega. You are my *enemy.*"

"Grandson," he said levelly. "To be accurate. And don't confuse me with my parents or my bloodline. I have lived my own life, away from their shit, for the majority of my adult—"

"Your *mahmen*. The demon, Devina, is your . . ."

The world started spinning so she threw out an arm to steady herself—and when he tried to help her, she recoiled away from his touch. This was *not* the magic she'd had in mind, this was *not* what she'd—

"You're pure evil," she hissed. "And you mask yourself in the world. You're worse than *everything* I've been trying to get away from. You're a violent, murderous illusion—"

"When have I *ever* hurt you!"

"Now! You're hurting me *now!*" Abruptly, she slapped both hands over her mouth as her stomach rolled. "Oh, God . . . I had sex with you. You came inside of me—"

As that muffled banging continued, Dev squeezed his lids closed like she'd stabbed him in the chest.

"I can't do this," she mumbled. "I can't—I've got to get out of here, I have to—"

Just as she went to take a step back, something locked on to her ankle, and she felt a searing pain. As she yelped and looked down, blood welled through the hem of her blue jeans—

Laughter bubbled up from the *lesser* who, for some reason, was right at her feet. Even with a broken neck, it had managed to drag its body over and wield a knife with enough strength to cut her to the bone.

With a roar, Dev bared his front teeth. No fangs, but the fury was real. "You fucking bastard—"

On the attack, he dematerialized onto the slayer, tore the knife out of that grip, wielded it over his head—

With a fresh wave of lurching nausea, Lyric fell to the floor, her hands going to the wound and all the blood.

Annnnnnnd that was when L.W. broke into the apartment by shattering the door. In a split second, she caught a glance of the wavy distortion she'd seen right before Dev's eye color had registered for the very first time, and she knew L.W. had somehow penetrated through the spell or whatever the barrier was. And then right behind him, out in the hall, she saw that Shuli and Rhamp were dealing with an elderly woman holding a tray of food.

Except then the door mystically re-formed, as if it had never been hit by that powerful shoulder.

Before she could say a thing, the heir to the throne looked down at her and across at Dev. The roar that came out of the male next was surely something that everybody in the building heard—maybe all of Caldwell. But there was no stopping L.W., stopping any of this.

With two running leaps, he slammed into Dev, spun him around, and shoved him into the wall. Forcing Dev's arm back, he made him drop the knife.

From out of her swirling confusion, she groaned. "He's not human, he's—"

Right beside her, at floor level, the *lesser* locked eyes with her and that demented smile came back. And he had something else in his hand.

Lyric told herself to pull it together and focus—

As another rhythmic thumping started to sound out at the door, the gun in the slayer's hand came into sharp focus.

The *lesser* didn't point it at her.

It smiled even wider and swung the weapon around. At L.W.

"No!" Lyric screamed.

Before she could think better of it, she jumped up and threw herself in front of the slayer, just as she heard the gun go off. There was some shouting after that, but she was suddenly cold and numb so it was impossible to detangle who was yelling.

Except she heard the enemy's laughter.

That was the last thing she was aware of as she fell to the floor for a second time—

No, that wasn't the last thing.

L.W. suddenly went flying across the room, the heir to the throne airborne and then some. As he crashed into the little table she and Dev had eaten at in another lifetime, chairs went on a scatter and Dev was suddenly right with her, his face in front of hers. His mouth was moving, those odd, all-wrong eyes he'd taken such pains to hide from her welling with tears.

In that moment, she split in half, one side remembering all the things they'd said and done together . . . the other thinking of how many innocent vampires had been taken down by slayers, how many nights she and her *mahmen* had worried about the males in their lives out on the streets hunting, how many horrors had happened over countless centuries.

An ancient, bloody feud defining her life.

She thought back to the beginning of everything with Dev, the pair of them outside at the construction site, his jacket around her shoulders, his hard hat in her hands—when he'd told her he hated his *mahmen* and that she was dead. And then she recalled what he'd just said, that he wasn't his parents, that he had lived away from them and their evil doings . . .

But even if all that was true, none of it could matter.

History and her loyalty to her King made him forbidden.

Abruptly, there was a bright light, a smell of something burning—

The slayer. Stabbed by a kitchen knife if she recognized the handle correctly. Sent back to its maker by Dev.

To his . . . father.

"Lyric," he said as he came back to her. "Stay with me . . . stay—"

Pulling up her loose sweater with a trembling hand, she looked down at the red stain blooming on the white turtleneck she had on underneath. The deadly wound was right in the center of her chest, the bullet meant for the heir to the throne finding her heart instead.

"Fuck you! This is about her!" Dev snarled over his shoulder.

Her eyes drifted over to whoever he was talking to. L.W. was growling like a guard dog, his tremendous fangs on full display, and yet he seemed to be frozen where he was, held in place by invisible restraints.

She opened her mouth to speak, and both males instantly silenced.

It took her two attempts to get the message out.

And she spoke to L.W. first.

"Get me home," she told him roughly. Then she looked at Dev. "If I live . . . through this . . . I don't want to ever see you again."

CHAPTER FORTY-SEVEN

Talk about a tits-up parade of bad shit going down. After Shuli disappeared the old lady with the food back into her apartment on a quick mental smudge, he jumped over to help Rhamp, who was ramming his whole body into a door that L.W. had just busted open, but which had, miraculously, reconstructed itself like it was brand-fucking-new. On the third try, Rhamp managed to break the fucking thing apart again and—

A nightmare.

That's what it was.

L.W. was up against the wall, splayed out like da Vinci's *Vitruvian* sketch, while a man—male? what the fuck was it—was kneeling next to Lyric like he was losing his whole life as he tried to keep her conscious. With her sweater wedged up to her neck, the alarming chest wound she'd sustained was bleeding at a fast rate—and of course, like all the tragedies Shuli'd ever had to witness, there was also the burning stench of a slayer having been sent home, as well as a discharged bullet casing on the wood floor.

Tunnel vision. Everything just collapsed for him into a pinprick of sight, and even though he wanted to fucking lose it, he brought up his phone so that the screen was right in the tube of vision he had.

He sent out the emergency call along with his location—

Meanwhile, Rhamp threw his big body forward, shoving everything out of the way to get to his sister—and somehow, that snapped some kind of magic spell that was in the air. As L.W. dropped off that wall and landed on his feet, the heir to the throne lost no fucking time. He went right for the boyfriend, picking up the guy, swinging him around, and throwing him down by the bed like he intended to drive him into the center of the fucking earth. Then L.W. mounted his prey, grabbed on to that throat, and started squeezing the ever-living shit out of the bastard.

Couldn't say he minded that one, Shuli thought as he knelt next to Lyric.

Taking her free hand, he said, "Help's on the way. We've got you."

The way her eyes rolled back in her head made him feel like he was going to pass the fuck out, too.

And then he heard the strangest thing.

"Take . . . you . . . to . . . him . . ."

While Rhamp stayed focused on his sister, Shuli looked over at the man who was under L.W. Even in the midst of the terror and the drama, it really hit him that whatever that vampire was sitting on . . . was not actually human.

He didn't know what that thing was. Not a *lesser*, no. But—

Even L.W. slowed down the strangulation as the guy kept talking.

The man—whatever he was—dragged in a breath. "That is what you want, isn't it. My father."

The statement—spoken in a remarkably level tone—brought even Rhamp's head around.

"Get off him," Shuli said in a guttural rush. "Get the fuck off him."

L.W. didn't budge. Until . . . he did.

Sitting back on the guy's hips, the fighter still looked like he was ready to kill his prey. But something was firing in his frontal lobe—and then his nostrils flared, in a way that his sire's had on many occasions.

"He's telling the truth," L.W. said, almost absently. "He intends to . . . take us to Lash."

Shuli did some quick math and then glanced at Rhamp. "You stay here with her. ETA on help is about two minutes."

The male was nodding as Shuli rose to his feet. Even though the last thing he wanted was to leave Lyric, her brother had dominion over her, both in terms of the Old Laws and every sense of well-duh. Stupid emotions of the misplaced-love variety had no place in this kind of crisis.

Because he knew what was coming next.

"L.W.," he barked, "get him up. You and I have to leave with him right now if you want what you've told me you want. Otherwise, the Brothers are going to take this over—"

He didn't get a chance to finish. The heir to the throne dragged the man—or whatever—up to his—its?—feet.

Leaning down once again, Shuli put his face in Rhamp's and mostly blinked back tears. "Take care of our girl."

He had no idea if the male was hearing anything. So he repeated: "Help is coming. ETA ninety seconds. You stay with her."

In what seemed to be a daze, Rhamp nodded. With that settled, Shuli went over to L.W. and the pair of them each grabbed an armpit and all but carried their target out of the apartment.

"There's a better way than this," the guy muttered in a bored way as his feet dangled.

Whatever, the Brothers were about to come in through the basement or the building's front door at any second, so Shuli nodded up the stairs and they hit an ascension as fast as they could go. Reaching the top floor, he glanced around—

Utility closet.

Tearing open the door, he was about to tell L.W. to—

L.W. handled the man like a Hefty garbage bag, tossing him inside. Then they both followed and shut the door.

Before the heir to the throne could start throwing insults—or punches, or maybe bullets?—Shuli put his palm in the fighter's face. Then he addressed their new, not-so-little friend.

"First, we talk this shit out. Now, what the *fuck* were you saying back there."

◆   ◆   ◆

Squeezed into a small closet with all kinds of brooms, buckets, and furnace filters, Dev's mind was not on the two vampires in front of him. All he could see was Lyric splayed out on his floor, that blood on her turtleneck at the sternum, her face losing its coloring.

And then she had said those words—

"I'm not going to be able to hold him back forever, asshole. So you better get talking."

As the syllables being spoken at him got through the fuzzy delirium that lessened his powers and his focus, he forced his eyes to get with the program. The shorter of the pair of males had a good haircut, handsome features, and a pair of diamond studs in his earlobes that were the size of quarters. The other one, the one with the braid down the center of his head and the long black hair, was the guy to worry about, and not just because of his tremendous size. With a face that was carved with aggression, and eyes that gleamed with hatred, it was clear he'd try to kill somebody just for jaywalking in front of his car, and that was not even close to what was going on here. To what had happened . . . back there.

Yet there was utility in this meeting, wasn't there. Something had been jelling for Dev, something that was radical, impossible, and dangerous as hell.

"There's nothing I wouldn't do for that female," he said roughly.

"Well, she's never seeing you again," the bigger vampire snapped. "*Ever.*"

Yeah, he'd heard that.

"You want to get to Lash." He looked directly into the taller one's pale green eyes and let the male's thoughts flow through him. "It's your first and only goal, isn't it. Except . . . no, there's a shadow, too. Of a female—"

The punch came flying from the right, and the follow-through was masterful. As Dev's head snapped back, he spat blood and slowly righted himself on his feet.

"Okay," he muttered. "We'll leave the female stuff alone. But like I can't read your thoughts clear as day? You want Lash, I can take you to him."

Even if Lyric had rightfully fucked him off, even if she'd all but banished him from what he feared might be her death, that didn't mean he couldn't help her, help her species. Meeting her, bonding with her—in the way of a male vampire—had transformed his world, shaking him out of his solitude, waking him up to a purpose he never would have contemplated before.

Because he'd been too busy being bitched at the cards destiny had dealt him. Or parents, rather.

Nothing like true love to change your course. Too bad this was going to be a solo flight, not that he blamed Lyric—oh, God, what if she was dying?

"I can take you to my father," he said because he couldn't bear where his thoughts were going. "In honor of her. I will . . . take you to my sire. Hell, I want him eradicated, too."

There was a tense silence as the pair of vampires did all kinds of shocked-to-the-core math. And all he could think of was Lyric, down on that floor, bleeding out while conventional medical help was "on the way."

It wasn't going to be enough to save her—

"Why would the heir to the Lessening Society want to give up his own sire," the shorter one demanded.

"The two of you are the very last people I should have to spell that out to."

"I don't trust you. At all."

Dev lifted his shoulder in a shrug. "I wouldn't either."

"What proof do you have that you're not going to fuck us—"

"He's trying to kill the female I love and everybody who's like her. What more proof do I need to have."

On that note, he got fed up with the stalling and was gripped by a sudden, prescient terror. So he dematerialized out from under them.

In a scatter of molecules, Dev traveled down through the floors that separated him from Lyric, returning to his studio. There were all kinds of people standing around her now, and for a moment, he kept himself invisible in the corner, wrapping his arms around his chest as he made sure no one sensed his presence . . . not the members of the Black Dagger Brotherhood who'd arrived—he recognized them by the blades holstered upon their chests. Not the medical staff who'd come—one of whom appeared to be a ghost? Not that male who did not leave Lyric's side.

So Dev was there.

When Lyric died.

CHAPTER FORTY-EIGHT

Conrahd Mainscowl the Elder hovered in the doorway of Whestmorel's bedroom. The male was still laid out upon the monogrammed duvet, but sometime during the day, his clothing had been removed and replaced with satin bedclothes that were like a dark stain upon the paler sheetings. The room had also been darkened, and something else had changed: There was a strange scent on the air.

A sickly sweet undertow that lingered in the sinuses.

As alarm bells continued to ring in Conrahd's mind, he took pains to calm himself with rational considerations. There had been many opportunities to take control of the movement along the way. Slipups of Whestmorel's leadership. Suspicions among the ranks. And then leaving Jenshen behind in that hidden room at their "leader's" house, still alive, just to punish the male for asking questions.

Alive.

That had been the most egregious fault thus far. There had been no reason to leave that loose end. If Whestmorel wanted the male out because he was a weak link, then kill him. But no, the ego had always been more important to their supposed overlord. He'd known damn well the Brotherhood would soon enough take possession of that mansion as the treasonous plot had come to fruition, and he'd been determined to provide them with proof of his cruelty, proof of his aggression . . . that he could torture someone to within an inch of death and walk away. Of course, he'd taken for granted that Jenshen would expire before he was discovered, but who could know whether that actually had occurred.

And what a loose end.

Following that? This move out here to this glass house on the shores of Lake George. They needed to be underground in a bunker, not drinking bourbon and staring out over the view like there was any kind of imperial horizon to contemplate. There was not *anything* to regard. Yet. There was nothing but plans and work, and the reach-out to the Omega's son.

Which had clearly not gone well.

Not that there were any details.

So now they were here, with Whestmorel overcome with some kind of exhaustion, and no communication, no plan.

"How goes he?"

Conrahd sensed the remaining members of the inner consortium standing behind him, and in the silence, he weighed his options. He might be able to assume power now, if he killed Whestmorel by smothering him with a pillow. But his sense was that the coalition was failing, the gentlemales lined up behind him rightfully concerned that two of their ilk had been killed recently, especially last night.

This was getting far too bloody for their constitutions.

Their participation was required, however. Their money was needed, their support was paramount, their commitment the only way to make any of this plot work.

Though there were many others on the periphery, these were the core of the plot.

"He is just resting," Conrahd lied. "The meeting went very well indeed, and the Omega's son and he will be in touch promptly to coordinate the raid on the Audience House."

There was a grumble that could have meant anything.

"We must bear up, fellows," he said levelly. "We shall give him the day to rest, and come nightfall the next, all will be well."

With any luck, Whestmorel would die of whatever ailed him and then the road would be clear to do this properly.

And if not? Then needs must and all that.

Conrahd pivoted around and smiled at his comrades. "Come, let us enjoy a bourbon by the fire."

As he led them off to the study, he was certain they would follow him, for they wanted to be led out of this whole situation. Separated from their families, enemies of the King and the Black Dagger Brotherhood, they were in way over their heads and all they wanted was relief. So he would provide it to them—as he himself took solace in knowing that if Whestmorel did not die . . . Conrahd, unlike the others, was not above getting his hands dirty.

Very, very dirty.

"Worry not, gentlemales," he said as he went over to Whestmorel's display of rare, collectible bottles. "Everything is in hand."

CHAPTER FORTY-NINE

Dev had always hated where he came from. Who his parents
were. What they did, what they were doing, and what they
would do in the future. He had recognized them by inches
as he had grown up, his realization starting with the vicious little games
they played with each other and then propagating properly to the dark
magic that had surrounded all three of them, the evil that had seeped
from their pores, the hatred they had shown the world and others.

In secret, he had developed his own powers.

And then when he'd felt like he was ready, when he was confident in
his ability to mask himself in their presences, to hide in thin air, to disappear from their senses . . . he had gotten the fuck out.

There had been no big blowout, no coming to them hurt and in
search of explanations he knew would just be lies to calm him down—
and no looking back, either. In the aftermath? Just the dull, solitary life
he had lived for so long, and been prepared to continue to endure, using
only enough magic to make sure they never, ever could find him.

They would know he still existed, however. He was sure to leave
just enough of a footprint so they were certain that he had chosen the
estrangement—and was keeping it in place on purpose, not because he'd
eradicated himself somehow.

Every day that dawned was a way to stick it to the pair of them. His existence, on the earth but not with them, was the payback they deserved, and he knew they were suffering. In their own fucked-up ways, they both loved him, and immortality being what it was, he was more than prepared to make them hurt for eternity.

Except then, one snowy night in Caldwell, New York, everything had changed.

And it was changing again now, as the blond female he had come to love in such a short time ceased to breathe.

The vampires clustered around her, all but one of them males, all but one of them armed, let out a collective explosion of grief as they recognized what had transpired—

"Come on, now," the female medic at Lyric's head urged. "We're not doing this. No, we're not doing this—"

She looked up to the dark-haired one who had not left Lyric's side. "Chest compressions on your sister. Now."

So that's the brother, Dev thought.

Just as the male started pumping her chest, the vampires Dev had been in the closet with skidded back into the room.

"And I need someone's vein—let's try to get some blood into her!"

The ghost brought forward a syringe full of something, and she injected whatever it was directly into the vein at the side of Lyric's throat. Then she pressed her fingertips in to check for a pulse—

The doctor did what she could to hide her expression.

And that was when Dev floated forward.

Keeping himself invisible to the lot of them, he settled himself at Lyric's feet. Then he raised his arm. Calling up that cursed nature of his, he did what he had always refused to do.

He intervened in the matter of life and death, and used the very thing that he hated most about himself.

Extending his palm, he summoned his very essence, concentrating it into an aura of light that was both black and white, a combination of evil and goodness.

Then he prepared to will some of his own life-force into Lyric, to give her a measure of himself. It felt like the right thing to do, but he wasn't sure, especially as he remembered her horror that she'd had sex with him. Perhaps the betrayal she felt went so deep, she would have refused the help? Too late, and there wasn't a way to ask her.

Anyway, she already had his heart. She might as well have part of his soul—

As he sent the spark into her, there was a crack of energy, the smell of ozone, and a series of concentric rings that vibrated through the air, riffling through peoples' clothing and hair, pushing their bodies around.

And then Lyric took a great, gasping breath, drawing in oxygen as her heart restarted.

I love you, Dev thought at her. *With all that I am.*

Meanwhile, as everybody recoiled in shock . . . her brother looked up and over his shoulder. At Dev.

As their eyes met, he thought that that was a neat trick of the male's. Except maybe he just sensed something was amiss—or maybe, because of the amount of magic required to do what he did, Dev had briefly revealed his presence.

In any event, time to go.

Dev backed up. Then turned away.

He passed through the apartment door as if it didn't exist, and then he threw up a screen in the hallway. They were going to have to get Lyric out somehow. The least he could do was make sure he covered them.

Then he would see about the rest of things.

He intended to make good on his offer to those two vampires in that closet: He was more than ready to bring his father's enemy directly to Lash.

After all these years, he was in a mind to join the fight now.

On the right side of history.

CHAPTER FIFTY

Floating.

Lyric was floating through a white landscape, fog roiling up around her, her body weightless in a way that reminded her of being up in the Sanctuary. When she came upon a white door, she had a sudden shock.

The Fade? Was she really . . . *here?*

Vague memories of what had transpired down below played through her mind, but they were like echoes of something that had happened to someone else, even as she remembered jumping in front of that gun to protect L.W., even as she recalled—

Dev.

Pain lanced through her, and she felt tears come to her eyes. In an impossibly fast series of images, she watched their entire relationship, from the start to where it had ended, everything playing out with a painful clarity. And as she got to that last argument, she knew he was right. She had kept her secret as well, but the magnitude of what he had not shared was . . .

Oh, what did it matter. She was here now, and she knew what it meant.

She had died.

And though she was so very sad for everyone she was leaving

behind, she found herself feeling rather done with life, like it was a problem she had tried to solve and the calculations had just gotten way out of her capabilities.

Confronting the door, she put her hand forward toward the knob, knowing that as soon as she turned it and opened—

Someone appeared in the closed panel, someone who made the tears in her eyes multiply until they were spilling down her cheeks.

"*Granmahmen.*"

The smile that came back at her was just what it used to be, joyous and strong, healthy and happy. Gone were the wasting and the pain, the sadness and the resignation that the bill had come due for a mortal's purchase of life.

All the vitality was back, and so was that beautiful face.

"Lyric."

Oh, yes, and that voice, that lovely voice, too.

"Do you really think it is your time?" Her namesake gestured toward whatever was behind herself. "It is beautiful there, nothing except peace and tranquility, but my dear girl, there's so much to keep you where you are down below."

"I miss you," she croaked out.

"And I miss you." Her *granmahmen* smiled again. "And I want you to know that I'm waiting for all of you here. I'm safe, and content to bide the time you are due upon the earth, each of you. Do not rush this decision just because of your heartbreak."

"I can't . . . be with Dev, *Granmahmen*. I never should have started this with him. He's not . . . who I thought he was."

"Are you sure about that? My child, do you not remember what I told you about him?"

Lyric wiped her tears and remembered back to the last conversation she and her *granmahmen* had had. "You, ah, you said that everything will be all right in the end . . ."

"And if it's not all right?"

When her *granmahmen* nodded for her to reply, she finished with:

"Then it's not the end. But I think you're wrong. I think this *is* the end, this *is* how it ends. Maybe what's right is just supposed to be painful in my case."

"And I believe you should listen to your elder." Her *granmahmen* smiled some more—and then looked down sharply. "Oh, it appears he is about to prove me right. How nice that he has exactly the magic you not only were looking for, but that you need in this moment. Alas, all that is for you to discover and do with what you will, though. You always have freedom of choice, my dear."

The vision began to recede and fade away. "Know that I love you, very much. Tell everybody I say hello!"

On that note, the spirit of her *granmahmen* disappeared.

Lyric looked at the knob—

A sudden bolt went through her, and she glanced down. Through the cloud cover at her feet, she could suddenly see a keyhole view of everything that was happening in that apartment of Dev's: She was lying where she had slumped to the floor after the gunshot, Rhamp and Doc Jane by her head, the Brotherhood all around her.

Some kind of injection had just been given to her. Clearly, that was the reason for the revival she was abruptly feeling, the connection with her body having been lost, but now reestablished . . . such that she could, if she wanted, follow the signal back to be reunited with her physical form.

Thus rejoining her family and friends, all of whom were looking absolutely heartbroken and horrified.

Instantly, she recalled the promise she had made to her *granmahmen* on that deathbed.

It was because of that vow, and for the people she loved, that she returned.

Not Dev.

Whatever he was.

Their end had occurred, and now it was up to her to make things "okay."

CHAPTER FIFTY-ONE

The following evening arrived with flurries, but oddly warmer temperatures. Not that anyone in the training center knew about either.

"It was a miracle."

As Blay spoke up, Qhuinn looked over at his *hellren*. His most favorite redhead on the planet was sitting beside him in the break room, the pair of them holding hands while they'd stared up at a muted TV screen and tracked absolutely nothing about the marathon of the old school *The Resident* episodes.

"It was." He lifted Blay's wrist to his mouth and pressed a kiss to the veins there. "Doc Jane said she'd never seen anything like it. Guess that shot of epinephrine really worked."

"You know something, I'm not sure . . . if I can take much more." Blay laughed on a short exhale. "Even if it's good news, my heart needs a break from shocks."

Nodding his head, Qhuinn kept the rest of his thoughts to himself. There were a lot of questions to be answered, main among them what his daughter and son had been doing in the apartment—although clearly it was owned by that human Lyric had apparently been dating. When he'd pressed Rhamp for details, he'd gotten stonewalled, and he was very certain his son knew all kinds of things he wasn't talking about. But whatever. At this point, though, it was still one night at a time. Lyric had somehow survived her gunshot wound, everybody was here safely, and there was only one urn of ashes to be picked up and brought home from the crematorium.

All things considered, Blay had it right. A miracle had been granted, and at least for now, they needed to just be grateful.

He glanced at the clock. "Let's go check on her?"

When Blay nodded, they got up. There were all kinds of brothers sitting around, and everybody glanced over like they were looking to be given a job: Rhage was eating ice cream, of course, while Z strummed on a guitar. Vishous had two laptops open in front of him, while Tohr and Xcor were at his side like the pair were comparing notes with the guy. Meanwhile, Phury, Xhex, John Matthew, and Butch were playing gin rummy, while Payne and Wrath were down the hall, sparring in the gym. And on the far side of the room, Lassiter was stretched out on two stuffed chairs, the TV remote in his hand. The angel had been the one to pick the show for the binge watch—so really, the distraction could have been much, much worse.

Out in the corridor, Quinn looked down the way to the room Lyric was resting in. L.W., Shuli, and Rhamp had been outside her door all night and into the day, and he had no complaints about their loyalty. At the moment, though, one of the Three Musketeers was missing.

"Hey, boys," he said as he approached. "Where's Rhamp?"

"In there with her." Shuli rubbed his eyes like they were burning from lack of sleep and an existential exhaustion. "We're getting ready to leave. He wanted to say goodbye—see you later, I mean."

"Where you going?"

"Oh, you know. Just out. She's stable, so we're gonna go food up and have showers back at my place."

"No field work," Qhuinn warned. "Everybody's off rotation. The King's orders."

Even L.W. nodded at that, which was a relief. Talk about your wild cards. The heir to the throne had been making everybody nervous for years, and now was *not* the time for any reminders of that dynamic.

Qhuinn cracked the door. Lyric was sitting up in the hospital bed, and Rhamp was in the chair next to her. The two looked impossibly old, no trace at all of the young they'd once been showing. He was proud of the fact that they were adults, but sad to see the maturity, too.

Their innocence was totally gone now, the final vestiges of it seeming to have been burned away in the last twenty-four hours.

"Let's give them a moment," he murmured as he let the door re-close without entering.

◆   ◆   ◆

Lying on a hospital bed she could barely remember being brought to, Lyric searched her brother's face and tried to understand what Rhamp was saying to her.

"What do you mean . . . he was there."

Sitting next to her on the clinic's chair, her twin shook his head. "I don't know what else to tell you. At the moment your whole body bounced back to life . . . I saw that guy standing over you at your feet, with his palm outstretched. I don't fucking know."

With a sense of heartbreak, she thought of being up at the door to the Fade. And what she and her *grandmahmen* had talked about. "Well, it doesn't matter if he was there or not."

"Doesn't it?"

"No."

"I think he was the one who brought you back, Lyric." Her brother put both of his hands forward. "I don't know what went down between you two, and it's none of my business, but I wanted you to be aware of what I saw."

"You know who he is, right? He told you, I heard him."

At least . . . she was pretty sure she had? Things remained blurry.

Rhamp shrugged. "There were a lot of things said last night. And you know, given everything that's happening right now, I think it's best that we should just let it all go. I mean, if you're serious about never see-ing him again—"

"I am."

"Then talking about it is just going to kick up a lot of drama that no one needs. Besides, like I'd be in a big hurry to tell everyone I'd just dated the Omega's grandson?"

"I wish you wouldn't put it like that," she muttered. "Although it is the truth."

"So we don't say anything. He was just a human as far as they know. By the time they got there, he was nowhere to be seen. Let's just keep it clean."

Lyric found herself nodding. At this point, she only wanted to put the whole thing behind her anyway. Her grief and sadness were so profound, almost as profound as her sense of betrayal, and she also found it difficult that she'd never guessed any of it. It was only now, as she relived certain exchanges on things, that she saw the clues that had been there all along.

Forgettable by design, wasn't that what he'd said in the beginning? Forgettable on purpose was more like it.

Brushing under her eyes, she listened to the steady beat of the mon-itor behind her, proof positive—her being conscious aside—that she was, in fact, alive and kicking.

"So I went to the Fade," she blurted. As her brother's head ripped up, she nodded. "I saw the door . . . the knob . . . the whole thing. And *Granmahmen*."

"She was there?"

Lyric nodded again. "And she smiled a lot. She wants us to know she's waiting for us, but to take our time down here."

She could still picture it all, hear that voice, see the buffering clouds all around. "It's beautiful up there. Better than mortal life, for sure."

Rhamp cleared his throat. "I, ah, I don't know what I would have done . . . if you hadn't come back."

Reaching out, she squeezed his hand. "Well, the good thing is, we don't need to think about that, do we."

"No, we don't," he echoed.

With a brisk nod, he released a breath, as if she'd given him permission to put the whole nightmare aside, stuff it down deep, and never dwell on those moments again. The radical compartamentalization wasn't quite what she'd been going for, but if that was the way he handled it, what else could she do?

Other than make sure she stayed alive.

"How did you three know I was there?" she asked.

"We tracked two *lessers* to the address."

"Ah. Yes. Guess they'd been called in for backup by the one who knocked on Dev's door."

With a sudden shiver, she wondered about the slayers they'd seen all around that property. Had Dev been recruiting them, working with the—

"I'm sorry," she said roughly.

"What for?"

"Everything."

She thought about him calling her a Barbie, and that had been an insult. But she also recognized that she was a long, long way from making any decision about going out in the field. Yes, she would do the training, yes, she would work hard, but transformations in life were about so much more than getting spoon-fed some insta-wisdom from a woman strutting around on a purple stage and telling you what you wanted to hear. Or at least, what you thought you wanted to hear.

Real change required work, not just inspiration, and true growth was more than some fantasy about being a hero. And yet . . . as she thought about what she'd done for Allhan, and then remembered helping Rhamp at their *granmahmen's* bedside—and as she recalled especially the moment she'd jumped in front of a bullet to save L.W., she decided the fallen angel and her dearly departed namesake were right.

She was capable of things that mattered, and others knew, too.

L.W. had certainly thanked her for saving his life, and so had the great Blind King himself.

"So we're going to keep going," she said, mostly to herself. "Because that's what the living do and the dead cannot. We . . . move forward."

No matter how much it could hurt sometimes.

"Anyway"—she sniffled some composure back into her face—"where are you off to? They're making me stay here for monitoring, but honestly, I feel fine."

"I'm just going to train—but you should absolutely hang here." Rhamp got to his feet. "Call me if you need me."

"Always. And you do the same, okay?"

He bent down and kissed her cheek. "You got it, sister mine."

As her brother headed to the door, she closed her eyes, thinking she might sleep a little. There was nothing else to do.

"Lyric?" When she popped her lids and looked over, Rhamp was hesitating by the exit. "For what it's worth, I think you're wrong. I think it does matter that guy was there."

Drawing her brows together, she tried not to be angry with her twin. "Why are you defending him?"

"'Cuz I believe he saved my sister's life." Rhamp opened the exit and stepped out. "I owe him."

CHAPTER FIFTY-TWO

Back in the heart of downtown, on the fourth floor of the apartment building that had been the epicenter of so much, Dev was waiting on his bed, hands in his lap, eyes on the floor where the bloodstain was.

The red one, where Lyric had lain.

Passing a hand down his face, he knew that this was the last time he would be in this space, and he didn't feel any type of way about it. The studio hadn't meant anything to him when he'd first taken it, and in spite of everything, it didn't mean much to him now. If there was any hint of nostalgia, it was just because the square footage had been a marker of time passing, an era over.

Marked in blood, as it were—

One by one, they appeared, the three vampires from the night before entering through the crack in the window across the way: Lyric's brother, fierce and dark-haired on the left. The tall one in the middle with the nasty expression and the braid. The diamond-studded one on the other end.

"She's okay, isn't she?" Dev asked.

Twinkle Lobes muttered, "None of your goddamn business—"

The brother elbowed the guy to shut up and then replied smoothly, "She's totally okay. She's resting and fine."

As the pair of vampires glared at the male, he didn't seem to care. He just kept staring straight ahead at Dev.

Ah, so the guy *had* seen the little sleight of hand and knew what had happened.

"I really want to kill you," the one with the braid muttered.

"I wish you would." Dev smiled coldly at him. "With the way I'm feeling now, death would be so much more preferable. But unfortunately, given who my parents are, that's not an option." He sat up straighter and cracked his knuckles. "We could go a couple of rounds with that dagger in your hand, though. Good exercise for you, and I think I'd like to have a little physical pain to go along with everything else that's banging around in my head. Except that would really just be a waste of time when there's so many other things you want to do, right?"

"Where are you taking us," the braided one demanded.

"To his presence." Dev shrugged. "I'm not Google Maps, asshole. I can't give you directions. All I can do is transport us into my sire's vicinity."

"Hold on," Twinkles cut in. "How do we know this isn't a trap."

"Call the Black Dagger Brotherhood. Call all the vampires on the planet." Not that he wanted that. Better to keep this limited in scope so there was less chance of people dying. "I don't give a shit, but I thought you wanted to try to kill him yourselves. Or was I wrong about that."

When there was no immediate reply, he looked at them one by one. "What's it going to be, boys."

Still no answer, so Dev shrugged and went over to that open window. For a moment, all he could see was a memory of Lyric standing in front of the drapes as she'd looked around that first time she'd been here, her blond hair so beautiful as it shimmered when she moved.

The searing pain that went through him made him wonder what she'd felt after she'd been shot. Too bad he couldn't have taken whatever agony she'd had from her. The shit in the center of his chest was late to that party, though.

Clearing his throat, he said, "Look, I'm leaving Caldwell after this and never, ever coming back. It's now or not at all."

✦   ✦   ✦

Up on the shores of Lake George in Whestmorel's glass house, Conrahd stood over the bed and watched the male breathe. The respiration had been getting slower. Slower. Slower . . .

Slower.

Yet the aristocrat just would not expire. Frustrated, Conrahd checked the clock on the wall. It had been like this for hours, the lingering, on the verge.

Glancing down, he tightened the grip on the pillow between his hands.

Do it, he told himself. *Just lean over the bed and suffocate the bastard. The others had seen for themselves that their so-called fearless leader had taken very ill, thus there would be no questioning of the passing.*

Then he could assume power—

Outside, something moved at the sliding glass doors, and he pivoted toward the expanse of transparency that provided such a panoramic view of the water and the snowy mountains. Staring out across Whestmorel's body, he frowned. There was a shape on the far side of one of the doors, looming like a ghost that had become corporeal—

Every bone in Conrahd's body, every inch of his skin, all the hairs on his head and each rib in his chest, screamed for him to *go*.

Now.

It was the kind of calling that he couldn't ignore.

With a quick shift, he bolted out of the room, and skidded into the hall beyond. As he realized he was running with the pillow, he dropped it and went straight for the study.

The instant he arrived, the four other males looked up at him. They were in various stages of recline on the sofas, the chair, at the hearth by the fireplace, the stasis they were in predicated upon the update that Conrahd had been planning to make.

"Do you trust me," he said roughly.

They straightened, each of them, the three who were sitting rising slowly to their feet.

"Do you," he repeated as all kinds of urgency pounded his heart. "Just answer the question, I will not ask it again."

When the halting yeses came, he pointed to the hidden door that was tucked in the south corner of the room. "We go now, we leave through the tunnel, and we do not look back."

Now, the questions bubbled up, exploding on waves of anxiety:

"Now here, whatever is going—"

"—quite apparent something is rather out of order—"

"—is going on with Whestmorel. Is he sick—"

Conrahd cut them off with the horrible truth: "We go now, because the Omega's son has just come unto this house."

That was when a scream rippled out from down the hall, from where the bedroom was.

"Now!" Conrahd hissed as he bolted for the secret entrance to the escape tunnel. "Stay at your own peril."

He didn't even care whether they followed him. All he knew was that he was going to save himself first.

And then deal with the fallout.

Whatever route Whestmorel had intented to take with the head of the Lessening Society, whatever plan that had been conceived between the two, it was clear that no good could come of it.

If they intended to take down Wrath, there was going to have to be another way.

Assuming any one of them lived to hide from the dawn at the end of this night.

◆   ◆   ◆

When Dev left his now-former apartment, he brought the others along, the three vampires traveling with him in a pocket of energy he created. He could sense their resolve and aggression even more easily now that their physical bodies were gone and they were in their essence form: Before they'd left, he'd been surprised they hadn't called for backup—but now he understood why as he read them with clarity.

They would sacrifice themselves to protect the greater good.

And they believed they could call for help at any moment.

He wasn't sure the latter was true. Guess they would all find out.

What they didn't know, and he had come to a firm resolution on, was that he was the one who was going to kill his father this night. To save the vampires, and most importantly his love, he was going to stand up to the Omega's begotten son, and he was going to battle.

And these vampires were going to help him by dealing with the *lessers* who came to his sire's defense.

He would handle Lash—

Arriving at their destination, he made them all corporeal once more—and he was intrigued by the rustic location. It wasn't a dark alley in the shitty part of town, it wasn't some hidden induction site, it wasn't even a place of worship where the fucking converted sucked up to their master. Nope, it was a plowed lane leading to a glass house perched on the side of a mountain—and his father did not own the property.

His dark mark would have stained the very molecules of everything on the site.

No, for some reason, Lash had come here.

As the vampires shook off the travel spell, Dev walked forward through the snow. The great concentration of evil was on the far side of the structure, so he cut around the fringes, finding his way by stepping through branches and the accumulation of drifts. Soon enough, a vast frozen lake was revealed, and then he joined up with a porch that ran the breadth and length of all that glass.

He made sure Lyric was nowhere near his thoughts.

His father would sniff her out immediately—

The open sliding door, way down at the end. Yes, that was where he needed to go.

Except then he paused. Glancing back at the males behind him, he recognized they were ready to fight, but he had a sudden awareness that he couldn't shake.

And that was when he saw the shadow. Off to the side. An angel with gossamer wings and long black-and-blond hair.

As if a memory block was being lifted, Dev suddenly remembered that the entity had been at the apartment the night before. In the far corner, as unseen as he himself had been.

And there was a message being sent to him now, an urgent warning.

Turning back to the vampires, he looked them over. And then he opened his mouth—yet what happened next had nothing to do with him.

"You're not supposed to be here," Dev heard himself say in a voice that was not his own, as if he were a channel for the communication. "You have to go."

The arguments were swift and sure, aggressive and angry. But then he locked eyes with Lyric's brother.

"I shouldn't have brought you here," Dev said in his own voice now. "This is a family matter between me and my father."

Because it dawned on him, sure as if the conviction had been placed in his brain by that other entity: He might not survive this. So he couldn't protect these mortals if things went badly.

In which case, he'd be responsible for the death of Lyric's own blood.

"No," he said abruptly. "I was wrong to bring you with me."

Before they could make even more noise, he extended his hand, bundled them up safely, and sent them off. What had he been thinking anyway—other than respecting their need for vengeance because it was what motivated him.

Dev glanced back at the angel. The shimmering apparition put its hand on its chest, and inclined its upper body in gratitude.

Then that other voice wove its way into Dev's head. *If you give all you have, all that is within you, your destiny and everything you wish for will come true.*

And then the angel disappeared.

In the aftermath, he took a couple of deep breaths—and after that, he approached the aperture, his heart starting to pound . . . especially as he arrived at the open sliding glass door and looked into a bedroom.

His father was as he had always been, tall and strong, with blond hair that was currently tied back. No clothes of leisure tonight. Lash was wearing a black ceremonial robe as he stood over a male who was straining on a bed as if in a seizure, the mouth open, the face twisted into a mask of horror and pain, the limbs of the body sticking straight out from the torso as it levitated off the satin sheets—

His father looked over with a sharp jerk of the head.

And then he actually did a double take. Which was a rather . . . human? . . . response.

Mortal, was more like it.

The vampire was instantly forgotten, cast aside across the space to crumple into an oozing mess of black blood and gore in the corner.

At which point, Dev squared off at the evil.

Lash.

The Omega's son.

His sire.

In an effort to block any intrusion into his mind, Dev kept the titles circulating over and over again in his thoughts. If he was successful in redirecting his every conscious awareness back at his father, there were no weak points to get inside, no chance of infiltration and manipulation.

"The prodigal son returns," Lash said in a low voice.

"Hello, Father."

There was a moment of sizing up, on both sides. And then Dev stepped into the house, making sure that he was hyperaware of his surroundings, ready for anything.

"You know," his sire said with an autocratic accent. "Of all the places I expected you to turn up, after all these years, some random aristocrat's house in the mountains is not it."

Blue pupils with black rims, the reverse of his own coloring, stared across at him. He'd brought no conventional weapons with him, and of course, his father didn't need any. But that didn't mean things weren't going to get very deadly, very quick.

"I cannot read your mind." The evil smiled. "You are very strong. Tell me, how ever is your *mahmen?*"

As the memory of standing in front of the demon and seeing her truly for the first time struck a chord, Dev felt an odd need to protect the female.

"I wouldn't know," he lied.

"Do not tell me you've come here for some Shakespearean reason." Lash lowered his chin and looked out from under lowered brows. "That would be so unoriginal of you—"

The evil stopped. And glanced out of the open glass slider.

"I think we have a visitor, son."

CHAPTER FIFTY-THREE

L yric would later wonder why she traveled the way she did, how she managed it—even though she would know the why of her magical trip in real time.

When it was all happening, however, she was aware of only that one moment, she was in the hospital bed at the Brotherhood's training center. And then in another, she started thinking of Dev and remembering things they had each said, the two of them arguing while he had looked so brokenhearted, her anger rising along with her own shattered dreams of what they could have been—

And then she was just gone.

It was not unlike the swirling trip to the Fade, the appearance up at the Sanctuary, or the twisty twirl of death itself. All she was sure about was that there was a spark of Dev inside of her, and it suddenly yearned to be reunited with the whole of him to such a degree that she was pulled along through the night air with it. Instinctually, she fought the tide, recognizing that she was out of her own control. And yet . . .

She wanted to see him. She needed the closure.

Rhamp's parting words haunted her.

When the trip came to an end, it was like stepping off a train's platform, the movement over, the disorientation gone as if it had never been. Yet she was in a totally different place, on a porch that overlooked a frozen lake and a mountain view.

Glancing down at herself, she was still in the same flannel night-gown her *mahmen* had brought from home to the clinic. Then she looked around and recognized nothing of the modern house that was mostly glass. She felt Dev's presence, however—and she followed it as a light in the darkness, a homing signal that she could not ignore.

Even though it was cold, she felt nothing of the wind or the chill, and she couldn't decide whether that was because she was numb or if it was part of this whole strange experience.

Putting her hand over her heart, she told herself she could feel the beat. But what if she'd died again and just been in a different version of the Fade all day long? Except then why had she seen so many living loved ones?

"Stop it," she said.

Maybe this was a dream—

Down at the end of the porch, Dev jumped out of an open doorway, looked at her with pure terror on his face, and put both of his palms forward. "Go! Oh, God, *go!*"

Something came out of his palms, some kind of energy—

All at once, a dark shadow covered him, sure as if he'd been grabbed by a mystical fist, and he disappeared back into the house like he'd been yanked inside.

"Dev? Devlin!"

Riding a sudden panic, Lyric rushed forward, her bare feet slipping over the ice and snow as flurries from out of nowhere blew into her face like they were also trying to warn her to go back, stay away. And then, when she got to the sliding door, it shut in her face. There was some kind of coating on the panes so she couldn't see inside, but in her fear, she pounded on the—

The flash of light was so bright that the interior lit up to a point that the tinting couldn't cut the glare. She had a brief vision of Dev surrounded by a ball of energy—

And then something broke out of the house to the right of her, glass shattering as whatever it was catapulted into the air.

Moving over to the ragged, jagged hole, she looked inside.

Dev was standing with both feet planted and his palms forward, his face full of such fury, he was, indeed, the son of evil, begotten of a demon, the grandson of the Omega.

Yet the energy he sent out was not dark.

It was . . . something else.

And then he focused on her with haunted eyes. "Lyric . . . you have to go. Nothing matters but you. *Nothing.*"

✦   ✦   ✦

Right before the evil grabbed him on an existential level, Dev prayed that Lyric would listen to him and get the hell out of there. Except there had been no time to talk sense into her—hell, he didn't even know what she was doing at the house at all. But then his father had reached out and snagged him, and he'd been pulled in by an undertow so powerful, there had been no fighting it.

Determined to keep her safe, at any cost to himself, he had ducked and rolled, sprung up and fired back at his sire, sending out a burst of energy that made them change places: He might have been sucked into the house, but Lash had been expelled.

It wouldn't keep his father busy for long, however. And he needed to get—

Lyric burst into the bedroom, going barefoot right over the broken glass. As he caught the smell of her blood, he rushed across and swept her up off the carpet—then rerouted for an interior door. Opening it with his mind, he was about to start running out of the suite when the lights flickered and went out.

He glanced around his shoulder.

Lash was coalescing in the night sky, like a flock of crows pulling together, and the rumbling underfoot was a harbinger of what was to come.

If you give all you have, all that is within you, your destiny will come true.

Dev stopped and looked Lyric right in the eyes. "I love you. And I'm sorry."

Before she had a chance to respond, he put her behind him, sheltering her with his body, and closed his lids. All around them, thunder rolled through the sky, and he could tell there was lightning, too, the reflections of the strobing registering and constricting his pupils.

But he had to ignore all that. He had to tap into the wellspring of what he felt for this female.

With grim resolve, he thought back to the way he'd spent his day, spinning a pathetic fantasy where he actually was the just-normal-mortal he'd pretended to be, and the two of them lived happily ever after like everybody else on the planet who was mortal. No curses, no magic—and not because he was shutting it all down as he'd been doing for the last decade.

No curses and no magic because there was none inside of him—

The pulses started with the beat of his heart and emanated out from there, great waves of energy gathering around him from the very origins of the universe, the power that had brought the first spark of life into being, the essence of the Creator, doubling and redoubling within him.

His soul purged everything that he'd been born with and hadn't wanted into a barrier that protected Lyric, surrounding her, fortifying her . . . protecting her.

And just in time.

Dev's eyes blinked open right as his father stepped back through the broken pane.

"Really," came a warped voice. "Over a *vampire?*"

And then there was no more talking. Lash let loose a barrage of dark magic, the power so great the whole house rumbled on the foundations that had been drilled into the very bedrock of the mountain—

As the force hit, Dev's metaphysical shielding of Lyric held, the evil diverted so that she wasn't hurt. But as the barrage continued, Dev could feel himself losing strength.

And he knew what he had to do. One shot. He needed to take his one shot—

Give all of himself, as the angel had said.

Summoning his strength, Dev yelled out a battle cry, and embraced the opposite of what he felt for his female. Instead of love, he accessed the deep hatred he had for his sire—and in doing so, he started to absorb the dark energy being sent at him, his corporeal being turning into a repository for the evil, until he felt his soul sicken and contort. But he took still more, the longer his father continued, the further down he sunk as he collected the root of all that was cruel and conniving and angry in the world—

When he couldn't hold it any longer, when he was full beyond bursting, he flipped the switch and sent the hatred back to its source.

The explosion of energy was so great, it blew out all the windows along the front of the house, the shards of glass mixing with the flurries that fell, the shock wave also felling trees and shearing rocks off the mountain's elevation.

Lash was swept off the porch and carried far, far out over the lake, his form spinning in the midst of the black energy, trapped in everything that he brought to fate and destiny, captured by the dense darkness that contaminated hearts and souls and condemned those who acted as evil to an eternity in *Dhunhd*—

There was a moment of suspended pause, the sky storming around the concentration of malevolence, lightning flashing.

And then the teeming mass of evil dropped into the middle of the frozen lake, the impact breaking the ice and creating a tidal wave that emanated out from the center hole, swamping boathouses all around.

After that . . .

Nothing.

There was nothing left of his father.

Dev collapsed to his knees and fell forward. When he was rolled onto his back, Lyric was leaning over him.

Her eyes were wide, her breath coming out in pants. "Dev . . ."

For a moment, he had a ringing sense of completion, the job well done as she was alive and his sire gone. But then he felt his strength start to ebb, and he realized, in saving her and her kind, he had sacrificed himself, just as her brother and those males had intended to do.

Just as the angel had foretold: He had given his all and gotten his wish for her.

With a trembling hand, he tried to reach up and touch her face. "I'm . . . sorry."

Yes, the angel had been right, but destiny had also been a kick in the balls. He was "dying" in the only way an immortal could.

There was no more soul left in his corporeal body.

Fine, if this was his fate, then he had finally done something important, something worthy of the love he had at last known, at the end of his destiny.

"Dev, don't leave me—"

"It's okay . . . better off . . . without me . . ."

"No! You have to stay," she stammered. "Please, we have to figure this out. We have to figure *us* out—you saved my life, you can't leave me now—"

"And you saved my soul."

Damn it, he wished he could touch her; he had to settle for looking at her.

"Live your life free and out loud . . ." he whispered. "And know that you are loved . . ."

That was as far as he got. His life-force was like a rope he'd been holding on to.

All of a sudden, his grip slipped.

And that was it.

CHAPTER FIFTY-FOUR

D ev!" Lyric moved his head into her lap. "Dev—no, no, no . . . Dev!"

She was drawing in a deep breath and getting ready to scream when she heard something outside the house. Ignoring whatever it was, she just kept saying his name again—until abruptly, the sound outside grew so loud she could no longer ignore it.

Lifting her head to the shattered glass sliders, she frowned as she focused on the lake beyond.

In the midst of the ice surface, there was a great hole, as if a rock the size of a football field had been dropped by the hand of the Creator.

As more lightning flashed, bubbles rose out of the black, oily water—and the force of them abruptly turned into a geyser. Something was emerging out of the depths, rising higher and higher, and as a ringing chorus of dread swamped not just her mind, but her body, she knew that whatever was coming for her, coming for Dev, was unlike anything she had ever seen.

Or anything she could survive.

She'd been looking for magic, but not this kind . . . dearest Lassiter, not like this. The enormity of the evil was incomprehensible as it manifested, so vast that it blocked out the mountains and the sky.

The heir to the Omega. The entity that existed only to hunt and kill her species—

Lash's essence rushed at the house, and as the great waves of darkness zeroed in on her and Devlin, she threw herself over him—for all the good that would do.

Besides, he was barely breathing.

Bracing herself, she knew that dark energy was going to wipe them both out, and she screamed—

All at once a figure appeared before them. A female.

Valentina Disserte?

From . . . Resolve2Evolve? Yes, it was, in all her purple-dressed glory, her dark hair up in a bun, the grapey perfume Lyric had smelled when they'd met saturating the air. Except . . . the face was different now. Very beautiful, yes, but the features were not exactly what they'd been.

After a moment of eye contact, the woman turned around.

And then a strong female voice reverberated through the entire Northeast, it seemed: *"No! He is my son, and you will not hurt him."*

The female planted her stilettos and surrounded them all with a shimmering force field. And then, as a great roar began, she separated herself out, took two running steps, and leaped off the porch at the dark energy.

And something . . . happened.

Just before the evil slammed into the house, some kind of merger occurred in the sky, and the resulting luminescent waves exploded across the horizon, northern lights except in red and gold and purple, so much purple.

After that there was only darkness, inside the house, outside at the lake with the hole in the center, over all of the whole world, it seemed.

But Lyric didn't give a shit.

Looking down at Dev's face, she felt the cold in his skin and panicked. She didn't have a phone on her, she had no idea where they were, and she wasn't sure whether anybody could help them anyway. This was not mortal business: It was in the realm of immortality, and the implications terrified her.

"I love you, too," she said desperately to him. "Dev, I love you . . ."

There was a great release speaking the words, but they were too late, he was too far gone—

Snap!

The female entity reappeared in front of them, still in her purple skirted business suit, but that long, luscious brunette hair was an absolute mess, and the silk blouse was untucked.

"Goddamn him," it muttered as she threw out her hand and a lit cigarette appeared between her fingers. "He always was a good fuck."

She looked down as she exhaled. And promptly her annoyed expression left her flushed face.

The female lowered herself beside Dev. "My boy. My beautiful boy . . ."

Devina. The demon. Dev's *mahmen.*

"Bring him back," Lyric begged. "With everything I've heard about you, I know you're powerful enough. You can raise the dead. You can bring him . . . back."

She was crying now, the tears flowing freely onto her flannel nightgown.

"He is the one thing I love most in all the world," Devina said. "And so I won't do that to him. I can't."

"*What.*" Lyric slapped a hold on that arm. "Please, you have to, he can't die like this—"

"If I bring him back, he'll have me in him again. He wouldn't want that, even if you were with him and you love him like you say you do—he'd be back where he started." A bloody tear formed at the corner of one of those black eyes. "He hates his father and me, and I don't blame him."

"You can't let him die—"

"But you can do something about this."

"What?" Lyric frowned. "I have no magic, I have—"

"You have a piece of him in you. I can sense it. I don't know how it happened, and it doesn't matter, really. But you . . . give that back to him. Let his essence flow from you back into him, a mixture of the two of you, your mortality cleansing me and his father from him, clearing the decks, so to speak."

There was such sadness in the female, but also a resolve.

"Take his hand, Lyric—and question nothing. Just feel and let it flow back into him." The demon glanced out toward the broken glass. "And don't worry, you're safe, because Lash isn't coming back here. He's an asshole, but I promised him a blow job later and I'm very good at that. Turns out he's missed me, the piece of shit—and I'm doing my damnedest to not be charmed by that."

The entity tilted her head as she rose to a full stand. "My son's chosen wisely in you. You're going to do well together. Now, wake him up with the kiss of life, and know that this is where you two end . . . and also where you begin. Save the one I love most in the world, for both you and me."

Riding a sense of fear and disbelief, Lyric refocused on Dev, staring into his sightless eyes. Then she took a deep breath, closed her lids, and pressed her mouth to his.

Prepared to attempt the most important thing in the world.

CHAPTER FIFTY-FIVE

Dev heard his name being called from a great distance. In the dark swill around him, the sound was a reassuring anchor, but he had to fight to focus on it and try to move forward. His effort became like swimming through sluggish, frigid water, great strokes getting him almost nowhere. Yet the voice became louder and presently he recognized it.

"Lyric . . . ?" he said into the void. "*Lyric*—"

A current flowed into him, and it peeled the black pressure away, but in the absence of the full-body constriction, pain flared as every part of him struggled to contain itself. Moving more freely at last, he started to ascend with a sudden buoyancy, going faster and faster, until, like an inflatable surfacing, he popped—

—open his eyes.

Lyric was kissing him, pushing life-force into him, while standing off to the side, with tears of red streaming down her face, was his mother.

Dev took a deep breath and coughed through a wretched suffocation. But his lungs got with the program soon enough and began to do their duty properly, pulling air in, expelling it out. And then he forgot all about that.

"I love you," Lyric cried as she pulled him up and held him to her heart.

Now he found the strength to reach out his arms and hold her back; now he had the strength to sit himself up and cradle her. Except he didn't know how this had happened . . . he didn't know how *any* of this had happened.

Except really, who the fuck cared.

He kissed Lyric back with everything he had. And then he said hoarsely, "I'm sorry, I love you, I'm so—"

Babbling. But again, who the fuck cared, really. He was alive, she was here, and . . .

Dev slowly eased apart from his female and looked over at his mother. "What are you doing here?"

"She helped me," Lyric said. "She protected us and told me what to do to save you."

Dev moved Lyric so that his body shielded her from the demon. "Why would you do that."

"It's very simple, really." Devina wiped her eyes and had to clear her throat. "There is nothing a parent won't do for their child. You needed me . . . and I came, and I made sure that in the end, you were free of your father and me, and everything we gave to you. You are mortal now, and you have her vampire nature within you. There is no more left of your father and me."

Glancing down at himself, he realized he did feel a void. He did feel very, very different than he always had.

"No more magic, no more immortality," she confirmed. "You're released from your legacy and can live as you choose, with whomever you desire."

The only thing he could do was stare up in speechless wonder. Sure, the demon might have shown him a glimpse of who she really was at that conference, but of all the acts he had ever thought her capable of, something selfless like this? Not even at the bottom of the list.

"Thank you, Mother," he choked out.

"She is the one who saved you." Devina smiled tenderly at Lyric. Then the expression was lost. "You have to be careful now, though. There is no going back from this."

Dev found himself exhaling in relief. Whatever came next, at least it was going to be on his own terms.

The demon took a deep breath, that beautiful face cast in deep sorrow. "And yes, I'll leave you alone going forward. But you two must leave here now—I'll keep your father busy for long enough so you can get off the property. And then provided you don't cross his path, he won't be able to find you anymore. Of course, the same is true of me. I will not be able to locate you, either."

She lifted up her manicured hand in goodbye. Then turned on her stiletto.

"Mother."

At the sound of his voice, she glanced over her shoulder.

"Thank you," he said hoarsely.

"Goodbye, son," she whispered.

And then she was gone.

Dev looked at Lyric, raising a trembling hand to her face. "I'm not special anymore."

"Oh, you're more than that." She smiled at him through her tears. "You're *everything*. And . . . I believe what you said, that you are not your parents."

"I'm really not your enemy."

"I know that now. And I'm sorry for jumping to conclusions when I was so panicked."

With that, they shared a kiss that seemed to go on forever. Then again, when things were deeply felt, time had little meaning—and wasn't that a kind of eternity for the mortal?

When they finally parted, he looked at all the broken glass. "We need to go."

Lyric helped him to his feet, then frowned as she glanced down at her own in confusion. "Um . . . I wasn't wearing these when I got here."

The Louboutins were beautiful, tall and black and sleek.

Dev had to chuckle. "My mother always did like her shoes. Guess they were a present."

As they started to pick their way around the shards, she said, "She also fixed all my cuts."

One more reason to . . . love? . . . the one who'd borne him. Yes, that was the word. *Love.* And as the conviction came over him, a big part of him was healed, the anger that had always roiled inside of him disappearing.

Then again, not only had he made peace with one of his parents, he was with the female he loved. That set so much to right.

Now all he had were daddy issues. But hey, nobody got everything in life.

"You know what," he conceded. "Maybe my mom wasn't that bad after all."

Lyric chuckled as they hit the hallway. "Actually, I kind of like her . . . who knows, maybe we can see her again sometime. She's on a lot of billboards, right?"

He thought of where this had all started, back in the middle of a snowy city street, a one-in-a-million accident gifting him a once-in-a-lifetime love.

Proof that you never knew when your destiny was going to come and find you, or how it was going to land on your head.

"I think seeing her again is very possible." He kissed his female with total gratitude to the one of his parents who had done him right when it really counted. "Very possible indeed . . ."

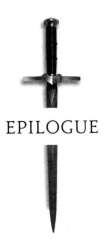

EPILOGUE

Two weeks later . . .

Okay, this was not rocket science, Lyric resolved as she stared into the abyss of an empty 9 x 15-inch baking pan.

Surrounding her on the counter, like a gauntlet she was going to have to get through, was a vat of meat sauce, a strainer full of lasagna noodles, a container of cottage cheese, a plate of shredded mozzarella, and a tub of parmesan powder. Behind her, the oven her *granmahmen* had always used to great fanfare was heated up to 350 degrees, and ready for whatever the hell she put together.

Please let this not be Franken-dinner, she thought.

"I can do this. I can totally . . . do this."

Just as she plunged her ladle into the sauce, male voices percolated down at the front door.

"Upstairs, yeah?"

"Yup," Dev answered her twin. "And then everything else in the basement. She wants to clean her weapons on the second-story porch so they don't stink up the house."

Heavy footfalls boomed an ascent up the stairs, and she looked overhead to follow the creaking of floorboards as the males made their way to the corner room that faced the back view. She imagined the two of them chatting back and forth about something, nothing, anything, as they unpacked the gunmetal that had recently come into her life.

Refocusing on her pan, she put a ladle's worth of sauce on the bottom to help things not stick, then she started laying out the noodles shoulder to shoulder, just like her *granmahmen* always had.

"Her weapons" was certainly a new phrase, at least as it related to Lyric. But she'd been learning all kinds of things in the Brotherhood's training center, like how to shoot a handgun, a rifle, and a shotgun, or throw a grenade, or fight with a knife or with only her hands. She didn't know where it was all leading, and if she was honest, she didn't see herself out in the alleys, hunting for *lessers*.

Not with Lash knowing who she was, not with the chance of her running across him. If the head of the Lessening Society got ahold of his seriously estranged son's mate? Yeah, nobody needed to think about that outcome.

Still, she was getting physically stronger, mentally tougher, and more secure in herself. She hadn't figured out what she was going to do long-term, but she was already helping her *mahmen* amplify her Etsy business with some good social media engagement. After all, she was well familiar with how the algorithms worked, and whaddya know. Using what she'd learned for a higher purpose, to help Luchas House and Safe Place?

Made her feel good.

"Okay, next . . ." As her voice trailed off, she went for the plate of shredded soft cheese. "It's the mozzarella and then the cottage cheese."

No ricotta. Her father Qhuinn was not a ricotta guy, and she was making this especially for him—

"Are you sure you guys want to do this?"

She looked up at her grandfather. Rocke had just come out of the bedroom, his hair wet from a fresh shower, his flannel shirt pressed, his khakis, the same. As he settled himself onto the stool in front of her, Lyric's heart ached for him. He was having a hard time of it, which was not unexpected. All those years of a happy mating? For godsakes, she and Dev hadn't even been together for a month and she would be utterly lost without him. After a hundred years or more?

"We're very sure," she said with a smile as she glanced out toward the hearth.

The beautiful cloisonné urn that contained her *granmahmen's* ashes sat in a position of honor in the center of the mantel, right under a photograph of the gazebo and the pond that had been enlarged and framed. They'd had a beautiful celebration of life last week, and everyone from their little community had come. Seeing all the people standing around, hearing stories and sharing laughter and tears, had been a reminder of how supported they all were—and she had caught Dev standing off to the side, staring over the males and females with a banked expression of humble surprise.

It was as if he had been alone for so long, he'd forgotten what being in a crowd of family was like. Or . . . perhaps he had never known that closeness, and didn't that make her glad he was with all of them.

"Well, I'm happy you're here," Rocke said. "You two fill the house up. But I don't want you to think you have to take care of me."

Lyric started on her next layer, working with the noodles again. "Oh, I promise it's not that. He and I want to live together, and your basement is perfect for us. We're grateful you're taking us in."

And okay, sure, fine, it was a *little* to take care of her grandfather. He'd lost some weight, and though he was resolutely composed in the old school way of things, the dark bags under his eyes were the telltale that he was not sleeping during the day. She also had the feeling he just wandered around a lot, going from room to room, no doubt reliving happier times. They kept finding cans of Coke or half-eaten sandwiches or books that were cracked open in all these odd places in the house.

Like he kept trying to find a place to settle, and never quite got one.

The truth was, they'd all been a little worried about him, and with her and Dev here to keep an eye on the male? It was a good thing, all the way around—

More voices percolated down from the front entrance, and Rocke turned to the sounds with a happy flush, his eyes lighting up.

Yup, she thought as she went for more sauce. *This is a very good thing.*

Xcor and her *mahmen* came into the family room first, and Qhuinn and Blay were right behind them. The quartet were speaking in a rapid-fire doubles match, completing each others' sentences, skipping from subject to subject, and she had to grin. She'd grown up with them like this, and recognized that she was lucky. Her family wasn't just blended, it was a damn smoothie.

"Lyric! You're doing so well!" Layla came around and inspected what she had made so far. "It's perfect—"

Xcor swooped in for a hug. "Absolutely, and I'm ready to eat—"

"Just like my *mahmen* would have done," Blay tacked on as he got misty.

While the comment registered, there was a moment of silence, and it was like that now. From time to time, someone would say something, or point at a picture, or mention the way the moon draped the gazebo in gentle, wintery light—and the quiet would come as the elder Lyric was remembered.

"I can't wait to have some," Qhuinn added softly.

As Lyric's own eyes welled up, she hugged him and then brushed her tears away with the inside of her forearm. "She always made it for you. And now, I will."

It was what she had promised, after all. And she was a female who kept to her word.

"—say goodbye to my sister."

Rhamp entered while talking over his shoulder, and in response to the announcement, he received one big frown from everybody.

"You're not staying?" Lyric asked.

"Nah, I've got plans I can't change."

As their eyes met, a sliver of unease rippled through her. "I thought you were off schedule tonight."

"Training." He came around and gave her a hug. Softly, in her ear, he whispered, "You worry too much."

While he said goodbye to everybody else, she zipped her lip and got busy again with the lasagna. She had a bad feeling about whatever her brother was doing, and it made her think about the aftermath of everything that had happened on Lake George. She and Dev had been honest with everybody, especially the King and the Brotherhood, about who he really was, who his parents were. She hadn't been sure whether or not she would be banished, but Wrath, the great Blind King, had stared at Dev for the longest time. And then he had nodded once, and that was done. Her mate was accepted.

Well, and maybe Rhamp's testimony about what had happened when she'd been shot had something to do with it. Her twin had been clear that without Dev, she wouldn't be here.

Go figure, that had opened a lot of minds and hearts—and so had the fact that she'd put her life on the line for L.W.

Glancing up again, she looked down to the front door. Dev was coming in with another box just as Rhamp hit the threshold. There was a pause as they talked, and then the two males embraced, clapping each other on the back. She was glad to see their closeness.

When the time came, maybe Dev could help her talk some sense into the fighter.

After Rhamp stepped out, Dev shut the door and came down to the kitchen. As he went along, he peeled that construction jacket of his off his heavy shoulders, and she had to smile as he hung it on a peg next to her grandfather's parka. Everyone greeted him, and while he returned the hi-hello's, his eyes were only on her.

His beautiful blue eyes . . . that had lost the black rim around the iris.

As he came over to her, and dropped his head for a kiss, she leaned into him, keeping her messy hands out of range like she was a surgeon.

"Everything's inside," he said as he straightened. "We can sort it after Last Meal. Oh, and Fritz wants to come pick up the van, but there's no need. I can take it back—"

Instant silence, all the way around, to the point where he looked up in alarm. "I'm . . . sorry?" he hedged.

While Lyric tried to find the right words, Qhuinn spoke into the shocked silence. "Listen, son, you've been doing great. I mean, really. Taking care of our girl, moving her things—"

Xcor cut in with, "You're a good sparring partner."

"Always willing to lend a hand," Rocke murmured from his spot on the stool. "And you're a Jets fan, no matter how hard that is."

"Very respectful," Layla added. "Lovely manners."

Blay nodded. "A good listener, too."

"And we trust you," Lyric concluded. Which, given the circumstances, was everything.

"Buuuuuuuut . . ." Dev intoned.

Over at the refrigerator, Qhuinn dipped in and came out with a beer. As he brought the Sam Adams across to Dev, he popped the cap with an opener.

"Here's the deal." Her sire handed the bottle over. "There's one thing you *cannot* do in our little world, one thing that's right under treason against the King in terms of the fuck-around-and-find-out. Am I clear?"

"Yeah," Dev said. "Yeah, totally. Just tell me what it is."

The answer came from all corners of the kitchen: "You don't—"

"—don't help the—"

"—the butler—"

"—*ever*."

They all said it at once. And for a moment, Dev lifted a brow like surely this was a joke and the pause that followed was for the punchline.

"Never ever," Lyric said. "It'll make him cry and you won't get over that. Trust us. That's a nightmare you do *not* want to volunteer for."

There was all kinds of muttering agreement, with everybody shaking their heads ruefully as personal memories of the one mistake made clearly haunted the assembled.

"Wow," Dev murmured as he lifted his lager in salute. "Well, even though it feels rude as hell, I will *not* help the butler."

The clapping and approvals burst out, and Dev shrugged, all when-in-Rome. As conversation re-bubbled and Lyric set about finishing her layers, her mate fell into talk with Qhuinn and Xcor, the three males becoming instantly animated as they discussed who was making it into the Super Bowl. Then there was Blay, who was chatting with Layla, the Chosen nodding and gesturing with her elegant hands, and finally, Lyric's grandfather, sitting on his stool with a banked half smile, like he was getting a break from his mourning.

It was all so beautifully . . . normal. So perfectly ordinary. So sublimely non-dramatic. Which didn't mean there weren't stressors. For sure, the war and the plot against the King loomed as always in the background, and then there was whatever crap her twin was getting himself into. But this right here, all of them together in the house, a lasagna about to go in the oven, people talking and laughing? *This* was what she had always re-membered and loved about this home, this family . . . this Sunday night Last Meal—

And that was when Lyric saw her *granmahmen.*

Over by the hearth, in the glow of the warm fire, the female was standing off to the side, wearing one of her handmade flowered dresses, her short hair tucked behind her ears, her carriage straight and proper, as it had always been.

Instantly, tears sprung to Lyric's eyes, but she got with the program, tilting the now-heavy lasagna-filled pan in that direction so her name-sake could inspect it. In response, the elder Lyric beamed and gave a round of silent clapping. Then her *granmahmen* nodded at Dev and smiled in a knowing way.

"You were right about him," Lyric whispered.

"Right about what?" Dev said.

Jerking to attention, she lowered the pan back down onto the counter and glanced at Dev. When she looked to the hearth once again, the apparition was gone. Ah . . . but the presence remained. Her *granmahmen* was all over this house and always would be, for however long the rest of them were here.

And knowing the female, she might well haunt whoever moved in later, may that be many, many, many years in the future.

Dev frowned. "Lyric? Are you okay?"

"I love you," she managed to choke out.

Emotion bloomed on his face and especially in his eyes . . . a reflection of what he felt in his heart, down to his soul. "And I love you. Always."

As Lyric took a long, deep, easy breath, she smiled up at her mate and plunged her fingertips into the tub of parmesan.

Making it snow over the top of the lasagna she'd made for the very first time, she said, "Everything turned out all right. In the end . . . everything's worked out, just as it should."

ACKNOWLEDGMENTS

With so many thanks to the readers of the Black Dagger Brotherhood books! This has been a long, marvelous, exciting journey, and I can't wait to see what happens next in this world we all love. I'd also like to thank Meg Ruley, Rebecca Scherer and everyone at JRA, and Hannah Braaten, Carrie f'n Feron, Jamie Selzer, Sarah Schlick, Jennifer Bergstrom, Jennifer Long, and the entire family at Gallery Books and Simon & Schuster.

To Team Waud, I love you all. Truly. And as always, everything I do is with love to and adoration for both my family of origin and of adoption.

Oh, and thank you to Naamah, my Writer Dog II, and Obie, Writer Dog-in-Training, and Jerry, who's the new man on the block! All of them work as hard as I do on my books!